MAVIS BITES

BLUE FEATHER BOOKS, LTD.

As always, for Heather.

ALSO WRITTEN BY
MAVIS APPLEWATER:

- MY SISTER'S KEEPER
- THE BRASS RING
- PLOT? WHAT PLOT? I
- PLOT? WHAT PLOT? II

AVAILABLE NOW FROM
BLUE FEATHER BOOKS, LTD.

www.bluefeatherbooks.com

MAVIS BITES

A BLUE FEATHER BOOK

by
Mavis Applewater

NOTE: If you purchased this book without a cover, you should be aware that it is stolen property. It was reported as "unsold and destroyed" to the publisher, and neither the author nor the publisher has received any payment for this "stripped book."

This is a work of fiction. All characters, locales and events are either products of the author's imagination or are used fictitiously.

MAVIS BITES

All stories copyright © 2005 by Mavis Applewater.

Cover design by pinfeather

All rights reserved. No part of this book may be reproduced in any manner whatsoever without written permission from the publisher, save for brief quotations used in critical articles or reviews.

A Blue Feather Book
Published by Blue Feather Books, Ltd.
P.O. Box 5867
Atlanta, GA 31107-5967

www.bluefeatherbooks.com

ISBN: 0-9770318-3-7

First edition: October, 2005

Printed in the United States of America and the United Kingdom.

Acknowledgements

I would like to thank the members of YoMavis, my little, little e-group, who inspired the Wednesday Afternoon Series, and The Royal Academy of Bards and The Bard's Village, for posting my first stories. Also Lisa Raymond, Joanne Forbes-Murphy, Mary Phillips, Catherine DeLeone, Toni Zulig, Brunnhilda, Theresa Nezwicki, Heather Stewart, David Crowder, Rae Haggerty, and Caitlin and everyone at Blue Feather Books for their endless patience. Very special thanks to Ma Kessler who gave birth to me, and to Ma Bardsley who accepted me as her daughter-in-law. Also to Nana and Sunny, for telling me to let my light shine no matter what anyone said.

The Price I Paid

I'm standing in my studio apartment in New Orleans, looking down at a pile of ashes. The gray heap is illuminated by bright sunlight flooding in through the French doors that lead out to a tiny balcony. I gaze at my hand and find a delicate gold ring, set with a large ruby and engraved with the most intricate carvings I've ever seen. I'm puzzled. I know this is my apartment, I know where I work, and I even know my name. What's truly bizarre is that my only clear memory of the past year is that of a night almost a year ago, when I was one of the nameless, faceless masses that lived on the streets of New York City.

I clutch the ring tightly, as though it can bring me some answers. I glance at the clock, knowing that I need to get ready for work. Rummaging up an old shoestring, I slip the ring onto it and place it around my neck. Strange that I know I need to keep it close to me; stranger still that I know I should keep it hidden. But neither is as strange as not having any memory of how I went from being homeless to being employed and living in a nice little studio in New Orleans, yet knowing where I work and how to get there.

As I spend my day doing my job, which is simple data entry, I'm plagued by the fact that I know how to do it and know the names of my co-workers, but have no clear recollection of just how I came to live in this city. My last clear memory is of Halloween night one year ago. It was cold in the city that night. When you don't know where you're going to be sleeping, the city can turn even colder.

For years, I had been on the streets; I had run away from home as a teenager. The dangers I faced paled in comparison with the hell that was my family. But the city streets were harsh, and I paid a price for my freedom. By that Halloween night, I had already endured the back alleys and learned what to do to keep safe. I found an abandoned building that, according to a dilapidated sign, was about to be torn down.

I figured it would be infested with rats and other vermin, but two-legged vermin troubled me the most. I was careful not to make my presence known. Under the best of circumstances, a woman out alone at night wasn't safe; a lost soul like me was a walking billboard for trouble.

I avoided the floors that were already inhabited by junkies and other lost souls. Climbing a stairway that reeked of urine and despair, I made my way up to the top floor and stepped carefully into an empty room. The floorboards creaked beneath my feet. I held my breath, knowing that rats and rapists weren't the only dangers to be found in a condemned building.

Air burst from my lungs as the floor crumbled beneath me. I could feel my limbs being torn as I crashed through the old wood and fell into the darkness. The pain was immeasurable, and I smelled my own blood. I looked down and discovered that one of the floorboards had impaled me. My blood seeped from my small body, and I knew I was going to die. I felt a strange sense of relief that my torment was finally over. I could stop fighting the good fight and finally find peace.

I didn't fear death. In truth, I had prayed for it many times. I heard the sound of flapping wings above me. The flapping wasn't soft, like a bird; it sounded more leathery, like a large bat. As I chuckled at the absurd notion of a very large bat hovering above me, the shadow of wings covered me. I was still laughing when the wings became a cloaked form with a pair of piercing blue eyes. Then darkness encompassed me.

That was my last conscious memory before this morning. Perhaps something traumatic had happened. But what could have been more traumatic than my childhood? My co-workers stop by and tell me I'm looking much better, and I finally have some color back in my cheeks. Perhaps I've been sick. Would that explain my loss of memory?

That night, I sweep up the ashes from my carpet and store them in an old coffee tin. I don't know why I choose to save them. After I complete the task, I begin searching my tiny apartment for some clue as to how my new life came about. I discover that I have a limited number of belongings. Not surprising, since up until a year ago, I was reduced to dumpster diving just to find something to eat.

Among my belongings are a few simple outfits, a driver's license, my birth certificate, a Social Security card, a copy of my

GED, a business card from my present boss that's marked with the date and time for an interview, a leather travel bag, and a note. I don't know how I came to be in possession of a Louisiana driver's license or a copy of my birth certificate, much less a Social Security card. I don't recall buying any of the clothing or the travel bag. I hoped that the note, written on very elegant paper that crinkled when I touched it, would hold some clue.

Samantha,

I've given you what you've asked for. You have your freedom. The gifts I have left should prove helpful. You paid the price, and now the rest is up to you.

K

"What price have I paid?" I wonder out loud, running my fingers along the elegant script. My fingertips burn as they slowly trace the ink, and I am more confused than ever. Who is this mysterious K, and what did I do to earn a new life?

Over the next few days, I continue with my simple life. This new life is truly a gift. My small home might be considered shabby by some, but after literally living in a cardboard box, the studio seems like a palace to me. I just wish I could remember who K is, and how I got here. The only thing I know for certain is that my co-workers keep telling me that I'm glowing, unlike the anemic look they say I had possessed a few weeks ago. I wonder if my memory loss has anything to do with the strange scar I discovered at the base of my neck? At first, I thought the scar might have been from the accident back in New York, but now, after examining it carefully, I notice that it closely resembles the crest on the ring that I keep around my neck.

"Samantha?" Betty, who works in the cubicle behind me, breaks me out of my thoughts.

"Yes, Betty?" I quickly tuck the ring back into my shirt.

"I was just going to catch lunch at that new sandwich place down the street. Do you want to join me?" she asks cheerfully.

"Okay," I say, thinking that lunch with a friend might help me fill in the gaps of my life. I'm eager for another reason. This will be the first time I've ever participated in what most people would consider a mundane activity. I may have shared a meal with a friend during the past year, but since I have no memory of it, this is a new experience for me. Betty looks surprised at my response; perhaps I wasn't a very social person.

"Betty, you seemed startled that I accepted your lunch invitation," I say carefully as we dig into the large sandwiches.

"You never have before," Betty explains with a shrug and a warm smile. "I knew that if I kept trying, you'd come out of your shell."

"I was afraid of that," I mutter as I tug on my shirt collar in an effort to hide the unusual scar on my neck.

"Don't be afraid, kiddo." She laughs, misunderstanding my statement. "I can't help myself. My kids are all grown up, and I have to butt into someone's life."

"I wish you'd gotten through to me earlier," I say with a heavy sigh. "This is going to sound odd, but I can't remember the past year of my life. I know my name, where I work, and where I live. Hell, I even know what Jell-O is, but I can't remember how I got to New Orleans."

She gasps so loudly that her large body shakes. "You're kidding!"

"No, I'm afraid I'm not. How long have I been with the company?"

"Almost four months. Maybe you should see a doctor. A few weeks ago, you weren't looking very good. You were tired, drawn out, and pale as a ghost."

"I think you might be right." We gather up our belongings, and I groan when I knock over my cup. As I bend over to pick it up, the ring slips from the safe confines of my shirt. A dark-haired woman passes by as I'm tucking it back in. She halts when she spies the ring and the mark on my neck. Her mesmerizing hazel eyes widen in a look of fear as she stares at me, and then she glances up at the sun, blinks, and seems surprised.

"It can't be," she mutters, as she shakes her head and goes on her way.

"What was that all about?" I ask in exasperation.

"Oh, don't mind her." Betty dismisses the quirky woman's actions. "That's just Carlotta."

"Huh?" I say. We start walking back toward the office.

"You know, Madame Carlotta," Betty answers. "She has a shop just around the corner from the office."

"Let me guess—tarot cards and voodoo dolls." I snicker at the idea.

"Don't be knocking the mojo ladies. The tourists love that kind of crap. Plus, I wouldn't mess with Carlotta. She's the real deal."

"Don't tell me you buy into that stuff."

"Hey, I'm a real Cajun, honey, and I've seen some things that would scare the pants off the devil himself," Betty says. "Maybe you should have her do a reading. You never know, it might help. But I'd see a doctor first. I'll give you my son's number."

"Your son is a doctor?"

"My oldest." She beams with pride. "The other one, Randy, well, let's just say we spent twenty-six thousand dollars a year on tuition so he could drink heavily and chase girls. Now he lives in our basement and makes ink for a living."

"At least he has a job and a loving family." I feel a pang of remorse for the years I've lost.

"Amen to that. Now I want you to promise me that you're going to take care of yourself."

"I promise." I feel slightly overwhelmed by her generous nature. "Betty, could you not mention this to anyone?"

"Don't you worry about a thing, child," Betty reassures me, and for the first time in years, I find myself actually trusting someone.

The following night, I go to see Betty's son, Fred. After a long series of tests, blood work, and x-rays, he informs me that I'm in very good health. "Your memory loss does concern me," he says. "And I'm worried that you've obviously suffered from malnutrition in recent years."

"I was homeless for a long time," I confess with embarrassment.

"That would explain it," he says in a gentle tone. "You seem to be fine now, but these things do have a lingering effect. I'm going to prescribe some vitamin supplements."

"What about my memory?"

"From what I can see, it's purely psychological. Maybe something happened, like you were mugged. Your memory could come back at anytime, or if you want, I can refer you to a competent psychiatrist."

"That might be a good idea," I say. "A lot saner than what your mother suggested."

"Why, what did she suggest?"

"A trip to Madame Carlotta's parlor." My response earns me a hearty laugh from the young man. Then he gets serious.

"Off the record," he says in a hushed tone, "I dated one of her daughters when I was in high school, and that old lady really knows what she's doing."

"I bet she kept you from messing with her little girl," I say with a laugh.

"You have no idea." His face pales as he answers. "I'd rather face a shotgun-toting dad than that old priestess again."

"Yeah, like you'd have to be a mystic to know some teenaged boy wants to get into your daughter's pants," I say, teasing him.

"True. In the meantime, you get plenty of rest and exercise, and keep eating right. Maybe your memory loss has to do with your time on the streets."

"Thank you, Dr. Fuller." I take the prescription and make my exit, smiling as I leave. His advice warms my heart. The things he has instructed me to do seem so basic. A year ago, I wouldn't have been able to follow his instructions. I had nowhere to sleep, I never knew from one day to the next if I would find anything to eat, and the only exercise I got was running from the police or worse.

Later that night, I'm standing on my balcony, drinking in the sweet scent of magnolias as my fingers twirl the ruby ring that is dangling from my neck. I think about everything Dr. Fuller and Betty have said to me. My memory loss could be post-traumatic stress syndrome, although it's a bit late for it to creep up on me now. But perhaps finally leading a normal life has set it off. Living with my parents for seventeen years was a nightmare. The beatings and verbal abuse were nothing compared to the wretched treatment I received after they discovered I was gay.

"Do I really want to know what I've forgotten?" I ask the almost full moon, as the distant sound of wings flapping in the breeze echoes in my memory. When the moon fails to respond, I decide to just let go and enjoy my new life.

My resolve lasts only until Saturday night, when I once again tear through my meager belongings in search of some answers. I'm frustrated when I fail to discover anything new. I clutch the travel bag tightly as my irritation grows, and suddenly I feel something. I grope the bag furiously and feel it again—the slim outline of something. Opening the bag, I search along the inside. I tug at the bottom stitches and smile when they give way. Sewn inside the bottom is a thin notebook. I open it and discover, much to my surprise, a journal written in my own hand.

I sit down on my bed, and eagerness wars with trepidation as I begin reading.

* * *

My name is Samantha Timmons. I'm writing down these events to help me understand them. It all started on Halloween night when I fell through the floor of an abandoned building. One of the floorboards had pierced through my body, and I knew I was going to die. I welcomed the end of my miserable existence. The idea of no longer having to endure cold, hunger and hostile glares gave me a strange sense of peace. Then I heard the sound of wings flapping. It was a strange sound, not like a bird, more like the leathery clapping of a bat's wings.

The wings unfolded into a cloaked form, and a pair of piercing blue eyes looked into my soul and captured me. I was encompassed in darkness. At the time I thought it was death, finally come to claim me. I was wrong.

When I awoke, it was still evening. I was in an elegant room, lying completely naked on a soft down comforter. A fire was burning in the fireplace and the windows were completely covered by long red velvet drapes that blocked out the slightest hint of light. I was aware that it was nighttime only because of the sounds of crickets chirping in the distance. My nakedness and the lack of wounds on my body startled me. I jumped from the bed and quickly scanned the room for some clothing and a way to make my escape. There was no clothing, but I spied a large mahogany door.

"Try this," a sultry voice called out to me. I spun around to find a tall, raven-haired woman, clad from her boots to her top in black leather and wearing a long black leather coat. She was holding out a black silk robe.

Her lips curled into a smile as her electric blue eyes drifted down to my breasts. I tried to cover my body with my hands. I was embarrassed by the way she was looking at me. Her gaze drifted up to my eyes, and my knees buckled as her smoky gaze captivated me. "You don't have to get dressed if you don't wish to," she said, toying with me in a rich tone that sent a shiver down my spine.

I snatched the robe from her long fingers and wrapped it around my body. I tore my eyes from her gaze. "How... how did you get in here?" I stammered, realizing that I had been looking at the door, yet hadn't seen her enter the room. "And for that matter, where is here?" I was suddenly angered by the situation.

"This is my home," she said in a casual manner, lowering herself onto the bed. She stretched out and leaned on one elbow, watching me as I nervously paced about the room. "Samantha?" Her voice beckoned me.

The air escaped my lungs, and I almost fell to my knees when her tongue peeked out and she slowly licked her ruby-red lips. I forced my eyes to look away from her lips, only to see her palm caressing the bedding. I was mesmerized until a glint of red broke my trance. On her ring finger was a gold ring set with a very large ruby.

"Samantha?" Her voice once again sent a shock wave through my body, and I quickly stepped away from her. When I felt the door pressing into my back, I reached for the knob. It turned, but the door failed to open. I closed my eyes. "Why am I here?" My voice shook as I squeaked out the words.

"I brought you here." The words were murmured in my ear. My eyes snapped open, and I found her standing directly in front of me. Somehow, she had closed the distance between us without my hearing her movements. "You were hurt," she continued, her long fingers caressing my neck. My skin prickled from her touch.

"I'm not hurt now," I said in a voice just above a whisper, as I felt her body leaning into my own. Her touch warmed me,

"No, you've been healed, bathed, and given a very nice room," she said, her hot breath caressing my ear. I whimpered as her tongue traced my ear. "Now it's up to you whether or not you wish to stay," she said with a purr, and dipped her tongue into my ear.

My entire body quivered with desire as her hand drifted to the back of my neck. I tried to fight against the passionate urges coursing through me. "And what is my debt for your kind hospitality?" I said, already knowing the answer.

"The price I will ask for extending your visit isn't what you think it is," she said. "Look at me." My heart beating wildly, I looked up into her eyes. "You can leave now, wearing the filthy rags I found you in, with a simple thank-you. Or you can pay the price for enjoying the comforts of my home for a while longer. All I ask in return is that you share your smile with me."

My head fell back as she pressed the length of her body against me. I was lost in an emotional tug-of-war. She felt so good, and it wouldn't be the first time I had given myself up for a warm meal and a bed to sleep in. I shivered as the robe I wore was opened and her fingers danced along my skin. "The gift of your smile is a small price to pay," she said, in accord with my thoughts, as her fingers brushed along the swell of my breasts. "In the past, you've paid much more for far less than I'm offering."

"Damn you!" I cried, pushing her away. I wanted her, but the harsh truth of her words sickened me.

"Too late," she said, releasing a deep, throaty laugh.

I looked at her in puzzlement before I noticed the glimmer of a mirror on the opposite wall. My eyes widened in horror as I looked past her shoulder and saw only my reflection. "Hmm," she said, following my gaze, "I don't know why I bother hanging those things." Sighing, she once again reclined onto the bed.

"This can't be happening," I said in disbelief, and looked over at her. "Wings. I heard wings. It was a bat… a vampire bat?" I gasped in fear.

"Don't be ridiculous," she said with a laugh. "Vampire bats are only found in South America. Why would one be flying around New York City?"

"It wasn't a bat?" I tried to make some sense out of the situation.

"Yes and no." She sighed, seeming to grow bored with the conversation. "I can take many forms."

"Oh, peachy," I blurted. For some reason, I suddenly found the situation funny. I think I was convinced that I had finally gone off the deep end, and none of this was real. "I must be insane to think I'm in a mansion being seduced by Dracula's daughter."

"Vlad the Impaler was never one of us." She rolled her eyes in disgust. "That guy was just a big psycho."

"Knew him personally, did you?" I found myself laughing again.

"No," she said, and smiled. "He was a bit before my time."

"And just how old are you?" I asked as I sat down on the bed.

"Let's just say I'm older than I look," she said in a droll tone. "You're not imagining anything."

"Of course I am," I answered, and gave a heavy sigh. "I have to be. If I'm not, then I really am having a chat with a vampire."

"Would that be so bad?" Once again, I found myself captivated by her piercing gaze. "My name is Khristina Belcourt. I've been alive for over four hundred years, so of course, I'm not mortal. I was born a creature of the night, and I'm not able to walk in the daylight. I'm not going to harm you. My only wish is to bask in the sunlight of your smile. Your body is your own, to be given or taken only as you desire. When I said I wanted to see you smile, that's all I meant. If you refuse, then you're free to go back to New York."

"I'm not in New York?"

"No," she said. "I will return you to where I found you."

"And if I stay, you won't hurt me or drink my blood?" I pondered my unusual situation, and wondered just why my hostess seemed so flippant about everything.

"I said I wouldn't hurt you," Khristina corrected me. "But I have to eat." Her tongue glided over her pearl-white teeth, revealing sharp fangs for the first time.

"Oh, like that isn't going to kill me or turn me into one of you."

"You'll die only if I drink too much, and you can't become one of us unless we drink from one another at the same time," Khristina said.

I gave her a skeptical look. Despite her sincere expression, I doubted her motives. I would have been a fool not to. "Right. And all I have to do is smile, and we can just cuddle," I scoffed. "And if I want to, I can just walk right out of here? Then why is the door locked?"

"Go," Khristina waved her hand and the door opened. "It's true I desire you, but I will only take what you offer."

"You'd let me just walk out of here?" My skepticism grew. "Aren't you afraid I'd tell someone?"

"Go right ahead," she said and laughed, adjusting her body so that she was leaning against the plump pillows lined up along the headboard. "Walk up to the first cop you find, and tell him that a mean old lesbian vampire took you home and made a pass at you. Either way, you'll get three meals a day and a bed to sleep in."

The gravity of her words hit me hard. "Yeah, and I'll be heavily medicated." I moaned and buried my face in my hands.

"I don't need to hide who I am," Khristina continued. She sat up and began to rub my weary shoulders. "No one would believe you. One of the joys of progress is that no sane person would believe that I exist."

I began to weep. I cried harder than I had in years. She cradled me in her arms and held me as I sobbed. "Stay," she whispered in my ear as I curled up in her embrace. "If just for one night, let the pain go. A few hours ago, you were welcoming death. Tonight, just welcome a blissful slumber."

Much to my surprise, Khristina only held me during the night. She could have done anything she wanted to me and I wouldn't have refused; yet she simply held me as I cried myself to sleep. When I awoke the following morning, I did what she asked me to do. I smiled. For the first time in years, I smiled. Sadly, she was fast asleep and failed to see it. "I owe you one," I whispered as I climbed out of bed and gently pushed back the drapes.

The room echoed with a fierce growl that sounded like a jungle cat and the drapery snapped shut of its own accord. I jumped back fearfully and spun around to find my benefactor rubbing her tired eyes. "Sorry, I'm not much of a morning person," she apologized wearily, and gave a deep yawn.

"Right," I said, crossing carefully back to the bed. "I forgot."

"This bed is very comfortable," she said absently, releasing another yawn.

"This isn't your room?" My eyes widened in realization. "Of course it isn't! You need to sleep in a coffin."

"Where do you mortals get this stuff?" she said, shaking her head. "I sleep in a bed. I just don't usually sleep in this bed. This is the guest room. And for the record, I love garlic."

I couldn't help myself; I laughed at her joke while I climbed back onto the bed. "Now that's what I wanted to see," she said, and sighed deeply as she cupped my face in her hands. I leaned into her touch, enjoying her warmth.

"Why are you doing this for me?" I asked, unable to accept that someone could simply be kind to another person. But then again, she wasn't really a person.

"Why do you doubt that you deserve kindness?" she asked. I felt myself being drawn to her again.

I couldn't answer her question. In my heart, I truly believed that I didn't deserve kindness. The dark glimmer in her eyes trapped me in her spell. I licked my lips, eager to taste hers. She brushed them softly against mine, and that simple touch sent a tremor through my body. As her arms encircled me, I kissed her again and was greeted by the soft fragrance of magnolias mixed with leather.

Her long leather coat slipped from her body, and I caressed the leather clothing that encased her, suddenly feeling as though I were embracing fire. My fingers became entangled in her hair as the kiss deepened. I remember moaning as our tongues met. I find it hard to explain, but her kisses felt as though she was giving me life. Suddenly, for the first time in years, I wanted to live.

I still wonder if perhaps she had indeed cast a spell over me. At that moment, I didn't care. Touching and being touched by this woman felt far too good. Each time my tongue grazed one of her sharp fangs, I felt a void that only she could fill. I had spent years not feeling anything, but at that moment, all I could do was feel.

Pure desire possessed me. I was gasping for air as her lips broke away. My head fell back, and I felt her hot breath on my skin as her tongue caressed my neck. My stomach clenched when her fangs dragged along my skin.

I lay back on the bed, pulling her along with me. I pressed her mouth closer to my neck and begged her to drink from me. A soft growl filled my ears and then sharp fangs pierced the skin at the base of my throat.

When she drank from me, it felt as if my entire being had burst into flames. I clawed at her body, needing to become one with her, as she opened my robe and filled her hands with my breasts. My body bucked beneath her as I climaxed. Then the moment was over, and she was licking droplets of blood from my throat. "More," I pleaded.

"No," she whispered against my skin. "You are still weak."

"Please," I begged once again when I felt her rising. Dark blue eyes gazed down at me as she hovered above my quivering body. Her leather-clad thighs straddled me, and she caressed my breasts. "How did you find me?" I asked, giving in to her touch.

"I was hunting," she said and moaned when the tips of her fingers brushed lightly across my nipples. "I could smell your blood."

"Why did you heal me?" My body arched against her touch. "I've already lost my soul. Why not feed on me and let me die?"

"You haven't lost your soul," she said. "Perhaps I saved you because of your soul. You have a bright light inside of you that I will never know."

I reached up and began to unlace the ties of her leather vest. "How did you heal me?" I asked, in an effort to fully understand what was happening to me.

She raised her left wrist, which bore a strange scar, and pressed it to my lips. "You drank from me," she explained. Her deep, sultry voice called to me like a siren. I kissed the scar and traced it with my tongue. I slipped the vest off her body. The vision above me was poetry. Her body was sheer perfection. Her movements stilled as my hands explored her skin.

My gaze followed the shy, sweeping motions of my hands. It had been a lifetime since I had touched another woman this way. I didn't want to waste a single moment, knowing that I could awaken to find myself back in that building, bleeding to death.

"This is real," Khristina whispered softly, encouraging me to continue my exploration.

"It can't be," I said, not truly believing that I was really feeling her skin responding to my touch. Her flesh was so warm and smooth, and my hands needed to feel all of her. I felt a sense of freedom as I touched her. Perhaps it was the first time in my life that I had been granted the choice of touching and being touched by someone I truly wanted. And yet my wary mind still didn't believe that anything I was experiencing was real.

My hands caressed her firm, full breasts as she leaned closer, allowing me to play with her. The feel of her rose-colored buds hardening against my touch sent another shock wave through my system. My movements paused for a moment and I stared at my hands on her body. I felt dirty, and unworthy of her touch. It was then that I realized my body had been bathed for the first time in years.

"You're beautiful," she said in a tender voice, covering my hands with her own and guiding them down to her flat stomach. She leaned closer and pressed one of the hard buds against my trembling lips. My tongue snaked out and flicked lightly against her nipple. I felt her hands caressing my body; each touch was like a loving kiss.

She purred like a contented lion and slipped away from me. I looked up at her, confused. She licked the traces of my blood from her lips. "You must be starving." Her voice seemed to caress me. "I'll have the cook bring you up some food. Feel free to rest or walk around the grounds. Do whatever you wish to do today."

She closed my robe and knotted the sash before climbing off the bed. I stared, astonished, as she dressed herself. "Wait," I called as she opened the door. "Don't you want to make love?"

"Yes," she said, with a brilliant smile that once again revealed her fangs. "When that's what you're offering."

"I don't understand," I said, whimpering like a child.

"I know," Khristina's voice was sad. "I need to rest. I hope you'll stay and join me for dinner." Then she was gone. I jumped from the bed and opened the door, just to assure myself that I could. I looked down the long, barren corridor, searching for her. Unable to find any trace of her, I returned to my room and climbed back into bed.

At the time, I failed to understand the depth of her words. I didn't understand why she didn't just take what she wanted. Of course, back then I didn't know that what she wanted was more than I thought I was capable of giving. I thought that "making love" was just a polite expression for sex. The raw physical act was something I understood. I had no concept that there could be something deeper, more meaningful.

The only thing my weary mind could focus on was how comfortable the bed I was nestled in felt, and that Khristina was sending food up to my room. My stomach growled at the thought of having a hot meal. My last meal had been a half-eaten Big Mac I had retrieved from a trash can two days ago.

I drifted off to sleep, only to be awakened by the delightful aroma of food. I was drooling when I opened my eyes and saw a plump woman placing a tray of piping hot food on the dresser. The woman, I eventually found out, was Nettie, the cook and maid. Nettie didn't bother to hide her distaste for my presence. She didn't like having to deliver my breakfast, and made sure I knew she was unaccustomed to waiting on the lady of the house's guests. And I clearly understood that by guest she meant whore.

Nettie's treatment was more like what I was used to. I was worthless, and she didn't feel the need to pretend otherwise. The sad thing was that at the time, I agreed with her assessment. Nettie and I never took to one another. Our mutual dislike was never very well hidden from the other members of the staff and Khristina.

How can I describe my life at Belcourt Manor? I felt imprisoned, though in many ways, I had been set free. Khristina made certain that I was fed, clothed, and cared for, and I was free to come and go as I pleased. Her manservant saw to my every need and was even teaching me how to use the computer.

When I first met the tall, thin, brooding man I expected him to introduce himself as Igor. I laughed outrageously when he told me his name was Biff. Khristina still doesn't understand why I think it's so funny. She doesn't always get my sense of humor. Of course, I was only just finding out that I had one. It had been far too many years since I laughed.

Nestled among the willows just outside of New Orleans and away from curious eyes, Belcourt Manor was elegant, to say the least. My hostess was more than gracious and often absent. So why was I so unhappy? I was gaining skills that would enable me to find work if I left the safety of Khristina's home. But could I leave her? And did I really want to?

She rarely drank from me. When she did, the feel of her fangs piercing my skin sent me into a euphoric haze, and her drinking my blood was pure ecstasy. When she was around at night, she would hold me, caress me, sleep beside me; yet she never made love to me.

I wanted to feel all of her, but I was afraid to touch her. I was too afraid that my need to be with her was born of a sense of obligation. I knew she felt my hesitation. I could see her eyes cloud with sadness when she looked at me, and I knew I was the cause. Every day, I wondered if this would be the day she finally grew tired of my fears and cast me out, sending me back to the streets.

There were nights when she would return late. I knew that she had fed upon or been with another, and I was filled with a bitter rage. Strange to feel jealousy when I couldn't decide if I wanted Khristina, or just what she gave to me.

I entered my bedroom late one evening, and the balcony doors were wide open. A gentle breeze and the scent of magnolias filled the room. Suddenly, there she was, perched on the rail. I wasn't surprised to see her; I had quickly become accustomed to her sudden appearances.

She floated into the room as though she were carried on the wind. Her movements always made my heart beat faster. She moved with the sleekness of a panther and gathered me into her arms. Again I questioned whether I was drawn to who she was, or what she was.

"Always questioning," she said, purring deeply, and my body shivered in response. I hated that she seemed able to see my innermost thoughts.

I pulled away and glared at her. I could smell another on her. "Would you deny me my pleasures?" she asked, and my inner torment returned.

"Why am I not enough?" I said, my voice bitter.

"You don't offer what I need." She sounded unhappy. "Samantha, when you know what you want, only then will we have a chance."

She reached out and cupped my face. I pulled her closer and kissed her deeply. I loved the way she kissed me. Each time our lips met, I felt as though our souls were touching. Of course, I was the only one who had a soul. Still, I felt as if I were part of her.

"I want you," I murmured against her lips.

"Do you?" Her hands roamed along the curves of my body. "Or are you simply offering your body because you feel obligated to do so?"

"You can see inside me," I said, slipping her long leather coat from her body. "Can't you feel my desire?"

"I can." She moaned, and her hands drifted up to the swell of my breasts. "I can also feel your fear." My hands busied themselves with the laces of her vest. "You have the skills now to find work. If you wish to leave, I won't send you back to the streets. I've spent centuries amassing enough money to ensure that I'll never want for anything."

"What are you saying?" I guided the vest down her arms and dropped it to the floor.

"I can give you a new start." She moaned again, leaning into my touch. "An apartment and a job. Whether you keep them and survive is entirely up to you."

My movements stilled when I realized just what she was offering me—a fresh start with no strings attached. Once again, Khristina had rescued me and asked for nothing in return. "Khristina," I said with a sigh, my hands returning to the smoothness of her skin. "You've quieted my fears, but not my desire."

I looked up at her. Khristina's eyes took on a mystical glow. She filled her hands with my breasts, and I inhaled sharply as I felt her touch gently exploring my body. "Ask me for your freedom," she said, tugging my shirt out of my pants.

I could feel that her request was breaking her heart. I didn't want to hurt her, yet I knew that I had to do as she asked. Neither of us would ever feel that our passion was true unless I was free. "Set me free," I said, and sobbed.

"It will be done." Her voice was filled with pain as she whispered her promise.

"Make love to me," I pleaded, and she did as I requested. For the first time in my life, I understood what it was to be loved. I'll never forget how her hands felt. There's no other way to describe her touch. She undressed me slowly; I watched as her hands glided along my body.

She guided me down onto the bed. Watching her, I couldn't breathe as she undressed and the leather slipped from her skin. Her naked body was the most amazing sight I had ever witnessed. She stood beside the bed, her eyes roaming along each of my curves. Her gaze touched me, and I felt as though her hands were already caressing my flesh.

My body arched beneath her fiery gaze; I was ready to explode, even though she still hadn't touched me. I felt a love and a sense of belonging that I had never known existed. My experiences with women had been limited to the youthful fumbling of the bi-curious girls I knew in high school and the tawdry paid encounters I had endured in the dank back alleys of New York.

Rarely had my soul been touched by those. I was simply there to provide a service and shamefully did what was asked of me. Until that night, I hadn't understood how it felt to be treated like a lover. Khristina made me feel complete simply by looking at me. I trembled as I reached out to her.

She accepted my hand. Her skin met mine and my body burned as I kissed her. Khristina's hands slowly traced the curve of my hips. I moaned and ran my tongue along her sharp fangs and quivered. Lacing my fingers in her silky hair, I drew her to me. Her fangs teased my neck. I pressed closer, begging her to feed.

Strangely, she hesitated for a moment before plunging her fangs through my skin. I remember crying out while my body quaked. I can still recall her scent filling me with desire as I clung to her while she licked the blood from my neck.

I dug my blunt nails into her shoulders as our bodies became one. I'll never forget the rhythmic movement of her body as she pleasured me. Everywhere she touched me, my skin burned. With her tongue and fangs, she teased my nipples until they ached with pleasure. Her fingers inside of me felt like heaven. I rode against her gentle touch, crying out her name until I was exhausted.

She cradled me in her arms; the feel of her body touching mine re-ignited the fire. Soon I was exploring her with my hands and my mouth. My touch was slow; I tried to memorize every inch of her. We gave and took throughout the night. I feared the morning, thinking that I would never see her again. Our lovemaking had brought me to heights I had never known existed, and I wasn't ready to be released from my bliss.

Khristina shared my unspoken desires, keeping me in her arms well into the following evening. It wasn't until I drifted off to sleep that the magic began to fade. I awoke the next day in a strange apartment. She had left me the keys, some money, new clothing, furniture, and a note. She had given me my freedom. The rest, as she had said, was up to me.

I went to the interview she had arranged, and I got the job. It was simple data entry, something I was now trained to do. I'm certain that many would scoff at my meager paycheck, but to me it was more than enough. It paid my bills, kept a roof over my head, and put food in the refrigerator. I had a new life. It was slow, adjusting to living in comfort that I provided for myself.

I still felt uneasy around my co-workers and neighbors. Before Khristina flew into my life, I had very little interaction with other people. At times I felt claustrophobic. It was harder at night, when I was all alone, staring up at the night sky and missing her.

One night, I left the balcony doors open in an effort to catch a breeze. The scent of magnolias filled the air and I smiled, knowing that when I turned around, I would find her. Khristina's long leather coat billowed as she breezed into the room.

"I've missed you," I cried, wrapping my arms around her slender waist.

"You're doing just fine without me." She kissed the top of my head.

"Thanks to you."

"No. I gave you an address, got you an interview, and that's all I did."

"You're my landlord, aren't you?" I already knew the answer. "That's how you can enter my home without an invitation, isn't it?"

"True," she said. "But paying the rent is entirely your responsibility. I don't get involved with the running of my properties."

"It feels good to say, 'my home'." I guided her to my bed.

"You deserve it." She smiled at me as she reclined onto the bed.

"I've started school," I said, taking her hand.

"Tell me all about it."

I began to prattle on until I noticed the lateness of the hour. "We don't have much time," I said as I began to undress her.

"This isn't what I came for," she whispered, capturing my hands as she spoke.

"Don't you want to?"

"Of course I want to." She smiled and kissed the back of my hand.

"So do I," I said, before claiming her lips.

We made love until she was forced to flee the sun-fire springing into the sky.

* * *

Khristina visits me almost every night. She has no other; I coax her to feed from only me. My body is growing weaker, yet I can't stop myself. She needs to feed, and I can't bear the thought of another touching her. She fights with me. Perhaps that's why I've begun this journal.

My life is slipping away. Soon, either I will perish or she will stop visiting me in order to save me. Each time I pull her to me, we argue. "I'm killing you!" she screamed at me the other night. "If you bonded with me, drank from me and became one with me, you would be safe."

"I can't," I said. "I've just discovered the light in this world. I can't give it up now. And I can't give you up."

Every night is the same. We love, we laugh, and I give her my essence. She tries to stay away, but neither of us can breathe without the other's touch. What she has said is true; she's killing me. I can't leave the joys of the morning light and she's trapped in the darkness. I've found my soul, and it belongs to her; yet the way things are, we can never really be together. Our different worlds are tearing us apart, so I've decided that if she comes to me tonight, I'll leave my world and become a part of hers. It's the only way.

* * *

That's where the journal ends. I stare blankly at the pages. How odd it is to be reading about my love life and not recall a single detail. I read the journal over and over again, looking for some clue as to what happened next. It's always the same. If I had decided to bond with her, then why am I here? More important, where is Khristina?

I spend day after day reading each word in the blasted journal and come no closer to understanding what happened. Now it's early evening on Halloween. One year ago today, my life changed forever. I'm at my wits' end, and the need to find out the whole truth has driven me to the last door I ever thought I would enter.

A bell chimes as I step into the bustling little shop. The tourists have filled every nook and cranny. My eyes dart around in search of the mysterious Madame Carlotta. A voice whispers coldly in my ear, "Now why would someone with the mark of Belcourt step into a slayer's den?"

I jump with surprise and turn to find Madame Carlotta standing beside me. "And how is it that you traveled here with the sun still in the sky?"

"I don't know," I answer meekly.

"Come with me," she says. "I'll take no more clients this evening," she calls out to the younger woman working the cash register, and guides me away from the crowd.

We step behind a curtained area into a room filled with plush velvet furniture and a mahogany table. I spy the tarot cards spread across the table. When she motions for me to sit, I do, twirling the ring that still hangs around my neck. She sits across from me and eyes me as though I'm a circus attraction.

"So you're a slayer?" I ask.

"Not me," she says in a firm tone. The curtain opens, and the cashier steps in. "My daughter."

"Okay, Mother, I've locked up the shop," the tall brunette says in a tired voice. She looks down at me. "This had better be good."

"So you're Buffy?"

"I hate that." She scowls with disgust. "The name is Keren. And you are?"

"Samantha." I shift nervously, clutching the paper bag I've brought with me. Inside are my journal and the tin of ashes I've kept for the past year.

"Show Keren your neck," Carlotta says.

I wince slightly as I brush my long blonde hair from my neck. "The mark of Belcourt?" Keren says with disbelief. "Amazing. Slayers have a long history with the Belcourt line. We have an uneasy alliance. Each of us is trained to distrust the other, yet neither has had cause to interfere with the other's life. That is, until very recently. Stefan, the family elder, is very upset. It seems his favorite daughter is missing."

"Khristina?"

"Yes," she confirms. "And here you sit with her mark on your neck and her ring. Would you care to enlighten me as to just how it is that she marked you so deeply, and yet you still walk in the daylight?"

I fumble with the paper bag and extract my journal. I hand it to Carlotta. The old woman accepts it in her gnarly grasp and places it on the table. "I think that's my story," I try to explain.

"It is," Carlotta says in a sad voice, running her fingers along the unopened notebook. "Your words are true."

I ask myself how she knows this. Has she read my journal or is magic at work here? Some things are beyond my understanding, but I decide I don't care. I need answers about Khristina, not Carlotta.

"Please tell me what happened," I beg, as her daughter looks on.

"Everything happened just the way you wrote it," Carlotta says in a direct manner.

"But it isn't the whole story," I argue. "Why do I feel something is missing besides my memory? What happened to me? What happened to her?"

"You offered to bond with her, and she refused. You made love that night. While you slept, she removed her ring and placed it at your bedside. She walked over to the balcony and drew open the curtains. For the first time in her existence, she felt the sun on her skin." Carlotta's voice is filled with sadness as she tells my story.

"That would have killed her," Keren looks startled.

"It did," Carlotta says.

"But why?" I ask, sobbing.

"To save you," Carlotta explains. "When she left this world she took your memory with her. Now you're free."

"Wait," Keren says. "Khristina Belcourt committed suicide? I don't buy it. Why would she?"

"True love." Carlotta nods toward her daughter. "This one doesn't understand," she says to me. "She has the worst taste in men."

"Hey, not so," Keren tries to object.

"A matter for another time." Carlotta calmly ignores Keren. "For now, the question is, would you do what she did, Samantha? Would you sacrifice everything to save her?"

"I don't even remember her." It's true. I read the words in the journal as though they had been written by a stranger. Still, something in my heart screams out my answer. "Yes!"

"Give me her ashes." Carlotta begins to light a series of candles and the strangest smelling incense.

"Betty was right about you." From the paper bag, I remove the coffee tin and hand it to her.

"Mother, what are you doing?" Keren asks.

"Hush, and fetch me the ivory urn," Carlotta says. "I'll need her ring too."

I listen to Keren's grumbles as she storms out of the room. Slipping the shoelace from around my neck, I place the ring on the table. My eyes grow fearful as Carlotta rummages about, placing an odd array of items on the table. They include an animal bone; a lock of hair; and most disturbingly, a dagger.

"This rarely works," Keren says to her mother as she places the urn on the table, "and you've never tried it before."

"You've never done this before?" I struggle with a feeling of horror as I try to understand what the old woman is up to.

"Best to prepare yourself then," Carlotta tells Keren as she places the ashes in the urn. "We don't know who or what will be joining us."

"Son of a..." Keren is muttering and digging through a leather sack. The items she retrieves are like something from a movie: a wooden stake, a vial of holy water, and, of course, a cross.

Carlotta kneels, pulls me down beside her, and chants as she burns more incense. The aroma is disgusting. She grabs my hand and holds the dagger above the palm. "What would you give to save Khristina from hell?" Carlotta asks with a moan.

"Everything," I say, praying that my words are true.

"Her blood is in your veins." She moans again, and I feel the dagger piercing my skin.

I watch in disbelief as my blood flows freely. I have no idea why I'm doing this. I simply allow Carlotta to guide my bleeding hand over the urn. I feel the room spinning, and her chanting grows louder.

I close my eyes, and bell chimes fill my ears. I'm crying, and I don't know why, as the sounds in the room grow louder. I hear a monstrous clap of thunder. I blink open my eyes and the room is as dark as night with the exception of an ethereal glow hovering above the urn.

The table snaps like kindling as the glow becomes a bright light. The disjointed sounds of a weeping child fill the room. "She isn't coming," Carlotta says weakly and collapses.

"No," I cry out, jumping to my feet. I still have no understanding as to why I'm doing this. I feel deep sadness wash over me as I reach out to the light. "Take my hand!" I yell. My heart feels an essence near me. "Take my hand!" I call out again, my eyes filling with tears. The air escapes from my lungs as I feel something—someone—clutch my hand.

It's Khristina. I feel her warmth, sense her pain, and I remember everything. "Come back to me," I beg from the very depths of my being. In a flash, the room explodes. I shield my eyes, tightening my hold on her. I open my eyes, and the only change in the room is a wondrous one. Khristina stands before me, looking very tired and very naked.

"Samantha? I can't believe it!" she cries before wrapping me up in her arms. "Why did you do it?"

"Why did you leave me?" I say, trying to quiet my sobs.

"You shouldn't have remembered me."

"I didn't, but still I felt the void of your absence. You left me wounded." It's the truth. All this time I thought I was searching for my past, but in reality, I was searching for her.

She smiles at me, and I blink with surprise. Her brilliant smile is brighter than I recall, and the fangs are absent. "What?" she asks. I grin at her as she runs her tongue along her teeth.

She turns toward Keren. "Slayer," she hisses at the smirking woman. "What have you done?"

"Your father is going to be pissed," Keren says with a saucy grin.

Grabbing the first thing I can find, I wrap a long curtain around my lover in an effort to conceal her naked body from the others.

Seemingly unconcerned about her nakedness, Khristina looks at Carlotta. "I'm mortal?"

"You were pulled from hell." Carlotta acts as if these things happen every day. "You could have returned as the vampire you were or even as a demon. Human isn't that bad."

"Our worlds have met," I say, suddenly feeling shy. "But you could go back to yours."

"I could never bond with another," Khristina says, taking me by the hand. "I love you. Now all I need to know is how you feel."

"I didn't bring you back into this world just to be your friend," I say with some passion. "I love you too. I'm just afraid that I have nothing to offer you."

"Your have your smile." She beams one down at me.

I can't help it; I smile up at her. "That's all I ever needed," she reassures me.

"We need to get you dressed, and quickly," I say.

"Why the hurry? We have a lifetime."

"I want to walk you home before the sun goes down," I explain, as Carlotta and Keren go in search of some clothing. "Today's your birthday as a human, and I want to share your first experience in the daylight."

Khristina dresses quickly. Her clothing doesn't fit, but it's Halloween, and I'm certain no one will notice. As we step out onto the bustling streets, she looks as excited as a little kid. The sun's beginning to set, but we bask in the few moments of daylight left. "Let's go home," I say, giving her hand a tug.

"Yes, let's go home," she echoes, following willingly behind me.

We hurry along the street, eager to begin our new life together. Each of us has paid the price for our freedom. The price we paid was very simple, yet very dear. We gave our hearts to each other and placed unwavering trust that the other would treasure our gift.

The Wake of Night

Wales, 1534

"'Tis never good to start your day crawling out of your own grave," Elisabeth Belcourt snarled, clawing at the muddy soil covering her body. Her major concern at that moment was to be certain that darkness had fallen, pulling its curtain over the blazing sun. For almost two hundred years, Elisabeth had walked in the night, the sun no longer allowed to caress her body. It was the year of Our Lord 1534, nearly three hundred years after a branch of the Belcourt line had fallen into the clutches of Alexandria—seduced, tricked, and sired by the lascivious vampire who had preyed upon the family one by one, until the family began preying on one another.

Elisabeth had grown up hearing the rumors of the family's descent into darkness. She was mortal and did not heed the warnings, sniffing at them as fanciful tales invented to scare children into obeying their parents. Too late, Elisabeth discovered the truth behind the stories. Now she walked only in the darkness. "I have only myself to blame," she admitted, recalling how easily she had disregarded the admonitions not to travel the woods or the moors at night. She gritted her teeth and punched her arm through the soil, knowing the world was a mere pile of sod away.

She murmured with delight when the cold, dark night greeted her. Digging the rest of her way out of the grave, she was disgusted that she had allowed herself to be captured so easily. Fortunately for her, the silly villagers had not realized that she was a creature of the night. Assuming that she was a witch, they had opted to lynch her. "Fools," she sneered, trying to scrape the mud from her cold body.

"You need a bath," a familiar voice taunted her from the shadows.

"Cousin," Elisabeth said and sighed wearily as she spied the teenager. Khristina wasn't really a teenager in earthly terms. The youngster was well over the age of fifty, but Khristina was of a rare breed, born to creatures of the night, never having known the joys or sorrows of mortality. Khristina was blessed, or cursed, by aging differently than her mortal counterparts. "What brings you?"

"Father sent me to fetch you and deliver you to safety. We are traveling soon," Khristina informed her cousin.

Elisabeth's very distant Uncle Stefan was the undisputed leader of the Belcourt clan. He hadn't seen the trouble brewing when his brother Ronan had arrived at his doorstep with a seductive guest. Alexandria had seduced the elder brother and his family, begetting the new line of vampires within a fortnight.

Born long before Kristina's conception, Elisabeth was a very distant cousin. "I do not wish to leave this land," she said, in a fury.

"Why?" Khristina spoke with youthful arrogance, guiding the slender redhead toward the carriage that was awaiting them.

"It is my penance, Khristina." Elisabeth's green eyes darkened with anger. "We all pay a price. Even for lost souls, every action has a consequence."

Khristina's brilliant blue eyes studied her cousin as they climbed into the carriage. "You've been walking this land for almost two hundred years. Surely your debt is paid," she said.

Elisabeth motioned for the driver to hurry. They needed to distance themselves from the unruly mob that would seek her once they discovered the empty grave.

Bracing herself against the carriage's jolting, Khristina continued. "I shall never understand you, cousin. The family works hard to ensure a comfortable existence for all of us, and yet you turn your back on us. Wandering the isles, living in filth like a scavenger and feeding on vermin. Shall you never be free of your debt?"

"No. I have sinned."

"We all sin."

"Mine was a dark sin—that of betrayal," Elisabeth said, her voice dismal. "Taking a life is said to be the darkest sin. I say it is breaking a heart."

"We set sail tomorrow evening." Khristina ignored her cousin's gloomy outlook. "The new land is promising. It is a long ride, so you'll have time to tell me your story."

"Why?" Elisabeth sneered.

"So I may learn. If we all owe a debt, I wish to know what price I am expected to pay. If you share your folly, perhaps I can avoid paying such a dear one. You are like me. I understand that the heart you stole was that of a woman. Help me avoid falling into the same snare."

"Wise beyond your years," Elisabeth noted with a small laugh. "No small wonder you are your parents' favorite. No, the price you pay is to never know the daylight. Your sin was your birth. You have a kind heart, though. Even if it fails to beat, there is goodness deep inside it."

"I fear you are mistaken," Khristina said in a thoughtful tone. "Though I wish I could feel the warmth of the sun as most of my family has done, I sense that I too will be called upon to pay a price. One born from love, and not from duty."

"I pray you are wrong," Elisabeth said, her tone and features grim. "My story began in the year of Our Lord 1334. I was a mere lass, and foolish. 'Never travel the woods at night, never trust a stranger, beware of the Belcourt curse, and heed our warnings—do not fall into the darkness.' My parents' words fell on youth's deaf ears. Her name was Marjie, and I loved her. Yet the young heart is not to be trusted. I was easily swayed to travel the road that led to betrayal. She lived just beyond the woods, and I lived with my father and mother near the cliffs. Our meetings were clandestine from the very start."

"Marjie? Not Marjie Kraig? She was a slayer," Khristina said, amused.

"We were star-crossed before our births, yet I loved her from the first moment I spied her walking alone in the woods," Elisabeth said. "We were mere children at the time. She had yet to discover that she was the chosen one, and I was cursed by my birth into this family.

Elisabeth continued her tale while her cousin sat back, listening. "I was about eighteen when I finally succumbed to my desire for her. Marjie disappeared quite often, and I had no knowledge that when she left our little village she was fulfilling her destiny. She was wary of me. She knew of the Belcourt family, as all slayers did. Still, we are not murderers, which allows our strange alliance with them. She never told me she was a slayer, and I never believed the stories, so why couldn't I share my love with her?"

Scotland, 1334

I was quite smitten with Marjie Kraig. I had been carrying a torch for the dark-haired lass with the hazel eyes since the first moment I saw her. I was just a child then, as was she, yet I was drawn to her when I saw her wandering the woods that day. The fire only grew as I aged. I didn't understand the strange stirrings I felt whenever I saw her, but I was bright enough to keep my attraction to her a secret.

Marjie was an enigma, to say the least. She rarely ventured into the village. She lived in the woods, in a small thatched cottage, with a man whom I had mistakenly assumed was her father. Over the years, I heard many stories about him. I was uncertain what to believe; the only truth I knew was that he was not her father, but he had raised her. I was more than curious; my consuming desire to know more often led me to venture into the forest to spy on her.

My parents went into a rage whenever they discovered I had been roaming about the wooded area just outside our tiny village. In an effort to keep me home, they tried to scare me with stories of ghouls and demons. I thought the fanciful tales of vampires and such were nothing more than fables, manufactured in an effort to keep me close at hand, and assumed that they had somehow discovered my secret.

I was growing older, and soon I would be expected to marry. If my parents' wishes had been granted, I would have already been a bride. I was obstinate to the very end; Marjie was the only person whose ring I wished to wear. Yet I knew I could not reveal my unnatural desires to my parents, who would never accept them. Instead, I fended off every would-be suitor, slipping away to stroll about the woods in search of Marjie.

It was funny how she always sensed when I was about, and I was wounded each time she fled my arrival. In the summer of that year, I heard that Liam, the old man who lived with her, had passed on. His death was cloaked in mystery. Once again, my curiosity was piqued. Late one evening, I slipped from the bed I shared with my two younger sisters and made a fateful trek into the woods.

With every snap of a twig and soft flutter of owls' wings, my heart leapt. I made my way to Marjie's home in the moonlit darkness. Despite my bravado, tales of wild creatures preying on innocent maidens dominated my thoughts. I was covered in sweat by the time I reached the cottage. My hand trembled as I raised it to knock on the door. It was the first time I had ever had the courage to approach her home directly.

Before my shaky fist could strike the withered wood, a voice greeted me. "What is the meaning of this visit?" My breathing seized as I spun around to discover Marjie standing behind me.

"Goodness, you gave me a fright." I gasped and clutched my chest as her hazel eyes seemed to study me. "I only wish to call upon you."

"Belcourt," she muttered in the most untrusting manner.

"True." My knees quivered as her eyes bore into me. "Elisabeth, daughter of Rory and Lesley. I came to pay my respects. I heard of the passing of your..." My words trailed off.

"Liam, my guardian," she said, and I watched her body tensing. Beneath her dressing gown, I spied a shimmering cross that was nestled in her ample bosom. "Why come calling at such a late hour?" she asked, closing the distance between us. My senses reeled at the heat radiating from her.

"My parents are quite superstitious," I said, my eyes still locked on the cross and the gentle rise and fall of her breasts. "I was forced to steal away under the cover of darkness."

"You should heed your parents." She brushed past my trembling form, and my heart nearly shattered at her dismissing me so easily. I reached out to halt her and gasped with surprise when she quickly deflected my advances, almost hurting me with her forceful movement.

"My apologies." I held up my hands to assure her that I meant no harm. "I only wished to speak with you." I felt foolish standing there, practically begging a lass who was probably no older than I was myself for a moment of her time.

"It is late. The woods are much too dangerous for you to be traveling alone," she said in a resigned tone. "Allow me a moment to change, and I will escort you home."

"If it is too dangerous for me, then why is it safe for you?" I asked, disturbed by her condescending manner.

"I'm not like other girls," she said, opening the door to her abode.

"'Tis true," I said and sighed, my eyes wandering along the beauteous curves that the moonlight revealed to my eager gaze. Yes, Marjie was like no other. Perhaps that was what had drawn me to her.

"Wait here," she said. Once again my shoulders slumped, my heart breaking from her callous rejection. "So innocent," she said. Sighing, she stepped past me, delivering another blow to my fragile heart.

I suddenly felt like a child. "No need to trouble yourself. I shall find the path home."

"It is dangerous!" She hissed this time, and the feeling in my heart turned to anger. My eyes narrowed and I reached out, placing a hand on her shoulder. Her body quivered, surprising me. My fingers burned from touching her, and my gaze once again betrayed me, drifting to the swell of her breasts. I licked my lips, unaware of my actions as my fingers drifted to her soft flesh. I ignored her sharp gasp and my fingertips drifted along her neck, slipping lower until they brushed against the cross.

"You are mortal," she whispered, her eyes fluttering shut as I traced the cross.

"What?" I asked, filled with a need I had never experienced before. At the time, I dismissed her statement as foolish, my mind focused only on the softness of her skin. I felt her hands on my hips as I stroked her breasts. "Am I dreaming?"

"No, but this cannot be," she said in a hushed voice, her confidence seeming to fade with every touch.

My eyes filled with tears. Her words of rejection rang in my ears, but she had not pushed my clumsy fumbling aside. Instead, she laced her fingers through my long red locks and I murmured with pleasure. My body filled with a warmth I had never known before. Licking my lips, I felt a sudden insatiable urge and dipped my head to inhale the exhilarating aroma of her flesh.

When I shyly brushed my lips against her neck, my knees buckled and she drew me closer. My face was flushed, my lower body pulsating as our bodies pressed together. I had never felt such joy as when I buried my face in the valley between her breasts. "I have seen you before, craved your touch," she whispered as my lips stole kisses, drinking in the taste of her skin. "We cannot," she gasped, though she pulled me closer and guided me into her home.

I was filled with confusion. Her words were those of rejection, yet her hands spoke another story. She caressed me, tearing at my clothing to feel more of me. My mind was spinning. I gazed up at her, my heart soaring as she captured me in a smoldering gaze. We kissed. Not a shy greeting or a playful peck. We kissed as lovers, as if we were trying to devour each other's soul.

Her tongue flicked against my parched lips, encouraging me to accept her desires. I eagerly granted her request and moaned when her tongue slipped inside the warmth of my mouth. I greeted her touch, and soon we began teasing and taunting each other, both struggling to breathe, yet unable to end the passionate kiss.

We stumbled deeper into the cottage, and I yelped when my hip struck the rickety table in the center of the room. We laughed at the strange turn of events. One look into her stormy eyes, and I knew I would never be free. I trembled against the table I was clinging to and fought to control my breathing, allowing her hands to roam my body.

My thighs quivered, and Marjie slowly removed my simple attire. I was anxious to be free from my bindings, to rip her clothing from her, to share a passion that was forbidden. I wanted her that night and every night that followed. I did not care if we were damned; I only cared about feeling her body, her passion, and all she had to offer.

My nipples hardened when the cool night air caressed them, and my clothing fell to the floor. Marjie's eyes filled with wonder and fear as she tenderly explored my newly exposed flesh. I clenched my thighs in a vain effort to ease the demanding throbbing that was clouding my thoughts.

I was so captivated by her touch that I hadn't noticed that she had managed to undress me completely. I blushed when I realized that I was standing naked before her. My hands trembled, and I reached out to slip her nightgown down her shoulders. I needed to see her, to feel her flesh burning against my own. I shuddered from the feeling of her mouth sucking on my neck. I pressed eagerly against her and her touch grew bolder.

I was ablaze, clutching at her gown, my need screaming inside me. My body arched as her mouth captured my nipple. Drawing her closer, I pressed my breast deeper inside her mouth. I gasped when our hips began to sway, our bodies rocking against each other in an urgent need to release the fire burning inside us. By the love of all that was sacred, I needed every bit of her. I tore open her gown. She trembled as she lowered me onto the table.

Her mouth still teased my breast while her hands groped over me. I drew her closer, offering my innocence, my body and my soul. I cried out when her teeth grazed my nipple and her hand cupped my womanhood. My passion spilled from me, and I knew she could feel how much I wanted and needed her. I rolled my hips, responding to the feel of her palm grinding against me.

Enthralled by her touch, I wrapped my legs around her waist. I clawed at her back, my body thrusting wildly. Her fingers slipped between my slick folds while her mouth worshiped my breasts. She feasted on them savagely, teasing one, then the other. "We are not meant to be," she wailed, pinning my hands above my head with one of her own. I was amazed by her strength, and willingly surrendered to her desires.

"We belong together." I gasped as her free hand glided along my wetness. "Make me yours." It wasn't a request. I was demanding that she take my virtue, my need burning out of control from the feel of her breath on my skin and her fingers dancing against the nub of my most intimate place. I was throbbing, and she teased me harder as my body thrust against her.

"Elisabeth," she murmured, her voice filled with tenderness, her fingers teasing me, pressing against the opening to my maidenhood. "I have watched you, followed you, and spied in your bedroom window." Her voice was shaking as her fingers slipped inside me. "But I am not destined to give my love."

Her voice had grown desperate. I jerked my hips against her touch in an effort to impale myself on her fingers. "Love me," I pleaded, my eyes filling with tears. The rough wood of the table bit into my flesh. I cried out when she plunged inside, tearing my veil. Marjie quivered as I lay beneath her. We gasped for air as her fingers stilled inside me.

I watched her; the vein in her neck pulsating, her breasts peeking out from the tattered remains of her nightgown. My body ached. I lifted my head and captured one of her rose-colored buds between my lips, and the primal groan she released fueled my desires. I arched and pressed against her, demanding that she take all that I had to offer.

The pain ebbed, and her fingers slid deeper inside me. I suckled her nipple like a starving child while she held me captive. She called out my name, over and over again, her fingers plunging in and out in a frenzied rhythm. I loved it and I loved her; I matched her demanding touch eagerly. My screams of pleasure were muffled against her flesh, and the world spun out of control as everything exploded and my heart shattered.

Outside, the world was dark, but I basked in the light of her touch. I nipped at her flesh, urging her to take me higher. I reached the crest; still she pleasured me with wild abandon. My body jerked, aching for more even after her fingers had slipped from my body. She held me in her arms; my vision blurred; our hearts beat as one.

I had crossed the threshold, given in to my hedonistic desires, sinned, and still I craved more. I had foolishly believed that one kiss, or merely standing in her presence, would sate my needs. Now that I had known her passion, I knew that I could never be without her. I began kissing her, my lips burning as she returned the fiery kisses.

I was driven mad by her touch. She gave in to me, allowing me to climb off the table. I tore off the remnants of her clothing, kissing her as I pulled her toward the simple bed nestled by the fire.

My heart skipped a beat when I drank in her glorious, naked form bathed in firelight. I guided her down onto the bed, which was nothing more than a straw mattress supported by a rustic bed frame. I could smell her desire filling the room. Kneeling before her, I buried my face between her creamy white thighs and tasted her. I can still remember the guttural groan I released upon savoring her nectar for the first time.

My tongue teased and tasted her passion, her body grinding against mine as she pleaded for me to take her. I could feel her nub pulsating as I drank from her. I captured the throbbing pearl between my lips and sucked it urgently, wanting to drown in her desire. I clasped the firm flesh of her backside, guiding her closer, pleased by the way she was begging for my touch. I gave in to her, slipping my fingers inside her and tearing her veil as she had torn mine, while I continued to feast upon her.

I felt her hands clawing at my flesh, her passion painting me with her wetness. I couldn't yield to my passion; I kept pleasuring her even when her body tightened against me. Finally, I gave in to my wanton desires and nestled into her embrace. At that moment, I thought it was all I would ever need. I dressed, and she escorted me safely out of the woods, making me vow that I would not return. Even as I uttered the pledge, I knew it was a falsehood.

I returned two nights later. Once again, the fire consumed us. She was all I needed, all I dared hope for. We were separated only by the outside world. On those nights when I would slip away, stealing through the forest, we gave ourselves to one another freely. The passion we shared was wild, untamed, and free from any thoughts of sin or damnation.

Each time the moon lit the night sky, I went to her. It was bliss, except for the nights when she was away. I never asked, even though her absence filled me with doubt and insecurity. I would pay a dear price for my lack of trust. The cold winds of September had blown in. My beloved had been away for a fortnight, and I was desperate to see her. My heart demanded to know where she had been and if there was another.

I saw through young eyes, blind to reason. I slipped from my bed that night, the moon riding high in the sky. I was filled with doubt and the insatiable need to feel her touch. I plodded on my way through the dark forest, my doubts still weighing heavily upon me. I just needed to see her, to hold her, and all would be right. You may imagine my surprise when I happened upon a stranger lurking in the forest.

The tall, pale woman had golden locks and cold gray eyes. "I knew you'd follow her," the stranger taunted me. I was stunned, held captive by her lilting tone. My heart was screaming at me to flee, to run as fast as I could and find solace in Marjie's tender embrace. My feet, however, remained firmly planted in the damp soil. It was as though they had taken root in the ground.

My will was no longer my own. My lips remained frozen; no words could escape. Somehow, I sensed that it would displease the woman if I dared to speak. I was terrified, chilled to the bone. Still, there was something about her that held me.

Before I could form a coherent thought, I was in her arms, giving in to her searing kiss. My mind was devoid of thought; only the guilty stirrings in my heart spoke to me. She quieted their urgent warnings of impending betrayal without uttering a single word. No, she did not speak. Her mouth was far too busy kissing me. Not only did I willingly kiss her in return, but I lifted my dress, pulling up the flimsy shift I wore beneath my clothing.

"Belcourt," she murmured, pushing my trembling body against a tree. With my mind still clouded, I didn't understand her words, and was only dimly aware that she was speaking. Her hand slipped between my thighs and I moaned against her touch. My flesh burned as she sucked my neck, and my body erupted when sharp fangs pierced my skin. I was hers. My body reached the pinnacle just from the sensation of her drinking from me.

I did not need to feel her loving me; the fire of her teeth and her bite were all it took for my helpless body to fall over the edge. "Drink from me," she said, pressing her wrist against my mouth. This was blood; I knew what it was, still I drank from her as she fed upon my neck.

I paused only when I saw Marjie's smile in my mind. "She'll hunt you," the stranger said and cackled, erasing all thoughts of my lover from my heart. We drank from one another, my body soaring, filled with an uneasy passion. I gave away my soul and bonded with the stranger.

I fell to the ground, weak and filled with a dark coldness I had never known before. "A Belcourt sired me." She laughed as I curled up, my body screaming with pain. "My quest is to repay the favor to all of you." Her cruel voice taunted me as I clawed at the ground, wrenching with agonizing pain. "Your family will be next, but first the slayer. You are the key."

I failed to understand her words, or what I had done; I was only aware of the pain. The sun was barely peeking over the horizon, yet I felt as though it were burning me. My face and clothing were bathed in her blood and mine. As I crawled on my hands and knees in agony, I felt a strange hunger. I needed to feed. All day long, I hid in the brush, covering my body. It was demanding the taste of blood. I was still in pain, even when the blinding sun slipped from the sky and I stumbled from my hiding place, adrift and unaware of the world. All I could feel was the hunger. I have no recollection of how long I wandered or when I captured the small bird. I only remember finding its ravished body in my hands, the innocent creature's blood on my lips.

Falling to my knees, I wept. The stranger reappeared. "You learn quickly," she gloated, a cruel gleam in her haunting eyes. "You need to feed."

"Who are you?" My stomach churning, yet I was still drawn to her.

"Lucetta," she said in a disturbingly merry tone. "You are mine. Bring me to her."

"No," I said, whimpering like a frightened child. I knew she was seeking Marjie.

"No?" She laughed and yanked me to my feet. "We can share her," she whispered hotly in my ear. I was wet with desire as the vivid image of the three of us naked played out in my mind: my lover tied to her bed, Lucetta's face buried between her thighs, drinking from her as only I had; my hands caressing my lover's breasts, watching as Marjie screamed in ecstasy, willing the both of us to pleasure her.

"I know how you love it when she mounts you from behind, when she makes you beg as she rides you. Do you want me to watch her taking you, pleasuring you while you taste me?"

"Yes!" I screamed into the darkness, giving in to the erotic image. My sharp fangs gleamed in the moonlight as Lucetta opened her cloak, revealing her naked body. Snarling with pleasure, I lowered myself to the ground. I growled like a wild animal when I breathed in the musky aroma of her passion. I parted her, running my tongue along her sex before curling it and plunging it deep inside of her.

"Oh, yes, my sweet." She moaned as I glided my tongue in and out of her. I slipped it from her warmth and began suckling her throbbing nub while she pressed me closer. I shuddered with pleasure as her passion spilled over me. Sinking my fangs into her thigh, that still trembled from passion, I drank from her. Lucetta's blood made me stronger, forcing the pain that was muddling my thoughts to recede.

"Drink," she said, running her fingers through my hair. "You are still weak. Soon you will be strong, and you can make her yours for eternity."

I have no idea what happened next. I awoke the following evening nestled in a large, comfortable bed. Lucetta was by my side. My body had been cleansed and was now filled with a hunger for passion and blood.

"Drink this." Lucetta smiled and handed me a crystal goblet filled with a dark red substance. The scent of blood invaded me. I drank, and felt alive. I licked the last drops from my lips, savoring the taste. "Now, one craving has been sated. Is there anything else you desire?" She dragged her nails along the curve of my body, taunting me. My mind was still adrift; I could only focus on the primal needs stirring inside of me. *Tie me to your bed and ravish me!* I silently screamed.

"So eager, broken so easily." She laughed and captured me in a savage kiss. I gasped when she overpowered me, and my body hummed as she guided me to my hands and knees. I cried out when her hand slapped my bare backside. My hips jerked back, eager to feel her strike me again. She did so, sharply. Neither blow caused pain, only pleasure. I was shameless; each time I felt her hand striking my flesh I thrust my hips backward, silently begging for more.

My only thoughts were of how good I felt, and that if I gave in to Lucetta's passion I could make Marjie mine forever. Lucetta bound my hands to the bedpost with a silk scarf; my senses whirled as she knelt behind me. My cries of ecstasy echoed throughout the bedchamber as her tongue glided down along my spine. I willingly parted my thighs as she straddled my hips, pressing her wetness against me.

She seemed to hear my thoughts, granting my inner desire and riding wildly against my backside as I eagerly rocked against her touch. The moment I thought I wanted her inside of me, she plunged her fingers deep inside my wetness. Strange that I failed to notice that my heart wasn't pounding; in fact, it wasn't beating at all. I lost myself in her touch, begging her for more, ignoring all else, lost in the pleasure of ecstasy.

Our passion continued every night for a week. Still I failed to understand what I had become. I simply gave in to her desires as she trained me. That was her explanation for the passion we bestowed on each other: she was training me. I still cannot help but question why I failed to see through her, even though I know that when you are sired, the one who bonded with you bewitches you. That is cold comfort for forsaking Marjie.

The week was over, and it was time for me to go to Marjie and make her mine for eternity. Lucetta told me this was what I wanted, and I believed her. I wasn't listening to my heart. Even though it had stopped beating, it still spoke to me. Lucetta's spell held me so tightly I could hear only her lies. I went to Marjie's cottage, eager to make her mine, to seal our love for the ages.

Marjie was shocked when I knocked on her door, beckoning her to come to me. "By all that is sacred, where have you been?" Marjie said, greeting me frantically as I shielded my eyes from the glimmering cross that dangled between her breasts. I felt sick, and I averted my eyes and tried to hide my face.

"Elisabeth," she choked out. I could feel her heart breaking.

I looked at her, and it was at that moment I realized what I was, and what I had done. "Kill me," I whispered. Lucetta's voice wailed with displeasure from her hiding place.

"You're already dead," she said, tears cascading down her cheeks. I could see it in her expression; she could not perform her duty and end my miserable existence. "Name the one who sired you." The need for vengeance was brewing in her eyes.

"Lucetta," I said. She looked past my shoulder and sneered, and I turned to find my owner perched behind me.

"Hello, Slayer," Lucetta growled, her gaze murderous.

All at once, I understood everything. By claiming me, Lucetta had taken her revenge on my family, and she was one step closer to tasting the blood of a slayer. The clouds had lifted; my place in the world became clear. I was a creature of the night, but that did not make me a monster. I held Marjie back as she tried to attack Lucetta. "I shan't return," I said, turning my back on the only person I had ever loved, the person I had betrayed.

Because I hadn't delivered Marjie to her, Lucetta's anger was like wildfire. She vowed that my penance would be to watch my family die and then watch her kill my beloved. My heart may have stopped beating, but it still had feelings. Lucetta was never afforded the opportunity to carry out her promise. She was turned to dust by my hand before the next sunrise.

I was filled with a strange sense of satisfaction when I drove the stake through her heart. Not long after that night, a Belcourt sought me out and taught me the ways of our kind. Marjie never smiled again.

I would come to her in different forms so she would not know it was me. I might be a bird, or a cat. Often, I sat perched on her window in the form of a raven. I just needed to see her, to know that she was safe. One night, she granted me the pleasure of crossing her threshold. "Enter," she said, staring at me perched on her window. "I know it is you. I grant you permission to enter my home."

I flew into the humble room, my body changing, my wings becoming arms as I floated down to her. I stood before her, human and not quite human. I now wore dark leather clothes that hung loosely from my body. "Your family has fled. I told them you perished," she said, unable to look at me. "Lucetta's cronies are hunting them. They are safe in a new land, far from here and the curse that haunts your line."

"Thank you." I shifted nervously, my heart aching to see her inability to look at me. "I am hideous," I said and sighed, accepting my fate.

"No," she whispered, turning to me, tears filling her once brilliant eyes.

"I betrayed you." I reached out for her, then quickly withdrew my hands, knowing that she would not accept my touch.

"You were bewitched," she said. I could hear the pain in her voice. "When you saw me, she no longer held you. Our love finally set you free, and because you listened to your heart, you saved my life. I forgive you for losing your way. Forgive yourself."

"I cannot." I rubbed my face with my muddy hands.

"You need a bath," she said awkwardly.

"You are a slayer. Do your duty. End my existence," I pleaded with her, as she began heating water.

"The Belcourt family do not kill or feed on innocents," she said while she continued preparing the bath. "Slayers do not harm those that mean no harm. Most of your clan is like you—there is no malice, just the need to survive. The water should be ready soon. Take off your garments."

My fangs flared as my body filled with carnal desire. I shook my head, trying to vanquish my lustful urgings. "Take off your garments," she repeated sternly. Again my body burned with desire.

"I shall not," I said, my eyes coveting her sensual body. "I cannot have your hands on me." I released a feral growl that exposed the tips of my fangs, but I turned away quickly when the cross slipped from beneath her dressing gown. To my surprise and horror, she removed it. "I will prepare your bath, and if you fail to remove your clothing, I will be forced to strip you."

I snarled, completely baring my fangs, driven wild by the knowledge that she was offering herself to me. My eyes gleamed, turning dark and fierce as she went about her business. I fought an inner battle, wanting only to ravish her as I had done so many times in the past. But I was no longer human, no longer worthy of her touch. Perhaps I never had been. "You want me?" I asked, and then growled and wrapped my arms tightly around her waist. My fangs scraped against the soft flesh of her neck. I could feel her blood pulsing beneath my touch; I could smell it. I was consumed by the need to taste her, to drink from her, to make her mine for eternity.

"One last time," she said, leaning into my touch. "But if you bite me or try to feed on me, you will suffer. I do not care how much I love you; that will never happen."

I purred like a jungle animal, drinking in her scent, fighting the need to taste her blood. "I should go," I finally cried, tearing myself from the warmth of her body. I stumbled backward, needing to distance myself from her before I gave in to my desires. "I am no longer the person you loved."

"I still see my sweet Elisabeth lurking inside of you," she said softly. "Lucetta robbed you of your life and your soul, but not your essence. Take off your clothes."

"Kill me!" I demanded.

"Never. I will wash your smelly body, which would be a much easier task if you'd rid yourself of those ridiculous garments. What is the attraction between vampires and leather?"

"You are impossible," I said, beginning to shed my clothing.

"My sweet love, my dear Elisabeth, I was always impossible," she said, giving me the ghost of a smile.

"True." I dropped my tattered garments to the floor and purred contentedly when I slipped into the warm, lavender-scented water. "Ah," I sighed, enjoying the feeling of the warm water engulfing my weary body. I released a sharp gasp when I felt Marjie's hot breath caressing my ear and her hands gliding along my body. She knelt beside the tub, washing away the dirt and filth, but not my sins.

My body flailed in the water when her hands cupped my breasts and teased my nipples. Her lips captured mine and when her tongue scraped against my fangs, I growled fiercely. I grasped the wooden edges of the tub in an effort to keep my hands at bay. I dragged my fangs along her neck. She gasped with pleasure, her fingers kneading my scalp as she cleansed my soiled locks. Our lovemaking had always been wild and raw, but now that wildness could prove dangerous.

"You must bind me," I said as her hands roamed down the front of my body under the guise of washing me.

"I do so enjoy that," she whispered huskily, and captured one of my nipples between her lips.

"I know, but now it is necessary, not a game." I gasped, and my body thrust forward in the water as she suckled the erect bud.

I dug my fingers deeper into the side of the tub, and they ached painfully. I was on fire as she guided me from the water and slowly dried my body. I reached out, clasping the back of her head, drawing her to me. I kissed her deeply; my body hummed with desire. I tore off her nightgown, just as I had done the first time we had loved. Her hands were all over me, each of us helpless to refuse the other.

She led me to her bed and bound me tightly with leather straps. I was eager for her to have her way with me. Her hands roamed my body, the musky aroma of our passion filling the room. Her touch was magic, unlike the torrid experience I had shared with Lucetta. I suddenly understood that what I had with Lucetta was like a drunken encounter, paling in comparison to making love.

I struggled against my restraints, driven by the need to feel her flesh as she rolled my nipples between her fingers. She kissed me long and hard, and I squirmed beneath her naked body, my senses giddy from the feel of her passion brushing against my flesh. She loomed above me, pressing her nipple against my lips. I fervently captured the bud, suckling it, careful not to pierce her flesh. Marjie ground her passion against my stomach, and pressed her breast deeper inside my mouth.

Much too quickly, my mouth was deprived of her taste when she pulled away. Whimpering as she straddled my body, I watched in amazement as her hands glided down her own form. The leather bindings creaked as I yanked against them, watching her part herself. I could see her glistening desire begging for my touch. I released a feral hiss as I watched her slip a single digit between her slick folds.

My body jerked wildly, fueled by the vision of her stroking her own sex. My eyes were transfixed, watching her. I was on fire as she painted her passion over and around her nipple. Once again, she pressed it against my lips, and I licked away every drop. Soon she was climbing up my body. The sweet nectar of her passion hovered over my mouth, then she lowered herself to me and I feasted on her. She clung to the bedpost, her hips rocking against my frantic rhythm.

Her thighs quivered against me, inviting me to take her. I nipped at her sweet flesh. A single drop of blood spilled, and I licked it up. I savored the taste, knowing it was all I could take from her. My eager tongue slipped back into her wetness, flicking against her throbbing pearl. I sucked her harder as her screams filled the room.

She collapsed, consumed by waves of ecstasy. But she did not pause. Instead, she began kissing me. Our kisses grew deeper, and her hand slipped between our bodies. I wrapped my legs around her, inviting her to take me. I moaned into the warmth of her mouth when I felt her fingers slip inside me. I rose eagerly, greeting her touch until I, too, was screaming as my body erupted.

Morning crept closer, and our lovemaking turned furious. All too soon, she freed me. I gathered up my clothing and took flight from her bedroom window. It was farewell for both of us. At least, it was supposed to be. We were weak and unable to release each other.

We loved the fire still burning inside of us, yet our hearts were darkened by my betrayal. Many nights, when the moon was bright, I'd find comfort not from loving her, but from spending time with her as a small cat. I knew she recognized me, even in a different form. I would sleep on her bed, content to hear her breathe and listen to the beating of her heart as she slept.

A slayer's life is far too short. I was with her the night she left this world, at the hands of a coward unworthy to claim her spirit. He did not linger long enough to enjoy his victory. I hunted him, pleased that he made such easy prey, and for a second time erased one of our own.

* * *

"Now I walk this land that was once my home, searching for Marjie's soul," Elisabeth concluded grimly. "I know she is out there. I must find her."

"You were bewitched," Khristina said. "No mortal can resist a dark power."

"My love should have been stronger than magic," Elisabeth said, giving a tired groan. She had walked the earth for centuries, and she was weary.

"You need to forgive yourself." Khristina tried to reason with her. "Did Marjie forgive you?"

"Yes, but I will never forgive myself. Mordecai claimed her soul before he killed her. If I find her soul, maybe I will find peace. Until then, I will not stop searching this land. Khristina, you are so very young; you do not understand that a heart is fragile. Someday you will."

"Let me help you search," Khristina said. "Perhaps, when my time comes to pay my price, I will be better equipped to handle my payment."

"This I must do alone." Elisabeth gave a weary sigh, then kicked open the carriage door and jumped to the ground. Before Khristina could stop her cousin, Elisabeth had flown away.

September 16, 1975
Edinburgh, Scotland

Khristina walked into the noisy pub. "Still lurking in the shadows, I see." She smirked down at the scruffy-looking woman hiding in the corner. The woman ignored her, taking a long drag on her cigarette. "Now, is that any way to greet your long-lost cousin?"

"Buy me a drink and I might be more hospitable," Elisabeth said to the youngster who had planted herself in the seat next to her.

"Is that all it takes to win your favor? A pint?" Khristina said, taunting her. "You're living like a beggar when the family has more than enough money to provide you with shelter and comfort. Why?"

"I told you my story once. I don't wish to repeat it." Elisabeth waved for the barmaid to bring another round.

"Yes, I recall your tale of woe." Khristina paid the barmaid for her cousin's pint of ale. "If you joined the family, you might not have to waste anymore of your time. You were right. Mordecai was not worthy to claim the life of a slayer. Your Marjie was careless that evening, already wounded by another. Mordecai was nothing more than a lackey serving the one who sired him. He was sent after the slayer only because his master wished to be rid of him. No one expected him to succeed. His master was stunned when Mordecai presented him with Marjie's soul."

"Who is he?" Elisabeth slammed her fist on the table.

"Sheridan," Khristina's voice was solemn. "He left this land more than two hundred years ago. You will find him in Nova Scotia."

"All this time, I've been searching the wrong bloody continent," Elisabeth said, disgusted.

"Apparently," Khristina replied, a tad too pleased with herself. "I make my home in New Orleans. Come back with me, and I will help you. But only if you promise that once you succeed you will finally put the past where it belongs—in the past."

"Does he have her soul?" Elisabeth's mind was spinning at the thought that her quest might finally be over.

"I imagine he keeps it near him," Khristina said. "The power of a slayer's soul is not something to trifle with. If we can obtain it, you can set her free, give her peace, and perhaps allow her to be reborn. That doesn't mean she will return to you."

"I've known that for quite some time," Elisabeth said. "I simply want to give her peace. I don't expect to win her heart."

"I don't understand. You've spent centuries searching for her, but if you found her, you would let her go. Is that what love is?"

"Yes," Elisabeth said with a laugh. "Someday, you will understand that when you love, sometimes walking away is the right choice."

"Seriously?"

"Yes. When do we leave?"

"Now, if you wish," Khristina said. "I have a plane waiting. But promise me one more thing."

"For this, I will gladly promise you anything," Elisabeth said.

"Take a bath before we leave. Frankly, you smell."

Over a week later, they arrived in Halifax, Nova Scotia. First, they had gone to inform Stefan, Khristina's father, of their intentions. He didn't approve, but he was unable to refuse Khristina anything. Just outside of Halifax, their limousine pulled up at a grand estate.

"Apparently the centuries were good to Sheridan," Khristina said as they approached the front door.

"What did he say when you offered to buy her soul?" Elisabeth asked.

"He said no. Remember, dusting him is not an option."

"Why not?" Elisabeth rang the bell.

"By the rules, he hasn't done anything wrong," Khristina said. A butler answered the door, and after learning who they were, showed them to a sitting room.

"Two ladies from the house of Belcourt," Sheridan said, greeting them in a cavalier manner. Brushing his long black hair from his shoulders, he entered the room. "Now, why would I be honored with such a visit?"

"Do you remember a certain business transaction I suggested some months ago?" Khristina asked. Elisabeth sat silently, reminding herself that she couldn't stake the arrogant pissant. Marjie's soul was near; she could feel it in her bones.

Sheridan laughed. "Why are you so interested? I thought such magic was beneath the honorable Belcourt clan. But I would still be interested in those IBM stocks I mentioned."

"Not a chance," Khristina said. "Come now, Sheridan. We all have a price."

"For a slayer's soul?" He shrugged. "I don't even know where it is. Again, I am surprised by your interest."

"It is near," Elisabeth said. She hated it when people lied to her.

"Very good. I'm keeping it. I don't know you. Why haven't I seen you before?"

"I like to keep a low profile," Elisabeth said, sneering.

"Very low." Sheridan eyed the redhead. "The sewers I'd say. In London, Scotland, or perhaps Ireland. You are the mistress—the one Lucetta stole from the slayer. Why is it that your clan is so determined to be honorable? What a foolish concept."

"Are you quite certain I can't dust him?" Elisabeth said as she glared toward Khristina.

"A threat?" Sheridan raised an eyebrow.

"A promise," Elisabeth retorted with an evil grin. "I took care of Mordecai and Lucetta without batting an eye. You should be easy."

"I really should thank you for Mordecai. As for Lucetta, she hasn't been missed. Still, that doesn't earn you my most prized possession."

"And what would?" Elisabeth asked, wearying of the game.

"Your servitude would be a nice start," Sheridan said, beaming.

"Not going to happen." Khristina held up her hand. "There'll be no war over this matter, on that you have my word. And since you don't wish a monetary reward, perhaps I can offer a challenge."

"A challenge?"

"Well, not a challenge as such, more of a wager."

"And what do you have to offer?" he asked.

"What I bring to the table is the chalice of Danu." Khristina smiled, and Sheridan gulped.

"The chalice from the temple of Avalon? I thought Gwyneth held that." Sheridan seemed amazed, and Elisabeth gaped at her cousin.

"Gwyneth had it, and as we all know…" Khristina paused.

"You had Gwyneth," Sheridan grumbled, his brilliant blue eyes turning dark.

"You're not still angry about that, are you?" Khristina laughed. "I warned you that you weren't her type. Interested?"

"The chalice, blessed by one of the Goddesses of Avalon, that holds the power of life and death? Yes, I'm interested," he said. "What shall we wager on?"

"I've heard of your fondness for baseball. The World Series is next month," Khristina said casually, while Elisabeth glared at her. "I also know you've bet a small fortune on the Boston Red Sox. Now, if by some miracle they make it to the World Series, I'm willing to wager they won't win. Cincinnati will. No trickery, magic, or feeding. Just a good, old-fashioned ball game."

"Deal," Sheridan said.

Once they were back in the limousine, Elisabeth coughed loudly. "What?" Khristina asked, her expression innocent.

"I don't wish to seem ungrateful, but did you just wager the soul of the only woman I have ever loved on a sporting event?" Elisabeth asked angrily.

"I believe I did," Khristina said. "Not to worry, Boston won't make the playoffs. Well, let's hope they don't, because that chalice is very dear to me."

"And if they do?"

"Then we'll be forced to steal Marjie's soul," Khristina said, and her tone turned serious. "I'd rather do this openly, but if we have to, we'll go against my father's wishes and free her soul however we can."

"You're an idiot," Elisabeth said.

"Possibly," Khristina acknowledged.

"I realize that I don't understand baseball, but you seemed quite certain that Boston wouldn't even be playing in the World Series!" Elisabeth shouted, barging into her cousin's bedroom.

"I know," Khristina said, "but they have to win four games in the best of seven series. We still have a chance."

"I've searched for Marjie's soul for centuries. Waiting this long has been the most arduous part of my quest, and now it could slip through my fingers," Elisabeth said. "I failed her once. I can't allow that to happen again."

"No interfering," Khristina warned. "So many already know about the wager that if we try to change the outcome there will be hell to pay, and I mean that literally. Just be patient."

For the first six games of the series, Elisabeth was on pins and needles, constantly pestering Khristina to explain the strange game to her. By the seventh and final game, Elisabeth was a wreck. "One run?" she gasped when the ball clipped the foul pole, ending the series. "How am I ever going to explain to Marjie that her salvation came about because of one run in a game that wasn't even invented when she was alive?"

"I'd leave that part out." Khristina was trembling, shocked that they had come so close to disaster. "Up for a trip to the north?"

They stood in the darkness of the wooded area that had once been Marjie's home. Most of the trees were gone, replaced by cheap housing. Still, a small part remained; it would have to be enough.

"Do you know what to do?" Khristina asked.

"Yes, I've been studying and preparing for this moment for hundreds of years." Elisabeth set an urn on the ground and knelt beside it, offering her prayer to the moon. "Peace," she called out and smashed the urn with her fist. A bright light lit up the dark forest. She smiled for the first time in centuries as she watched the embers floating up toward the sky. "Forgive me?"

"I already have." She heard the words whispered on the wind, and as it became dark once again, "I love you."

"And I you," she called out, a wave of warmth encompassing her.

"That's it?" Khristina asked. "You just had to break the pot?"

"Yeah, that's it," Elisabeth said and laughed. "I just had to find it first."

September 16, 2003
The London Offices of Belcourt Enterprises

"Don't you ever knock?" Elisabeth grumbled as her cousin walked into her office.

"Should I?" Khristina said, teasing her yet again. Elisabeth was about to offer a witty retort when she looked up at her cousin and noted the darkness that seemed to hang over the younger vampire.

"What's wrong?"

"Nothing." Khristina sighed, her eyes dim. Clearly, something was weighing heavily on her. "I just felt the need to visit."

"Liar," Elisabeth said. "I have a meeting, but I could cancel it. You look like you need to talk."

"No." Khristina released another heavy sigh. "I wanted to ask you something."

"Go ahead," Elisabeth said.

"Was it worth it?"

"Was what worth what?" Elisabeth asked, confused by her cousin's sullen mood.

"The price you paid. Was it worth it?"

"You mean freeing Marjie, knowing that I would never see her again?" Elisabeth smiled. "Yes, it was. Perhaps someday I'll fall in love again. I don't know. But letting her go was the right choice. You've fallen in love?"

"Yes," Khristina said with a shy smile.

"She's not one of us, is she?"

"No, she's mortal."

"You say that like it's a bad thing," Elisabeth said. "I was human once. Granted, it was a long time ago."

"She has no place in our world, and I can't walk in hers."

"Follow your heart," Elisabeth advised. "If I had done that, then perhaps Marjie and I would have grown old together."

"Thank you." Khristina nodded, and turned to leave.

"Hold on. That's it?" Elisabeth said, laughing. "You hop on the Concorde just to ask me advice about your love life and then split? I don't think so. Come on, we're going out. I know a place where we can feed without harming anyone, and then there's a pub not far from there."

"Well, that was fun," Khristina said when they arrived at the airport. "Thank you again." As they tried to avoid the hordes of people milling about the airport, something, or rather someone, caught her eye. "Witch," she said with a nod of her head.

"White light." Elisabeth smiled, noting a woman with long dark hair, whose back was to them. "Pure energy. I wonder if she knows."

"There's only one way for you to find out." Khristina wiggled her eyebrows. "I have a plane to catch."

"Safe journey," Elisabeth said, hugging her cousin. She stumbled as she stepped back, seeing the witch turning toward them. It was the young woman's eyes and her smile that gave it away. "It's her," Elisabeth whispered, and a brilliant smile appeared on her face.

"What?"

"Nothing." Elisabeth shook her head. "Go, already. The sun will be rising soon."

"Right." Khristina gave her a searching look. "Follow your heart, remember?"

"Go," Elisabeth said, nudging her.

She watched as Khristina disappeared into the crowd. Once her cousin had vanished she looked for the witch. She was gone. "At least I know you made it safely to the other side." She sighed happily.

"Took you long enough," a familiar voice taunted.

"Excuse me?" She spun around, her jaw dropping when she encountered a familiar pair of hazel eyes.

"I said it took you long enough," the woman repeated. "Do you have any idea what it's like being trapped in a jar for hundreds of years?"

"Can't... can't say that I do," Elisabeth stammered, her mind spinning out of control. "Wait, how did you—?"

"That's a fine greeting after all this time." Marjie shook her finger at the confused vampire. "I came back. Not reborn, just back. I needed to be with you... and I'm needed."

"Pure white light," Elisabeth said, drinking in the sight of her long-lost love.

"Speaking of light, shouldn't we get you home?" Marjie said in a hurried tone.

"Yes," Elisabeth agreed, and laughed unsteadily. "It wouldn't do, having you travel the expanse of the universe only to have me turn to dust the moment you arrive."

"No, it wouldn't." Marjie smiled at her. "Take me home, and I'll explain everything."

"A bit dark, but very nice," Marjie said, looking around Elisabeth's elegant home.

"Yes, well, it's hell on the plants, but if I don't want to go to hell, I have to keep the drapes drawn," Elisabeth quipped, but her mind and body were still reeling from Marjie's sudden reappearance. "Why are you back now?"

"The world's entering a troubled time, and I'm needed," Marjie explained. "I didn't think about coming back at first, but when I realized that you and I could have a second chance, I moved heaven and earth, and not just figuratively, to come back to you. I had to wait because you took so long to forgive yourself. And I wasn't very forgiving at first, either. Before I died, I was angry that you had allowed another to touch you. Knowing that you were bewitched was small comfort. But when you staked that bitch, I knew it was never your heart that left me."

"I was young and stupid," Elisabeth said. "I still love you. Hundreds of years have come and gone, and it's still your smile I see when I sleep."

Marjie took her hand and squeezed it. Then she grimaced. "Your cousin is in for a difficult time."

"I feared that was the case. She was born to the darkness and has never been in the light. I can't imagine what her life has been like. I still remember those rare days when I was able to sneak away—how you and I laughed and played in the sun. It's funny what you take for granted. Now I'd give anything just to go back to those days and undo what I did."

"You can't," Marjie said, sighing. "But we have blissful memories, and now we have a future. I certainly don't plan on harboring a grudge for an infidelity that happened hundreds of years ago. That doesn't mean I'll tolerate another indiscretion, of course." She looked at Elisabeth sternly.

"Understood," Elisabeth agreed, gulping. "I can't believe you're here. I searched for you. Decades turned to centuries as I wandered the isles looking for you. If I had been smarter, or better educated, I would have realized that your soul wasn't there. I'm sorry it took me so long to set you free."

Marjie silenced her, pressing her fingers to Elisabeth's quivering lips. "You never gave up. You lived in squalor, feeding on vermin just to find me, and never strayed from the goodness that still burns inside of you. I knew. Just as I knew that even if Lucetta hadn't seduced you, our time together would have been short. I was the chosen one, and it's a short life. Now we have eternity. That is, if you still want me."

"Want you?" Elisabeth gasped at the absurd question. "Never did you stray from my thoughts, not once."

"So?" Marjie trembled, shyly glancing at her lost love.

"Kiss me," Elisabeth said, her fangs gleaming.

"Oh, yes." Marjie wrapped her arms around Elisabeth and dipped her head to capture her lover's lips.

"Wait!" Elisabeth blurted, jerking her head away. "Do we need to confine me?"

"Not unless you want to," Marjie said with a seductive purr. "I'm not among the living. Like you, my heart no longer beats and no blood flows through my veins. Even if you wanted to turn me, you couldn't."

Elisabeth smiled with relief before capturing her lover in a searing kiss. No breath escaped the immortal beings as they kissed, their hands roaming each other's bodies. Elisabeth sighed happily and nuzzled her lover's neck, scraping her fangs along the soft white skin. She was pleased when Marjie shivered with pleasure.

Marjie clasped her hand. "Take me to your bed." Elisabeth smiled and guided her lover through her home and up the staircase to her bedroom. Elisabeth stood behind Marjie, encircling her waist, still unable to believe that they had been granted a second chance. She murmured happily as Marjie leaned into her embrace.

"This should feel strange, after so many years." Marjie sighed, turning in her lover's arms so she could face her. "How is it possible that I still feel the same way? In life, I knew I should have sent you away that first night, yet I was unable or unwilling to do so. Now here I am again, helpless to refuse you."

"Because we were meant to be together." Elisabeth suddenly understood that this was indeed the truth. "The timing just sucked." She placed a feathery kiss on her lover's cheek, and then luxuriated in the feeling of Marjie's fingers caressing her neck. Elisabeth slipped her hands up Marjie's arms and began caressing her shoulders. Tonight, she planned to take things slowly. She had waited almost a millennium for this moment, and she had no intention of rushing things now.

Apparently, Marjie shared her lover's sentiment. She kissed Elisabeth tenderly, caressing her slowly, her happiness showing in the gentle way she held her. Elisabeth kissed the fingers that lightly brushed her cheek. Then she tilted her head, nodded toward the fireplace, and smiled brightly when a fire ignited.

"That's handy," Marjie said with a laugh.

Elisabeth took a step back. "Wait till you see what else I can do." She waved her hand, and Marjie gasped as her clothing fell to the floor. "Much better," Elisabeth beamed.

"Pity I have to do most things the old-fashioned way." Marjie stepped closer and ran her fingers along the buttons of Elisabeth's blouse.

"Slow is good," Elisabeth said with a grin, watching her lover's nimble fingers releasing each tiny button. "I've waited so long."

"As have I." Marjie removed Elisabeth's blouse, pausing to kiss the newly exposed flesh. Elisabeth quivered as her lover's lips teased her skin. Her knees threatened to buckle when Marjie dropped the garment to the floor and focused on her bra.

Marjie cupped Elisabeth's firm, full breasts, her fingers playing with the lacy border of the bra. Elisabeth happily enjoyed her lover's slow, tantalizing attention to detail. As each garment fell from her body, Marjie worshipped her flesh with long, lingering kisses.

Elisabeth was quivering by the time the last of her clothing was removed. Marjie was kneeling before her, caressing her creamy white thighs, dragging her blunt nails along Elisabeth's trembling flesh.

Cupping Marjie's face in her hands, Elisabeth guided her to a standing position. She glanced at the large bed and the bedding turned itself back, folding neatly as it opened to greet the lovers.

She brought her lover to the bed and gently lowered her onto it. She smiled and her fangs glimmered as she covered Marjie's body with her own. The lovers moaned softly when their flesh met for the first time in ages. They melted together, kissing one another softly as hands roamed, gently reacquainting themselves.

"Blessed be," Marjie murmured, and flicked her tongue against her lover's sharp fangs.

Elisabeth nestled against Marjie's neck, trailing the tips of her fangs against her lover's flesh. She paused before piercing her skin, and Marjie's body arched as she clung to her lover and accepted her bite. There was no blood, no pain; only pleasure greeted them as their bodies began swaying together.

Each could feel the other's clit pulsating in a needy rhythm. Elisabeth missed the feel of Marjie's breath on her skin as they fell into a sensual haze. She was always amazed that her body could still hum with desire despite the fact that her heart no longer beat.

They held each other captive in smoldering gazes as they slipped their hands between their bodies. They moaned in unison when they felt each other's passion Their eyes remained locked as they slipped inside each other's warm, wet center, each stroking her lover's clit with her thumb while their fingers glided in and out.

Passion consumed them, and their bodies surged. Never breaking their gaze, they screamed with pleasure. Even after their bodies tightened and exploded in ecstasy, their touches continued.

"I can't stop touching you," Elisabeth said, her hands once again growing demanding.

"Then don't!" Marjie cried. "We finally have eternity. Let's not waste it this time."

Elisabeth could only nod in response. They rolled across the bed, pleasuring each other long into the night. "Bloody hell, you've exhausted me, woman," Marjie groaned, finally collapsing against her lover.

"Rest," Elisabeth said, as she nestled into her lover's arms and licked the beads of sweat from her. "I plan on exhausting you even further. We have so much lost time to make up for."

"Then you shall need your rest as well, my love," Marjie murmured, tightening her embrace around Elisabeth's weary body. "Come nightfall, I plan on ravishing you."

"If you must," Elisabeth said. She laughed, happy to be basking in Marjie's smile.

"Oh, I must." Marjie beamed as she made her firm answer. "Sleep."

The Forgotten

It is said that she led an unremarkable life. Not a soul can remember her passing, and very few remembered much about her life. Her name was Shauna McQue, and she lived and died sometime during the nineteenth century, in the small New England town of Manchester. She was a maid. Those who remembered anything about her recalled that she was a quiet girl who did her job well and rarely spoke. Unnoticed in life and forgotten in death.

A sad tale, or was it? Cara Temple wondered. Cara had first encountered Shauna over a hundred years after the quiet maid's death.

Two months earlier

Cara was a sensible woman, newly divorced and trying to find her way in the world. She had purchased a very small house in Manchester, or as the locals insisted on calling it, Manchester By The Sea. Cara quickly learned that it was considered blasphemy not to add the 'by the sea' part to the affluent town's name. The house had once been the carriage house and servants' quarters of a grand manor. Given its location, not far from Singing Beach, it was surprisingly affordable. Real estate prices in that area were insanely high, so Cara quickly put in a bid. It was accepted, and she became the new owner.

The house was buried behind what had once been the main house. The Phelps family had owned the estate for hundreds of years. A snooty stockbroker and his trophy wife now owned the larger, better preserved home. Cara had tried to be friendly with her neighbors, since she would be living so close to them, but they seemed to have no interest in forming a friendship with the quiet bookkeeper. *So be it,* she thought.

The carriage house had fallen into a sad state of disrepair, and Cara had a lengthy list of things to be repaired before she could move into her new home. She assumed that this was the reason the price had been so ridiculously low.

When the workmen finished restoring the carriage house, Cara moved in. It was a cool, crisp, late-summer day, and she was thrilled to finally begin her new life. The town's strict guidelines had demanded that she didn't alter the structure's historical value. Thus, she had converted the lower portion, once meant for horses and carriages, into an expansive living room and a kitchen that was wide open, filling the house with warmth. The upstairs had once housed a few servants, probably including a couple of maids and, of course, the footman; now it was her bedroom. She had the old fireplaces restored, opened up the tiny quarters that barely passed for the staff's living space, and put in a luxurious bathroom—complete with a Jacuzzi.

This was her home now, and she chose to furnish her new home with new things, determined to leave the past behind and embark on a fresh beginning. For the first time in her thirty-some years, she was on her own.

The first night in her home, she was lounging on the sofa eating a simple dinner. When the lights flickered on and off, she grumbled that the electrician had screwed up. It happened a few more times during the night. She checked the switches and circuit breakers each time, but could find nothing amiss.

At length, she climbed into her new bed, content and exhausted from unpacking. Around three in the morning, she awoke feeling cold. She checked the thermostat, confused by the lack of heat. "Okay, tomorrow I'll call the electrician and the heating guy," she muttered, and then climbed back into bed and bundled herself up in a large feather comforter. She felt a small pang of fear as she made a mental list of things that needed to be done. Normally, Jack had handled such matters. Then again, Jack had handled everything. "I should have listened to my parents," she admitted, recalling how they had cautioned the couple that they were much too young to consider marriage.

Throughout her marriage, she had endured, refusing to acknowledge that her parents had been right. Jack was a good man, a good husband, and a good provider. He also bored her, for which she blamed herself. She kept trying, however, long after ennui had devoured both of them. Then, after almost fifteen years of marriage, Jack had announced that he was leaving her for another woman. As usual, Jack handled the details of the divorce. He was surprised by how well Cara accepted the breakup. The truth was that she wanted to jump up and down, shouting "Thank God! I'm finally free!" She refrained, not ever letting the man whose bed she had shared since she was a teenager discover that she had never loved him.

When Jack walked out, Cara realized that the two of them were strangers. She also realized that she had no idea who she was. Now was her time; this new beginning would help her find out. The sudden coldness seemed to disappear, and Cara sighed, feeling at peace for the first time in her life. The peaceful feeling was shattered when the hair on the nape of her neck stood up, and she heard a woman's voice from the other side of the room. "Come back to me," the voice pleaded.

Cara shot up, jumped out of bed, and dashed to the kitchen for a weapon, flipping on lights as she ran. Knife in hand and every light in the house blazing, she searched every nook and cranny. She was alone. For an hour, she paced around her new home before she finally calmed down, managing to convince herself that she had fallen asleep and that what she had heard was nothing more than a dream. Still, she didn't sleep that night. Perhaps it was because she had left all of the lights on, or perhaps it was because deep down she knew she had been wide awake when she heard the voice.

The following day, she called the workmen, who found nothing amiss with the either the heating system or the wiring. She reasoned that it was an old house. These things happen. That, or her repairmen were ripping her off. Later that day, the lights flickered again. She grumbled and rolled her eyes, then scoured the yellow pages for a new electrician. She decided to call in the morning, and after a simple meal settled down for the night.

She was just about to drift off to sleep when she heard a loud noise, as though something had gone crashing down the staircase located only a few feet from her bed. Once again, she sprang from her bed, turned on every light in the house, and discovered... nothing. She told herself it was probably thunder, or the neighbors, and returned to bed. After another sleepless night, she went to work. When she returned home, she checked the alarm system to ensure it was working. Everything seemed fine, except for the rocking chair she had placed by the bookshelves. It had been moved to the other side of the room, by the fireplace.

She had postponed calling a new electrician, hoping things would settle down. Now she questioned her decision.

Cara couldn't shake the uneasy feeling that someone was in her house. She searched everywhere, only to confirm that she was alone. "I'm going crazy," she said, her mood grim. She failed to sleep for yet another night, once again leaving all the lights on. The only difference that evening was that nothing out of the ordinary happened. The following night she was convinced that it was simply the wind or an overactive imagination playing tricks on her. Still, she spent another evening with every light on, choosing to stay awake all night watching television. Nothing happened.

As she sat searching for something to watch, her mind raced. She prayed that she hadn't made a mistake in purchasing the carriage house. Despite the recent events, she truly loved both the space and the surrounding area. This was her home. She had fallen in love with it back when she had first visited what was then a crumbling structure. She had seen beyond the ramshackle appearance, and now it resembled the vision she had carried with her.

She continued to play with the remote control, silently hoping that the problems with her home would prove to be minor and temporary.

She had so many questions to face, now that she was finally finding her way. She didn't need or want the distraction of whatever was lurking about her home. She had wasted too many years of her life questioning her heart, wondering who she truly was. Hiding behind her marriage vows and pretending had been an easy way out. The answers to her questions frightened her, yet for the first time in her life, she felt she was almost ready to face the truth.

"Almost." She sighed, thinking of how even her mother had questioned her sexuality many years ago. The possibility that she was right had terrified Cara deeply; so deeply that she had started dating Jack. Her mother's query hadn't been judgmental or accusatory, but Cara had been a scared teenager, still in high school. "I'm not a kid anymore," she reminded herself, smiling when she discovered an old episode of Cagney and Lacey playing. "Okay, I can say it, Chris Cagney is hot. There, that wasn't so hard."

The following day she was exhausted and felt completely foolish. That night she went to bed very early, leaving only the lamp in her bedroom switched on. Finally, she slept. For more than a week, nothing strange occurred and Cara managed to push the troublesome events of her first few nights from her thoughts.

Then one night, while she was trying to read in bed, the lights and television suddenly turned on and off. She sat in her bed paralyzed as the temperature in the room dropped, and then nothing happened. Poor Cara spent another sleepless night. When she returned home from work one day to find the stereo on, she was at her wits' end. "Okay. I know that wasn't on when I left." She trembled as she tentatively approached the sound system, which was playing loudly, and turned it off.

By the time she washed up for bed, she had managed to convince herself that there really must be some electrical malfunction causing her problems, and that maybe she should have called a new electrician. But when she emerged from the bathroom, she saw the misty figure of a young woman looking out of her bedroom window.

A scream froze in her throat, and she was just about to pass out when the indistinct figure vanished. She stood rooted in place, staring at the window and trembling with fear that the apparition would reappear. Eventually, she retreated under the bedcovers and hid there until morning.

In the light of day, she once again convinced herself that her new home had bad wiring, and that what she thought she had seen lurking by the window was nothing more than a figment of her overtired mind. Being the ever-practical woman that she was, she finally allowed her friend Mary to set up an appointment with an electrician.

After work that day, she hurried home to meet the service person. The commute to her new home was much longer than her previous one, but it was a small price to pay for the beautiful scenery. She hoped straightening out the wiring would help her find peace in her new home. She pulled into her driveway next to the van awaiting her arrival. "Damn," she muttered, knowing that she was late. "I hope he doesn't charge me for the time he spent sitting here."

"Hi," she said, feeling sheepish as she approached the van. Her jaw dropped when a leggy brunette emerged from the vehicle. She couldn't stop gaping at the tall woman standing before her. "I'm sorry I'm late." The woman flashed a brilliant smile that sent a shiver down her spine.

"Not a problem," the woman responded brightly, removing her sunglasses and revealing the most amazing blue eyes Cara had ever seen. "I'm Sam. Mary Duggan called me. I hear you're having problems with your heating and lights."

"Cara," she said, unable to tear her gaze from the attractive stranger. "Yeah, I had the whole place renovated just before I moved in, and a lot of really odd things have been happening." She began to explain some of the problems with the lights and electrical devices, skipping over the misty image in the window and the furniture moving about. The last thing she wanted was for Sam to think she was insane.

"That's odd." Sam picked up her toolbox and followed Cara into the house. "Wow! I love what you've done with the place," she said.

"You've been here before?"

"Long story." Sam shrugged. "Why don't you go about your business, and I'll have a look around? Maybe I can figure out what the problem is."

"All right." Cara grabbed a quick breath as Sam wandered off to have a look at the new wiring. Her heart was racing and her palms sweating. "Not again," she muttered. This wasn't the first time an attractive woman had thrown her off kilter, and Cara shook her head in an effort to vanquish her troublesome thoughts. Yet another reason her marriage was less than she had hoped for. She just couldn't feel anything for poor old Jack. She blushed with shame as she raced up to her bedroom. While changing into more comfortable clothing, she couldn't erase the nagging doubts that reminded her that one of the reasons she had rushed into marriage so young was because she had a crush on her best friend. *I'm not ready to deal with this*, she thought, and cowered in her bedroom until it was time for Sam to inspect the upstairs.

When Sam entered her bedroom, Cara made a quick excuse and retreated downstairs. She pretended to work on her laptop while Sam roamed about, humming a delightful tune. "All done," Sam announced over an hour later, startling Cara. "Sorry," Sam said with a little smirk. "Well, I have good news. There is absolutely nothing wrong with the wiring or anything else."

"There has to be."

"I wish there was. I could use the business." Sam's face lit with a brilliant smile. "What did the realtor tell you about this place?"

Sam listened patiently while Cara recited the history of the carriage house. "Well, that's almost the truth," Sam said. "Except that this was a summer home for the Phelps family. Back in the 1800s, Manchester was considered a vacation town for the idle rich. What the realtor forgot to tell you is that the main house is fine, but no one has managed to live in this carriage house for more than a couple of months. It's changed hands more times than anyone can count. It was a rental for years, because the last owners refused to live here and they couldn't find a buyer. Back when I was in college, I rented part of the upstairs, and despite the phenomenally cheap rent, I didn't stay past the first week. I don't know how to tell you this, other than to say it right out. Your house is haunted."

"You're kidding," Cara couldn't help laughing. "Really, that sounds absurd."

"Hey, that's what I would have said too. The first couple of days, I thought my roommates were screwing with me by moving my stuff around. One of them accused me of talking in my sleep. I know I snore, or so I've been told, but chatting in my sleep isn't something I've done before. Still, I didn't think anything of it until I rolled over in bed late one night and saw her standing by the window. I moved out the next day."

"Saw who?" Cara could barely choke out the words.

"I have no idea," Sam said with a slight shiver. "All I know is that she was blonde and her body didn't go all the way down. I have to admit I almost didn't take this job because of what happened back then. I guess I was a little curious."

"You're serious?"

"Oh, yeah. If you want, I could help you research the place." Something in Sam's voice made Cara feel warm. "I live just over in Beverly."

"No, that's okay." Cara was a little leery of Sam and her strange ideas. A small part of her wanted to accept the electrician's offer, but it was far too ridiculous to even consider she had seen a ghost.

"Okay." Sam shrugged, the slightest hint of regret lingering in her voice. "Before I go, I just have to ask about one more thing. Did you know about the grave behind the house?"

"Excuse me? A grave? Um, no. I haven't ventured very far out there because of all the overgrowth. I was planning on clearing out the mess in the spring. It was too overgrown to check out completely."

"Come on, I'll show you."

Cara shook her head in disbelief as she followed the quirky woman. Sam put her toolbox in her van before guiding Cara around the back of the house. As they pushed through the mass of weeds and fallen trees, Cara regretted her choice. Her hazel eyes widened when they finally came upon a dilapidated iron fence that surrounded a tiny gravestone. Cara's jaw clenched when she spied the stakes the county surveyor had left behind. The tiny plot was most definitely a part of her property.

"I can't believe no one told me about this." She felt a slight pang in her heart for whoever was buried beneath the plain gravestone, forgotten by everyone. She cocked her head, and her jaw quivered when she finally noticed that, despite the wild shrubbery that had sprung up everywhere else, the grave was pristine.

"Weird, huh?" Sam's warm voice broke the silence. "No wildflowers, weeds, or trash. Nothing but leaves and grass. Kids used to come out here to party. That's how I knew about it. I've often wondered if it was her. You know, the blonde in the window. Well, now that you're convinced that I'm completely nuts, I guess I should get going."

They strolled back to the house in silence. Cara was trying to understand what was happening. None of it made any sense. She stood in the driveway as Sam shifted nervously, fiddling with the keys to her van. "I hope I haven't scared you," Sam muttered.

"No," Cara said, her mind still trying to grasp what Sam had told her.

"Well, nice meeting you. Again, I love what you've done with the place." Sam opened the door to her van.

"Wait," Cara blurted out. "I... I saw her, too," she said. "Standing by the window. I saw her. I thought it was my imagination. Does anyone know who she is?"

"No," Sam softly answered. "Are you going to be all right? I mean staying here alone?"

"Oh, sure. It will be like having a roommate." Cara laughed, suddenly finding her situation funny. "Oh, man, I should have known the price was too good. Jack would have asked questions."

"Jack?" Sam crinkled her brow.

"My ex-husband," Cara replied.

"Oh." Sam coughed, her eyes widening with surprise. "Didn't see that coming," she muttered under her breath, as Cara gave her a curious look.

"See what coming?" Cara asked.

"Nothing. Well, I think my work here is done. Your wiring is perfect, and I've scared you half to death. I think I'll just run along now, before I cause any more problems."

"Wait, what do I owe you?" Cara wasn't eager for Sam to leave or to be alone.

"Nothing." Sam laughed, and her laughter once again spread warmth through Cara. "You didn't need me, and I've managed to do more harm than good."

"Nonsense," Cara protested. "I mean, it is a little funky, and I'm not sure I believe any of this, but it would have been nice if someone had told me before I bought the place. What am I saying? I wouldn't have believed it then, either."

Sam apologized again before driving off. Cara found she was more upset by Sam's departure than by the possibility that she was sharing her home with a ghost. Once again, she scoffed at the notion that her home was inhabited by something not among the living, until she walked back inside and discovered that the rocking chair had once again been moved next to the fireplace. "I'll just leave it there," she said, shuddering. Grabbing her wallet, she suddenly decided to dine out for the evening.

She sat alone in the small restaurant, not far from her new home. Hiding in the back, she ignored the merriment that surrounded her as she drank a glass of wine after completing her meal. "So, do you think I'm crazy?" a familiar voice asked. Cara gaped up at Sam, who took the seat beside her.

"The jury is still out," she answered. "Buy you a drink?"

"Thank you," Sam said. "I'm sorry about this afternoon. Lunacy isn't something I usually display when trying to woo a potential client."

"No? I found it endearing," Cara teased as they ordered drinks. "Can I ask you something?"

"Sure." Sam offered a shy smile that made Cara's heart flutter.

"Why were you surprised that I'm divorced?" Cara asked bluntly, already sensing the answer.

Sam chewed on her lip for a moment before giving her response. "I made an incorrect assumption."

"Which was?"

"I'd rather not say." Sam shifted in her seat as an older gentleman approached them.

"Sammy! What're you doing out tonight?" he asked in a boisterous tone.

"I thought I had a client, but it turns out I don't. This is Cara. She just moved to town. Cara, this is Captain Bill. He's older than dirt and knows everyone and everything about this town."

"You always were a smart-ass, Sammy," Bill said with a grunt. He turned to Cara. "You'd be the gal that bought the carriage house."

"Told you." Sam laughed as Cara raised her eyebrows.

"What were you thinking? That old place is haunted!" Bill prattled on.

"No one told me," Cara said. "Oh, hell, I can't believe this. So if you know everything, who's buried in the backyard?"

"Shauna," he answered. "I think she was one of the Phelps's maids. Died suddenly one summer back in 1887 or thereabouts."

"You never told me that," Sam said. "This isn't one of your wild tales, is it?"

"Might be," Bill said in a teasing tone. "No, I'm pretty certain that was her name. My grandfather used to talk about it."

"Why did she die?" Cara asked.

"A lot of folks found her sudden passing odd. She was young and healthy. The family claimed she fell down the staircase in the carriage house," he continued as they ordered another round of drinks. "Then the Phelpses bolted out of town right afterward. They never used the house again."

"Wait. The maid dies accidentally, and they just bury her in the backyard and don't come back?" Sam was frowning.

"They never used the house again," Bill said. "No one did until the grandkids sold it, back in the twenties. But ever since Shauna took that fall, folks have seen and heard odd things in the carriage house. Lights burning when the place is empty, the sounds of a woman crying. I remember back when I was about sixteen, a bunch of us decided to take a look around. It was late, and when we broke in, there wasn't anything there—just dirt, piles of dust, and the sound of a woman crying. Got the hell out of there and ran off. We didn't stop until we were halfway home."

"Oh, yeah, this is going to help me sleep tonight," Cara said, giving Bill a wry look.

"Sammy could always keep you company," he suggested with a wink.

"Bill?" Sam said.

"Yeah?"

"Shut up."

Bill laughed heartily before walking away. "Sorry about that," Sam apologized softly.

"I'm sorry too," Cara said.

"What, that Bill thinks I'm making a pass at you?" Sam inquired, as the waitress brought them a round of drinks, compliments of Bill.

"No," Cara said and laughed. "I'm just buzzed enough to let myself enjoy that. I meant about Shauna being dumped in the yard like a stray animal, and no one even bothering to put her name on the headstone."

"It's sad, but if it makes you feel any better, Bill's been known to spin some pretty wild tales. And for the record, I'm not making a pass. Although I'm curious as to why you look so disappointed that I'm not. Perhaps that's a subject for another time," Sam said graciously, and Cara heaved a sigh of relief. "For now, why don't you tell me about yourself? Then I'll walk you home, since neither of us is in any condition to drive."

They talked until closing time, and Cara was in heaven. Sam was indeed quirky, but sweet, not to mention gorgeous. Cara smiled happily as they strolled up the winding street that led to her home. It wasn't the first time she had been attracted to another woman, but it was the first time she was just drunk enough and free enough to allow herself to simply enjoy the feeling. Sam was an enigma. She was bright, loved what she did for a living, open about her life and lifestyle, and despite her generally level-headed attitude, completely convinced that the carriage house was haunted.

They arrived at the driveway, and Cara froze. Her home was brightly lit up. "Oh, goodie," she muttered, gaping at the sight.

"I need to call a cab," Sam said. "Do you mind if I use your phone? There are no repeaters way out here, so you can forget about using your cell phone." She took a closer look at Cara. "What is it?"

Cara couldn't speak. Her body trembled, and she swallowed hard in an effort to calm down. "I didn't leave any lights on," she said, still staring at her home. She was rooted in place, unable to move, terrified to walk into her house. When a hand came to rest on her shoulder, she yelped and jumped, only to discover that it was Sam's hand. "Sorry," she muttered, and laughed nervously.

"May I suggest plan B?" Sam said. Cara stared deeply into Sam's mesmerizing gaze and her fears vanished.

"Plan B?" she said in a breathy whisper, fighting against the rush of emotions that suddenly overwhelmed her. It was so tempting; the wine had lowered her inhibitions just enough to encourage her. She reached up, surprised when Sam took a step back.

"Plan B," Sam said, "is that instead of trying to get a taxi at this ungodly hour and paying a small fortune to get home, I crash on your sofa. I can get my van from downtown in the morning, and you won't have to spend the night alone."

"The sofa?" Cara felt an odd sense of sadness.

"The sofa." Sam motioned toward the front door.

Taking a cleansing breath, Cara fought the urge to wrap her arms around Sam's warm body. "The sofa," she grumbled under her breath, not missing the snicker that came from behind her as she opened the front door.

"Shauna, we're home," Sam called out boldly once they had crossed the threshold.

"Oh, you're a riot." Cara rolled her eyes and she locked up behind them.

"All part of my charm," Sam said, shoving her hands into the front pockets of her faded jeans.

"Yes, you must have women falling at your feet." Cara looked around the living room, fearful that she would find the mysterious Shauna wandering about. Her heart fluttered when her gaze stopped at the sofa. "I bet you do," she added with a tinge of sadness, knowing that she wanted Sam to stay, but not on the sofa.

"No, I don't, but thank you," Sam murmured, and the rich tone of her voice made Cara quiver. "Cara?"

Feeling the heat from Sam's body, just behind her, made Cara tremble. She wanted to invite Sam to spend the night upstairs with her. Frightened by her desires and hurt by Sam's obvious rejection, she was on the verge of tears. Her body tensed when she felt Sam's hands resting on her shoulders. "Spare me the 'it's not you, it's me' speech," Cara said.

"I wasn't going to say that," Sam answered. "Your life is in upheaval. You just got divorced, your house is scaring you, there's a body in the backyard and you're half drunk. You're not thinking clearly."

Cara stood numbly. Sam's words were no more than the truth, but that didn't quell the desires stirring inside her. She parted her lips, ready to agree with Sam, when the rocking chair creaked.

Sam's arms wrapped around Cara's waist, and they watched the chair slowly rocking back and forth. Cara couldn't breathe; her only source of comfort was Sam's embrace. "I was... um," she sputtered, "I was just about to agree with everything you said," Her eyes were fastened on the steady rhythm of the chair. "And offer to get you some blankets for the couch, but now I'll pay you to sleep upstairs with me, and not because I want to get fresh with you. Keep your clothes on. Whatever. I would really rather not be alone up there."

"Good idea," Sam whispered.

They slowly stepped backward, never taking their eyes from the rocking chair as they climbed the staircase. They were still trembling when they reached the top landing and peered down over the rail. The chair slowly came to a halt as they watched, yet Cara's body was still covered with goose bumps. Suddenly the house was plunged into darkness. Cara squeaked and stepped backward, colliding with Sam.

"At least she waited till we were up here." Sam's laugh sounded hollow, and the tremor in her voice betrayed her fear.

"I'll get the light." Cara's voice and body shook as she pried herself away from Sam's embrace. They both released a sigh when Cara clicked on the lamp by her bed. "That was fun," she said, kicking off her shoes and feeling a small sense of relief when Sam did the same.

"Yeah, I'm a fun date, aren't I?" Sam laughed, still visibly shaken.

"The best," Cara answered, nervously running her fingers through her hair. She wriggled out of her slacks, and her heart fluttered as she watched Sam unbutton her faded jeans. She released a tiny whimper when Sam's long legs were revealed. "Damn," she whispered, once she finally managed to stop ogling Sam's body.

"I'll take that as a compliment," Sam said, grinning as they climbed onto the bed.

Cara searched her mind for some witty remark as they nestled on top of the bedding, still half dressed and maintaining an appropriate distance from each other. "Thank you for staying with me," she managed to say.

"My pleasure," Sam's voice was subdued, and she moved slightly farther away. "Want to talk, since I doubt either of us is going to get any sleep tonight?"

"Sounds like a good idea." Cara tried to work up the nerve to move a little closer. "I really enjoyed talking to you back at the pub. Sam, when did you know that you're gay?"

"When didn't I?" Sam countered playfully. "When did you?"

"Know you were gay?" Cara hedged, knowing that wasn't what Sam had meant. "When you told me."

"That wasn't what I meant," Sam said, nudging her.

"I know. I've had my doubts since I was about fifteen. Every time I, or someone else, suspected something, I ran out and got a new boyfriend... or got married. Poor Jack. I don't think he ever suspected. I'm still not ready to—"

"I've noticed," Sam cut her off. "Which is why I'm staying way over on this side of the bed."

"Party pooper," Cara quipped, relieved that Sam seemed to understand her predicament.

"No, just a realist," Sam said. "Trust me, I was tempted more than once today. But if anything had happened, I think it would have freaked you out a lot more than Shauna's shenanigans. Instead, I'm happy to have made a new friend with a really cool house."

"A cool house?" Cara laughed. "Why? Because the lights turn on and off all by themselves?"

"No, because of the old brick, beamed ceilings, fireplaces and walking distance to the beach, not to mention that Jacuzzi I saw in the bathroom," Sam replied. "Frankly, I think you need a pet so I can housesit for you whenever you go out of town."

"Are you this helpful with all your clients?" Cara asked, laughing.

"Oh, but you're not a client," Sam corrected. "Although electrical work isn't all I do. I'm a handyman, or handywoman as it were. If it makes you feel better, you can hire me next spring to clear out the back."

"You'd charge a friend to help with yard work?"

"Oh, so now I'm a friend? I see how this works."

"We could wait until spring, and judge it by just how friendly we are," Cara suggested hopefully.

"Lucky for you I'm a patient woman."

The two women chatted the night away, only stopping when they heard a creak or other strange noise. Fortunately, no other eerie events occurred. The only problem Cara encountered was the occasional urge to close the distance between them and kiss her companion. More than once, she thought she spied the same longing in Sam's eyes. Still, they managed to simply rest side by side and talk.

When morning arrived, Cara's head was aching from the wine and the lack of sleep. Her body was agitated from sharing the night with Sam and having nothing transpire except stimulating conversation. "What's that look for?" she asked, noticing that her companion's brow was furrowed and she was drumming her fingers nervously against the blankets.

"Nothing," Sam replied. "You know, exhaustion, hangover, and—" she mumbled the last part so softly that Cara couldn't understand what she said.

Cara searched her mind in an effort to fill in the blanks. She knew she was hung over as well, and exhausted from lack of sleep. She was also frustrated. She smiled, hoping that was the part Sam was omitting. She reached out, ready to test her theory, and grimaced when Sam caught her wandering hand.

"Don't," said Sam. "This is hard enough. I don't like to rush into things anyway, and your life is particularly complicated just now."

"Less and less so," Cara said, rolling onto her side. She was pleased that Sam was still holding her hand. "But you're right. I've spent over thirty years avoiding my feelings. This is going to take time."

"Sucks, doesn't it?" Sam laughed and gave Cara's hand a squeeze before releasing it. "In the meantime, I was serious about helping you find out what we can about Shauna. Maybe knowing more about her will help quiet things down around here. You said you heard her speaking. What did she say?"

"'Come back to me.'" Cara finally accepted that the strange happenings were real.

"That poor girl. Brokenhearted and forgotten," Sam said in a sad voice. "Let's hope we can find out something that will help.

Meanwhile, I hate to say it but I need to go. I'm sure my van has already been ticketed, and if I don't get it now it'll be towed."

Finally, the missing pieces of Cara's spirit were falling into place. True to her word, Sam stopped by frequently, offering to spend the day scouring the town library or some other place in an effort to find out about Shauna, or to at least confirm that was the woman's name. Cara suspected that Bill had indeed told them the truth, since whenever something strange happened, she would call out Shauna's name and things would quiet down.

Shauna seemed fascinated by anything electrical. One morning she played with the coffee maker, and her curiosity ruined Cara's morning coffee. Shauna must have felt remorse for her transgression, since when Cara returned from work that day, there was a fresh pot of coffee waiting for her. "Thank you," she said rather fearfully. Later that evening she relaxed by the fire, wryly wondering if she could convince Shauna to do a little housework. "Now I'm just being silly." She laughed, but the laughter died on her lips when the rocking chair began moving again. She quickly retreated upstairs, praying that Shauna would simply enjoy sitting by the fire and leave her alone.

A few nights later, Cara was startled awake by the sudden coldness and the sound of a woman crying. Her heart felt heavy as she listened to the muffled sobs and the now familiar words, "Come back to me," called into the darkness.

"It's heartbreaking," she confessed to Sam the following evening, recounting the recent events over dinner at a local restaurant. "She seems so sad," she continued. "Although she does seem to enjoy playing with the appliances and sitting by the fire."

"I can understand her enjoying the warmth of the fire," Sam said. "Remember when we found the original plans for the place? The servant's quarters were tiny, and the only heat was from the fireplaces. If she lived here year-round, the winters must have been torture. The horses were kept warmer than the staff."

"Maybe she lived somewhere else? You said this was a summer home." Cara was surprised at how easily she was accepting the strange goings on in her new home. "I did find something," she added, sliding a photocopy over to Sam.

"'Shauna McQue died suddenly at the home of her employer.'" Sam read from the obituary Cara had stumbled across while surfing the Internet. "'No services.' That's it? Jesus, didn't this woman have any friends or family?"

"That was all I could find. I'm not even certain it's the same woman. I ran into Captain Bill at the market the other day and got the same story he told us before. He thinks her name was Shauna and that she worked as a maid for the Phelps family, but he isn't certain."

"Yeah, I talked to him last week."

Cara sat back, watching her friend. Her eyes were riveted to every move Sam made. *This is bad,* she thought, mentally sighing.

"It's so sad." Sam seemed unaware that Cara was more interested in watching her speak than in listening to what she was actually saying. "Her life was condensed into a single sentence. Makes you wonder why anyone even bothered putting up a gravestone, or fencing off her grave."

"I'm more curious about who did that," Cara looked away, suddenly aware that she was staring. "Maybe it was the person she keeps calling for."

"Perhaps," said Sam. "But that seems odd, too. He loved her enough to mark her grave, but not enough to pay a few pennies and have her name engraved?"

"'It is said that she led an unremarkable life. Not a soul can remember her passing, and very few remembered much about her life. Her name was Shauna McQue, and she lived and died sometime during the nineteenth century, in the small New England town of Manchester. She was a maid. Those who remembered anything about her recalled that she was a quiet girl who did her job well and rarely spoke. Unnoticed in life and forgotten in death,'" Cara read from the photocopy Sam had given her. "Who wrote this?"

"Sarah Phelps," Sam said, leaning back against the sofa cushions. "I found a copy of her diary buried in the stacks at the town library."

Cara gave Sam a curious look. They had searched for weeks, to no avail. Tonight was Halloween night, and Sam had showed up on her doorstep with bundles of take out, a bottle of wine, and a stack of papers. Cara sighed and poured herself another glass of wine. She glanced over at Sam, who was shuffling through the stack of papers. She studied the woman who had been helping her and confusing her since the moment they met. The emotional tug-of-war was beginning to take its toll on both of them. Somehow, dealing with the strange happenings in her home was much easier than dealing with the overwhelming attraction she felt for her friend.

A few days ago, they had begun sniping at one another, the tension from pretending they were nothing more than friends finally emerging. Cara felt brokenhearted when Sam finally said, "I can't do this anymore," and walked away.

Tonight, after handing out candy to the few children who had ventured out, Cara was wallowing in a sea of self-pity. She had just turned off her outside light, ready to call it a night, when there was a knock on her door. She was stunned when she discovered Sam waiting on the other side.

Sam politely asked to come in, offering the food and wine as a bribe. She said that she had found something about Shauna. Other than that, she offered no explanation as to why she was there.

Cara glanced over when the rocking chair creaked. "You know, I'm getting used to it." She laughed, even as she wondered what was going on with Sam. "Why are you here?"

"I found Shauna's story. It might help if someone finally told it," Sam explained, a curious gleam in her eyes. "Plus, I feel like an ass for storming out of here the other day. Let me tell you Shauna's story?"

Cara nodded, simply happy that Sam was there, and curious to hear about Shauna. "The rest of the entry for that day is this," Sam continued softly.

> I remember Shauna. She worked for my family as a maid during the summers we spent in Manchester. I was young, and didn't understand that the quiet woman who had always been kind to me was a servant. She lived in the carriage house year-round, simply waiting for us to arrive.
>
> Father normally stayed in the city, except for a few scattered weekends during the summers. What I remember most about those summers was how happy my mother was. She looked forward to our summers by the sea. The only times her mood darkened was when father arrived. The other times, she laughed and played with Shauna and us.
>
> The days we spent at our home in the city, my mother was never happy. Shauna seemed to light up her world. I never questioned why she brought out the best in my mother.
>
> One summer day, in early August, everything changed. I awoke to my mother's wailing and my father's screaming. Suddenly everything was quiet, and the staff was quickly packing up our belongings. I fussed, confused as to why we were leaving in such a hurry. I searched for

Shauna, confident that she could explain things to me. I failed to find her, and we never went back to Manchester.

My mother was so despondent when we returned to the city that she retired to her bedroom permanently. Years later, I would learn through hushed whispers that Shauna had died the night before we fled. It was a curious accident. I never understood why my father chose to bury her in haste and flee Manchester.

After my father's passing, when my mother was nearing the end of her life, I learned the truth. It was a sad tale, which I am forced to carry to my grave. My children have sold the old summer home. I pray that Mother and Shauna rest peacefully, and that my father is paying for his crime.

Cara stared at Sam. Her jaw dropped as the story sank in. "It stops there," Sam said. "Are you thinking what I'm thinking?"

"I think that Sarah's mother and Shauna were very close," Cara noted. "And Sarah's father found out, and Shauna's accident wasn't an accident. I hope the son of a bitch is burning in hell."

"That's what I thought." Sam nodded, smiling at Cara as she stood and tended to the fire burning brightly in the fireplace. Sam was still smiling when Cara curled back up on the sofa. "So, being the busybody I am, I did some more digging. I have a friend who works in the archives at the Athenaeum in Salem, and she found a letter that Mildred Phelps, Sarah's mother, wrote just before her death. Care to read it?"

Cara snatched the photocopy from Sam's grasp, almost knocking the taller woman over in her eagerness to read the letter. "I'll take that as a yes." Sam laughed.

"'August tenth, nineteen sixteen,'" Cara read aloud. "'It is the anniversary of her death. I pray each day since she was taken from me that I will finally join my beloved.'"

August 10, 1916

It is the anniversary of her death. I pray each day since she was taken from me that I will finally join my beloved.

Summering in Manchester had been my husband's idea. I saw no need to leave the city, although I was intrigued by the prospect of not having to spend my days and nights with Thomas, my husband. He claimed that the family summer cottage was being wasted. A staff was hired, and the children and I were packed off to enjoy the shore. Manchester was pleasant enough, that first summer. The most enjoyable part was meeting a shy lass named Shauna McQue, who was the maid.

Miss McQue was only two or three years my junior, and very competent when it came to performing her duties. The girl was so quiet that at times I didn't even notice that she was about. Still, there was a light about her, and she seemed to bring sunshine to my dreary existence. The children simply adored her. Perhaps it was because she not only listened to them, but also joined their games. I found myself inviting Shauna to join more and more family activities.

Thomas was most displeased with this change in her duties. So many things displeased Thomas. After his first visit, he fired the footman and made Shauna a nervous wreck. I found it quite distasteful that my husband would openly leer at the girl. I worried when the new footman, Frederick, was hired. Since Frederick had a residence nearby, Shauna was given the luxury of living alone in the carriage house. What concerned me was that after the staff changes had been made, occasionally Thomas would go for a stroll and linger around the carriage house. I mentioned to Shauna that she should keep the doors locked, and as far as I know, she did.

Thomas was never a vulgar man. He seemed to accept that the girl was not interested in his attentions. His evening strolls ceased, but he continued to leer at the shy woman. I was quite brisk with him the night I brought the matter to his attention. He seemed surprised by my meddling. Thomas and I have never pretended to be more than we were. We married within our station, and once our third child, William, was born, we no longer shared a bedroom. Like most women, I did not really care to know who comforted my husband or warmed his bed. I was honestly relieved that I was no longer required to do so.

He was so annoyed by my behavior that he cut his visit short and returned home. I was positively giddy when he departed. When Shauna helped me undress and prepare for bed that evening, I spoke out of turn. I told her that if Mr. Phelps so much as looked at her inappropriately, she had my permission to knock him in the head with a fire poker.

The poor girl was so startled by my suggestion that she blushed from ear to ear. I laughed merrily, and hugged her. Both of us were stunned by my familiarity. I had not only spoken freely in front of a domestic, I had hugged her like an old friend. I immediately apologized for my forwardness. Shauna simply nodded and went about her duties.

I could not sleep that night. I was troubled by my actions and by the curious way it felt warm and right to hold the girl in my arms. The following morning, Shauna cleaned the house before joining the children and me for a stroll along the sandy beach. I loved the beach near our little hideaway. The sand would literally sing when you stepped upon it. The delightful sound had become quite a game for the both the children and the adults, each trying to make the beach sing the loudest.

It was a joyful day; the only dark cloud was my mood. I was still terribly troubled by my behavior of the previous evening. So troubled that when Shauna helped me that evening, I rambled on and on, trying to apologize. She just smiled up at me with deep blue eyes that resembled the crystal waters not far from our home.

My heart fluttered when I brushed a stray strand of hair from her face. I gasped when I felt her leaning into my touch. It was truly amazing. For the first time in my dreary existence, I felt like a woman. How can I explain that this simple girl stirred something in my soul?

In my youth, I endured listening to my friends' prattling about romance. I played along, doubting that love existed. Now, with one brush of my hand, I discovered passion. By the rapid beating of my heart, one would have thought I had just discovered Paradise. Perhaps I had. Shauna smiled up at me, and my heart swooned.

I was so unsettled by the experience that my knees quivered. Shauna moved quickly, clasping my hips to keep me from falling. My body quivered from the warm feeling of her hands resting on my hips and the sweet way she was smiling up at me. "Shauna," I whispered. Her darkening eyes mirrored the emotions swirling through my own body and soul.

"Missus," she said simply. The word reminded me of our stations and that I belonged to another.

I wanted to curse and bang about like a child at the cruel reality of our predicament. I was a married woman, her employer. Nothing could ever happen between us. Yet the longing in her eyes drew me in. I threw caution to the wind, dipped my head, and brushed my lips against hers. It was a sweet kiss, filled with innocence despite the fire raging inside of me. Her lips were soft and inviting, moving tenderly against mine. Her sweet breath tickled my face; her hands caressed my hips. I was confused by the rush of warmth that encompassing me.

My eyes fluttered open, and I gazed down at her. Shauna's eyes were still tightly shut, and her lips parted as I watched her pink tongue peek out to lick her soft, full lips. I could feel her body trembling, our hearts pounding in unison as we clung to one other. My transgression should have ceased at that moment, but her eyes slowly opened and I knew that I could never resist her.

Her eyes burned brightly. We tried to pretend that nothing untoward had happened, and she went about undressing me. Under the guise of preparing me for bed, her hands drifted to places she had never previously explored. I accepted her roaming fingers willingly, my flesh tingling from her touch.

I stood before her completely exposed, as I had so many times before. That night, however, she did not avert her eyes. No, that night her eyes seemed to covet my flesh. I reached out, gently tugging at the ribbon that held her long blonde hair bundled upon her head. I gasped as I watched her hair cascade down and caress her shoulders.

I laced my fingers through her long, silky locks and drew her to me. I was nervous, yet the soft moan she released against my body filled me with confidence and desire. I was stunned when a feral groan escaped my lips as I felt her lips brush tenderly against my bosom. I felt giddy listening to her soft murmurs and feeling her .shy, curious hands stroke my hips.

I moaned, and my body filled with immeasurable pleasure when I felt her tongue slowly trace the swell of my breast. My thighs clenched in an effort to control the passion slipping from my body, but my sweet Shauna had opened the gates.

My fingers dug into the thick cloth of her uniform. I was frustrated; my only desire was to feel her. Nagging voices deep inside of me screamed for me to keep these impulses at bay. I tried to pull away from her, afraid that I was corrupting her or forcing my wayward desires upon her innocent person. "We should stop this," I murmured, my heart aching at the thought of releasing this magnificent woman from my embrace.

"Is that what you wish?" Her words hitched, and I could hear the pain in her voice.

"No," I confessed, clinging to her, "but I cannot bring myself to take what is not mine. We must cease before we sin."

I was firm, filled with the conviction that I was taking advantage of her. Still, I was unable to release her from my grasp. I nuzzled her long hair, breathing in its sweet scent, and tried to convince myself that it would be enough. Strong arms wrapped around my waist and hot breath teased my nipple. I was lost. I released a loud cry when I felt her tongue tease the bud, coaxing it until it hardened against her touch. "You are my undoing," she said and moaned as her lips captured my nipple and she suckled like a starving child.

Clearly, I was not forcing Shauna to do anything. She desired what I desired, and nothing could come between us. That night belonged to us, and we were helpless to stop the tidal wave of desire. The feeling of her mouth devouring my breast drove me insane. My body began to grind shamelessly against hers and I begged her for release.

Dear, sweet Shauna teased me in ways I had not known were possible. My flesh was damp from her kisses; my fingers clawed at her dress while my body melted against hers. I was breathless. My body was on fire. I drew her to me, holding her face in my hands. I kissed her passionately, plunging my tongue inside her mouth, moaning when her tongue greeted my own. I was dimly aware of the sound of cloth tearing as I wrenched at her dress.

The kiss turned savage. My hands ripped her clothing while her fingers teased my quivering flesh. I yanked the bodice of her dress aside and cupped her firm breast in my hand. The jolt of pleasure I felt was indescribable. Her nipple hardened against the palm of my hand while her nimble fingers brushed against my passion.

I was filled with a strange sense of delight knowing that she could feel the excitement she had inspired. Her fingers slipped inside me, and my body began thrusting urgently against her touch. I teased her nipples, capturing them between my fingers, and my hips rocked wildly as I allowed her to love me. Had these desires been brewing all this time? All these years later, I still have no answer. I only know that once she touched me, I was hers. I needed to feel her pressing against me. My hands retreated reluctantly from her firm breasts, eager to rid her of her remaining clothing. She plunged deeper inside me even while we stumbled toward the bed. My mind was spinning, my body filled with unfamiliar pleasure as I gave myself to her.

I fell onto the bed, Shauna drifting kisses down my body. I shuddered when her hair tickled my thighs. I gazed down my naked body and saw her brilliant blue eyes looking back at me, and I could feel her breath across my womanhood. For a moment longer, she held me in a smoldering gaze. I was shocked when her tongue parted my swollen nether lips and she began to drink from me.

My shock was quickly cast aside when her tongue glided along my sex, teasing my engorged nub. She sucked the pulsating bundle, fighting to hold my thrashing form steady as she feasted on me. Her fingers plunged deeper inside my wetness and my body arched, eager to feel all she offered. I felt a sense of wild abandon and I press harder against her, my passion spilling from my body as my screams echoed in the room. I collapsed from the sheer ecstasy she bestowed upon me. The world vanished, and I struggled for air as my lover continued to pleasure me.

The room was spinning when I finally managed to escape from her talented touch. I needed her; I silently prayed that she would allow me to pleasure her as she had just pleasured me. I was quick to finish removing her clothing, and my hands explored her flesh, teasing and caressing her.

I hovered above her naked body, basking in her beauty as my hands explored the wonders lying beneath me. She clasped my wrist and guided my inquisitive touch between her quivering thighs. I gasped when I discovered her passion. She guided me deeper, and I followed willingly, pleased by the sight of her body arching and the sound of her voice begging me to love her.

I gave in to my hedonistic desires, slipping inside her warm wetness. My touch faltered when my fingers met resistance. My Shauna was innocent! The revelation filled me with fear, but her firm grasp guided my touch. Her hips thrust hard, and I watched as she impaled herself on my fingers. I was shaking from the knowledge that I had just taken her innocence. "I wanted it to be you," she whispered, her eyes filling with tears. "I wanted you from the beginning, but I tried to hide my sin."

"You have not sinned," I said, sobbing as my touch turned gentle and I slid my fingers deeper into her womanhood. I kissed her gently, my senses in a whirl as I tasted myself on her lips. I made love to her slowly, tasting and touching every inch of her body. I felt that I, too, was a virgin that night. The pleasure she shared with me was a delightfully foreign experience.

I selfishly kept her in my bed, so I could hold her as she slept. I was filled with trepidation when morning arrived, but Shauna's kiss quieted my fears. We belonged to one another from that moment on.

For over four years, I reveled in her passion. I grew impatient whenever I was forced to return to the city, and counted the days until we would be together again. I tried in vain to convince Thomas to hire my love for our home in Boston. He refused, thinking it foolish. I never ceased trying, dismayed that I only knew happiness from mid-May to early September. I feared that Shauna would find another during my extended absences, but she never strayed. Each time I left, she would kiss me and beg me to return to her soon.

Then came the morning of August 10, 1887. Thomas had somehow discovered my secret. I do not know how; perhaps he had finally noticed the longing looks Shauna and I exchanged during his visits. As I lay in my lover's bed, I was unaware that he had returned that evening. It was near dawn when he stormed into the carriage house and tore me from my Shauna's embrace.

He never uttered a word as he dragged me back to the main house and locked me in my bedroom. I screamed and pounded on the door until my fists were bleeding. Finally, he returned. He spewed out a litany of curses as I begged him to simply walk away and allow me to stay with her. Then his laughter rang cruelly in my ears, and I noticed that his clothing was covered with dirt and blood.

Horrified, I was forced to listen as he vented his disgust at what I had become. His eyes turned dark and evil, and he told me what he had done. He sounded pleased when he described how he had beaten her, and the way she had screamed for me all the while. Then he boasted that he had thrown her down the staircase and her neck had snapped, stopping her sniveling cries.

I fell to my knees, wailing with grief, and he went on to say that he had buried her in the back like the dog she was. The horror overwhelmed me, and I was unable to think or speak. I felt numb as our things were packed and we fled the house. I did manage to give some money to Frederick, pleading with him to place a marker on Shauna's grave. The poor fellow begged to know what had happened. I was unable to speak, consumed by guilt and the knowledge that I had caused Shauna's death.

During the journey back to Boston, I tried to console myself, knowing that I had my children to look after. They were the only reason I had not revealed my husband's crime. The shame of what had happened would have ruined their lives. If not for them, I would have gladly given my life to see Thomas suffer. The guilt and grief proved too much for me. Upon returning home, I retired to my bedroom. At the time, I foolishly thought I needed time to grieve, or work up my courage to avenge Shauna's murder.

I never spoke, nor did I leave my bedchambers. My mind and spirit died with her. I languished in bed, numbly watching my children grow. Finally, my daughter came to me and told me that Thomas had died in his sleep.

"Bastard," I said, breaking my years of silence and shocking my now grown daughter.

My callous reaction frightened her and my two sons. During one of her visits a month later, she demanded to know what had happened. I told her everything. I do not know if she understands, or has forgiven me. It was the last time I spoke; now I pray for my own death. I feel that my wait is nearing its end, which is why I am writing this letter. I need to write it, even though there is no one to mail it to. I pray that Shauna has forgiven my cowardice. I know I shall never forgive myself.

Mildred Phelps

"'...I shall never forgive myself. Mildred Phelps.'" Cara brushed a tear from her cheek. Something stirred in the air as she set the paper down. "I don't know whether to sympathize with Mildred or bitch-slap her."

"I know how you feel," Sam said. "When I read the letter, my initial reaction was that she was a coward, and that she and Thomas got off way too easy. If she kept the secret for the sake of her children, then why leave her children's upbringing in the hands of a murderer? Then I read it again and again, and I wondered what I would have done. It was the 1800s. The word gay wasn't even a label yet. These women couldn't even vote. Hell, I'm not sure they had indoor plumbing, and I freak out if the cable goes out. I came out almost a hundred years after Mildred's sexual awakening, and it still wasn't a picnic."

"She gave up everything," Cara said.

"Yes, including herself. Mildred snapped. If she'd turned her husband in, everything would've come out, and she might have ended up in jail herself for being a deviant. I live in the twenty-first century, but at times I cross paths with someone who doesn't approve of my lifestyle. I live in a state that permits me to marry a woman. I slap rainbow flags on everything, and still the other day I bolted. This dance we've been doing, and your uncertainty, it scares me. If I'm afraid, I can only imagine how terrifying all of this is to you. Now, imagine going through this over a hundred years ago."

"I wouldn't have taken the chances they took," Cara admitted. "I'm afraid my cowardice runs much deeper than Mildred's." She studied Sam carefully, suddenly understanding why she was there. Sam needed to know if Cara was finally going to follow her heart.

"No more," she whispered, closing the distance between them. She was terrified that she had misinterpreted everything, and that Sam would reject her. "I'm tired of being afraid." She held Sam's face in her hands and swallowed hard, deciding it was time to start living.

Their breath mingled as Cara drew Sam closer. Her eyes fluttered shut and she gave in to her desires, brushing her lips tenderly against Sam's. Her heart soared at the sounds of light laughter echoing in the house. "Apparently, Shauna agrees," Sam said, then she reclaimed Cara's lips. The passionate embrace made Cara's heart race. She melted against Sam's tender touch.

"That was worth waiting for." Sam smiled and tightened her arms around Cara.

"You did say you're a patient woman," Cara said. "I don't blame you for running. I wasn't offering you a reason to stay, but I'm ready to now."

"Really?"

"Yes, really. I had a long talk with my mother after you took off. I told her that I'm gay."

Sam's eyes widened. "What did she say?"

"She said, 'No kidding,'" Cara answered and laughed at herself. "She's known for years. Then I told Mary at work. Her reaction was very similar to my mother's. Other than that, I've only told Shauna. I don't know if that counts."

Cara yelped when they were plunged into darkness. She jumped into Sam's warm embrace.

"I think Shauna counts." Sam laughed and called out, "She's sorry." They waited for Shauna's reaction, snuggling closer and exchanging kisses until the lights blinked back on.

Cara was far too interested in tracing Sam's features with her fingers to care that the lights were back on. "Stay?" she asked, her heart racing as she waited for Sam's response.

"Afraid of Shauna?"

"No." Cara's fingers drifted to the nape of Sam's neck. "Strangely enough, I've gotten used to Shauna lingering about. What frightens me is giving in to my fears and letting you walk away. I've wasted most of my life trying to be someone that I'm not. I can't do that anymore. I have feelings for you, and I refuse to be an idiot. I'm not playing games. I'm not curious. I am simply completely and utterly gaga over you."

"Do you have any idea how beautiful you are?" Sam asked.

"Show me." Cara stood and offered Sam her hand.

She led the way up the staircase and to her bedroom, and soon she was nestled in Sam's arms, kissing her soon-to-be lover tenderly. Her anticipation built as they slowly undressed each other. She shut out the horrible events that had happened in her home so many years ago. Instead of recalling Shauna's horrible fate, she focused on the fact that two people once shared a great passion in what was now her home.

Sam's kisses and gentle touch made her body hum with desire. Everything about this enigmatic woman was exciting. Cara's breath caught as she gazed at Sam's naked body for the first time. She was amazed when Sam blushed in response. "You're so beautiful," Cara gasped in wonderment.

"No, that's you." Sam's eyes raked up and down Cara's body. Bolstered by her lover's smoldering look, Cara guided Sam to the bed. She moaned deeply when their naked bodies touched for the first time. The softness of Sam's breasts brushed against her own, making her heart pound as they fell on the bed. It was pure bliss. Cara's hands roamed along Sam's body, exploring every curve, her fingers tingling when she felt Sam's flesh quivering beneath her touch.

Their bodies swayed in a slow, mesmerizing rhythm. Cara was lost in sensation, and she groaned when she felt Sam's passion painting her flesh. Her body was throbbing. Sam's lips teased her neck and skilled hands caressed her thighs as their bodies became one. The soft murmurs escaping Sam's lips enticed Cara to touch her lover. She quickly became enthralled with teasing Sam's nipples, rolling them gently between her fingers as they became erect.

She cupped Sam's firm, round breasts, feeling their weight, amazed at how good it felt to caress her lover. Lifting her head, she flicked her tongue against the hardened buds. The feeling of Sam's hair tickling her skin filled her with a sense of warmth. In the background, she thought she heard the soft sounds of music. Perhaps Shauna was helping; perhaps the music was simply playing in her head, born from the ecstasy encompassing her soul.

The night was magical. Her body swayed in perfect rhythm with Sam's, each slipping a hand between their bodies to stroke the other's engorged nub. They kissed deeply, their tongues entwining while they slipped inside each other's passion. Cara felt like a child on Christmas morning, filled with awe as they pleasured one another until their screams filled the night.

For the first time in her life, she was completely happy. She trembled as Sam kissed a trail down her burning skin, and arched her body as her lover cupped her backside and drew her in. Sam's breath caressing her sex was maddening, and she cried out when her lover's tongue parted her. Wrapping her fingers in Sam's long tresses, she drew her closer, eager to give her anything she desired.

The room was spinning. Sam's touch was driving her to the brink of ecstasy for the first time in her life. She called out Sam's name over and over again, until her throat was raw and her body sated.

She curled up in her lover's arms, and could feel their hearts beating in unison. How amazing Sam's touch had been, and why had it taken her so long to experience such bliss? She smiled as her hands explored Sam's exquisite body. She slipped inside her wetness, slowly gliding her fingers along Sam's sex while nuzzling her breasts. She was pleased by the passionate moans her lover gave as she drove her to the edge. Her heart swelled when Sam's body erupted, spilling her passion against Cara's touch.

Sam kissed her tenderly, the taste of Cara's passion still lingering on her lips, her eyes glazed over with desire. "Happy Halloween," she sighed. Cara blushed.

"Happy Halloween," she said happily, noticing that a fire was burning in her bedroom fireplace. She shook her head, knowing that she hadn't lit the fire. She hoped it was Shauna, showing her approval of their coupling.

"Funky," Sam said when she saw the fire, and snickered. "So, is your new home everything you hoped it would be?"

"And more. A ghost and a beautiful woman, both in my life. This isn't what I was expecting, but now I can't imagine things any differently. Either I've completely snapped, or I'm where I should be. I'm happy."

"So am I." Sam pulled Cara in for another kiss.

O'Connor's Pub

"What was that?" Zousa yelped, when the animated skeleton dressed in a tattered tux sprang to life. The Halloween decoration had been sitting in one corner or another of the bar for weeks, singing and dancing whenever someone had the bad manners to push the purple button on his base. It was the first time the waitress had seen Johnny spring to life without someone activating him.

"Oh, Johnny's been doing that all day," Marissa, the bartender, explained to the frightened young waitress. The staff at Molly's, the quaint little Irish Pub where Zousa worked, were known to be pranksters. The petite brunette who waited tables for extra money to help with college expenses had enjoyed, the bartenders' stunts—until that moment. The problem was that neither she nor Marissa were anywhere near Johnny when he sprang to life.

"And you don't seem upset by this... because?" Zousa asked, watching Johnny sing *Born to be Wild,* his beady red eyes flashing and his hips swaying in a most undignified manner.

"Because I'm assuming that Johnny has a sensor, like most Halloween gizmos," Marissa explained calmly. "Granted, he's never gone off all by himself before, even though he's been on display since the first of the month, but I'm going with the sensor theory. Just in case, however, I've been talking very nicely to him all day. Especially since he hasn't been doing it when there have been loud noises or when someone walks by, which is what normally activates a sensor, so I'd stop flipping him off," she warned Zousa, who was giving Johnny the finger. "Look, it started before I opened. I was on the opposite side of the room checking my bank and he just started singing. I looked at his wiring. Nothing seemed different, and it didn't happen again until I changed the channel on the television."

"What did you do?" Zousa asked.

"I put the movie back on," Marissa said. "I'm not an idiot. It's probably just his sensor. Then again, it is the season. Weren't you the one who told me that Claire heard strange noises the other night when she was locking up? All I'm saying is that it's Halloween tomorrow, and I wouldn't be surprised if Molly decided to pay us a visit."

"Molly? The owner's kid? Is she the one the bar's named after? I mean, I just assumed Ryan named this place after some relative."

"So did I," Marissa said and shrugged. "He's Irish and it isn't that uncommon a name for an Irish pub. Turns out it was the name of the original owner's daughter. She saw Zousa's puzzled expression. "Oh, come on, you must know this story. You've been here longer than I have." Zousa shook her head, certain that the barmaid was trying to put one over on her. "You've seen the handprints in the dry room floor, right?" she said, referring to the room in the back of the basement where nonperishable items were stored. "Next time you go downstairs for napkins, move the boxes of Christmas ornaments. There's a set of handprints embedded in the cement."

"Stop yanking my chain," Zousa said, rolling her eyes and thoroughly convinced that the bartender was playing her. She liked Marissa, who had only joined the staff a couple months ago, after tending bar for nightclubs in the city.

"Fine, don't believe me," Marissa said. "Want me to get your ice, or are you brave enough to go in the basement?"

"Fuck you." Zousa snatched the large white ice bucket from Marissa's grasp. She could hear the other woman laughing as she ventured down the narrow staircase. She shivered slightly when she passed the walk-in cooler and turned into the room that housed the ice machine. "I'm not falling for it," she muttered, thankful that the room next door was the office, and the dry room was at the very end of the basement. Despite her brave words, she filled the bucket and raced back upstairs in record time. She growled under her breath when she heard Marissa chuckling.

While she set up tables for the dinner crowd, Zousa glanced up at the old tin ceiling and wondered how old the pub was. On the opposite side of the room hung an old black-and-white photo of the pub, back when it was called O'Connor's. It looked like it had been taken in the fifties, based on what the people were wearing. She had heard that O'Connor's was the original name. Over the years, the pub had taken on many names and identities, including a deli at one point. The current owner had finally restored the pub to its original grandeur, pulling down the false ceiling and paneling and revealing the beautiful tin ceiling and brick walls.

"Do you want to hear the story?" Marissa asked when Zousa approached the bar to order a round of drinks for her patrons.

"No." Zousa jumped when Johnny suddenly sprang to life. "Stop that!" she shouted at the animated decoration.

"I really wouldn't be yelling at him," Marissa said. "Just in case," she added eerily.

"You're a freak."

"True," Marissa agreed with a wry smirk. "Your drinks are up."

All throughout the evening, Marissa seemed to take great pleasure in taunting the young college student, and Johnny's sudden free will wasn't helping calm her jagged nerves. Somehow, Zousa managed to endure her shift. At the end of the evening, the kitchen was closed, the cook had departed, and she and Marissa set about cleaning and counting out.

Marissa was behind the bar; Mickey, one of the other bartenders, who had stayed to help, was perched at its end. Zousa was just about finished, and dreading having to go down to the basement to gather supplies for the next shift. "Hey, Mickey," Marissa called out. "You've heard the story about Molly, haven't you?"

Zousa was ready to fire back a nasty barb when Johnny started singing. "Forget it, Mickey," Zousa said. Despite Johnny's sudden animation, she was certain her co-workers were playing with her.

"You mean Molly O'Connor?" Mickey played along, laughing at Zousa's distress. "That's a really sad story. They say she used to come in, long after the family had sold the business, and sit at the bar or start waiting on tables. They finally had her committed."

"You're both a couple of assholes," Zousa growled, tearing off her black apron and running her fingers nervously through her spiky brown hair.

"She doesn't believe me," Marissa said and sighed dramatically. "Guess she doesn't want to hear the story."

"Fine, tell me the story." Zousa plopped onto a barstool.

"I don't know…" Marissa started to tease, only to have Zousa smack her with her apron. "Okay, I'll tell you. The building was built in 1890 by Innis O'Connor, after one of the big fires took out half the city. Innis sank every penny he had into the place. He was a widower, and the burden was so great that he had to sell his home. He and his children, Seamus and Molly, moved into a boardinghouse that was across the street."

"And after daddy died, Molly hung around and her handprints are in the basement," Zousa cut Marissa off.

"Oh, no, those aren't her handprints," Marissa said. "No one knows whose they are. Only that no matter how many times the floor is redone, within a couple of days the hands reappear. Some people believe they belong to Bridget Boothe, a barmaid who worked for the O'Connors. In the beginning, it was just Innis and his children, trying to keep the fledgling business afloat. Later, Innis hired Bridget, who just happened to disappear suddenly on a Halloween night, around 1894."

"You don't know the year, but you know it was Halloween night?"

"Do you want to hear the story or not?" Marissa asked the girl, who sighed in response. "Okay, now where was I? Innis hired Bridget, a fetching brunette, who was eager to stop working at one of the shoe factories. Part of her pay was free room. Since the family didn't own a home, Innis offered Bridget a small room in the basement of the pub, which is now the dry room. It was small but warm, dry, and, most important, rent-free, so Bridget accepted.

"By all accounts, Bridget was a beautiful woman. She caught many a man's eye, including Innis's. The pretty barmaid brought in a lot of business and was happy to have a steady income.

"Molly and Bridget became close friends, and quite often Molly would spend the night with Bridget, keeping her company. Bridget became like a member of the family, and people said that Innis was planning to ask the girl to marry him. They also said that Seamus had the same intention.

"On the morning of November first of that year, Molly arrived to begin her day at work, only to discover that the doors to the pub were locked. The young woman was terrified, since her father opened the pub promptly every morning, even on holidays or when he was in poor health. She banged and banged on the door until finally her father opened it. He told her to go home; the pub would not be opening that day. She was stunned by the news and the wild look in his eyes. When she raced across the street to fetch her brother, Seamus told her to go to her room and forget about it. She protested, explaining that her father looked like a mad man and his clothes were covered with paint and dirt. Seamus demanded again that she go to her room and forget the matter.

"Molly was confused, but did as her brother instructed. The following day, the pub opened on time. Molly's questions were met with cold stares. Desperate to learn what was at the heart of her father's troubles, Molly raced downstairs to Bridget's room. She was shocked once again when she found the room empty, freshly painted, and with a brand new floor.

"She dashed upstairs and asked where Bridget was. She received varying answers from her father and brother. Sometimes, they said

Bridget had met a beau and eloped. Other times, they claimed she had found a better job in a different city. Molly was heartbroken that her friend had taken off in the middle of the night, without so much as a word of farewell. In the days that followed, she would often stop by the room where Bridget had slept and stare at the emptiness. One day, about a week later, she ran screaming up the staircase.

"She refused to speak, only crying like a child. Her father hurried down to the basement and discovered a frightening sight. There, imprinted in the new floor, was a set of handprints. Innis spent the day covering the floor with another coat of cement, a task he would perform many times over the years, only to have the imprints quickly reappear.

"Molly continued to work for her family, but she never spoke again. The O'Connors kept the pub going even during prohibition, operating it as a restaurant and selling contraband beer and liquor clandestinely to trusted customers. In the late fifties, the family sold the business, but that didn't stop Molly from coming in. She'd sit at the bar, wait on tables, and often make a trip down to the basement. Finally, when she was an old woman, the family sent her to a nursing home. She died soon after. That's the whole story."

"You made that up," Zousa said accusingly. Marissa smirked at her.

"Maybe. Come on, we have to lock up before the cops show up and ask what we're still doing here."

The others agreed. Zousa decided to wait until tomorrow to fetch what she needed. She wasn't eager to go into the basement after listening to Marissa's wild tale.

She went into the dry room the next day, filled with trepidation, to gather the supplies she needed for her shift. Looking around the room curiously, she took a calming breath and set down the napkins and other items she was carrying. She shivered and glanced over her shoulder before shifting the large boxes filled with Christmas decorations. Her heart pounded when she spied the dusty pair of handprints etched in the cement floor.

A scream caught in her throat, and her body was shaking as she grabbed up the items and dashed out of the room. "Where's the fire?" Marissa asked when Zousa almost knocked her over.

"Hand… handprints," she sputtered, and almost dropped the armful of supplies.

Marissa moved quickly to take the items from Zousa before they were scattered on the barroom floor.

"Calm down," Marissa said. "I never should have told you that story. You do know, don't you, that anyone could have put those there? Some workman, or one of the former owners, for instance?"

"Yeah, right. Anyone." Zousa didn't sound convinced.

"Relax, it's Halloween night and we're going to be slammed," Marissa told her. "It was just a story. Are you going to be okay?"

"I'm good," Zousa lied.

True to Marissa's prediction, the pub was packed that night. The constant demands of the crowd kept Zousa from thinking about the eerie story and strange handprints in the basement until it was time to close. Once the last of the drunken crowd had been kicked out of the pub and the doors locked, Zousa was filled with uneasiness again.

"Stop it," she said to Mickey, who was laughing at her.

"I made it up," Marissa finally said, as she went about cleaning the place. "The story, I made it up. There wasn't a Molly or a Bridget, I was just teasing. Molly is the name of Ryan's granddaughter. I thought you knew that."

"You suck." Zousa was angry that she had been made a fool of. "Clean up quickly, I want to go home. Thank God tomorrow is my day off. I am so going to pay you back for this."

"Yeah, yeah, I suck, but we made money tonight," Marissa said with a laugh. "Tomorrow, Johnny and the rest of the crap Ryan bought go into storage and all will be right with the world. Tonight, I just want to go home and sleep."

The three of them made quick work of cleaning the messy pub. "Hold on," Marissa asked, when they stepped outside, ready to lock up. "I forgot my cell. Wait for me?"

"Hurry, it's cold," Zousa said, still angry about Marissa's teasing.

Alone in the dark pub, Marissa snatched her cell phone from behind the bar. She wasn't surprised when Johnny's head turned and faced her. "Okay, so I didn't lie," she tried to reason with him. "There's no way she was going to show up for her next shift if I told her it was the truth. Then again, it wasn't the whole truth either. No one knows the whole story, except for you, maybe." Marissa felt a chill fill the room as Johnny's eyes lit up and his head quirked once again. His jaw clapped open, and he shut his eyes, blinking. "Man, I am going to have some serious nightmares tonight." Marissa grimaced, wishing she didn't believe in such things and could ignore the fact that the decoration, which had been purchased at Wal-Mart, was reacting to her words. "Well goodnight, whoever you are." Her breath caught when she spied an elderly woman sitting at the end of the bar. She knew all the customers had left long ago.

Marissa rushed out and joined her co-workers on the sidewalk, locking the door behind her. "Home," she choked out, choosing not to tell her friends what she had just seen. "Who needs a ride?"

* * *

Molly O'Connor sat at the bar looking around the dark, empty room. "I know," she whispered, and her green eyes filled with tears. She stared at the door that led to the basement. Finally, she stood and walked across the room and through the locked door without bothering to open it. She floated down the dark, narrow staircase, through the narrow basement, and stopped at the door to the room that had been Bridget's bedroom. She didn't notice the boxes and supplies that now filled the room. Molly saw only the bare room, freshly painted, and Bridget's handprints marring the floor. "I know," she sadly repeated, her thoughts returning to that spring morning in 1892 when she entered the pub and met the new barmaid.

* * *

"Good, you're here," Innis greeted his daughter, oblivious to her curious gaze. "This is Bridget. She's going to be working here."

"Working here?" Molly said, unable to tear her gaze from the tall brunette with the amazing blue eyes. "Doing what?" she finally managed to ask. A surge of warmth spread through her as Bridget greeted her with a brilliant smile.

"A little bar work, waiting tables and such," Innis explained, a slight hitch in his normally confident tone. "You and your brother can finally have a night off now and then. I've already fixed up a little room for her down in the basement. Show her around, will you? I need to start setting up. The mill workers will be wanting breakfast soon."

Molly blinked with surprise as her father stumbled toward the kitchen. *Now, what's gotten into him?* she wondered, before returning her gaze to the new barmaid. "Oh." Understanding dawned. Apparently her father had taken a shine to Bridget. Molly was troubled by the thought of her father taking an interest in a woman who was probably close to her own age. *Then again, Da's been alone for such a long time,* she tried to reason, her lips curling into a grimace at the thought of the attractive woman becoming her stepmother.

"Bridget Boothe," the tall woman said warmly, distracting Molly from her disturbing thoughts.

"Molly O'Connor. It's a pleasure to meet you, Bridget," she responded, her grimace turning into a bold smile as she shook the woman's hand. She held Bridget's hand for a moment longer than necessary, turning it over and running her fingers along the calloused palm and fingers.

"Factory work," Bridget explained softly, running her fingertips against Molly's. "Serving drinks is a step up, as is having a room of my own."

"It's in the basement," Molly said, wondering just what her father had done, and if Bridget would be happy living in the cellar of a pub. *Then again, the rooming house is no picnic either*, she thought, silently vowing to inspect Bridget's accommodations to make sure the new employee would be comfortable. "Welcome to O'Connor's. If you can pour a pint half as good as you look, you'll be retiring to Lake Shore Drive in no time."

"You flatter me." Bridget laughed, warming Molly's heart.

I'm trying to, Molly thought wistfully as she showed Bridget around the pub, explaining the rules and prices.

Molly was a bundle of energy that day, hovering over Bridget under the guise of teaching her what to do. "A private bath," she said when Bridget showed her the room in the basement. It was tidy, a small bed in the corner and a bathtub set up across from it. "When did Da do all this?"

"He only offered me the job last week," Bridget said. "Believe it or not, this is the nicest place I've had in a long time."

Molly stared at the ceiling, through which the noise of the night crowd pounded from above. "Complete with entertainment," she said with a wry grin. She worried that Bridget wouldn't be able to sleep on her nights off. "We should head up," she said. "It's pay day, and Seamus must have them lined up at the bar."

She shivered as she noticed how close Bridget was standing. Her shiver turned into a tremble when the tall woman reached out and clasped her hand, squeezing it as they stepped out of the tiny room in the back of the basement.

From that first day, Bridget proved to be an asset. The men tripped over themselves to get her attention. Molly was troubled by the way seemingly intelligent men acted like buffoons just to catch

Bridget's eye. More troubling than the patrons' antics was the way her father and brother were fawning over her.

"Men are idiots," Bridget whispered in Molly's ear. Molly trembled when the warm breath caressed her. She felt her face flush as she watched Bridget stuffing a wad of money into her bosom.

"I need to fetch another keg," she blurted out, quickly ducking away in an effort to conceal her blush.

"I'll give you a hand," said Bridget.

"No need." Molly scurried to the basement stairs. She muttered a curse when she found Bridget standing behind her.

"I have to learn where things are."

"Right," Molly reluctantly agreed, and they headed down the stairwell.

They struggled with the cask, giggling at the dust as they rolled it toward the stairs. "I can't believe you can lift one of these by yourself," Bridget said, brushing an errant strand of hair from Molly's cheek.

"We all pitch in." Bridget's knuckles drifted lower, brushing against the swell of Molly's breast. Molly inhaled sharply, and her eyes darted up, captured by Bridget's smoldering gaze. The tiny space was made loud by the din from upstairs, but the thudding of Molly's heart drowned it out.

"Hurry it along!" Seamus bellowed from above.

Molly swallowed hard as she looked down to find Bridget's fingers still resting against her breast. Her body felt cold when Bridget jerked her hand away. "Bugger off!" she screamed up to her brother. She was dismayed when Bridget turned away. "Him, not you," she murmured. "Now grab an end." She hesitated. "Of the cask." She smiled when Bridget blushed.

"Survived your first night, have you?" Molly asked Bridget as they cleaned the pub after closing.

"Barely."

"Da?" Molly called as she put stools up on tables so Bridget could sweep. "I'll stay and help Bridget clean up. Why don't you and Seamus go on home?"

"I could help her," Seamus offered eagerly.

"No, Seamus," Innis said sternly, glaring at his son. "I can stay."

"Da," Molly cut off the contest that seemed to be in the making. "You know how loud the rooming house gets on payday. I'm in no hurry to get back there just so I can barricade my door and be kept awake all night by drunken hooligans. I'll stay and help Bridget."

Innis nodded and continued his own chores. "Barricade your door?" Bridget said.

"The rooming house rents mostly to men," Innis explained, embarrassment clear on his face. "Nights like tonight, Seamus and I keep a watch on Molly's door."

"Molly could bunk with me," Bridget said, and Molly's stomach fluttered. "I wouldn't mind. I used to share with my sisters. It would be much safer for Molly, and I wouldn't feel so lonely on my first night."

"Molly?" Innis asked, happy to see the two women getting along.

"All right," said Molly. "I'll just dash across the road and grab some clothes." She darted to the boardinghouse, dodging the drunken guests, and grabbed a change of clean clothing and an extra quilt. She was breathless when she returned to the pub.

"Good God, girl! I've never seen you move so quickly," Innis exclaimed.

Molly could feel Bridget watching her while they cleaned and locked up for the night. She turned off the lights and then followed Bridget down to her tiny room. They faced away from each other as they shyly prepared for bed. Molly bit down on her bottom lip and steadied herself, then turned, half hoping Bridget would still be changing. She smiled to hide her disappointment when she saw that Bridget, clad in her nightgown, had already turned down the bedding and added the quilt. "We should be warm enough," Bridget said, climbing into the small bed. There was a tremor in her voice.

"Of that I have no doubt." Molly turned down the lamp and climbed in next to Bridget. "Small bed," she whispered, as their bodies pressed together.

"I could—"

"Move closer?" Molly interrupted boldly before Bridget could offer to sleep on the floor or upstairs. She held her breath until she felt Bridget's hands wrap around her waist and pull her closer.

"Closer is good," Bridget said, and they giggled nervously "I'm a lucky woman. A new job, my own room, and I've met a beautiful lass, all in one day. I'm not wrong about you, am I?"

"No." Molly laced her fingers in Bridget's long, dark tresses. "Although this is very fast. I don't normally just climb into bed with a woman."

"Nor do I," Bridget said. "And I am not planning on being overly brash on the first night."

"Pity," Molly said with a teasing laugh. She snuggled closer to Bridget's warm, inviting body. She could feel Bridget's breath caress her face. They kissed shyly and cradled each other tenderly. Molly sighed happily, and kissed Bridget once again. She released a soft moan, enjoying the lips moving against her own as Bridget's fingers played with the lace on her nightgown.

The kiss grew deeper, and their hands shyly explored each other's bodies. Molly was in heaven, her touch growing bolder until Bridget captured her wandering hands. "Molly O'Connor, I plan to woo you slowly," Bridget said in a tender voice. "You deserve that."

"As do you," Molly softly agreed. She curled up in Bridget's embrace and drifted off into blissful slumber. When she awoke the following morning, her body was agitated but her soul was at peace. She kissed Bridget tenderly before they climbed out of the warm bed and once again turned away from each other to change their clothing.

Molly was surprised at herself. She would have made love to Bridget on their first night, so she was thankful that Bridget had the foresight to slow things down. Hurried passion had never been Molly's style; it was hard enough to conceal her true nature without the risk of having her secret revealed by a woman she barely knew.

Over the next few weeks, Bridget attracted a great deal of business and an equal amount of unwanted advances. It was painfully obvious to all that Innis O'Connor fancied his new employee. Seamus and everyone else stepped aside each time Innis bristled over some other man paying too much attention to Bridget. For Molly, her father's attention was a double-edged sword. The large Irishman kept unwanted suitors away, yet what Innis and everyone else failed to notice was that Bridget had eyes only for Molly.

Their shy glances and covert touching went unnoticed. Molly found it amusing that no one remarked how long it took the women to fetch anything from downstairs. They spent the extra time caressing and kissing, driving each other closer and closer to the point of no return. "This is madness," Bridget whispered in Molly's ear one morning, when they were pretending to check stock. Instead, the amorous women were locked in a passionate embrace.

"You are so beautiful," Molly whispered, slipping her hand along the curve of Bridget's breast. They stumbled away from each other, their faces flushed with desire. "I don't know how much longer I can resist you," she said, her voice husky. "Today is payday. May I stay with you tonight?"

"Yes," Bridget promised, her eyes smoldering with desire. "But we need to get back to work before someone notices that we're gone."

"What's wrong with you, girl?" Innis asked, when Molly dropped another glass.

"I'm fine," she said, sneaking a glance at the snickering Bridget. Molly had been jittery all day; she knew that once closing time came, there would be no one to interrupt them, and they could finally consummate their passion. The realization that she was finally going to make love to Bridget filled her with elation and terror. "Don't forget that I'm staying here tonight."

"I saw that you packed your bag last night," Innis said. "Lord, girl you'd think you were sailing to Europe instead of sleeping in the bar. I'm pleased that you and Bridget are getting on so well."

"Why wouldn't we?" Molly said. "She's only a year older than I am," she added, reminding her father that Bridget was young enough to be his daughter. She felt a sharp pang when she saw the embarrassed look in her father's eyes.

At closing time that evening, Bridget and Molly hurried through their chores and waited until Seamus and Innis finally left. "Thank heavens." Molly bolted the door and turned down the lights. "Sorry," she said, seeing a curious look in Bridget's brilliant blue eyes.

Bridget cupped Molly's face in her hands. "I wanted to throw everyone out even before the sun had set. Are you as nervous as I am?"

"More," Molly said, leaning into Bridget's touch.

"We don't have to do this." Bridget smiled when Molly gave her a dubious look. "You've stolen my heart, Molly O'Connor."

"And I've fallen in love with you, Bridget Boothe." Molly beamed and wrapped her arms around her lover's waist. "Take me to bed."

They laughed, stumbling down the stairs in their hurry to reach Bridget's room. Bridget spun Molly in her arms, pinned her against the kegs of ale, and kissed her deeply. Molly gave in to her lover's fiery kiss, caressing her tongue with her own. Her hands roamed along the curves of Bridget's body and they ignored the fact that Bridget's bedroom was only a short distance away.

Molly moaned into the warmth of her lover's mouth. When Bridget tore open the front of her dress, Molly responded by hiking up the hem of Bridget's. Her head fell back as Bridget's body swayed against her. She reveled in the feel of eager hands cupping her breasts while she caressed her lover's backside. Her hips ground against Bridget when she felt her lover's mouth capturing her breasts. She pressed her breast deeper inside the warmth of Bridget's mouth and gasped for air as her lover suckled her erect nipple while pressing her harder against the wooden casks.

She tore at Bridget's undergarments, eager to feel her flesh. Her body pulsated with desire as the firm, round backside filled her hands. Her skin felt cold and wet as Bridget's mouth began to devour her other nipple. Bridget's teeth nipped at the erect bud, swelling Molly's desire.

Her stomach clenched when she heard a fierce growl escape her lover's lips. "Bed," Bridget gasped, stumbling away from Molly's overheated body. "I'll not have our first time together be a tawdry encounter in the hallway amongst casks of Guinness."

Molly smiled sweetly as her lover took her by the hand and they walked through the basement until they stepped into the simple surroundings of Bridget's room. She held Bridget's face between her hands, her lover mirroring her actions. The air felt heavy, filled with nervous energy as they stared deeply into each other's eyes. "I wish I could give you more," Bridget said, her words throbbing with passion.

"Do I have your heart?" Molly asked, caressing her lover's chiseled features.

"Now and forever," Bridget promised, slipping Molly's dress down her smooth, creamy shoulders.

"That is all I shall ever need or desire." Molly's fingers stroked her lover's neck. Finding companions had always been torture for Molly. First there was the attraction, then the dance of testing the lady in an effort to discover if they were indeed kindred spirits. More often than not, Molly was left wanting, walking away when she discovered that the woman didn't share her interests. And if she did, the need for discretion and secrecy proved overwhelming. With Bridget, she had felt an overpowering connection from the very first moment. The first time their hands had touched, she had felt it. She had not only found a companion, she had found her mate.

She shivered with anticipation, her dress falling to the floor, and stood in utter surrender as her lover slowly undressed her. It was ecstasy and agony both, standing there with her body quivering from Bridget's touches until she was naked in the cold room. Bridget stood before her, and seemed to struggle to catch her breath as her eyes, filled with love and raw desire, raked up and down Molly's naked body.

Molly licked her lips and stepped shyly toward her lover. She reached out and slowly untied the ribbon that barely kept Bridget's ample bosom captive. Her heart soared as she slowly undressed her, and she felt Bridget quivering beneath her touch. Her jaw dropped once her lover's glorious, naked form was finally revealed.

"How is this possible?" she asked in amazement, her emerald eyes drinking in every inch of Bridget's body.

"How is what possible?" Bridget closed the gap between them until their bodies met.

"That I have managed to win the heart of the most beautiful woman on earth." Molly trembled as Bridget's soft breasts brushed against her.

"You haven't," Bridget murmured. "I'm the one who has been granted that honor."

"Oh, sweetness," Molly said, her hands gliding along the supple curves of Bridget's body. The world spun out of control as Bridget took her in a searing kiss. She moaned, and her tongue wrapped around her lover's. Her hand slipped between their bodies and explored her lover's firm stomach. Eager hands traveled up and down Bridget's form as they stumbled toward the bed.

They fell onto the small bed, laughing merrily. Molly expelled a needy groan as she covered Bridget's body with her own. They melted together, their kisses growing deeper, curious hands exploring forbidden pleasures. Molly's kisses drifted lower, worshiping the tender flesh of Bridget's neck. As she sucked her lover's neck, she could feel the blood pulsating beneath her lips. Her hand slipped between Bridget's trembling thighs, and her fingers brushed against her lover's passion.

Her teeth sank into yielding flesh, and Bridget's desire filled her hand as her body wriggled beneath her. She teased Bridget, cupping her mound, pressing the heel of her hand against her lover's throbbing desire while her mouth drifted lower. She slowly traced the swell of Bridget's breasts with her tongue, savoring the taste of the sweet flesh.

Molly nestled her body between Bridget's long legs, glancing down at her lover and parting her with her fingers. She was filled with elation as Bridget's face flushed with desire, her wetness greeting Molly's tender touch. Molly slowly stroked Bridget's swollen sex, dipping her head and capturing one of Bridget's rose-colored nipples between her lips.

Bridget's legs wrapped around her, and Molly eagerly suckled her nipple, loving the way it puckered against her touch. Her fingers danced against Bridget's throbbing bundle, bringing wild thrusts as she begged Molly to pleasure her.

"I will, my love." Molly brushed her thumb against Bridget's aching nub, and her mouth drifted lower, licking and kissing every inch of Bridget's body. She nestled her slender body between Bridget's thighs. The musky aroma of Bridget's passion filled her senses as Molly draped her lover's long legs over her shoulders. She cupped Bridget's firm backside, drawing her closer.

Bridget's desperate pleas called out to her while she caressed her, drawing her passion to her lips. She parted Bridget, dipping her tongue deep inside her. Tasting her lover for the first time, she murmured with pleasure. She slowly slid her tongue along Bridget's sex, driving her into a frenzy. "Molly, Molly," Bridget cried over and over again, as Molly feasted upon her.

Molly fought against her own growing need to find release, suckling her lover's throbbing clit urgently. Bridget's body thrashed beneath Molly's slender fingers, that had slipped deep inside her warm, wet center. Molly sucked harder, her fingers plunged deeper, and her body reeled when Bridget's passion spilled over her.

Bridget's cries of pleasure echoed through the basement, fueling Molly's desire further. She was ravenous, and the only thing that could sate her aching need was pleasuring Bridget until her lover had nothing left to offer. She held Bridget's thrashing body, suckling her harder, sending her deeper into a euphoric haze.

Molly was resting blissfully against Bridget's trembling thigh when the air was driven from her lungs and she found herself lying on her back. She laughed up at Bridget, who hovered over her with a devilish gleam in her eyes. She began begging her lover to do whatever she wished, but she need not have bothered. Bridget bestowed savage kisses upon her while her fingers plunged deep inside Molly's center.

Molly's body erupted, and her mind filled with wondrous colors as she willingly gave herself over to the marvelous things Bridget was doing to her. They made love through the night, their wild passion clouding their judgment until they were almost caught when the upstairs door was unlocked. They tumbled out of bed, frantically washing and dressing before Innis could come downstairs and see the hedonistic scene.

They could barely keep their eyes open that day, despite their euphoria. If anyone noticed their elation, and the knowing smiles they exchanged, it was never mentioned. Their love affair continued for over two years, and no one seemed the wiser, despite the numerous times Molly would trump up some excuse to sleep at the pub.

During the day, they would steal kisses and familiar touches. Their nights were spent making love and promising each other that some day they would run off together, far from prying eyes.

Molly's dreams were shattered in the early morning hours of November 1, 1894, when she arrived at the pub and found the door still bolted. She knocked repeatedly. The knocks turned to pounding, and still no one answered. At last, her father emerged, almost knocking her over when he flung open the door. Molly was shocked by his unkempt appearance and the wild look in his eyes. She tried peeking past him, searching for her lover, regretting that she had obeyed her father the night before and slept at the boardinghouse.

Fear gripped her heart when her father sent her on her way. She pleaded with her brother, who also had a strange look in his eyes when she kept telling him that something was amiss. Again and again, her pleas were dismissed. She sat in her tiny room all day, and found no sleep that night. The following morning, when Seamus summoned her for work, her first thought was not of her family but of her lover.

She raced to the basement, and her heart shattered when she found Bridget's room empty, freshly painted, and with a new floor. She begged for answers, only to receive various stories from her family. She was distraught for more than a week, fearing that Bridget had just abandoned her, or that her father had discovered the truth and sent her beloved away. Then one day, she wandered into the vacant room just as she had done every day since Bridget had vanished. She shrieked in horror when she saw the handprints embedded in the floor. It was then she knew that Bridget hadn't left her.

Horrified, she raced upstairs and into the barroom, ready to exact her revenge. Instead, when she saw the pleading look in her father's eyes, she collapsed and wailed like a wounded animal. In that instant, her mind and soul were broken and she was left speechless. From that moment on, she lived in a world that no longer existed, looking for her lover, who would never return to her.

What the world failed to see, as Molly wandered the pub, both in life and after her death, was that Bridget's body was trapped beneath the floor, but her spirit waited. She would continue to wait, feeling Molly near but never seeing her. Others might see one or the other of them, over the passing decades, but they never found each other. Over the years, staff and customers alike spun wild tales about the strange events that happened from time to time. Yet none of them knew the truth.

* * *

"What exactly are we doing here?" Cat looked around the empty barroom. It looked gloomy in the dim lights left burning. "It isn't like we don't spend enough time in this hell hole as it is."

Marissa cast a weary glance at the co-worker she had dragged out of bed. Cat was the only one other than Marissa herself who didn't get freaked out when it came to ghosts. In fact, Cat was into the whole subject. "Come on, you do cleansing," Marissa said. "Haven't you ever wondered what's going on around here?"

"Personally," Cat said, "I think it's an old employee still looking for a tip."

Marissa was having trouble explaining her actions. She didn't quite understand why, after dropping Zousa and Mickey off tonight, she had raced over to Cat's apartment instead of simply going home. Okay, so the story, or rather the multitude of stories, about who or what was wandering around Molly's Pub had piqued her curiosity. Maybe someone who knew something about spirits could find out what had really happened to Bridget. Cat, another bartender at the pub, was the only person Marissa knew who worked in the realm of the spirit world. She also knew that Cat was one of the few friends she could awaken in the middle of the night.

After Cat finished spouting a lengthy stream of curses, Marissa managed to convince her to join her in an effort to find out the truth. In addition to making a mean martini, Cat was a tarot reader and part-time ghost hunter.

"I hope we don't get in trouble for this." Marissa looked out the pub windows to ensure that the police weren't about to show up. What would she tell them? "Sorry, I know it's against the law to be here after hours, but I really want to know why the skeleton decided to do a jig." That excuse wouldn't fly with the cops or her boss. She was putting both their jobs on the line, but she couldn't shake the uneasy feeling that she should at least try to do something. Just then Johnny sprang to life, singing and dancing. "Well, that's disturbing," she noted dryly, watching him swinging his hips. "I unplugged him before we left."

Cat didn't even flinch. She simply strolled over, checked the wiring, and confirmed that Johnny shouldn't be doing what he was doing. "Haven't you felt it the past few days?" Marissa asked. "It's way beyond the usual things that go bump in the night. That happens all the time, here. I just feel so—"

"Sad," Cat cut her off in a knowing tone. "She's trapped."

"Who?"

"Both of them." Suddenly, Cat looked interested. "It is the time of year for spirits to act up."

"Halloween?"

"Uh huh. Not just that, actually" Cat said. "One of them passed away, but failed to pass on. She's Irish, and being denied a proper burial left her soul trapped on this plane. We should go to the basement." She headed toward the door to the basement.

"What?" Marissa hoped Cat could explain things. She was the one who had told Marissa the story she had related to Zousa earlier that evening. When Marissa asked how she knew the real story, Cat simply stated that she had picked up on things. Marissa soon figured out that when Cat said she picked up on things, it meant she saw and heard things most people couldn't.

"Hey, this was your idea." Cat snickered as she swung open the door to the basement and clicked on the downstairs lights. "She's calling to you because you're a kindred spirit."

"Oh, don't get all Anne of Green Gables on me." Marissa closed the door behind them so the light wouldn't be seen when the police did their nightly checks on the building.

"She's one of yours," Cat said as they descended the staircase. "You know, working for her toaster oven."

"You could have just said that she was gay," Marissa grumbled and followed her friend. "So, Molly was a big lesbo."

"And so are you, and you're in tune with the other side even if you try to hide it." Cat stopped in front of the walk-in cooler. "I've never felt it so active down here before. This is where they used to meet to steal kisses and hugs. Very sweet."

Marissa held her breath when a dark shadow passed by them. It continued on down the hallway, turned at the end, and disappeared at the dry goods room. "Who was that?" Marissa squeaked.

"Molly," said Cat. "So much is coming to me. I've felt it before, but never this strong. She comes here night after night, looking for her one true love. She never finds her. Bridget wanders about here constantly too, but their souls never meet."

"Okay, you're the Goth chick who knows how to send people to the other side." Marissa nudged Cat with her elbow. "Just do it, so we can get out of here."

"I can't."

"What? Why not?"

"Bridget is trapped," Cat tried to explain. "She was denied a decent burial, and her killer was never brought to justice. Unless we can release her and have her murderer publicly named, she and Molly will continue to wander, searching for one another until the end of time."

"Well, isn't that just dandy," Marissa said and then scowled. "No way is Ryan going to let us dig up the basement. And just how do you know she was murdered?"

"She told me." Cat beamed.

"Well, that's why I brought you," Marissa grumbled. "Did she happen to tell you who killed her?"

"All I'm getting is Da or David or something like that. It isn't clear. Neither is the reason why he did it. All I can sense is that whoever it was surprised her. He was angry, and she'd never seen him angry before. It was then she realized that he knew."

"He knew what?"

"I don't know," Cat admitted.

"Then there's nothing we can do?" Marissa asked. The feeling of sadness in the room was overwhelming.

"Got a shovel?" Cat said flippantly.

"Yeah, that might be a little hard to explain. I can just hear us, 'Oh, we had a great crowd tonight, but somehow the basement ended up with a big-ass hole in it. Gosh, I don't know how that happened.'"

"You could always claim it was an invasion of mutant fruit flies," Cat quipped.

"Oh, right, that'll work," Marissa scoffed. Frustrated, she agreed to Cat's suggestion that they leave.

Time passed slowly at the pub. Marissa couldn't shake the sadness that came over her every time she went into the basement. One afternoon, after working a tediously slow day-shift, she was in the office counting out her meager earnings when someone passed by and greeted her.

"Hey," she muttered without looking up, only glimpsing the dark-haired woman out of the corner of her eye. She vaguely wondered why Cat was downstairs and why she was wearing black. She didn't stop to think that she had seen Cat moments before, wearing a neatly pressed white tuxedo shirt and black slacks, the required staff outfit.

After balancing her drawer, she put the till in the safe, locked up, and went back upstairs. She shook her head, noting that the only people in the building were the cook, Zousa, and Cat. She went behind the bar to gather up her belongings.

"Were you just downstairs?" she asked Cat, who was checking the inventory.

"No."

"Zousa, did you go downstairs?" She recalled that the passerby had been clad in black lace, and that the upstairs door was locked when she came up.

"No," Zousa responded in a flat voice. "Oddly enough, I've tried to avoid going down there ever since you decided it would be fun to freak me out. Why?"

"Oh, nothing." The figure had passed by the office, greeted her, and then headed toward the dry goods room. She almost said something, but refrained. Zousa had been skittish enough over the past couple of months.

"What happened?" Cat asked, after Zousa had gone to the far end of the room.

"Someone with long dark hair passed by the office, said hello, and walked into the dry room. At least she's polite." Marissa sighed heavily and ducked out from behind the bar. "I still wish there was something we could do. Forget it." She shrugged and took a seat at the bar. "What about you, Cat? Just another month or so, and you're out of here."

"I can't wait," Cat said with a smile. "New job, new city, and a whole new life."

"New city?" Marissa laughed. "Hell, you're moving to a different country. I'm going to miss you. But I'm happy that you finally found something more interesting than this place."

"Some things about this place have been pretty interesting," Cat happily retorted. "Maybe we'll find all of the answers soon."

"Huh?"

"Nothing," Cat said with a sly smirk.

Marissa's body was aching the following afternoon, and she was cussing. The pub manager had phoned her early that morning. For some unknown reason, the building's basement had flooded overnight, and she and some of the other staff had been called in to clean up the mess. "Great timing! We're all finished," she said to Cat, who was just arriving.

Marissa's jaw dropped when she caught the mischievous gleam in Cat's dark brown eyes. "What did you do?" she demanded under her breath, dragging Cat out of the barroom.

"Who, me?" Cat asked, giving her a wicked grin.

"Now it makes sense," Marissa said. "Most of the flooding was in the dry goods room. Kind of strange, since that room doesn't have any plumbing."

"No, but the air conditioning pipes do," Cat whispered. "And if you twist the water pipes in the office just right…"

"You're a freak!" Marissa had wanted to help Molly, but wanton destruction of property was way out of line.

"Did it work?"

"You could say that. Mickey told me they're going to have to dig up the whole floor. I don't even want to know how you managed to cause that much damage to a cement floor."

"The hard part was making the broken pipe look like an accident," Cat confessed, grinning like an idiot. "Then I had to damage the floor, and making that look like an accident. My back is killing me, and I'm sore in places I forgot existed. It wasn't easy. I had to do a lot of online research, too."

"And just what website did you find this info on, www.officevandalism.com? What good is this going to do?" Marissa said. "Even if they find the body, how are we going to find out who killed her?"

"Maybe when her spirit is freed, she'll tell us," Cat reasoned.

A few days later, Marissa stopped by the pub to find out if she would be working that night. Cat's scheme to flood the basement had been so successful that they'd had to close the bar for repairs, which meant no work for the staff. A very excited Zousa greeted her, ranting and raving about how the workmen found a body buried in the basement.

"You told me you made that story up," Zousa said, visibly shaken.

"I lied." Marissa shrugged. "Well, not exactly. I just repeated one of the multitude of stories I'd heard. It could have been a work of fiction. So, are we opening tonight?"

"No, you twisted freak. The workers had to call the cops. Who, of course, had no idea what they should do. The basement was finally roped off as a crime scene, and they brought in a bunch of people. You just missed them taking the body away."

"Bummer," Marissa said, teasing her. "Is the yellow tape still up?"

Zousa groaned. "You are seriously twisted."

The entire bizarre event caused quite an uproar. For over a month, Marissa followed the reports in the newspaper. Things calmed down slightly after it was determined that the woman's body had been resting beneath the basement floor for a very long time. Bridget was finally laid to rest in the local Catholic cemetery.

The calm didn't last very long. The media took an even greater interest in the story soon after the pub reopened. Suddenly, the bar was packed night after night with curiosity seekers. Everyone wanted to know who the mystery woman was and how she ended up buried in the basement.

Almost two months had passed since the night Cat decided to flood Molly's Pub.

"Thanks for helping me close," Marissa said to Cat. "It's been a zoo ever since Bridget turned up. I still can't believe that you got the city not only to give her a Catholic burial but also to put her name on the grave marker."

"All I did was put a bug in a couple of reporters' ears," Cat explained. "They ran with it until no one questioned her name. But that was only the first step. We have more work to do."

"I knew you had a reason for hanging around here." Marissa watched as Cat extracted some things from her oversized handbag. "A candle, and let me guess, those would be your tarot cards," she noted, pointing to the item wrapped in a dark cloth.

"Very good, grasshopper," Cat said, smirking. "Turn off the lights. It's time for you and me to make another trip to the basement."

"I was afraid you were going to say that." Marissa groaned before complying with Cat's instructions.

What happened in the basement was surprisingly dull, at least for Marissa. They huddled in the cold, dark dry goods room, lit only by the tall, white candle Cat brought with her. Marissa's boredom increased while she sat there among the boxes of napkins and cups and watched Cat turn over tarot cards. The silence was broken every now and then when Cat asked a question.

"Who is Davis?" Cat seemed to be troubled by something.

"Not Davis." Marissa fussed about and stretched out her legs. "Da."

"Duh?"

"No, Da. You said it on Halloween night. Da." Cat stared at her in confusion. "Okay, I know you and I are the only two people who work here who don't have a smidgen of Irish blood flowing through their veins, but even I know that Da is an Irish nickname for Dad."

"How did you know that?"

"Well, you know those online stories you're horrified that I read? It was in one of those."

Cat quirked her head slightly, and her brow furrowed. Marissa leaned forward, suddenly eager to see what would happen next. Cat's eyes fluttered shut, and she continued to lay out the cards. Then she stopped. Marissa held her breath, her eyes darting from the odd look on Cat's face to the cards lying on the floor. Finally, Cat's gaze lifted. Her eyes were dark and troubled.

"I know what happened," she said.

Marissa looked around, hoping to see something. "Just like that?"

"What were you expecting, a bolt of lightning?"

"Well, yeah, or a clap of thunder," Marissa said. "You know, something dramatic."

"Believe me, it is." Cat grew more animated. "This is what happened."

* * *

The beginning of the end began on an uneventful autumn afternoon when Innis was restocking the bar after the morning rush. Since Halloween was always a long night, he sent Seamus home for some rest. The girls had gone downstairs. A smile formed on his lips as he thought how nice it was that Molly and Bridget were getting along so well, though his daughter's constant reminders of just how close she and Bridget were in age sometimes troubled him.

He had hoped that his sweet angel would see past the age difference between his age and the attractive barmaid's. Innis had tried very hard to keep his feelings a secret. He had overheard the tongue-wagging about hiring Bridget in the first place, and it bothered him that he had taken the girl on simply because of her good looks and charming personality. Still, she turned out to be an asset. Now, if he could only get the local cads to stop trying to bed the girl.

At least his son had stopped trailing after her. Innis sighed heavily, silently praying for the day Molly would see Bridget in a different light. She already viewed the older girl in a sisterly manner; perhaps she could someday truly welcome her into the family. He just had to give it time, and then hope Molly would understand that he had been alone for far too long.

Then there was the matter of convincing Bridget. He could see it in her eyes; there was someone she was fond of. "He must be gone," Innis reasoned, since he had never witnessed her taking an interest in any of the young men who hung on her every word. *Blackguard probably broke her heart,* he thought angrily.

His brow furrowed when he heard laughter coming from downstairs. He glanced at the clock, tempted to stomp his foot on the floor as he had often done before. "They have time," he said aloud and smiled, wondering just what shenanigans the two women engaged in whenever they were alone.

"Da?" Seamus stepped into the pub. "Should I ask what you're smiling about?"

"Mind your own business," Innis playfully cautioned the boy. "And mind the bar. I need to fetch some stock from the basement."

Innis stepped out from behind the bar and paused as he went to open the door that led to the basement. *Maybe I can understand them better,* he thought, and stepped quietly onto the landing. A large man, Innis normally plodded down the staircase causing a ruckus with each step he took. That afternoon, he tiptoed down the stairwell like a thief. At the bottom, he caught hushed whispers and giggles echoing from the end of the hallway. He felt mildly foolish, watching his footing as he set about gathering the stock he would need for the evening crowd. He lingered close to the office, however, not really selecting anything.

His neck ached from the strain of leaning toward the sounds coming from Bridget's room. *What the devil are they doing?* he wondered as he inched closer to the barmaid's room.

"Tell me again, Bridget Boothe," he heard his daughter's lilting voice say. "Who has captured your heart?"

Of course. Why didn't I think of this before? Naturally Bridget would confide in Molly. If he wanted to know who Bridget fancied, he should have simply asked his daughter. Innis inched closer, and beads of sweat formed on his brow. He strained to hear Bridget's answer, which for some unknown reason was muffled. Noticing that the door was ever so slightly ajar, he peered into the tiny room. His heart stopped and his body froze in place when he saw why he could not hear Bridget's words. The barmaid's face was pressed against his daughter's neck. *I must be seeing things!* his mind screamed, horrified by the sight.

Innis frantically tried to think of some reason why Bridget was nuzzling his child's body. His gaze drifted, and he felt as if he'd been turned to ice when he spied Bridget's hand buried beneath Molly's dress. Then anger consumed him as he watched his child's body rock with forbidden pleasure. Bridget's face emerged, a lustful smile gracing her lips.

"Oh, how you taunt me, Molly O'Connor," Bridget cooed.

"Hush," Molly whispered, and pressed her fingers against Bridget's lips. "We don't have much time. Love me as no other."

Innis stood there, stunned. It couldn't be possible. His daughter, his sweet innocent angel, was asking this creature to violate her. Still, there she was, her body gently rocking while Bridget was doing God knows what beneath her bloomers. Then it hit him. Molly had said it clear as day. She wanted Bridget to love her as no other had. The wicked woman had seduced his precious child. Disgusted by the sight, he stepped away. Bile rose in his throat as he mounted the staircase.

Innis felt so numb that he forgot to be quiet, and he was unaware that his daughter had heard his footsteps. Molly broke away from her lover's embrace, promising her she would stay at the pub that evening.

"Da, you're pale as a ghost," Seamus said in a worried tone.

"Hush, boy," Innis snapped. "Get to work."

Seamus was startled, but not so foolish as to question his father's sudden mood change. Innis was muttering under his breath when Molly and Bridget emerged from the basement. The sick feeling churning inside of his stomach grew when he noted the happy looks on their faces. He sneered as he stalked over to the bar. *It can't be true,* his mind pleaded.

To everyone's surprise, he poured himself a shot of whiskey. "Da?" Molly questioned, horrified by his actions.

"Get to work, all of you!" he barked, and retreated inside his dark thoughts.

Innis O'Connor never stopped watching his daughter or Bridget that evening. All of the innocent gestures and touches the women had shared suddenly turned sinister. He grew quiet, fuming inside as his only daughter fawned over this stranger. The night was an endless torture, watching them giggle, smile, and touch each other. He managed to hide his anger when Molly asked to spend the night at the pub.

"Not tonight," he muttered.

"Da?" Molly was puzzled.

"Not tonight, child," he added, softly cupping her angelic face in his large hands. "I want you to go home. Seamus and I will close up tonight."

"Da?" she repeated, her eyes widening.

"I said go home," he gently persisted, burying his inner rage. *I have to save you, child* He didn't miss the woeful look she offered Bridget.

He did little to help with the nightly cleaning. His thoughts were consumed with guilt as he watched the sickness he had brought into his family flitting about. By the time she excused herself for the evening, he had reached the breaking point. He had to be rid of her.

He had to free his child from her depravity. "Seamus, finish locking up," he said.

Seamus didn't question his father. Innis's dark mood had frightened him to the core, and he was fearful of what might be revealed if he pried. He stood in the barroom, helplessly watching his father disappear down the stairwell. Whatever was amiss, Seamus prayed that the storm would quickly pass.

Innis had felt such an all-consuming rage only once before. That was the dark night his beloved Maeve was taken from him. If it had not been for the two precious children she had blessed him with, he would have been lost. Now one of his children was in danger, and it was up to him to save her.

"Mr. O'Connor," Bridget said, fear filling her face when he burst into her room. "Sir, did I forget to do something?"

"Pack your things," he ordered, his eyes burning with anger.

"But why, Mr. O'Connor?"

"I will not have your kind near my daughter!" he shouted.

"Dear sweet Jesus," she gasped. "Mr. O'Connor, you do not understand," she said in a pleading voice.

"I understand that you molested my child." Innis reached out and grabbed her by the front of her blouse. "I should turn you over to the authorities, but I'll not put her through that torture," he spat. "Get what you can carry and be gone!" He gave her a hard shove and she tripped over a small footstool. As she fell backward, there was a dull thud as her head smacked against the edge of the bathtub Innis had installed for her comfort. Blood gushed from the back of her skull as her body slumped over in a heap. Innis stood there above her lifeless form, watching in horror as her blood seeped into the floor.

He was still there, unable to move, when he heard Seamus's horrified scream. "Da! What have you done? We must help her!" Seamus darted past his father and knelt beside Bridget. "Da, she's dead," he choked out. "What have you done?"

Something dark inside of Innis emerged that night. The sight of Bridget's body covered with blood did not disturb him. Instead, it filled him with a sense of peace. "Da?" Seamus pleaded again.

"Hush," Innis said. "We're rid of her now. Help me clean up, there is much to do."

"What are you saying?" Seamus asked, gasping.

"I am saying that she was evil and now the evil is dead." Innis's eyes gleamed with delight. "She buggered your sister."

"No! It can't be true." Seamus began wringing his hands.

"It is," Innis persisted, ignoring his son's distress. "I saw it with my own eyes. She touched her as no woman should. I'll not have Molly's name soiled. We have work to do."

Seamus followed his father's instructions, working like a man in a trance. The O'Connor men set about hiding what had happened that night, and neither spoke of it again ever after. When Molly demanded answers, they brushed her off with vague falsehoods. When she stopped speaking, Innis considered it a blessing. And each time those handprints reappeared, they buried their sins anew beneath a slab of cement and a thick layer of paint.

* * *

"Innis killed Bridget?" Marissa said. "And Seamus helped him cover it up?"

"They never spoke of it again," Cat grimly answered. "She never knew what had happened; only that Bridget hadn't left her. The only time either of them spoke of it was on their deathbeds. Confession is good for the soul."

"Are you telling me those two got salvation by telling their sins to their priest?" Marissa asked bitterly. "Molly and Bridget are doomed to be separated for eternity, and those two are in heaven?"

"I wouldn't say heaven," Cat corrected her.

The air around them suddenly felt very still. "It is time." Cat tucked away her cards and picked up the candle. "Bless Bridget Boothe, who was taken from this world by the hand of Innis O'Connor."

Cat continued blessing Bridget and her lost soul. A dark figure appeared, standing next to her. Cat smiled at the dumbfounded look on Marissa's face. "Yes, they are both here," Cat informed her. Molly floated into the room, seemingly unaware of the mortals who stood in her path. Marissa shivered violently as Molly passed through her.

They heard Bridget speak. "Molly, my love," she said, ghostly tears filling her eyes. For the first time since her violent death, she could see and touch the love of her life.

"My love," Molly echoed.

"Forever," Bridget responded, as she wrapped her lover in her arms.

"Forever," Molly blissfully repeated, losing herself in her lover's touch. Clinging to each other, they dissolved into mist, never to be separated again

Trick or Treat

October, 2005

    Raquel Albright lay snug in the tiny twin bed in her dorm room, considering her prospects of becoming a member of the Sigma Kappa sorority. She had just endured an entire month of catering to every whim and antic the sisters of Sigma Kappa could toss at her and the other pledges. Hell Night had been that evening, and the encouraging words Justine had offered her at the end of the night gave her hope.
    Justine Henning was a tall, slender redhead with amazing green eyes. She had been selected to act as Raquel's honorary big sister, to watch over her during pledge month. Even though Justine had told her how well she had done, and that she looked forward to being her sister, Raquel understood that all it took was for one of the other sisters to vote against her. One negative vote and she wouldn't become a member of Sigma Kappa. Being a member of the sorority meant many things. For the naïve Raquel, the most important was living in the grand Kappa house on Higgins Hill, just a stone's throw away from the main campus.
    She would no longer need to hide in the library so she could study in peace, away from the loud parties that filled the dorm every night. Sigma Kappa encouraged academic excellence, and built strong ties that would prove helpful not only during Raquel's four years at the university, but also later in life when she was facing the real world.
    She was thrilled to have been selected after the Rush Party, where prospective candidates presented themselves to the sorority. Out of twenty girls, she was chosen to be one of the ten pledges that had a chance at becoming a member of the exclusive sorority.
    It made her even happier that Justine was chosen to be her big sister. She didn't understand what it was about Justine, she just really enjoyed being around her and tried to do anything she could to please

the confident sophomore. When Justine gave her a big hug at the end of Hell Night, Raquel felt ten feet tall.

Still, there were only five openings available this term, and Raquel was certain that Claudette Michelle didn't care for her. For some reason, the tall blonde made her very uncomfortable.

Raquel's last thought before she drifted off to sleep was that she hoped she wouldn't be living in the dorm for much longer.

A loud knock on the door stirred her out of her slumber. She grumbled as she climbed out of bed, assuming it was her roommate. Ginny possessed the most unpleasant habit of getting drunk and losing the key to their room. She didn't stop to think that anyone else would be knocking on her door at one in the morning, even though it was Friday night.

She jumped back in shock when she saw five mysterious figures, cloaked in white hooded robes, lurking in the hallway. "Come with us," one of the figures commanded in a muffled tone. Raquel was ready to slam the door shut when she spotted a familiar pair of green eyes twinkling at her.

She nodded, and a black pillowcase was pulled over her head. Stumbling along in the darkness, she wondered if perhaps this was yet another test for Hell Night. A pair of hands guided her gently, and she heard the sounds of the others moving away. The wet grass and leaves clung to her bare feet as they crossed the campus.

Raquel stumbled nervously along, wondering what task awaited her. She didn't need to see it was Justine who was carefully leading her now. She held onto Justine tightly while they mounted a staircase, and her body warmed as she stepped out of the cold night air. Briefly, she wondered if the surge of warmth she felt had more to do with the way Justine's hand was lingering against the small of her back than with the warmth of the room.

They stopped, and she stood there in silence, waiting to find out what was going to happen next. She could hear footsteps and the sounds of hushed voices mingling around her. Justine's presence kept her fears at bay, but she felt the tension filling the room. "Who among you wishes to pledge their allegiance to the sisters of Sigma Kappa?" a voice boomed.

"I do," Raquel responded. She recognized the voice—it was Sarah Moorehouse, the pledge master. She heard similar responses around her.

"Then show yourselves and join your sisters," Sarah commanded.

Raquel paused for a moment until she heard Justine whisper, "It's okay." Raquel tore the pillowcase from her head and her long blonde hair went everywhere. She blinked her eyes in an effort to adjust to the lighting. When her vision cleared, she smiled at the sight of Justine smiling down at her.

"Welcome, sister," Justine said, and wrapped the smaller woman in a warm hug. Raquel wasn't sure why she allowed the embrace to linger as Justine hugged her tightly. When Justine finally released her, she felt cold.

"I... I made it?" Raquel stammered as Justine fastened a small gold pin sculpted into the shape of the Greek letters, S and K, onto her pajama top.

She turned and was greeted by more hugs from the rest of the sorority, including Marla, Dorothy, Vivian, and Kate, who had also survived alongside of her to become members of Sigma Kappa. Then the five of them were led into the center of a circle the other girls had formed, and they made their pledge. They remained in the circle as their new sisters sang the sorority song before breaking into applause and welcoming them into the Sigma Kappa house.

Since they were all in their pajamas, they were offered blankets, and hot chocolate was passed around. For the next hour, they were regaled with tales of Hell Night and the trials of pledge month, and then they listened carefully to the rules of the house. There were to be no drugs, alcohol, smoking, or loud music. Overnight guests were never allowed, and each sister was expected to help with the household chores, pay her monthly dues on time, participate in charity events, and keep her grade-point average at 3.0 or better.

They were given their room assignments and the option to sleep either at the house that night or go back to the dorms. Raquel was eager to settle into her new room. "I put sheets on the bed already," Justine said, as she led Raquel up the staircase. "Your room is at the very top."

"Why aren't I sharing, like the others?" Raquel asked as they climbed up higher and higher.

"The room's too small." Justine escorted Raquel up to the narrow attic. "Sometimes we don't even use this one. So, enjoy the alone time. You won't get a single again until you're a senior. The others are just one floor below. Marla and Kate's room is the one on the right, and Vivian and Dorothy's room is on the left. I'm on the floor below that with the rest of the sophomores and juniors. The seniors have private rooms on the second floor."

"You weren't kidding. This is tiny," Raquel said, and then smiled as she looked around the room. "I think I'm going to love it up here. It's so cozy."

"Yeah." Justine looked around the room almost nervously. "Why don't I stay with you for a few minutes? In the morning, we'll go over to the dorm and I'll help you move your stuff."

"Thank you," Raquel said, and Justine shrugged out of the long robe she was wearing. Raquel's eyes lit up as she drank in the sight of Justine in her faded jeans and tight-fitting top. When she realized she was staring, she averted her gaze. Luckily, Justine hadn't seemed to notice the way Raquel was looking at her. She was still looking around the small room in a nervous fashion.

Raquel had hoped that moving away to college would break her of the habit of staring at other girls. For the life of her, she didn't understand why she did it. She sat down on the bed and wondered why Justine seemed so skittish all of a sudden. "So, do you like your pin?" Justine finally said. "I must say, it looks rather fetching on your jammies."

"I can't believe you made us walk across campus in our pajamas." Raquel wondered who had seen the parade.

"You lucked out," Justine said with a laugh, and sat on the very edge of the bed. "On my Hell Night, I was wearing nothing but a T-shirt and a pair of skivvies."

"Oh?" Raquel gulped as her mind conjured up the image of a half-naked Justine being led across the campus.

"Yeah," Justine said, sighing. "I hate wearing anything to bed, but you have to put something on when you're sharing."

"Uh huh." Raquel gulped again.

"Enough about me," Justine said, maintaining her position at the very edge of the bed. "Tell me about your classes. If you need help with any of them, feel free to ask. I'm a history major, too."

Raquel glanced down at her hands, which were folded neatly in her lap. For some reason, knowing that Justine liked to sleep naked made it impossible for her to look at the girl while they talked. She found herself prattling on and on while Justine offered her advice about her course load. Even though they were chatting away like old friends, Raquel still found it difficult to look at Justine. Then Justine gave a deep yawn. "I should let you go and get some sleep," Raquel said, the image of Justine's naked body flashing across her mind.

"Yeah." Justine yawned again. Her nervousness seemed to return as she stood to leave. "If you need anything, my room is the last one on the third floor."

"Thanks," Raquel said, giving a yawn of her own.

"I mean *anything.*" Justine lingered in the doorway. "If anything happens, or, well... anything."

"Okay," Raquel said, puzzled by the emphasis.

"Good night." Justine left, closing the door behind her.

"That was odd," Raquel mumbled to herself, then crawled wearily under the covers. Her eyes closed tightly the moment her head hit the pillow. They snapped open again when she felt the mattress move. She shrank back when she spied a girl she didn't recognize lying next to her. She was a dark-eyed brunette, wearing a dark green Sigma Kappa T-shirt.

"Hi," the stranger said in a husky voice, and her fingers brushed along Raquel's cheek. Raquel stared at the stranger, who moved nearer, closing the gap between them. Raquel could feel the other woman's hot breath tickling her skin. "I just wanted to welcome you, Sister."

"Who are—" Her words were cut off as the brunette's mouth covered her own. Raquel's hands flew out and pushed against the other woman's shoulders, but as she felt soft warm lips moving delightfully against her mouth, her resistance ceased. Instead, her hands slipped up and caressed the broad shoulders as a tongue parted her lips. Raquel gave in to the sensations. The kiss deepened, and the other woman explored the warmth of her mouth. She moaned as she felt a jeans-clad thigh pressing against her and parting her legs. Soon she was on her back, with the other woman covering her body.

Raquel felt her body rising to greet the brunette's touch while their tongues battled for control. She rocked her hips against the woman's thigh, and strong hands explored the curves of her body. The sound of the window shade snapping up, allowing the morning light to flood into the room, broke them apart, and the stranger's head jerked up. Raquel was mystified as she gazed into the dark brown eyes staring down at her. "Time to go." The dark-haired girl laughed merrily and climbed off of Raquel's body.

Raquel reached up to the retreating form. The sound of the window shade rolling itself back down turned her attention to the window for a moment. "What the hell?" she said. Her jaw hung open as she looked around her empty bedroom. The brunette was gone.

October 31, 1994

The young coed smoothed her dress nervously. Tonight Candy would be officially inducted into the Sigma Kappa sorority. Everything she had worked for was finally coming true. The hair on the nape of her neck prickled as the temperature in the tiny attic room suddenly dropped. Her heart beat a little faster as she recalled the stories the other girls had tried to frighten her with when she had first moved into the house. "Silly," she told herself, thinking it was absurd to believe that some dead Kappa was roaming about her room.

She turned back toward the mirror to have one final look before going downstairs to meet Fred, her boyfriend, and join the party. A scream caught in her throat when she glanced in the mirror and saw someone standing behind her. She spun around, looking for the dark-haired girl whose reflection she had seen.

Candy's fingers trembled, and she felt cold as she looked around the empty room. "Jackass." She laughed, thinking she had imagined the whole event. "I guess I've had my Halloween scare for the night." She laughed once again, reasoning that the room was cold because of the weather, not some ghostly encounter. She felt silly that her hand was trembling as she touched up her lipstick.

"Don't come back to this room tonight," an ominous voice whispered in her ear. Candy's hand froze. "No matter what, don't come back tonight." Candy dropped her lipstick and raced out of the room. Her heart was beating wildly as she stood at the top of the staircase that led from her attic room to the rest of the house.

Just as she began to calm down, thinking that either her mind was playing tricks on her or one of her sisters was having a good laugh at her expense, the door she had just left wide open slammed shut. "Okay, you win," she said, sprinting down the stairs. "You can have the place to yourself tonight."

Candy tried to enjoy the party, but she just couldn't shake the uneasy feeling from what had happened earlier. While she didn't really believe what she had seen and heard, she still didn't return to her room that evening. The next day, she felt nothing. The room was just the same as it had always been. She never told anyone what had happened, and over the years, she tried to forget. But the memory of the voice warning her to stay away lingered with her. Five years later, she heard that a freshman who was living in her former room had been attacked by something on Halloween night. Candy silently thanked whomever or whatever had warned her to stay away.

October, 2005

Raquel jumped up and frantically searched the empty room. Heading downstairs for breakfast, she wondered if she had imagined the entire encounter. "How did you sleep?" Justine asked, stepping into the foyer. There was a cautious note in her voice that made Raquel wary.

"Fine," she replied.

"Good. Why don't we get some breakfast? After we clean up, I'll lend you some clothes and we can go get your stuff."

Something's up, Raquel thought as she followed Justine into the kitchen, where some of the other girls were already eating. She barely touched her meal, instead looking around to see if any of them could have been her mysterious visitor. During the morning chatter, each one of the older girls made a point of asking her how she slept. Each time, Justine would intervene, glaring at them.

As they made their way over to the dorms, Raquel had a sinking feeling that she was being played with, and she didn't like it one bit. Confusing sexual feelings had plagued her for the past few years. Apparently, someone had discovered her secret and decided to toy with her.

By the way Justine was tiptoeing around, Raquel thought she was in on the joke, and she felt betrayed. She had thought they were becoming friends, and this sudden distance hurt her feelings. "So why is everyone so concerned with my sleeping habits?" she asked, her voice sarcastic, as they taped up the last box.

"It's stupid," Justine muttered.

"Why not let me in on the joke?" Raquel felt her anger steadily rising.

"Raquel, trust me. No one is goofing on you." Justine sounded sincere. "It's just that there have always been rumors about that room. Did you see or hear anything last night?"

"No," she blurted, just as Ginny stumbled into the room reeking of alcohol and cigarette smoke.

"Whash up?" Ginny asked, her words slurred.

"I'm moving out." Raquel looked at her ex-roommate and sneered. She wasn't going to miss either Ginny or her slovenly behavior. Even when Ginny was sober, the girl was a pig.

"Fuck." Ginny grunted, and flopped onto her bed. "So you're joining the freak show on the hill. Good riddance," she muttered, and passed out.

"She's charming," Justine said dryly as they picked up the first load of boxes. "Are you sure you don't want to stay?" Raquel forgot about the earlier tension and laughed.

It took them three trips to move all her belongings over to the sorority house, and not once did Ginny stir from her slumber, no matter how much noise they made. Raquel couldn't help noticing that each time they entered her new bedroom, Justine seemed edgy.

"That's the last of it," Justine said, dumping the final box in the corner of the room. She was bouncing on her heels as she glanced around the room. "Need help unpacking?"

"No, I should be fine. Thanks for the help."

"Okay," Justine said, seeming eager to make her escape. "If you want, we could go shopping tomorrow for a dress for your party. I could take you downtown."

"I bet that's not all she wants to take," a husky voice said from behind Raquel.

Raquel's head snapped around. The mysterious brunette was standing in the corner of the room with her arms folded across her chest and a cocky smirk on her face. "What the—"

"Raquel?" Justine said, drawing her attention away from the strange woman. When Raquel looked back at the corner where the dark-haired woman had been standing, she was shocked to find it empty.

"Raquel?" Justine sounded nervous again.

She looked at Justine quickly before glancing over her shoulder once more at the empty corner. "Are you all right?"

"Um, yeah," Raquel replied, beginning to doubt her sanity. "Just tired. I think I'm going to unpack now, but tomorrow sounds good."

"The welcome party is a very special night," Justine said, her tone brightening. "Are you inviting someone special?"

"Mark Justus," Raquel said, suddenly shy.

"Oh." There was a hint of disappointment in Justine's voice.

"We've gone out a couple of times," Raquel continued, wondering why she felt guilty.

"Oh," Justine repeated. Her smile looked forced.

Raquel decided to change the subject. "Justine, what is it about this room that makes you so uncomfortable?"

"Like I said earlier, it's stupid. There have been stories, over the last forty years or so, about some of the girls seeing or hearing strange things in this room."

"Are you trying to scare me?"

"Not much," Justine said with a playful smile.

"So what are you trying to say then? My room is haunted?" Raquel scoffed at the idea, then recalled the woman she could have sworn was standing in the corner a few moments ago.

"That's the rumor," Justine said. "But only a handful of girls have said they saw anything."

"Tell me the story."

"I... um... I need to get down to the kitchen. I have cooking duty tonight," Justine said quickly, her emerald eyes darting around the room. "Catch you later," she added, and bolted out of the room.

"A good old-fashioned New England ghost story, huh?" Raquel laughed as she went about unpacking her belongings. "I do believe my sisters are trying to scare me. Probably an alumna helping out with the prank," she reasoned, shrugging off her discomfort as she continued to fix up her new surroundings.

Dinner was fun, and later she enjoyed lounging in the study with the other girls. She kept looking for the mysterious brunette, eager to catch her sisters in their little game, but didn't see anyone who resembled her. Every time one of the other girls mentioned her room, Justine quickly changed the subject.

Climbing the staircase, she caught sight of Justine and her roommate Maggie speaking in hushed whispers in the hallway. "You should tell her," she overheard Maggie say.

"There isn't anything to tell," Justine fumed, and stormed off.

"Should I ask what's bothering her?" Raquel inquired tentatively as Maggie approached her.

"Oh, she's just being her grumpy old self." Maggie shrugged, a slightly worried look darkening her features.

"Does this have anything to do with my room?"

"Kind of."

"Well, tell me the whole ooky spooky story about the ghost, so I can be properly frightened."

"All I know is that very few people have seen her, and they won't talk about what happened," Maggie answered. "Supposedly, she was a Kappa sister back in the sixties or seventies. The story keeps changing, but you don't want to be in that room on Halloween night. The last girl who saw her freaked out completely and moved back to the dorm."

"It's going to take more than things going bump in the night to make me move back into the dorm." Raquel laughed, but Maggie shook her head.

"Just the same, watch out for Bonnie," Maggie said, and walked away.

August, 1964

"How old are you?" Christina Morris asked the dark young woman who'd had the nerve to perch herself on her desk.

"How old do you want me to be?" Bonnie said, with a brilliant smile and a mischievous gleam in her dark brown eyes. "Can I get some tickets?"

"Now I know you're joking." Christina laughed, studying the teenager carefully. *Damn, this girl is hot,* the older woman silently moaned. "Or are you just teasing?" she said, unable to resist the young girl's charm.

"I never tease." Bonnie's sultry answer sent shivers down Christina's spine. The twenty-four-year-old secretary watched the slender brunette slip off her desk. "I just want tickets to the concert." Bonnie playfully brushed the hair from the nape of Christina's neck. "My best friend's in love with Ringo."

"Along with every other woman on the planet," Christina scoffed, unable to keep from trembling as Bonnie's fingers slid along the curve of her neck. "The concert's sold out. I can't help you."

"Now it's you who is toying with me," Bonnie said, sighing. Christina shivered at Bonnie's hot breath assaulting her ear while the young woman's fingers drifted to the swell of her breast. "Can you help me? I'd be grateful, *querida*."

"How old are you?" Christina asked again.

"*Qué lástima.*" Bonnie sighed again, slipping away from Christina.

"Huh?" Christina ached to feel more of the younger woman's touch. "Look, I'm not a pervert. I just want to know before—"

"I'm eighteen," Bonnie said, with a huge grin. Christina's doubt evidently showed on her face. "I am," Bonnie insisted, showing the stunned secretary her driver's license. "In fact, next month I start college. I'm old enough to vote, to drink, and to kiss you."

"You're a teenager!" But Christina's body was screaming that Bonnie was legally an adult.

"Would you prefer to wait until I'm twenty-one?" Bonnie gently caressed her face. "Even if we wait three years, our passion would still be illegal. I don't want to wait." Bonnie sank to her knees in front of the swivel chair and ran her hands up along Christina's thighs. "And you don't have to get the tickets... just kiss me. Please, just once?"

Christina watched helplessly as Bonnie closed the gap between them and captured her in a searing kiss. As she moaned into the warmth of the younger woman's mouth, Bonnie's fingers slipped under her skirt. "My boss..." Christina gasped when she felt Bonnie's body settle between her thighs. "He could walk in. Anyone could walk in and catch us."

"I know," Bonnie said, a mischievous gleam in her eyes. She rested her face between Christina's breasts. "Show me," she whispered against the older woman's skin. Christina's fingers trembled as she began to unbutton her blouse. Before she could finish, Bonnie was nestled in the valley of her breasts. Christina gasped when Bonnie captured one of her nipples between her lips.

Christina's hips jerked forward when her young lover's fingers slipped inside her panties. She bit back her passionate cries as eager fingers slid into her wetness. "God," she said, panting desperately. Bonnie suckled her eagerly, her fingers gliding in and out of slick folds. Christina dug her blunt nails into Bonnie's shoulders; her body reeled from the younger woman's touch.

Bonnie's touch became more demanding, and she felt the young woman's breath on her thighs. Christina's eyes rolled back, and she clasped Bonnie tighter, lost in the incredible sensation of her lover's tongue gently exploring her passion. Bonnie might be younger, but she certainly wasn't naïve.

Christina's brilliant blue eyes snapped shut as Bonnie's tongue flicked her throbbing clit. She fought to keep silent, knowing that at any moment one of her co-workers could enter her tiny office. She had worked hard to hide her sexuality, since she would almost certainly be fired, or worse, if anyone found out. Now she was allowing this captivating teenager to take her to new heights in a very dangerous setting.

The danger seemed to fuel the fire burning inside her. Christina's body rocked wildly against Bonnie's mouth, and waves of passion consumed her. She wanted to scream, to beg Bonnie to never stop as she thrust ecstatically against the demanding touch. With a final surge, her climax overtook her like a huge wave breaking in a rush to the shore.

Her chest heaving, she tried to calm her body. When her vision cleared, she almost laughed at the self-satisfied smirk Bonnie sported while she licked Christina's passion from her long, slender fingers.

"Wow, you must really want to see the Beatles," Christina said, her body still trembling as she adjusted her skirt.

"It would be nice, but as I told you, it's my friend who wishes to see them," Bonnie said. "That isn't the reason I pleasured you, Christina. You're a beautiful woman." Bonnie's dark eyes still smoldered with desire. "You don't have to help me with tickets. This I did for me."

A week later, Christina met Bonnie at a tiny bar, hidden away from prying eyes. Bonnie thanked her for the tickets in the most delightful manner. Christina basked in Bonnie's touch, thinking she had finally found the one. After one glorious night of making love, however, Bonnie walked out of her life.

Teneil squealed like a child on Christmas morning when Bonnie showed her the concert tickets. Bonnie's parents were less enthusiastic. "Two girls, driving alone all the way to New York City?" Rafael Sanchez bellowed. His oldest child simply smiled up at him. "No. It is too dangerous," he flatly refused.

Bonnie could usually count on her natural charm and persuasive manner to get around her father's objections. She glanced over at her mother, who was preparing the evening meal. Maita Sanchez shook her head, refusing to assist her.

Bonnie considered the situation. Tension in the little apartment was already running high. Roberto, her younger brother, was having trouble in school and would have to endure summer school again, since he had failed most of his classes. Bonnie hated the way her parents pushed her young brother and expected him to fly through his courses as easily as she did, and she knew he resented the way their parents held her academic success over him.

Her quick mind was already formulating an argument. It would be foolish to point out that she was eighteen and owned her own car, which she had worked hard to buy. If she were a typical teenager, she would simply ignore her father's objections and drive down to New York. But Bonnie was never typical, and her family meant the world to her. She just had to find the right way to convince her father that she should be allowed to go.

From the pleased look on Roberto's face and the scowl on her mother's, she deduced that neither would prove helpful to her this time. "I understand you need time to think this over," Bonnie said.

"Bonita, I said no," There was an edge in her father's voice. "I don't understand why you would want to waste your time driving all the way to New York to hear these boys. They have long hair."

"Papá," Bonnie laid her hand on his arm. "I want this one adventure before I leave for school a couple of weeks from now. I will be with Teneil, and I promise to call Tío Roberto the moment we arrive in New York. You traveled all over the country when you were younger than I am."

"That's different, you're a girl." He scratched his chin for a moment, and his resolve seemed to falter. "Teneil's parents are letting her go?"

"Yes. Actually, Mrs. Watts suggested I take her, instead. She thinks Paul is cute. What do you think Mamá? Paul or Ringo?"

"Bonita," Maita said with a mock scowl, "George is the good-looking one. How did you get tickets?"

"A friend." Bonnie shrugged, and her mother glared at her casual response. "It's the truth. Her name is Christina. She works for the ticket agency downtown." Bonnie almost laughed at the way her parents worried that some boy would take advantage of her.

"Papá," Bonnie continued, "it's a five-hour drive. We can stay with Uncle Roberto and drive back in the morning. Knowing Tío Roberto, he'll be waiting outside the concert with a baseball bat just to keep boys away from us. Honestly, I doubt there will be any boys at the concert anyway, just a bunch of screaming girls like Teneil and me."

Bonnie rested her case, knowing her father was wavering. She had a more important mission to handle. Her brother had snarled and stormed off into his bedroom, and she followed him, knowing her parents would discuss the concert for a while before agreeing to let her go. "Roberto?" She stepped into his room without bothering to knock. "Wipe that sneer off your face. I'm doing this for you. Each time they let me do something like this, it opens the door for you. By the time you're my age, they'll be so worn out they'll let you date a *gringa*."

"Why wouldn't they?" Roberto spat. "You already date so many white girls."

"I know you don't mean to hurt me," Bonnie said, as his scowl deepened. "If you did, you'd tell them the truth about me and I'd be out on the street."

"No, you wouldn't. You're perfect."

"What's going on?"

"Nothing. You're perfect and I'm stupid," Roberto said angrily, not for the first time.

"Never say that again," Bonnie ordered.

"Why not? Our parents say it, even my teacher said it." Roberto, knocked his schoolbooks off the bureau.

"Which teacher?"

"Mr. Goldsmith." Roberto sounded so sad now that Bonnie's eyes filled with fire.

"Mr. Goldsmith obviously doesn't know you very well," she said. She was pleased when Roberto's sadness seemed to lift a little. Her next words lifted her own spirits. "Maybe someone should straighten him out."

The following day, Bonnie was angrier than she had ever been in her life as she stormed down the hallway of her former high school. She should have been ecstatic since, as she had predicted, her father had given her permission to go to the concert. She clenched her fists, waiting for the last class of the day to let out. "Roberto," she beckoned to her surprised brother. "Go wait in the car, I'm driving you home. Right after I talk to Mr. Goldsmith."

"Bonnie, don't," Roberto said. "He's right, I am stupid."

"Go to the car," she told him again, and watched as he walked away down the hall. Once the classroom was empty, she went in. "Mr. Goldsmith?"

"Bonnie! My favorite student." The tall, lanky man greeted her warmly. "Did you miss school so much you felt the need to visit during the summer? I hear that you're off to college in the fall."

"Did you call my brother stupid in front of his entire class?" Bonnie's voice was controlled, but there was no mistaking the anger in it.

The teacher swallowed uneasily, "I was only trying to prod him into trying harder."

"By insulting him? My brother doesn't lack intelligence. Have you spoken with him? Or did you just decide that the best course of action was to berate him? Telling him that he can't learn isn't going to inspire him to try. He does try. He studies every night, and I know he knows the work. What I don't understand is why no one is trying to figure out why his writing and reading skills are lacking. Something is wrong, and no one, including you, is trying to figure out why my brother can recite Shakespeare perfectly but can't write a sentence. Why is that?"

"Bonnie, I understand your frustration," he said, apparently trying to placate her. "Roberto's work is illegible. He can't read or write at a high school level. The only reason I can come up with is that he isn't applying himself."

"Mr. Goldsmith, it's you who isn't applying himself," Bonnie said grimly. "Choose your words more carefully in the future. Or do you want to discourage students who don't live up to your expectations until they drop out?"

Bonnie walked out, leaving Mr. Goldsmith with a shamed look on his face.

"Bonnie?" a voice called out. She turned to see her former math teacher, Mrs. Brinkman, running after her. "I heard what you said to Mr. Goldsmith."

"And?" Bonnie said, challenging her.

Estelle Brinkman shook her head. "First, I think that after you graduate from college you should consider running for office. But I wanted to tell you that you're right about your brother."

"I know," Bonnie said. "What I don't understand is why he's doing so poorly. I work with him almost every day. He can explain everything we go over, but when he writes his work down, it looks like a child wrote it. There has to be a reason."

"I agree," Mrs. Brinkman said. "His math scores are dismal, but his answers are correct. The numbers are just inverted. If you ask him to write down the answer to three times seven, more than likely he'll write twelve instead of twenty-one. When he writes his own name, very often the letters are backwards."

"Why, and how can I help him?" Bonnie was relieved that someone else finally understood that her brother didn't lack intelligence. There was something very wrong.

"I don't know," Mrs. Brinkman admitted. "But I promise that I'll try to find a solution. His grades in my summer course have gone up because I've been allowing him to take his exams orally. I ask him the questions and write down the answers he tells me. Since I've been helping him this way, he's been acing every test. Don't tell anyone, it might look as though I'm helping him to cheat."

"Thank you for helping him. My brother is under a lot of pressure, since my parents and most of his teachers blame him. They keep telling him how smart I am and that he isn't trying. It isn't fair to expect him to ace every class just because I did."

"I promise we'll figure out a way to help him," Mrs. Brinkman said.

"Thank you. I'm so grateful." Bonnie was filled with hope. From the moment her brother began his education, she was acutely aware of how her shadow hung over him. She could never understand why people expected Roberto to be a carbon copy of her academic success.

No one seemed to understand that the siblings were very different. Bonnie was outgoing and gregarious, and Roberto was shy and withdrawn. Her teachers wanted Bonnie to skip grades, but they wanted to hold Roberto back, blaming his poor grades on lack of effort. Bonnie was the only one who fought to help Roberto. He was the reason she refused to skip ahead, even though she was bored in most of her classes. If she had given in to the school's desires, she would have started college three years ago. At times, being able to learn quickly and remember everything she saw, heard, or read was a burden, not a gift. Other times, though, being smarter and quicker than most of her teachers amused her to no end.

"Good luck in college," Mrs. Brinkman said, patting Bonnie's arm. "Not that you'll need it, since you practically taught my class when you were in it."

Bonnie laughed with the kindly teacher, and then waved goodbye to her as she left.

October, 2005

"Who's Bonnie?" Raquel said to herself, as she stepped into her darkened room and closed the door behind her.

"You called?" A pair of warm arms encircled her waist. She recognized the ghost's touch instantly and was helpless to resist it. She leaned back and felt soft kisses caress her neck. "You smell delightful," the ghost whispered in her ear, drawing a whimper in response.

"Who are you?" Raquel moaned as the stranger nibbled on her sensitive earlobe.

She heard a throaty chuckle. "You know my name."

"Huh?" Raquel felt hands gliding up the front of her body. "Is this part of the prank?" Another chuckle was the only response, and the hands cupped her breasts. Her eyes fluttered shut as her nipples hardened against the arousing touch.

Hot breath tickled her skin while knowing hands massaged her breasts. Raquel's hips swayed in response as she felt the mysterious woman pressing harder against her. Her head fell back, and she was once again held captive in a fiery kiss. Raquel lost all sense of reason as she felt her shirt creeping up her body. Everywhere the woman's hands touched, her skin burned.

She no longer cared whether this was just a game or a prank—this woman was driving her insane. For a brief moment, Justine's face invaded her thoughts. "No thinking of others tonight," growled the ghost as she lowered Raquel onto the bed. "You belong to me."

How did this woman know what she was thinking? Raquel ignored these troublesome thoughts when she felt her shirt slipping away from her body. "You belong to me," the woman repeated, as she sucked Raquel's neck and cupped her jeans-clad mound.

"Yes," Raquel cried out, rocking her hips against the heel of the woman's hand. Only in the solitude of her bedroom had Raquel given in to her fantasy of touching another woman, and now she was living out her dream.

"I'm not a dream." The woman tore Raquel's bra from her quivering body.

Raquel gasped as the cool air met her skin and she felt the stranger's lips kissing their way down the front of her body. She thrust her hips more urgently against the woman's hand as once again Justine's smile invaded her thoughts. The woman let out another growl. "You belong to me," she insisted, as Raquel rocked harder against her touch. "Say it."

"I can't," Raquel sobbed

"You will." As the words were uttered, the window shade flew up. Raquel curled into a ball, fighting against the ache in her loins and the need to be close to Justine. She jerked up frantically once she realized she was alone. She looked down her half-naked body at her nipples, still puckered from the stranger's touch.

"This can't be happening," she whispered. She stayed up the rest of the night trying to come up with a reasonable explanation for what had transpired, all the while fighting the urge to run downstairs and hide in Justine's room.

August 28, 1964
Forest Hills Tennis Stadium, New York

"Bonnie, you're the best!" Teneil screamed over the noise of hordes of people, mostly young women like herself. "I can see the sweat on Ringo's face."

"Yes, very sexy." Bonnie laughed, covering her ears to block out the sounds of squealing young girls.

"I bet if it were Dusty Springfield up there, you'd think it was sexy," Teneil said, with a grin.

"If that were Dusty, I'd climb up on stage and lick the sweat off her."

"Groovy. I'd pay to see that," Teneil said. "Speaking of your charms, little Miss 'I have a surprise for you,' do I want to know how you got us free tickets to see the Beatles?"

"They just fell into my lap," Bonnie said happily, and shrugged at her friend.

"I hope you thanked her properly." Teneil knew quite well that Bonnie's charm was the real reason they lucked into the tickets. "Or did you just seduce her, grab the tickets, and split?"

Bonnie groaned, wondering if Teneil still harbored bad feelings about what had happened between them the summer before. It was a mistake, and in time Teneil would realize that her part in the brief affair had been nothing more than curiosity.

"Let me guess, it was all fun and games until she fell in love, and then you were long gone." Teneil was scowling. "You'll never change."

"Why should I?" Bonnie laughed off the comment, stung by the hint of betrayal that lingered in her best friend's voice.

"Fuck you." Then Teneil laughed, too. "Never mind, I already did."

"A little louder, I don't think Paul and John heard you." Bonnie was pleasantly surprised by Teneil's lighthearted comment.

"Hush! I can't hear the band." Teneil swatted her playfully.

"Hear the band? With all this screaming, I can't even hear myself think," Bonnie said. "My ears will still be ringing next week when we drive down to the college."

October, 2005

Raquel spent the following day moping around and avoiding Justine. The pledges' big night, when they officially became Sigma Kappa girls, fell on Halloween, and Raquel tried to convince herself to call Mark and make plans for the party. After last night, though, she couldn't bring herself to call him. Mark was sweet enough, but she'd felt more from the mysterious woman's touch than she had from any man's. This wasn't a new revelation, but it frightened her just the same.

Heck, I get more turned on when Justine smiles at me than I did when I slept with my boyfriend after the prom, she grumbled to herself. From her perch on the front porch swing, she stared out at the brightly colored leaves littering the campus.

"Hey," a voice called. She frowned when Justine sat down beside her on the swing.

"Hi," she responded softly, closing the textbook on her lap. She hadn't been able to focus on it, anyway.

"I thought we were going shopping today."

"I'm sorry." Raquel tapped the textbook and then set it aside. "I'm a little behind in this class. I started studying and totally forgot about shopping."

"You have old man Grimm, right?" Justine asked. "I took his class last year, and I still have all my old notes and tests. Maybe I can help you get caught up."

"Really?" Strangely enough, the thought of spending time alone with the person she had been avoiding all day thrilled Raquel. Nothing made sense to her except how good it felt to be sitting close to Justine.

"Yeah, really." Justine stood and held out a hand. "Maggie is off with her boyfriend, so we can study in my room."

Raquel's stomach tied itself in knots as she followed Justine up to her bedroom. Justine held her hand the entire time, and her body felt warm all over. She was filled with a profound sense of disappointment when they entered the room and Justine released her hold.

She was in heaven as they sat on Justine's bed studying the course material. It was late when Raquel blew out a heavy sigh. "I think I'm ahead of the rest of the class now, thanks to you," she said. It was true. Because of Justine's help, Raquel could probably float through the rest of the semester in Grimm's class. She'd had a hard time focusing throughout the afternoon, though, since she was much more interested in watching Justine's lips move as she spoke than in actually paying attention to what she was saying.

Justine stretched out against some pillows and looked over at Raquel with an amused expression.

"What?" Raquel said.

"Nothing." Justine shrugged and chewed on her bottom lip. "You've been a little tense the last few days. Are you sure everything's okay?"

"I'm fine," Raquel said defensively. There was no way she could tell anyone what was going on in her room at night, especially since she enjoyed it so much.

"You could tell me," Justine urged, her eyes filled with concern.

"It's nothing important. You know, school work, pledging. I'm just a little overwhelmed, is all."

"Come here." Justine pushed their books aside and beckoned Raquel to sit closer.

"Huh?" Raquel's eyes widened in alarm. Just the thought of sitting so close to the leggy sophomore was making her thighs quiver.

"I was going to offer to rub your shoulders," Justine said. "If you're not comfortable with that, I understand."

"I'm all right," Raquel said quickly, and scooted closer.

Raquel was certain she was going to pass out as Justine guided her to sit between those long legs. Then her body turned to Jell-O as Justine's strong fingers began to knead her shoulders and manipulate her muscles.

Raquel's lip hurt from her teeth biting down on it to stifle her moans. She could feel Justine's breasts brush against her back now and then, and an aching need was building in her lower body.

Their legs had become entwined, somehow, and one of Justine's hands wandered down along the curve of her body until it rested on her stomach. Feeling Justine's tickling fingers was making her stomach flutter. Her mind screamed for her to pull away, but her body gave in to the need to snuggle closer. Her eyes fluttered shut when she heard Justine release a contented sigh.

"Raquel," Justine crooned softly, wrapping long arms around her and nuzzling her neck.

Raquel moaned deeply.

"Hey guys!" The door slammed open. Raquel's eyes also snapped open, and she and Justine bolted off the bed, stumbling as they fought to extricate themselves from their tangle. Raquel stood trembling as she looked at Maggie.

"Yo, Maggie, what's happening?" Justine casually threw out the question as she plopped back down onto the bed.

"Not much." Maggie shrugged and flopped onto her own bed. "What have you kids been up to?"

Raquel felt like an idiot as she watched them bantering back and forth. "Just studying," Justine said calmly. Raquel's heart sank.

"Did you get your dress for the party?" Maggie asked Raquel, who was trying to gather up the pieces of her broken heart.

"No, we didn't have time," Justine answered for her.

"Bummer," Maggie said. "You've still got time. Don't forget to tell your escort to dress up as well." Raquel, gathered her wits, reconciling herself to the fact that Justine was only giving her a backrub and not offering anything else.

"Oh, I didn't invite him, after all," she said, focusing on Maggie, unable to look at Justine for fear she would break down. "We haven't been dating that long, and I don't really want to ask him."

"Oh?" Justine's expression seemed to brighten.

"Ahem." Maggie cleared her throat and glared at her roommate. "So how is life in spook central?"

"Oh, you mean Bonnie?" Raquel played along as she fought against the blush that was steadily creeping up on her. "Whoever claims to have seen her must have been full of crap, because there's nothing going on up there."

Raquel was confused by the odd look Maggie flashed at Justine. She looked over at Justine who now had a sorrowful expression on her face. "So, why should I avoid my bedroom on Halloween?" Raquel continued, pretending that there was nothing amiss.

"She died that night," Justine muttered.

"Or so the story goes," Maggie said. "And she's bitter about it."

"About dying?"

"Someone's bitter about something," Justine said so softly that Raquel almost missed it.

"Well, speaking of my bedroom," Raquel prattled, gathering up her belongings and darting toward the doorway, "I should go there and get some sleep. Good night."

She heard Maggie scolding Justine just as she was closing the door. "What were you doing?"

"Nothing," Justine answered.

September, 1964

"You wanted to speak with me, Dr. Graves?" Bonnie asked, walking into her advisor's office. She had only checked into her dorm room a few hours ago, so she was surprised when Mrs. Simmons, the dorm mother, informed her that her advisor wanted to meet with her. She hadn't even started orientation, but her advisor already seemed to be taking an interest in her. Bonnie studied the gray-haired woman, who kept pushing up her wire-rimmed glasses. *They don't fit,* Bonnie noted, thinking that the woman probably played with her glasses so often she had bent them out of shape. "I haven't signed up for my classes, I just arrived on campus this morning, and here I am. Now, why is that?" the cocky teenager asked.

Dr. Graves cleared her throat and seemed to be studying Bonnie carefully. "Your high school instructors were correct in their assessment. You certainly are an enigma, Miss Sanchez."

"I'm an eighteen-year-old girl. The two are synonymous," Bonnie said, smirking.

"These days, most eighteen-year-old girls don't know the meaning of that word," Dr. Graves said. "I wanted to speak to you regarding Mensa. You passed the test and were offered an opportunity to join. I'm curious as to why you haven't."

"I have no interest in joining."

"Why you would refuse to join such a prestigious organization? If you have no interest in it, why did you take the test?"

"I like taking tests." Bonnie shrugged. "I understand that having students who are members reflects well on universities, but I'm not interested."

"Mensa only accepts candidates whose IQs are in the top two percent, and you qualify," Dr. Graves said. "Certainly you must recognize how amazing that is? When you were twelve, your IQ score was one hundred and seventy-six, and you've scored near that on subsequent tests. There's no need to hide your light"

"IQ tests are culturally biased," Bonnie said. "The American chapter of Mensa fails to recognize this. Having a teenaged girl of Puerto Rican descent as a member would help the organization deny what is painfully obvious. Dr. Graves, I don't believe that any test can truly measure a person's intellect."

Dr. Graves, clearly irritated, tapped a pen on her desk. "Honestly, I've never given that much thought. If it's true, I can understand your reservations. Perhaps I can suggest an alternative group for you to join. I'd like you to consider Sigma Kappa."

"Sigma Kappa?" Bonnie said, hardly believing the woman's persistence. "Again, I fear you're wasting your time, Dr. Graves. I have no interest in joining an elitist group of women who only wish to party and find a husband."

"Good, because Sigma Kappa women strive for more, and I think you'd be perfect. Kappa women are interested in academic excellence and ways to help the community, not keg parties and boyfriends."

"Tell me more," said Bonnie, her interest piqued.

Dr. Graves smiled and laid down her pen. "Miss Sanchez, I think we're going to have a very interesting four years."

October, 2005

Raquel shook her head as she left Justine's room. "It's official, I've snapped," she muttered. It was the only reasonable explanation for thinking that the best-looking girl in the sorority house was making a pass at her. And then there were her delusions of nightly visitations from a brunette who didn't exist. And yet, when she stepped into her bedroom, there the young woman was, sitting on the bed and wearing the same green T-shirt and flared jeans.

"Who are you?" Raquel demanded as she closed the door.

"Love, you know my name."

"Bonnie?" Raquel tossed down her books and crossed the room.

She was ready to read her uninvited guest the riot act when Bonnie pulled her down onto the bed and savagely attacked her mouth. "See, you do know me," Bonnie murmured, as she caressed Raquel's hips.

Another woman's touch was too much for Raquel to resist. Her brief time in Justine's room had ignited a fire inside her, and now Bonnie's mouth worshiping her neck, as nimble hands drifted up and under her shirt, drove the flames higher.

She craved the sensations that flooded her when Bonnie captured and began pinching and teasing her tender nipples. "Feels good, doesn't it," Bonnie murmured. Raquel wrapped her legs around Bonnie's body. She rocked against her shamelessly, rubbing her clit against the seam of the other girl's jeans.

"Yes!" Raquel cried out, hating herself for enjoying what they were doing. Bonnie chuckled as she removed Raquel's shirt and bra. Raquel ground harder against the mysterious woman's body and Bonnie's tongue traced the swell of her breasts.

"She got you all hot and bothered, didn't she?" Bonnie slipped her hand between their bodies and cupped Raquel's mound. "Don't worry, I'll do what she wouldn't," she said, and captured one of Raquel's erect nipples between her lips. Raquel's body thrust urgently as Bonnie suckled her nipple while teasing her clit with the heel of her hand.

Raquel climaxed against Bonnie's touch. Her cries filled the room as Bonnie continued to pleasure her. "Baby, you need more," Bonnie whispered against her skin.

"I need her," Raquel said, tears welling in her eyes. Bonnie's movements halted, and the window shade flew up.

"Women." Bonnie grumbled as she retreated. "You will be mine," she said, and vanished.

The following day, Raquel left her bedroom as quickly as she could. She tried to convince herself that her intimate encounter had been nothing more than a dream, but she hid downstairs and studied in the lounge or the library rather than returning to her room.

Finally it grew late, and she had no other option except to go up to her bedroom. She braced herself as she opened the door. When she saw that the room was empty, she released a sigh of relief. "It was just a dream," she assured herself, closing the door behind her. Raquel yelped when she turned around and saw Bonnie lounging on her bed, flipping through one of her textbooks. "Should I have knocked?" the ghostly woman asked her playfully.

"It might be a nice change." Raquel fought down a whimper. "But no, you're not real."

"Depends on your point of view." Bonnie shrugged and beckoned the frightened woman to join her. "You look tired, *querida*."

"Small wonder." Raquel sat down and sighed with exhaustion as olive-skinned arms wrapped tightly around her body.

"Do I trouble you? Or is it perhaps the fair Justine?" Bonnie tenderly caressed Raquel's stomach.

"Leave her out of this."

"Relax," Bonnie cooed, "she's hot. I can't blame you for wanting her."

"I'm not like that." Raquel didn't believe her own words.

"Yes, you are," Bonnie scoffed at her denial. "And so is she. But I don't want to waste this evening talking about another woman."

"You brought her up," Raquel said, leaning into Bonnie's touch.

"Only because she's always in your thoughts." Bonnie let out a long sigh.

Raquel ignored Bonnie's words and relaxed into the woman's tender caresses. "Did you move my stuff around?" she asked, noticing that some of her belongings had been moved.

"I prefer it this way," Bonnie explained, her caresses growing bolder.

"Just my luck. Not only do I have a ghost in my room, but she's a horny control freak."

"You say that like it's a bad thing." Bonnie laughed.

Raquel gasped sharply when Bonnie's hands covered her breasts. Strangely, no matter how good it felt to be held by the brunette, it was Justine's touch that she craved. "Not tonight," Bonnie whispered hotly in her ear, playing with Raquel's nipples through the thin material of her shirt. "Tonight you belong to me."

Raquel squirmed against her body. She gave in to the passionate caresses, knowing that no matter what Bonnie did, it would be Justine's face Raquel would see when she climaxed.

September, 1964

Bonnie sat in the student lounge at the end of her first day of college life. Earlier that day, she and Teneil had unpacked their meager belongings in the room they would be sharing. Then Bonnie had decided to stroll around campus and check out the place that would be her home for the next four years. She knew she should head back and spend time with Teneil, but the blonde sitting across the room kept catching her eye. Bonnie smiled, not missing the way the girl would play with her earring or brush her hair back each time she stole a glance in Bonnie's direction. *Shy, blonde, and stacked. Just the welcome gift I was looking for.* Bonnie purred, and then chuckled to herself. *Whatever shall I do?* She stood and crossed the room. "Hello," she greeted the blonde stranger, who blushed when Bonnie took a seat beside her. "I'm Bonnie," she said, flashing the girl her most charming smile.

"T... Tonya," the young woman stammered, apparently nervous. "I'm a freshman," she added, brushing her hair back, her fingers trembling as she spoke.

"Me too," Bonnie said and sensed that Tonya was already relaxing in her presence. "What do you think so far?"

"It's so exciting. But I don't think my roommate and I are going to get along."

"Really? What dorm are you in?"

"Bowdich."

"I'm in Teasdale," Bonnie said. "Why do you think you and your roommate are going to have trouble?"

"I think she's a hippie," Tonya said, groaning. "Not that I mind, but we've only been here for a couple of hours and our room already reeks of Mary Jane."

"Oh." Bonnie cringed, familiar with the rank odor of marijuana. She suspected that Roberto already had more than a passing acquaintance with the infamous Mary Jane. "I've never understood the fascination with smoking weed. I'd much rather keep my brain cells intact."

"I agree. I just wish I'd gotten to meet her before we moved in. What about you? Are you hiding down here because of your new roommate, too?"

"No," Bonnie said quickly, already suspecting that Tonya would suggest switching rooms. "I'm lucky. My best friend and I both got in, so we're rooming together."

"Yeah, you're lucky."

We'll see. Bonnie checked her watch and calculated just how long it would take to convince Tonya that they should go off and find someplace more private. She loved shy women; they took forever to work up the nerve to speak to her, trying to drop subtle hints that they were like-minded. Yet once she kissed them and copped a feel, they turned into wild women. The problem was, they often mistook intimacy for love.

It didn't take Bonnie long to convince Tonya to go for a drive in her beat-up Chevy and check out the small town. Of course, the drive was short once Bonnie stumbled across Ford Hill, the local make-out spot. Her ruse of wanting to see the lights of the small burg from the top of the hill was flimsy. It didn't matter; she suspected that Tonya wanted to share more than the view of the town with her, anyway.

A few shy kisses quickly led to more lingering ones, and hands roamed as the windows of her car fogged up. She removed Tonya's blouse quickly, pleased when she discovered that she wasn't wearing a bra. "Do you want to get in the back?" Bonnie asked, panting, as Tonya began to wriggle out of her jeans.

"Yes." Tonya slipped her hand inside Bonnie's jeans while the brunette suckled Tonya's rose-colored nipple. They fumbled, still groping each other, while climbing over the front seat. Bonnie laughed when Tonya pinned her in the backseat.

Oh, yeah, I just love shy girls. Tonya yanked her pants down.

"I want to eat you," Tonya whispered and started kissing Bonnie's thighs. Bonnie moaned with pleasure, her back pressing against the door handle of the car. She sighed happily as Tonya nestled between her legs, and laced her fingers through her lover's honey-colored hair as Tonya's tongue parted her. Bonnie was very much enjoying her first night as a coed. She murmured softly, her body tingling from the feeling of Tonya's tongue flicking against her aching nub, then dug her fingers into the worn upholstery as Tonya urgently suckled her and slipped inside.

Bonnie shuddered with pleasure as Tonya repeatedly drove her over the edge. "*¡Querida!*" she cried, rocking her hips against

Tonya's tongue, which was now gliding in and out of her wetness. "Come here," she gasped at last, her body unable to give any more.

"What did you say?" Tonya asked, then captured Bonnie in a searing kiss. Bonnie moaned, tasting her own passion on the other woman's lips. "I think I should sign up for Spanish this semester," Tonya continued, and purred when Bonnie's hands slipped under her skirt. That was Bonnie's first warning that Tonya was already falling for her.

"No need," Bonnie whispered, tossing out her first hint that this was only for one night. She hoped Tonya would understand. In any case, she would deal with the emotional drama later; right now, she needed to see Tonya's naked body. They kissed passionately, and she quickly finished stripping her lover. "Tell me what you want," Bonnie said, slipping her hand between their trembling bodies, moaning as she found Tonya's overflowing desire.

"Fuck me," Tonya begged, much to Bonnie's pleasure. Her fingers slipped inside Tonya's wetness, filling her, stroking her long and hard. She teased her partner's throbbing clit with her thumb while their bodies thrust wildly until they were both crying out in ecstasy.

"Hello," Bonnie greeted Teneil, sauntering into their room.

"For heaven's sake, we haven't been here a full day and already you've got a hickey," Teneil said. Bonnie wiggled her eyebrows. "I thought you were just going to go for a walk around campus after your meeting with your advisor."

"I did." Bonnie shrugged and grinned broadly. "Then I went for a drive." She omitted the stop at Ford Hill and the fact that her little drive wasn't a solo trip. The time on the hill was more than enjoyable. However, on the drive back to campus, Bonnie had grown aggravated as she tried to explain to Tonya that their little encounter in the back seat of her car didn't make them a couple. She still had doubts that the other woman had listened to her.

"I hope you told her it was just a shag," Teneil said in an accusing voice.

"I did. I just hope she heard it."

"Have you ever considered just dating a girl?"

"Why?" The concept truly confused Bonnie. She didn't understand why everything had to be so serious. What she did was illegal. Not only could she get kicked out of school, but she might also end up in jail. Most of the women she spent time with weren't even lesbians. They were just curious. Bonnie didn't understand the concept of falling in love. The rare times she did feel more than desire, the object of her affections didn't return her feelings. Why bother with finding a girlfriend? For now, she needed to do well in school. Falling in love was something that would happen when it happened. *Still, it might be nice,* Bonnie thought, then dismissed the absurd notion.

"How is it that you can understand the mysteries of the universe and will probably single-handedly end world hunger or bring about world peace, yet you have no idea how fragile the human heart is?" Teneil asked.

"Perhaps I do, and that's why I keep my heart safely locked away."

"You're so full of crap." Teneil tossed her pillow at Bonnie, who was laughing.

"I know," Bonnie agreed, knowing that Teneil would never believe the shy, sincere act. *Because that's what it is, just an act,* she grimly realized.

"Bonnie, this is the beginning of our future. I don't want to spend it cleaning up after you the way I did in high school," Teneil said. "I swear, if one girl shows up crying about how you broke her heart, I will kick your Puerto Rican ass. And stay away from the Townie girls. I really don't want to deal with some redneck showing up on our doorstep because you stole his girlfriend and then dumped her."

"Agreed. No Townies."

"That's it? What about everything else I just said?"

"I'll try. You're a drag, Teneil. You know that, right?"

"You're impossible." Her friend sighed, knowing that a perky pair of tits was all it took. Bonnie couldn't resist.

"And you love me anyway." Bonnie laughed and tossed Teneil's pillow back at her.

October 31, 2005

Night after night, Bonnie visited Raquel. She seemed insatiable. They hadn't consummated things completely, yet Bonnie certainly seemed to enjoy touching her every night. Sometimes Bonnie popped in during the day, just to add a little commentary. Raquel had to admit that her uninvited guest could be quite witty. Whenever Justine was around, however, Bonnie taunted Raquel unmercifully. She also had more than a few annoying habits: she moved things around, she wouldn't answer any questions about herself, and she was very grabby whenever Raquel changed her clothes.

With each passing day, Raquel felt reality slipping further away, what with Bonnie's lascivious attitude and Justine's constant inquiries as to her well being. She wanted to move out of the room, or at least talk to someone about what was happening. But what could she say? She couldn't tell people—especially Justine, whom she was seriously lusting after—that she had been having sex with a ghost almost every night. Speaking of which, here she was again.

"Don't you look nice." Bonnie appeared, lounging on the bed, and sighed deeply as Raquel zipped up her gold and black evening gown.

"Thank you. I don't know which I find stranger, that you're here, or that I'm accepting it so easily." It was true. Sometime over the passing days, Raquel had just accepted Bonnie's presence.

"It's my room," Bonnie said.

"Not anymore." Raquel started to put on her earrings.

"Don't wear those," Bonnie said, wincing. "The diamonds would go with that outfit so much better."

"Now you're giving fashion tips?" Raquel shook a finger at her.

"Do you honestly think this is what I wore all the time? Had I known this was going to happen, I'd have picked a much nicer outfit to spend eternity in. If you must know, these aren't even my clothes." Bonnie looked thoughtful. "You know, you're a lot easier to talk to than the others."

"Why is it that only some girls have claimed to see you?" Raquel hoped Bonnie would answer one of her questions, for once.

"Did I tell you that I'm very proud of you for not asking that dweeb Mark to the party?" Bonnie said, avoiding the question.

"Why shouldn't I have invited him?"

"The same reason I don't bother every girl who shares my room," Bonnie explained. "Kindred spirits."

Raquel gulped, taking her meaning.

"She was right, you know," Bonnie said. She waved her hand and the nightstand moved.

"Stop it. I told you before; I like it where it was. I hate it when you move things around. Now, who was right about what?"

"Her," Bonnie explained as she nodded her head. "The one looking at you and not seeing me."

Raquel inhaled sharply and spun around to find Justine lurking in the doorway. "I was just talking to myself," she said quickly.

"She doesn't believe you," Bonnie taunted.

Raquel ignored the pesky apparition as she drank in the sight of Justine's long frame dressed in a silky black evening gown. "Wow! You look great!" she blurted.

"Thank you." Justine blushed a charming shade of pink. "So do you."

"What a couple of closet cases," Bonnie yammered. Raquel glanced over her shoulder and glared at her. "If you want my advice, skip the party and fuck her. I don't mind watching."

"I can't believe you," Raquel said, distracted by the chuckling ghost.

"Why, what did I do?" Justine asked, frowning in confusion.

"I can't believe how good you look," Raquel quickly amended.

"She's not buying it," Bonnie said. "You might want to ask her why."

Raquel rolled her shoulders in frustration. Normally, Bonnie's dialogue was entertaining, but tonight it was bugging her. Justine looked positively amazing, and Raquel needed to focus on the fact that she probably had some guy waiting for her downstairs. "No, she doesn't," Bonnie nearly shouted. "Hello! She has the hots for you. I can't be the only one who knows this."

Raquel groaned inwardly and tried to ignore Bonnie. "You know, she was really hot," Bonnie continued.

"The party's about to start," Justine said. "Can I walk you downstairs?"

"See." Bonnie winked. "I'm telling you, kid, she likes you."

"That would be nice, thank you." Raquel blushed as she tried to drown out Bonnie's crude suggestions.

"Um, before we go downstairs I wanted to ask if you would do me a favor," Justine said. "Maggie's staying at her boyfriend's tonight, and with all these Halloween rumors about your room, I'd feel better if you crashed in mine."

"Cozy." Bonnie's eyes crinkled, and she chuckled. "Say yes."

"I... um," Raquel stammered as her heart began to race.

"Say yes," Bonnie whispered in her ear.

Raquel felt flushed as she thought about spending the night in Justine's bedroom. "Please don't come back to this room tonight," Bonnie and Justine said in unison.

"Okay," Raquel agreed, shivering at the ominous tone in both women's voices.

"Go," Bonnie urged, her expression grave. "She'll be here soon."

"We should hurry," Justine coaxed Raquel as well, and as they left, Bonnie faded away.

October 31, 2004

"Will you stop that?" Justine growled, as her books flew off her computer table. She still found it odd that she had accepted Bonnie's antics. She hadn't ever believed in ghosts until she had moved into the tiny room in the attic of the Sigma Kappa house. Now, not only did she believe, she enjoyed her phantom roommate's company. Bonnie's only interests were having sex and helping Justine with her studies. The only annoying aspect was Bonnie's need to move things around to set up the room the way she liked it. "I said stop it," Justine demanded when her CD collection went crashing to the floor.

"Not until you listen to me," Bonnie said, appearing beside the flustered redhead.

"What is with you tonight?" Justine's voice snapped at her. "This is my big night. I don't have time for your temper tantrums."

"Justine, listen to me," Bonnie pleaded. "Don't come back to this room tonight."

"And just where should I sleep?" The drastic change in Bonnie's attitude confused Justine. Normally Bonnie was relaxed, quick-witted, easygoing, and a smart ass. Tonight she was none of those things; tonight she was angry, upset, and frightened.

"I don't care if you sleep on the steps of the town hall, just don't sleep here. I have to go," she whispered suddenly, her voice grim. "Listen to what I said."

Justine was startled when Bonnie vanished and the door to her room suddenly opened and then slammed shut. "Lucky me, a ghost with PMS." Justine dismissed Bonnie's silly suggestion. She had a great time at the party, but she was confused to see Bonnie in attendance. Adding to her confusion was that she was the only one who could see or hear the mischievous spirit. Bonnie had a good time playing with the lights and taunting the other guests by moving things around. Justine laughed at the wayward spirit's games, except when Bonnie kept harping on her about not returning to her room. "What, do you have a date?" she muttered, growing weary of Bonnie's meddling.

Sometime after midnight, Bonnie vanished. "Maybe she does have a date." Justine laughed at the thought, though she missed Bonnie's presence. A couple of hours later, she was exhausted. Ignoring Bonnie's warnings, she climbed the staircase. "Honey, I'm home," she announced, entering her room. When she flipped the light switch, nothing happened. "Peachy," she grumbled, ready to have it out with Bonnie.

The air in her lungs seized as an icy hand grabbed her by the throat. A sharp pain struck her in the back of the head, and she fell to her knees. "Whore," Justine heard an angry voice say, and someone choked her harder, beating her about the face. She fought helplessly to defend herself as the sinister voice spewed vile words and unseen hands beat her body. Ugly words were being whispered in her ears and cold hands seemed to be everywhere, choking and beating her until she lost consciousness.

When she awoke, her body showed no marks, yet still ached from the torture she had endured during the night. She couldn't stand, and bile rose in her throat as she crawled to the door. Maggie found her curled up at the bottom of the staircase, sobbing like a child. She couldn't speak, the ugly words still ringing in her ears. The unknown being knew what she was and had exacted its punishment for her sins. She rocked back and forth, silent and trembling, when her sisters tried to help her. She broke her silence and screamed wildly, "I'm not going back there!" when Maggie suggested taking her to her room.

She refused to go to the hospital; she couldn't tell anyone what had happened. She slept in the lounge that night, not speaking again until the following morning. Maggie packed her belongings and arranged to have her placed in one of the dorms until her room could be changed. Two weeks later, she was still living in the dorm when she finally tried to explain what had happened on Halloween night. She omitted the details concerning her sexuality and Bonnie's warnings. For the first time in her life she was ashamed, blaming herself for the attack. Maggie was the only one who heard the whole story, and that was months afterwards. Justine was crestfallen when most of the Kappa sisters dismissed her tale as nothing more than a drunken delusion or a fanciful story she had invented to get a better room.

October 31, 2005

Raquel felt giddy as Justine escorted her down the staircase. She stayed close by during the ceremony and party, and Raquel's skin prickled every time their hands brushed. She kept reminding herself that Justine was just being nice, and was not her date for the evening. The party was quite elegant, with the exception of lights going on and off and things being knocked off tables by unseen hands. Well, almost unseen; Raquel had been watching Bonnie's antics all night long.

Raquel almost burst into laughter as Bonnie yanked up the back of Claudette's dress, revealing to everyone at the party that she wasn't wearing underwear. "She's in rare form tonight," Justine whispered.

"Who?" Raquel asked.

"Bonnie."

Bonnie nudged Raquel. "Ask her how she knows it's me."

"How do you know that?" Raquel said.

"I had your room last year," Justine confessed. "I was the one who moved back into the dorm until they switched my room assignment. Claudette wasn't happy about moving up there, but she never saw or heard anything."

"So not my type," Bonnie said, disgusted.

"Claudette accused me of faking everything just so I could have a better room," Justine said. "I think she shoved you in there to get back at me. It's so strange to know that Bonnie's here and not be able to see her."

"Or touch her?" Raquel was surprised to feel jealous.

"She was a lot of fun," Bonnie said, grinning.

"Excuse me," Raquel said, blanching. "I need to use the ladies' room." She made a mad dash to the nearest bathroom, locked the door and buried her face in her hands. She felt sick. When she looked up and found Bonnie sitting on the sink with her legs folded beneath her, she squawked, "My God, can't I even pee alone?"

"You didn't come in here to pee," Bonnie scoffed. "And keep your voice down. Someone might hear you."

"Why is it that I can see and touch you, but no one else can?"

"How should I know?" Bonnie shrugged. "Now, back to why you're hiding in the bathroom."

"I'm not hiding," Raquel insisted.

"Yes, you are," Bonnie said. "Now, before you get all huffy and storm up to your room, there are some things you should know. First, I'm a total shit when it comes to women. I know I'm all possessive and demanding, but let a woman actually agree that she belongs to me, and I'm out of there."

"What an asshole."

"Yes, I'm an asshole, but it shouldn't have cost me my life. Now, promise me that no matter how mad you are at Justine or at me, you won't go back to that room tonight."

"Why not?"

"Because I'm not there, and something else is," Bonnie tried to explain. "This is the only night that something else is in that room. I'm here at the party, having a good time just like I was the night I died. I'm trapped here until just after midnight, when I sneak into the room that Jennifer Lowell used to live in."

"Let me guess, those are Jennifer's clothes."

"My dress got torn." Bonnie winked. "Jennifer is the only one I'm certain wasn't the girl waiting for me in my room when I sneaked back in just before dawn. I never saw who she was. She was wearing one of the ceremonial robes, though, and I saw a Kappa pin glimmering underneath. Oh, and she's very angry. She takes that anger out on anyone goes into that room before dawn."

"That's what happened to Justine?"

"She didn't listen to me," Bonnie said, her expression sad.

"How could you not know who it is?" Raquel asked, wanting to know the name of the person who had hurt Justine. "I mean, you couldn't have broken every heart in the sorority house."

"What can I say? I'm very friendly." Bonnie grinned saucily.

"Whatever, Casper," Raquel said, poking a little fun at the friendly ghost. "You're a pig, but you know that, don't you?"

"Fine, I'm a pig," Bonnie agreed. "I still didn't deserve what happened. You know, what really frosts my cookies is that she made it look like a suicide. Everyone in the house was given a 4.0 that semester because of the trauma. Not only did she get away with murder, but she got a free ride for the semester."

Raquel couldn't believe what she was hearing. Then again, she'd been carrying on an affair with a ghost for the past few weeks, so nothing should shock her at this point. "My pigdom aside," Bonnie continued, "no matter what has happened or will happen tonight, I can see the way you two look at each other. You have something special, so don't blow it. Well, I'm off. I don't have much time left. After tonight, I disappear and won't be back until next fall."

"You disappear every November first, the day you died?" Raquel asked, trying to put the pieces together.

"Every year. Then I'm back for Rush Week, just as I was here in life. It was all fun and games until fifteen years ago, when the attacks started."

"Sounds like your killer died, and she's still pissed at you," Raquel said.

"Women!" Bonnie shrugged. "I'm going to play, and I suggest you do the same."

"Wait! What year did you die?"

"1964," Bonnie said, and vanished.

Raquel stepped out of the bathroom and found Justine waiting for her. "Raquel, are you all right?" Justine's features were dark with concern.

"Yeah." Raquel said. "I was just having a chat with Casper."

Justine's concern changed to a smile. "I guess you mean Bonnie. I miss talking to her. You know, she used to help me with my homework."

"Among other things," Raquel quipped jealously.

"Yeah... about that," Justine said slowly. Her eyes darted around the hallway.

"Later. For now, just watch the punch bowl." Raquel saw Bonnie approaching the table. She placed her hand gently on Justine's arm, and they both watched as Bonnie toppled the punch bowl onto Claudette's date.

"Man, she so doesn't like Claudette." Justine laughed aloud. "I don't understand why she didn't bug her when she lived in the room."

"Bonnie leaves each Halloween night and doesn't come back until the next September," Raquel said. "And she said something about only playing with kindred spirits."

"I didn't know," Justine murmured, and her hand covered Raquel's. "I just couldn't go back up there. It wasn't Bonnie. Whatever was waiting for me that night wasn't anything like her. That thing was just dark and ominous. And vicious."

"I'm sorry you were hurt."

"It's in the past. Just tell me what Casper's up to."

"Right now, she's looking up Kate's dress."

"She's such a pig." The two women chuckled.

"And proud of it. You know, I think if I'd met her when she was alive, I would have slapped her face."

At that moment, Bonnie scampered by, pausing just long enough to goose Justine, who jumped with surprise.

"Hey!" Raquel glared at her.

"Sorry, *querida*," Bonnie said, with broad grin. "But the girl has a great ass."

"Yeah, well keep your grubby mitts off it."

"So, I'm not the only possessive girl in the room," Bonnie said, teasing her.

"Do I want to know what's going on?" Justine asked.

"Bonnie thinks you have a nice ass," Raquel said. "You do, by the way."

"Um, thank you." Justine blushed in response. "The party's dwindling down, why don't we head upstairs?"

"Yes," Raquel agreed, and Justine led her up the staircase.

September, 1964

"Bonita Sanchez?" The brunette with the lilting drawl addressed Bonnie, who was more focused on her morning cup of coffee than the older student's considerable charms. Bonnie yawned, finally looking up at the girl who was disturbing her bliss.

"Yes?" Bonnie asked, still weary from spending the night before getting to know another member of the student body up close and personal. *I really need to start pacing myself.* She finally took a moment to appreciate the attributes of the woman speaking to her. *Then again...* She smiled, and met the brunette's curious gaze.

"I'm Carrie Templeton," the woman said, politely extending her hand to the freshman.

"And a Kappa," Bonnie noted, seeing the pin on the older girl's lapel as they shook hands. "Please sit down."

"Thank you, Miss Sanchez. As you've probably guessed, Dr. Graves asked me to speak to you. Honestly, if everything she's told me about you is true, you'd make an excellent candidate for Sigma Kappa. Provided you survive the initiation, that is."

"Survive?" Bonnie laughed, wondering just what these girls did to ensure that a candidate was worthy. "Carrie, you don't even know me. Why are you so interested in me joining your sorority?"

"Pledging," Carrie quickly corrected the freshman. "There's no guarantee of being accepted unless you're a legacy. Simply being intelligent doesn't mean you're Kappa material. Did you really tell old lady Graves that IQ tests are culturally biased?"

"Yes, I did, and yes, they are," Bonnie said, her focus returning to her cup of coffee.

"I agree. I also know what it's like to be treated differently because you test well, or to do poorly in classes because you're bored. Sound familiar?"

"Yes." Bonnie sighed, thinking back on her first twelve years in school, during most of which she felt like an outcast.

"College is different," Carrie said. "You're no longer the best and the brightest. Now you're studying with the best and the brightest, and it can be overwhelming at times. Plus, the newfound freedom can be misguiding. Many women lose sight of their goals. There are a great many distractions that you will face. Sigma Kappa women strive for academic excellence. We help one another maintain focus, not just during the four years we spend here, but for life. Our alumnae go on to be leaders in their communities, not just wives and mothers. If that isn't something that interests you, then don't bother pledging. You'd be wasting our time and yours."

"You have my attention," Bonnie said.

"Good. Then stop looking at my tits and tell me what you want out of life," Carrie chastised the randy freshman. "And don't even try to outwit or charm me. You've been enrolled at this University a very short time, but your reputation already precedes you."

"And that intrigues you?" Bonnie purred, ignoring the older girl's warning.

"No, it troubles me." Carrie drummed her fingers on the stack of books and papers she had been toting around.

"You know what troubles me?" Bonnie said in a serious voice. "This paper." She slipped one of the papers out of the stack. "How did you get such a good grade on it when it's such a mess?"

"That's from last semester. What do you mean, it's a mess?"

"Here, in the second paragraph…" Much to Carrie's astonishment, Bonnie began noting errors.

Two hours later, Bonnie had completely reworked the paper, which Carrie had thought was well written. Now, Carrie felt like an idiot. When she began her college career, she went from being the best and the brightest to being one of many, but she still maintained a very high GPA and confidence in her intellect. At that moment, however, her confidence was shaky at best.

"Bonnie, do you remember when I warned you about suddenly becoming a member of the crowd?" she indicated the corrected paper. "Forget I said it. If you don't pledge, would you consider studying with me? I can't believe you haven't even attended your first class. I'm starting my senior year, and I thought this paper was brilliant. But I doubt the professor who graded it could comprehend the depth you've added to it."

"I'm sorry, I probably shouldn't have said anything," Bonnie apologized, suddenly bashful. "I can't stop myself. My mind just won't stay idle. Sometimes I wish it would."

"And here I thought you were only interested in my breasts."

"I was." Bonnie smirked, her bravado returning in full force. "That's also something I can't stop myself from doing. You don't seem to be troubled or offended, but you're not a lesbian, so why are you allowing me to ogle you?"

"I'm open-minded," Carrie confessed. Her heart fluttered as she gazed into Bonnie dark brown eyes.

"Ah." Bonnie smiled. "You've played in the garden."

"Yes," Carrie answered willingly. "Aesthetics aren't that much of a turn on for me. Intellect is what attracts me, regardless of gender."

"Interesting," Bonnie said. "This is the first time I've turned a woman on by correcting a term paper."

"Don't flatter yourself." Carrie collected her papers, apparently intending to leave.

"Tell me, do Einstein's theories make you wet?" Bonnie hoped to slow down Carrie's quick escape.

"Bonnie, think about pledging, and remember that college is a very close-knit community," Carrie said. "Everyone is exploring, trying things that maybe they shouldn't, and they talk about things. Word gets around."

"I never kiss and tell," Bonnie said, trying for a coy look.

"Everyone else does, so tread carefully," Carrie warned, and walked off.

"I'll try," Bonnie called after her, then sighed. "I really like college life."

"Yes, you do, and I want you to tell me where you slept last night." Teneil said, taking the chair Carrie had just vacated.

"No," Bonnie muttered, feeling slightly guilty for not listening to Teneil's advice. "You'd think less of me."

"Bonnie," Teneil said, an edge of anger in her voice. "Was that her?"

"No. That was, um, my new study partner."

"Finally you're focusing on something that has to do with school," Teneil exclaimed.

"Right now, I'm focusing on my stomach," Bonnie said. "Come on, I'll buy you breakfast."

"I'm honored." Teneil laughed. She could never stay angry with Bonnie.

October 31, 2005

Justine shut the bedroom door, and they stood looking at each other. "You look amazing tonight," Justine said. "I couldn't take my eyes off you." She stepped closer and put her hands on Raquel's hips.

"Please tell me this is really happening." As Justine's face neared her own, Raquel whimpered.

"This is really happening." Justine's whisper made Raquel's knees buckle. Lacing her fingers through Justine's long red hair, Raquel drew her closer and lost herself in their kiss. Bonnie had been an amazing kisser, but Justine's kisses were nothing short of magical. Raquel flicked her tongue across Justine's soft, full lips and felt weak when they parted in response.

Their bodies melded together as the kiss deepened. They were both breathless when the kiss ended, and they pressed their foreheads together. "I've been aching to do that since Rush Night." Justine took a step backward.

"You're such an amazing kisser," Raquel said.

"Raquel, you need to know something." Justine rested her hands on Raquel's hips. "Last Halloween, I was attacked by something, or someone, very dark."

"Did it... were you..." Raquel hesitated, praying that Justine hadn't been sexually abused that night.

"I wasn't raped," Justine reassured her. "But it was so hateful. It kept beating and strangling me while spewing horrible words about what I am. It drove me back into the closet. I haven't allowed myself to feel anything for another woman since then. Until the first night I saw you."

"I'm so sorry you were hurt so badly. I want to take that pain away."

"You already have," Justine said and smiled.

"Before I met you and Casper," Raquel said, "I didn't know I was in the closet."

"I had a feeling that might be so." Justine began to caress Raquel's hips. "How far did things go with Bonnie?"

"There was kissing and a lot of touching," Raquel blushed. "But it didn't go as far as it could have. Every time I was with her, I'd think about you and she'd get pissed off and leave. I wanted it to be you."

"That's what I wanted, what I still want." Justine cupped Raquel's face and drew her in for another lingering kiss. Her tongue's velvety caresses drove Raquel wild. Her face felt hot as Justine's hands held her tenderly. Spurred on by the desire pooling between her thighs, she allowed her hands to explore the soft, supple curves of Justine's body.

Justine leaned against her, guiding her across the room, and Raquel looked up into green eyes that were clouded with desire. Her heart swelled as she became lost in the lustful gaze. "Make love to me," she pleaded, running her slender fingers along the soft satin material covering Justine's breasts.

Justine's breathing grew ragged as she laced her fingers through Raquel's long hair. "You're so beautiful," Justine whispered, before flicking her tongue playfully along Raquel's lips. Raquel's moan turned into a fierce growl when she captured her lover's tongue in her mouth.

As Justine lowered her onto the bed, Raquel felt as though their souls had been united. Still fully dressed, they kicked off their high heels. Lying half on the bed and half off it, they caressed each other. Raquel's nipples hardened when Justine's hand moved up her leg and slipped under her dress.

"Raquel," Justine murmured into her neck, while her long fingers kneaded Raquel's firm, nylon-clad thigh. Delirious, Raquel could only whimper in response. Her body wriggled beneath Justine's as she clasped Justine's shoulders, digging her blunt nails into her lover's flesh.

Raquel's body refused to remain still, and she thrashed against Justine. Every fiber of her being cried out for more. She buried her face against the smooth neck and began to suck on it. Justine moaned with pleasure and rocked urgently against Raquel.

The taste of Justine's skin and the feeling of her body grinding against her drove Raquel to the brink. She cried out in frustration as she felt Justine retreating from her touch. "Shh," Justine whispered. "I just want to take things a little slower." She brushed her fingers along Raquel's cheek tenderly.

Raquel doubted that she would be able to comply with her lover's wishes, but she allowed Justine to guide her to a standing position.

"Slow is nice," she admitted, as Justine began to undress her, kissing and tasting every inch of her newly exposed flesh along the way. "Very nice." Justine nibbled and licked the pulse point on her throat.

"Incredibly nice," Raquel emphasized, mirroring her lover's actions and removing Justine's clothing. Her anticipation and desire grew as she lowered the zipper on Justine's gown. There was something sensual about how they took their time, enjoying the moment as their clothing fell to the floor. The best part was when they got down to their panties.

Raquel almost passed out as Justine kissed and tasted her way up her legs, pausing to savor sensitive spots like the backs of her knees. When Raquel knelt before her lover and returned the favor, she discovered the true meaning of happiness. The musky aroma of Justine's passion captivated her as she licked her lover's thighs. "There's no way I'm standing back up," she said, staring at the patch of red curls.

"Then don't," Justine said huskily. Raquel's gaze lifted to Justine hands and followed their movement as they slid down the front of her glorious body. Raquel gasped as her lover spread her own nether lips with her fingers and slowly began stroking her clit. She parted her thighs, inviting a closer look. Raquel licked her lips eagerly and leaned closer. When Justine offered her a passion-coated finger, she grasped her lover's wrist and plunged the finger into her mouth. She swirled her tongue around it, drinking in every last drop of wetness.

"More," she pleaded, her voice ragged with need.

Justine cradled Raquel's head. With a seductive purr, she said, "You can have as much as you want." She guided her lover to her wetness, and Raquel's tongue snaked out, gliding along the slick folds. When she tasted Justine's desire, Raquel murmured with delight. She could feel the swollen clit pulsating against her tongue as she teased it. Driven on by Justine's pleas for more, she suckled the throbbing bundle with increasing urgency.

Raquel refused to relinquish the pleasurable feast even after she felt her lover's body quaking against her. Finally, Justine pulled away. "My God." she choked out. "Are you trying to kill me?" She pulled Raquel to her feet.

"That was so amazing," Raquel said, panting for breath. She latched on to her lover, kissing her passionately, and Justine returned the feverish kisses eagerly. They giggled as they fell onto the bed. Their hands wandered again until they were pinching and teasing each other's nipples. Raquel could feel Justine's wetness painting her skin as their legs entwined. She straddled her lover's thigh as they began to rock urgently against one another.

Justine slowed their rhythm and kissed her way down Raquel's neck to the valley between her breasts. She pushed her lover gently onto her back, and her tongue slowly traced the curve of her cleavage. Raquel's body jerked and she pushed her nipple toward her lover's lips. Much to her agony, Justine circled the puckered bud with her tongue without touching it. "Please," Raquel said, pressing her breast more firmly against her lover's mouth.

Her body ignited when she felt Justine's teeth graze her nipple and her hands caress her hips. Raquel rocked against her lover's touch, her body screaming for release. Unlike Bonnie, who took pleasure in making Raquel climax as quickly as possible, Justine seemed determined to draw out her pleasure. Each agonizing moment took Raquel to new heights.

Her mind and body were afire as Justine guided her onto her stomach. She cried out when she felt Justine's passion against her ass. "I want to make you feel things you've never felt before," Justine said, pulling Raquel up until she was on her hands and knees.

"You already do." Raquel whimpered as her lover straddled her from behind. Raquel's hips jerked back when she felt Justine's wetness against her. "Oh! My! God!" she cried as they ground wildly against each other. Justine's breasts pressed into her back; strong hands clasped her slender hips and led them into a frenzied rhythm.

One of Justine's hands drifted along the curve of her ass, teasing the quivering flesh while her hips maintained the wild pace. Raquel's head fell forward as Justine explored each crevasse thoroughly until her slender fingers were buried deep inside Raquel's passion. Raquel's body pressed down, needing to feel her lover inside her. Justine slipped deeper inside Raquel's aching need, while her thumb teased her clit.

Justine never broke their frantic pace as she plunged in and out of Raquel. Passionate cries filled the room as Raquel became one with her lover. She was blissfully unaware that Justine was teasing her puckered opening. "Come for me," Justine ordered, and filled Raquel completely.

Raquel's body shattered and she erupted against her lover's touch. Everything blurred. Their bodies slapped together until they collapsed onto the bed, Raquel still convulsing. As her vision began to clear, she became aware that Justine's fingers were still nestled deep inside of her. She could feel herself shaking.

"Raquel?" Justine's voice was filled with concern. Her fingers slipped from Raquel's body and she wrapped her lover in a tender embrace.

"Can't speak." Raquel coughed weakly, and Justine chuckled.

Sighing contentedly, Raquel snuggled up against her lover, who kissed her brow tenderly. "I think I'm falling in love with you," Justine whispered.

"Good." Raquel smiled and snuggled closer to the woman she was certain she had already fallen hard for. As sleep claimed her, she listened to the steady beating of Justine's heart.

September, 1964

"Yes, God, yes!" Carrie screamed at the top of her lungs. Her body was covered with sweat as Bonnie took her harder. She knew she shouldn't have offered to study with the younger girl, knowing that Bonnie's mind and charm would override her senses. In less than an hour, the endearing Bonnie had swayed her. Now, she was in a dingy motel room on Route One, better known as 'no-tell motel row,' balanced on the bed on her hands and knees, while Bonnie knelt behind her, driving her over the edge.

Carrie's hips jerked back as Bonnie's fingers plunged deeper, her tongue tracing Carrie's spine. Carrie thrust harder against Bonnie's touch, needing to feel all of her. Bonnie's erect nipples scraped against her skin and she rocked harder against the arousing touch. "Yes! Fuck me!" she screamed, her body shuddering in unbelievable arousal.

Bonnie grunted with pleasure as she stroked Carrie's throbbing clit and pressed her wetness hard against the older girl. Carrie's ears were filled with a strange buzzing sound, her body arching as her mind turned to darkness. "Yes, baby. I want to feel you," Bonnie whispered hotly in her ear as Carrie fell into a whirlwind.

Carrie collapsed, her body exploding. She had suspected that Bonnie would be a giving lover, but she had never dreamed that behind the charming smile and quick wit lurked a fire that would drive her completely insane. "God, you're fucking unbelievable," Carrie said, still clutching the cheap blanket that covered the bed.

"¿*Querida?*" Bonnie whispered, cradling Carrie in her arms. "Are you all right?"

"I'm in heaven and I'm an idiot." Carrie's heart was still racing from the passionate encounter. "I told myself I wasn't going to sleep with you."

"Do you regret it?" Bonnie asked, teasing Carrie's quivering flesh with her nails.

"No." Carrie sighed, and caressed Bonnie's narrow hips. "You're an amazing lover."

"Thank you." Bonnie giggled and leaned into Carrie's touch. "Do you still want me to pledge?" she asked in a guarded tone.

"Yes. I understand this is just sex for you."

"Isn't that what you were looking for?" Bonnie asked.

"I guess." Carrie's hands drifted lower until she was cupping Bonnie's firm, round backside. *I can handle this,* she thought, drawing Bonnie's body closer. As they fell into a sensual rhythm, she moaned deeply, feeling Bonnie's desire on her flesh.

"Tell me what you want," Bonnie said, her breath tickling Carrie's skin.

"I want to feel you come," Carrie cried out, and their bodies gyrated wildly against one another.

"Touch me," Bonnie gasped, clasping Carrie tighter, parting her own thighs, and offering her passion to Carrie's touch. Carrie's heart leapt, and she rolled her passionate lover onto her back. She released a needy growl as she gazed down upon Bonnie's naked body lying beneath her, begging for her touch. "Take me, do whatever you wish," Bonnie whispered. Carrie cast off all sense of reason, dipped her head, and captured Bonnie's dark nipple between her lips. Her hands drifted down the front of Bonnie's body and she tugged on the erect nipple with her teeth, her fingers dipping into a pool of wetness.

"I'm going to lick you," Carrie said savagely, stroking Bonnie's throbbing clit with her fingers, her senses giddy from the feeling of her lover's body squirming beneath her own. "Long and hard, until you come all over me," she promised, her mouth attacking Bonnie's trembling flesh as she licked and tasted her way down Bonnie's body. She was on fire as the musky aroma of desire filled her senses. She parted Bonnie's slick folds with her tongue and began feasting upon her.

Carrie's tongue swept along Bonnie's sex and she began sucking the engorged clit fervently, needing to taste her lover's wetness and feel her climaxing. She grasped Bonnie's backside, drawing her closer, drinking in her passion as Bonnie's body rocked against hers. Bonnie guided Carrie deeper inside her, grinding her body faster, demanding release. "Harder," she groaned, rocking her body even more wildly. Carrie happily acceded to her demands.

Carrie could feel her body humming, nearing the edge, knowing that Bonnie was ready to give her what she desired. She sucked harder on the pulsating nub, and Bonnie's body tightened against her, trapping her inside the moist warmth. She screamed into Bonnie's wetness, climaxing as her lover's body exploded. Carrie was lost in a euphoric haze, licking the last drops of passion from Bonnie's thighs. They rested briefly, and then the tryst was over. A quick shower and a hasty drive back to the college, and the only promise Bonnie offered was to stop by the Kappa house for Rush Night.

Carrie couldn't understand why she felt heartbroken. She knew Bonnie was only offering casual sex. Still, the encounter had been so intense that she found it hard to believe that Bonnie wanted nothing more than a quick shag and a handshake. *How can someone offer so much fire and not feel anything deeper?* Carrie asked herself that evening when she found herself pacing by the telephone, trying to work up the courage to call Bonnie and invite her out for the evening. She finally called, only to have Bonnie brush off her invitation.

November 1, 2005

"Trick or treat!" Raquel was jolted from her blissful slumber by the scream. She looked up with horror to find a stunned Maggie standing in the doorway. She looked down at her naked lover, whose eyes blinked open.

"Close the door, Maggie," Justine grumbled, pulling the blushing Raquel back into her arms and covering them both with the blanket.

Raquel's heart was pounding as Maggie shrugged and closed the bedroom door before anyone else could sneak a peek. "I see we've already had our treats," Maggie teased the lovers, tossing her overnight bag onto her bed. "How about a trick?"

"Don't even think about it," Justine said.

"Spoil sport," Maggie grumbled looking at the horrified Raquel.

"She has no sense of decorum," Justine explained, tossing a pillow at her roommate.

"I do too," Maggie said, tossing the pillow back at Justine. "Relax, Raquel. I know all about Stretch and her wicked ways."

"You do?" Raquel pulled the blanket tighter against her body.

"I should. We grew up together," Maggie said. "You'll never guess who she used to date in high school."

"Don't go there." Justine's glare didn't seem to faze her roommate.

"My sister," Maggie said, cackling.

"You dated Maggie's *sister?*"

"Yeah, until she dumped my sorry ass for some cheerleader."

"My sister is a shallow jerk." Maggie shrugged. "I tried to tell you before you slept with her, but would you listen? No. Don't worry about a thing, Raquel. I'm not going to tell anyone about this. In fact, I'm very happy to see that you've finally fallen for Justine's considerable charms. She's been gaga over you for months now."

"Shut up," Justine said, scowling.

"I'm going downstairs, so the two of you can have some privacy and make yourselves decent."

"Thank you." Raquel sighed with relief.

She watched Maggie leave before turning toward Justine. "Good morning," Justine said, looking uncomfortable. "I'm sorry about Maggie."

Raquel cut off Justine's apology with a kiss. "Good morning," she said, a happy lilt in her voice.

Justine was stunned. "Good morning," she repeated, a goofy grin forming on her face.

"I guess we'll have to be careful," Raquel pointed out.

"Unfortunately, yes," Justine agreed. "As progressive as things are these days, not all the Kappa sisters would understand. The good news is that Maggie spends almost every weekend with her boyfriend."

"Danny? He seems nice."

"I would hope so." Justine laughed. "He's my brother."

"Are you guys from a really small town, or what?" Raquel teased. "Wait! He doesn't look anything like you, and you have different last names."

"Stepbrother," Justine explained.

"Oh." Raquel nodded. "Well, thank him for me for keeping Maggie busy on the weekends. I think you and I have a lot of studying to do together."

"I like the way you think," Justine said, beaming. "But as nice as this is right now, we need to get up and at least try to look respectable."

"Rats," Raquel grumbled, and they reluctantly got out of bed.

November, 2005

"What are you up to?" Justine asked Raquel, as she stepped into the library located on the main floor of the sorority house.

"Just a little research." Raquel greeted her lover with a smile, and glanced around to see who was near. She sighed when she noticed Kate and Sarah working in the corner.

"I was hoping we could do a little studying together before dinner," Justine said, giving a sly smirk. Raquel blushed at the suggestion. Ever since they had become lovers, this had been their little code.

"Maybe after dinner. I need to show you something." She slid the leather-bound book she had been investigating over to Justine.

"'Sigma Kappa Sorority, 1964,'" Justine read, and gave her lover a puzzled glance.

Raquel reached over, opened the book, and pointed to a space on one of the pages. "'Bonita Sanchez, photo not available,'" Justine continued reading. "Okay, I give."

"The reason the photo isn't available is because they're taken in the spring," Raquel said. "Bonita wasn't alive in May. There's no Bonita Sanchez listed in 1963 or 1965. It has to be her."

"Are you sure?" Justine asked, sounding excited. "I tried looking her up. I worked back to the early seventies before I gave up."

"I had a head start. The last thing she told me was the year she died. What I don't get is why she isn't listed as deceased."

"A suicide couldn't have been good for the sorority's image," Justine said. "Of course, if they had known it was murder, the house would have been shut down. So what does this mean?"

"Everyone who lived in this house in 1964 is in this book."

"And any one of them could be the murderer," Justine said.

"Maybe I can figure out who it was." Raquel propped her chin on her hand. "Bonnie said the attacks didn't begin until fifteen years ago. If I can find out who died around then, it might help stop what's happening every October thirty-first. Right now, the only girl I can eliminate is Jennifer Lowell."

"Why Jennifer?"

"Jennifer was the reason Bonnie was so late getting back to her room that morning," Raquel whispered.

"If you need any help with this, I'll be happy to do anything I can," Justine said. "It may not do any good, but I'd like to know who or what attacked me."

"According to Bonnie, it could have been any one of the girls living in the house that year," Raquel said.

"Wait a minute. At any given time, there are at least twenty-five girls living here. Based on what I went through, I got the distinct impression it was a jealous lover. She couldn't have shagged all of them." Justine flipped through the pages of the book.

"Why do you think I call her Casper the friendly ghost?" Raquel snickered.

"Man, she really was a randy dog. Speaking of which, are you sure we don't have time to study before dinner?"

A rush of warmth surged through Raquel's body, and she gathered her books. "Let's go," she said, tugging on Justine's arm.

"Good, no Maggie." Justine shut the door and wrapped her arms around Raquel's waist. "I've been thinking about you all day."

"We don't have a lot of time," Raquel warned.

Justine was already feasting upon her sensitive neck. "Maybe we could think of this as an appetizer, and later we can have dessert," she suggested hopefully, while Justine's nimble fingers began to lower the zipper on her jeans.

"I'll pay Maggie to go to the movies." Groaning, Justine sank to her knees and pulled Raquel's pants and underwear down with her. One look into Justine's sparkling green eyes was all it took to send Raquel's senses into overdrive. Justine's fingers glided along her slick folds, as Raquel guided her lover's face to her wetness. She parted herself with two fingers, still clasping the back of Justine's head as she felt her lover's flattened tongue running along her sex.

She teetered slightly as she watched Justine feasting upon her. "So good," Raquel whispered while Justine teased her clit with her teeth and tongue, before sucking it into her mouth. Raquel bit down on her bottom lip as Justine sucked her harder. "Hurry, baby," she pleaded, knowing that their time alone together was limited. Justine's tongue curled and pressed against the opening of her warm wet center. "Yes," Raquel begged, opening herself even further.

Raquel's hips rocked when Justine's tongue glided inside her, and she trembled as Justine thrust in and out. Justine gripped Raquel's backside firmly, and Raquel's pleas escalated as her body neared the edge. When she was about to fall into the abyss, Justine's tongue slipped from her body, her fingers quickly replacing it. Raquel exploded as Justine's fingers and mouth took her.

The bursts of sensation had weakened her until she could barely stand. She helped Justine to her feet and kissed her fervently, savoring the taste of her own passion on her lover's lips. "Tonight," she promised before they had to break apart and join the others for dinner.

"Tonight," Justine echoed.

September, 1964

"'Can't buy me love, love'" Bonnie sang boldly, walking into her dorm room.

"But you would if you could," Teneil teased her, without looking up from the textbook she was studying.

"*Querida*, I'm hurt." Bonnie faked a gasp and batted her eyelashes at her unconcerned friend.

"Save it for someone who'll fall for your smarmy line of bullshit," Teneil said with a snort. "I've known you too long."

Bonnie shrugged and climbed onto Teneil's bed, kneeling so that her shadow obstructed the other girl's view.

"Do you mind?" Teneil tried to move away from her playful roommate. "I know you can sleep through your classes and still ace them, but some of us have to study."

"Teneil, my dear old friend," Bonnie said, snatching the textbook away from her, "classes haven't even begun, and all you've done since we arrived is study. This is college! You need to lighten up."

"I just don't want to let my parents down," Teneil said, as Bonnie placed her hands firmly on the other girl's shoulders.

"You won't, I promise. Now, guess what we're doing tonight?"

"Don't you have a date?" Teneil asked. "Speaking of which, you really need to start being discreet, before you get your pompous ass tossed out of here."

"I'm just being friendly and enjoying my new-found freedom," Bonnie responded sweetly.

"You're a slut, and you know it."

"I come here to rescue you from yourself, and you insult my character?" Bonnie gasped with mock indignation.

"Bonita," Teneil said, as Bonnie stretched out on the bed, "you are my dearest friend in the whole world. I've known you since first grade, but you, my friend, are a pig. Who do you think you are, Rock Hudson?"

"Only if it means I get to sleep with Doris Day." Bonnie chuckled, snuggling up to Teneil, and caressing her stomach.

"Is there any woman you wouldn't sleep with?" Teneil asked.

"You," Bonnie said, her smile fading. "Because you like boys."

"That hasn't stopped you from trying." Teneil laughed.

"Or succeeding," Bonnie said, and nudged her, remembering the one night they had shared.

"Sometimes I wish I were a lesbian." Teneil sighed. "But you'd only break my heart."

"Never," Bonnie said.

"Liar."

"See, you know me too well." Bonnie laughed. She took a deep breath and returned to a kneeling position. "Sometimes I wish I could find love. To be as happy as you and Ronald are. Maybe when I grow up?"

"You are grown up." Teneil changed the subject. "So, what are we doing tonight?"

"It's Rush Night."

"And?" Teneil asked, looking confused until she grasped what Bonnie was implying. "You want to pledge? Have you lost your mind? I'm black, and you're Puerto Rican. There isn't a sorority house that would take either of us."

"The world is changing," Bonnie said. "Time to push for more changes. Isn't that what you told me the day President Johnson signed the Civil Rights Act?"

"Who's the girl?" Teneil asked suspiciously.

"No girl this time," Bonnie said, taking Teneil's hands in her own. "I want to at least try to get in. Sigma Kappa stresses academic excellence. And have you seen the house they live in?"

"The big one on Higgins Hill that looks like a plantation," Teneil answered. "How could I miss it, or the stream of white girls going in and out of it?"

"Two years ago, they accepted a Jewish girl," Bonnie said. "Sigma Kappa is for women who want to do well in school. They focus on academic success and charity work. No drinking, no late night parties, no boys in your room,"

"The last one should be a cake walk for you."

"I want to try. These girls make lifelong connections. They're nothing like Delta Gammas, who are only interested in drinking and finding husbands. Sigma Kappa is for eggheads like us."

"You mean like you," Teneil said.

"This will be good for us. Please? Come on. Who took you to see the Beatles last summer?"

"Who made me sit through Mary Poppins three times just because Julie Andrews has great tits?"

"Well, she does." Bonnie shrugged. "But Julie Andrews's tits aside, it'll be fun."

"All right, all right, we'll pledge."

December, 2005

Raquel was on edge. Coming home for the holiday had been a mixed blessing. She missed her family, but she felt trapped. Her parents still treated her the way they did when she lived with them. She had been on her own for months now, living a new life, not following her parents' rules. To add to the mix, she missed Justine. Being separated from her lover was unbearable.

She was caught in an emotional tug-of-war each time her mother asked her what was wrong, and if she had met any nice boys at school. *I have to tell them.* She braced herself for the inevitable fallout when she finally told her parents the truth. "It took me eighteen years to come out, okay? No need to rush things," she muttered under her breath when her mother once again inquired about her social life.

"Raquel, I know something is going on," her mother said, trapping her in the family room. "If you've met a nice young man, why not tell us about him?"

"Well..." Raquel felt the walls closing in on her.

"Raquel, telephone!" her brother, Simon, shouted from the kitchen.

"Sorry, Mom. I should get that before Simon hangs up on whoever is calling," she blurted, and raced out of the room. "Hello," she said, answering the call.

"Hello, beautiful." Justine's voice sounded like a purr over the phone line.

"Hey." Raquel couldn't stop the silly grin that appeared when she heard her lover's voice.

"You sound tense," Justine said. "Is everything okay?"

"No," Raquel answered. "I know I've only been gone a couple of months, but I feel out of place here, and I'm getting tired of dodging Mom's questions about my love life. I don't know what to tell her."

"Hey, who says you have to tell her? This is still new for you."

"Wait, what are you saying?" Raquel panicked.

"Hold on," Justine said "I'm not ditching you. I'm only saying you've just realized that you like women. That's hard enough, without adding in ghostly encounters and surviving your first semester in college. I know, trust me. I do know how hard going home for the first time can be. What I'm trying to say is, don't tell your family anything you're not ready to tell them."

"Well, there you go being all reasonable." Raquel sighed, and a wave of relief washed over her. "You know, I think I just needed to hear your voice. I miss you."

"I miss you too," Justine said, in a low voice. Raquel shivered at the deep, sultry sound. "You can call me anytime, day or night, whenever you need to talk or, well, for anything."

"What I need is to study," Raquel, said, and was pleased when Justine gasped.

"Oh, babe, I wish we could right now." Justine's panting carried clearly over the line. "Is your family close by?"

"Lurking all over the place," Raquel whispered, seeing her mother out of the corner of her eye.

"Bummer. I was about to tell you how much I want you. How I want to undress you and run my hands all over your naked body before I lick every inch of you."

"Stop!" Raquel cringed as her father entered the kitchen. She knew she must have turned a bright shade of red when he waved to her. Struggling to catch her breath, she raced away with the cordless phone, trying to find a place to talk in private.

"What?" Justine continued. "I was just saying how much I wanted to hold your naked body and roll your nipples between my fingers."

"Just…" Raquel ducked into the laundry room.

"Wow, you really can't talk. Sorry about that," Justine apologized.

"They follow me everywhere. The way they hover over me, you'd think I was lost at sea, not away at school," Raquel said wryly. "I really want to finish this conversation. How late will you be up tonight?"

"Late. I'm getting together with some friends," Justine said, and Raquel's heart sank. "Call my cell when you're about to go to bed."

"Really?" Raquel brightened.

"Yes, really. I meant what I said. I miss you. It's hard enough at school, having to be careful all the time, but not seeing you is killing me."

"Ditto," Raquel said as her mother popped into the laundry room. "I have to go," she added hurriedly, and exchanged a quick goodbye with her lover. "Yes, Mom?" she asked, clearing her expression.

"I just came to tell you dinner is ready," Mrs. Albright said, smiling at her frustrated daughter.

"So Albright, do you want to tell me what has you so agitated?" Toni, her best friend, inquired. It was only a couple of days before Christmas, and all Raquel could think about was how much she missed Justine, and what her parents going to say when they found out the truth. She had gone out a few times with friends from high school, but each time she felt strange; she had changed, and not only in her sudden sexual awakening. Things just weren't the same. She was growing in a different direction.

"I can't explain it," she finally said, her eyes darting around the familiar surroundings of the coffee shop. "I feel… alienated."

"I know. I feel it too. I went out with Connie and Gail the other night, and I don't know what it was, but I felt like I was hanging around with a couple of strangers, not people I grew up with. Maybe it's because they didn't go on to college or leave town."

"I don't get it either," Raquel said. "I went over to Maryanne's new apartment. It's nice, but I just felt out of place."

"All part of growing up, I guess." Toni laughed, putting Raquel at ease. Toni was the only one of her old friends she felt mildly comfortable with. "How is school going for you? You wrote about how well you were doing in class, and that you got into that sorority."

"That's not all that happened," Raquel said softly, bracing herself to tell the truth. She sensed that she could trust Toni; still, she wasn't certain that her old friend would be accepting of the news.

"What is it?"

Raquel bit down on her bottom lip as she mustered her courage. "I met someone," she finally blurted. Toni leaned back and gave her a knowing look.

"And?" Toni prompted, when Raquel didn't expand on her statement.

"And they're terrific." Raquel felt her courage slipping away.

"They?"

"She," Raquel managed to say. "Justine. She's terrific."

Raquel waited tensely for Toni's reaction. Toni just stared, her expression never wavering. Finally, she released a breath.

"It's about freaking time," Toni said. "I was beginning to think that you were a clueless idiot."

"You knew?" Raquel was startled that her friend had known and never thought to suggest it to her.

"Duh?" Toni laughed heartily. "Hey, chill. I'm just happy that you finally figured it out. So, tell me about Justine."

"But how did you know? I didn't even know."

"Let's just say your dabblings weren't as discreet as you thought they were," Toni said with a smug grin. "And I just knew, okay? So tell me about the girl."

"You just sucked all of the fun out of this for me."

"Oh, yeah." Toni laughed again. "Fun? You looked like you were ready to have a panic attack. Tell me about her."

"She's a sophomore," Raquel said, knowing she had a dreamy look on her face. "And one of my sorority sisters, which is very convenient. And not so convenient. She's smart and beautiful and amazing."

Toni listened to Raquel praise Justine's qualities for over an hour. Raquel was beaming by the time she finished. "She sounds fantastic," Toni said enthusiastically. "I can't wait to meet this wonder woman."

"I think the two of you will hit it off," Raquel said, relieved to have finally told someone. Not only had she shared her good news, but Toni had accepted it without question or judgment.

"Do you think I should tell my parents?" she asked, looking for guidance. If Toni could accept her lifestyle, perhaps there was a chance that her family might see the light as well.

"I honestly don't know," Toni said. "I mean, you know them better than I do. It must be killing you not to be honest with them."

"But what if they freak?"

"I wish I knew what to tell you. Maybe they won't, but then again, maybe they will."

"It would be easier if I could ease them into it," Raquel said.

Toni laughed and shook her head. "Just how does one ease one's parents into something like this?"

"I don't have a clue. I really wish Mom would stop asking me about the man in my life. It's killing me. I don't like lying to her. I'm just so terrified of how she and my dad will react.

December 25, 2005

Christmas dinner was wonderful. The entire family was gathered around the table, laughing and enjoying the festive occasion. Everyone that is, except Raquel, who was growing weary of her parents', and now her grandparents', constant inquiries into her social life. Raquel's sudden announcement that she wouldn't be joining the family for the traditional New Year's celebration only added fuel to the fire. She had told them she was going to a party with Toni, and would be spending the weekend with her. In truth she was meeting Justine and Toni was covering for her.

"Raquel, it's a family tradition," her mother said. "You know, your father and I aren't fools."

"What do you mean?"

"Sweetheart, I was young once," Mrs. Albright said. "There's no party, and you know it. If you want to see your young man for the holiday, I don't see any reason for you to lie. Invite him down."

"He can sleep on the pullout in the den," her father suggested.

"Um, Dad..." Raquel tried to choose her words carefully.

"Raquel, we want to meet him," her mother said firmly. "I don't know why you're hiding him from us. We don't care if he's one of these Goths with tattoos, or whatever you kids are into these days. We don't care if he's of color. Raquel, we trust you."

"Okay," Raquel said slowly. "Mother, there is no him."

"How can you sit there and lie to us?" Mrs. Albright looked hurt. "There's obviously a boy. Who else would you be talking to constantly? Whoever he is, we want to meet him."

"For the last time, I don't have a boyfriend," Raquel blurted in frustration. "I have a girlfriend."

All conversation stopped and the entire Albright clan stared at Raquel. They sat there in agonizing silence until Raquel broke it. "Please pass the butter?" she asked, and her brother quickly complied, but dinner carried on in an awkward silence.

There was no further discussion regarding Raquel's announcement, only a strange, uncomfortable feeling. Raquel's parents kept a close eye on her, preventing her from making any telephone calls that evening. The following day, after what began as a civilized conversation, it was decided that it would be best if Raquel didn't return home until she had, as her mother put it, come to her senses.

The rest of her vacation was spent trying to sneak out or use the telephone. Oddly enough, her younger brother became an ally. The only thing he wanted to know was whether or not her girlfriend was hot. Other than that, he didn't seem to care.

February, 2006

"Do you know that I never read the plaques they put up on the buildings around campus?" Maggie said, as she sauntered into her room and found Justine and Raquel studying on Justine's bed.

Raquel said a silent thank-you that they were really studying this time.

"Who does?" Justine asked, scowling up at her roommate.

"Today, I did," Maggie said.

"Goodie for you." Justine made a show of returning her attention to her textbook.

"It was at the crisis center," Maggie prattled on.

"The Sigma Kappa Crisis Center?" Raquel asked, seeming to take an interest in Maggie's ramblings. "I was thinking of volunteering there, since it's one of the Kappa alumnae's pet projects. Is the training hard?"

"The training's easy. It's the work that's heartbreaking," Maggie answered. "We can talk about that later. Right now I want to tell you about the plaque."

"Fine." Justine sighed, knowing that her old friend could be like a dog with a bone. "Gee, Maggie, will you tell us about the plaque outside the crisis center?"

"Did you know that the official name isn't The Sigma Kappa Crisis Center?" Maggie began to rifle through her backpack.

"Since I've never been there, no, I didn't know that," Justine said.

"Everyone just calls it The Sigma Kappa Crisis Center," Maggie went on. "If you read the plaque, you'll see that it's The Bonita Sanchez Crisis Center, founded by the sisters of Sigma Kappa in memory of their fallen sister."

"What?" Raquel perked up. What with the demands of school and her fledgling romance with Justine, her research into Bonnie's past had fallen by the wayside. Now, Maggie had stumbled on what sounded like a useful piece of information.

"I researched the center's archives in between calls," Maggie said, pulling out her notes from her backpack. "It began as nothing more than an extra telephone line here at the Kappa House, on November 1, 1965. Mostly due to the efforts of Jennifer Lowell and Teneil Watts-Johnson, it grew to become one of the most effective campus crisis centers in the country. The psychology department took over running it in 1978. That's all I could find out, except for a long list of awards, and that both Jennifer and Teneil have been very active in supporting the center over the years."

"Justine, Teneil Watts was on the list we found," Raquel said. "I think she pledged the same year Bonnie did."

"She graduated in 1968, so that makes sense," Maggie said. "You know, since I'm a psych major and crisis intervention is my main focus, it wouldn't be out of line for me to contact these fine ladies and ask them a few questions."

"Can I go with you?" asked Raquel.

"Since you're thinking about volunteering, it might be a good idea. Jennifer isn't a suspect, from what you told me, so why don't I try to find out if Teneil is still alive?"

"What?" She frowned at Justine, who was staring at both of them.

"I was just trying to figure out which one of you is Nancy Drew and which one is George."

"Screw Nancy Drew, we're Charlie's Angels," Maggie boasted.

March, 2006

"Try to act casual," Maggie whispered as they entered the elegant office. Raquel's eagerness had been almost rabid ever since Maggie had set up the interview. "Thank you for seeing us, Mrs. Johnson," Maggie said to the elegant, dark-skinned woman.

"Anything for a Kappa sister." Teneil offered them seats.

Raquel couldn't believe that the woman seated before them was almost the same age as her grandmother. "Remember that sisters help each other," Teneil advised the young students, smiling. "I understand you want to know about the crisis center."

"Yes," Raquel said, jumping in eagerly.

"Good. It's been a project of mine for almost forty years."

"How did you get involved with the center?" Maggie asked.

"I had personal reasons," Teneil said. "Bonita Sanchez was a very dear friend of mine. What you're probably not aware of, since the sorority doesn't like to discuss it, is that Bonnie committed suicide. What was so disturbing was that none of us saw it coming. To all outward appearances, she seemed to be truly happy and living life to its fullest. Her suicide shocked and devastated me."

Raquel bit her tongue to keep herself from blurting out that it wasn't suicide. "How close were the two of you?" Raquel asked, as Maggie elbowed her in the ribs.

"Very close," Teneil said. "We grew up together. I took her death very hard. She was the one who talked me into applying for college and pledging the sorority. I thought she was crazy. As a black woman, I didn't think any sorority would accept me. I didn't know I was actually the fourth woman of color to become a Kappa sister. Bonnie was the first Hispanic woman. Her death was such a waste. Everyone loved her."

"So I've heard," Raquel muttered under her breath, only to receive another sharp jolt to her ribs. "Please, tell us about her," she urged. Raquel couldn't help wondering why, if Teneil and Bonnie were so close, Bonnie couldn't cross her off the list of people who might have wanted to harm her.

Teneil's face clouded as she continued. "Bonnie was bright, beautiful, and full of life. She was pre-law, and wanted to become a civil rights attorney. She would have been damned good at it, too. It's funny when I think about how important the crisis center has become. The sisters had talked about starting a hotline before Bonnie died, but Bonnie thought there were more important issues to focus on. It was 1964, and the world was changing so fast. There was the war, the

Warren Commission was telling us that Lee Harvey Oswald used special bullets to assassinate President Kennedy, the sexual revolution was going on, and in the midst of all that, we were trying to grow up. It was a truly amazing time. She took me to see the Beatles," Teneil added the last with a smile.

"What?" Maggie asked.

"She took me to see the Beatles." Teneil laughed. "Ever since we saw them on Ed Sullivan, I was nuts over Ringo. She knew that, and got us tickets to see them. I don't know how, but she got fifth-row seats. Then again, Bonnie could be very resourceful. I just…" Her words trailed off. "I still can't believe she took her own life. Maybe if we hadn't had that argument…"

"Would you please tell us about the argument?" Raquel asked, though she didn't really want to push this woman, who was still in so much pain.

"It was about a week before she died. Bonnie was a very giving and caring person, except when it came to romance. She was gay."

"You didn't approve of her lifestyle?" Raquel bristled.

"Good Lord, her sexuality wasn't a problem for me." Teneil said. "I even fell victim to her charms once. It was the way she treated women. For someone so loving and caring, she was a real jerk when it came to women. She always had been, but I'd had enough of comforting her spurned lovers, and I told her off. Maybe if I hadn't, she wouldn't have done what she did."

Raquel listened as Maggie changed the subject back to the crisis center. She hated the way she had pushed the kindly woman for information. It was quite clear that Bonnie's death had wounded her deeply. Not for the first time, Raquel wondered if digging into the past was a good idea. If Bonnie's killer really was dead, what was the point?

"What an amazing woman," Maggie exclaimed on the drive back to campus. "She started her business with nothing but an idea and a lot of hard work."

"I hated bringing Bonnie up," Raquel said. "Can you imagine how she must feel?"

"She seems to still blame herself. One good thing that came out of this tragedy was the crisis center. They not only counsel potential suicides, but also help those who are left behind. Guilt is a common reaction."

"Bonnie didn't commit suicide," Raquel muttered. "But I'm not so certain that finding out the truth will do anyone any good."

"Mrs. Johnson would want to know the truth, and maybe it will bring some peace to Bonnie's family," Maggie said.

"I just don't know anymore."

"Someone got away with murder," Maggie stressed, "and that someone hurt Justine."

"You're right," Raquel finally agreed. She needed to know who had hurt her lover. Perhaps by discovering the truth, they could put an end to the attacks. When they returned to the sorority house, they filled Justine in on the details. Maggie made arrangements to meet with Jennifer Lowell the following week. Ms. Lowell was so thrilled by their enthusiasm that she offered to drive down to the campus to meet with them.

That night, Justine tried bribing Maggie to go to the movies. "I'm sorry, guys, I have a lot of studying to do," she said.

"Bummer," Justine replied.

"We could go up to my room," Raquel suggested.

"I'm sorry," Justine whispered. "I just can't get comfortable up there."

"I understand." Raquel placed a comforting hand on her lover's arm. "Anyway, I need to get some real studying done."

From the moment Raquel entered her room, she missed Justine's touch. She understood that her lover was uncomfortable spending time in the same room where she had been attacked, and besides that, it would cause talk. She resigned herself to studying. By eleven, she was caught up and very wide awake, so she decided to go through her notes on the class of '64. *Must have been quite an experience, being in college back then,* she thought, looking through the pictures she had photocopied from an old yearbook.

October, 1964

"A moment of your time," Bonnie said, panting as she caught up with the lanky student who was hurrying across campus.

"What?" Regina snarled.

"Nothing special, Sister. I just wanted to compliment you."

"Really?" Regina looked stunned.

"Yes," Bonnie said with a playful grin. "You're so smart, it's no wonder you're pre-med. I'm sure you'll make a fine doctor some day. But if I may offer you some information, it might prove helpful in your future career in medicine."

"What are you up to?" Regina's eyes narrowed.

"I just thought you should know that sound travels," Bonnie said in an innocent voice.

"Huh?"

"It's true," Bonnie continued, with a wide-eyed expression. "So when you call someone a spick or a dyke, other people can hear you."

"I... um," Regina stammered.

"My first instinct was to cause you physical harm," Bonnie said calmly. "But the great Dr. King teaches us that would be the wrong course of action. In the spirit of Dr. King's teachings, therefore, I wish to simply explain that, first of all, no more hand jobs for you."

"Keep your voice down." Regina glanced around quickly.

"Second, if you even think about using such hateful words again, I will tell everyone how much you enjoyed our mornings together," Bonnie said.

"Listen, you little—"

"Little what?" Bonnie egged her on.

"I could have you blackballed. You're not a Kappa yet," Regina threatened.

"Fine." Bonnie shrugged. "There are more important things in life, such as dignity and honor. I know you don't understand these things, just as I don't understand how those harmful words slip so easily from lips that once begged me to kiss them. The things you said aren't just words. They're weapons. You might want to think about that. Dr. King is right, I feel so much better, and I didn't need to beat the snot out of you."

Regina's voice was low and caustic. "I can't believe you have the nerve to blackmail me, especially when it's my word against yours. You'll pay for this."

Having already had her say, Bonnie simply shrugged and walked away.

March, 2006

"Let's see." Raquel perused the list she was preparing. "Jennifer Lowell was downstairs and couldn't have killed Bonnie." She glanced around the room, almost expecting to find Bonnie waiting for her. It seemed strange not to have the ghost visiting her any longer. "Next is Teneil Watts, not very likely, since she was Bonnie's best friend and is still alive. Next is Regina Becker," she continued, booting up her computer. She typed Regina's name into a search engine and found an old obituary from the Youngstown Journal.

Dr. Regina Becker-Hoffman died September 15, 1989, from breast cancer, leaving behind a husband, two children, and four grandchildren. "Could be her," Raquel said. *Dr. Becker received her undergraduate degree in 1966; in 1968, she left medical school to join the Peace Corps. Dr. Becker received her medical degree from Stanford University School of Medicine in 1976, and maintained a successful practice in Youngstown, Ohio, until her illness forced her to retire. In lieu of flowers, the family requests that donations be made to the American Cancer Society and to the Bonita Sanchez Crisis Center.*

"I wonder if she remembered Bonnie because she cared for her, or out of guilt," Raquel mused. Quitting for the night, she turned off her computer and climbed into bed.

A week later, she was sitting in the library at the sorority house reviewing her list of names when she heard a sultry voice speak in her ear. "Do I want to know what you're doing?" Justine sat down beside her, and Raquel handed over the list. "Regina Becker, Sheila Collins, Jerusha Davies, Carla Lipton, and Rita Summers. Let me guess—they all died in 1989?"

"Jerusha died in late 1988, run over by a snow plow," Raquel said.

"What a way to go." Justine shivered.

"Regina and Carla died of cancer, Rita had a heart attack, and Sheila was killed in a car accident."

"Anyone topping the list?" Justine asked.

"Hard to say, without having met any of them." Raquel tapped her pen nervously. "Regina was a doctor, but spent time in the Peace Corps—not exactly the vindictive type."

"Not unless you crossed her," said a commanding voice from behind them.

Raquel and Justine spun around and saw a husky, gray-haired woman standing next to Maggie. The woman spoke again. "Teneil said something was up. Do you want to explain to me why you're looking into my classmates' deaths?"

"This is Jennifer Lowell," Maggie said.

This is bad, Raquel thought.

October, 1964

"Don't even think about it," Sheila told the smiling freshman, who was watching a tall brunette walk across campus.

"And how is it that you know my thoughts?" Bonnie chuckled.

"Because you only think about one thing," Sheila said, sitting down next to her. "Jennifer Lowell is out of your league, and from what I understand, she's very spoken for."

"You sound jealous," Bonnie said.

"Why haven't I seen you?" Sheila asked.

"I've been busy with school and pledging. You should understand that." Bonnie wished Sheila would take the hint and give up.

She had stopped by Sheila's room late one night after completing a task, which was a nice way of saying that one of the sisters had given her a hideous assignment. She was looking for Carla, Sheila's roommate. Bonnie didn't miss the flirtatious hints that Sheila gave her from the moment she entered the room.

She sat down on the bed and brushed an errant lock of hair back from Sheila's face. The older girl practically swooned at the gesture. When Bonnie leaned over and brushed her lips lightly against Sheila's, the offer was eagerly accepted and they began making out. They rolled around on the bed, and Bonnie grew worried that someone would walk in on them. Her touches grew more insistent, and again, Sheila accepted her offer. Bonnie guided Sheila's hand under her skirt, and moaned deeply when she felt Sheila cupping her mound. Her own hand slipped under Sheila's skirt. They groped one another until their fingers reached past the elastic bands of their panties and they were stroking each other. After Sheila climaxed, Bonnie had thanked her for a delightful evening and left. Now she couldn't seem to get rid of the girl.

"Bonnie?" Carla called as she approached them. "Do you want to get a soda or something?"

"Groovy," Bonnie agreed readily, picking up her books to follow the blonde.

"My roommate?" Sheila became angry as she watched them walk away. "Damn her."

"According to the Bible, she already is," someone behind her said. Sheila was stunned when she turned to find one of her sorority sisters, Rita Summers. She stiffened, wondering just how much of the conversation Rita had heard. "Relax," Rita said. "Our newest pledge has been making quite an impression on the entire house."

"You too?" Sheila gasped.

"I was curious," Rita said, shrugging.

"The whole house?" Sheila felt completely miserable.

"Sally calls her Don Juanita."

"I believed her." Sheila started to cry.

"Hey." Rita put her arm around the sobbing woman. "Don't let her get to you."

"At least I don't have to worry about her becoming a Kappa," Sheila said, drying her cheeks with her palms. "Someone will blackball her for sure."

"I don't know. She's damned smart. Hell, she's even helping me with my calculus class."

"But she's only a freshman," Sheila said, her brows lifting.

"Told you she was smart," Rita said. "Even though she can't keep her pants on, I really like her."

"She's a bitch."

"Not really, but she *is* just a lowly pledge," Rita added, a mischievous smile lighting her face.

"What do you have in mind?" Sheila perked up.

"If a guy treated us this way, what would we do?"

"Get even." Sheila's eyes gleamed.

"Revenge it is." They shook hands on it and began to plot.

Later that night, Bonnie dragged herself into her dorm room dripping wet and covered with mud. "You look like shit," Teneil scowled.

"Good. I'd really hate to feel this bad then have the nerve to look good." Bonnie moaned, and yanked off her sopping wet tennis shoes.

"What happened?" Teneil tossed a clean towel at her.

"Damn task." Bonnie tried to dry off, but just smeared the mud around.

"They're really putting you through the wringer," Teneil said. "I thought some of the stuff I had to do was tough, but these girls are targeting you."

"It's personal," Bonnie agreed. "Women! I'll never understand them."

"Bonnie, you know I love you like a sister, but your callous attitude is wearing thin." Teneil's temper flared. "Maybe if you started treating women with respect, these things wouldn't happen."

"I do," Bonnie protested.

"No, you don't!" Teneil shouted. "You sweet-talk them until they fall all over you, then you cast them off. You need to stop. Promise me that you'll keep your legs crossed until Hell Night."

"You want to get into Sigma Kappa, huh?" Bonnie smiled.

"Yes, I do," Teneil said. "At first I thought the Kappas were nothing but a bunch of air-headed debutantes. But they aren't. They really want to make a difference, so promise me that you'll stop trying to sleep your way through the sorority. What you're doing is wrong."

"How is it wrong?" Bonnie asked. "I'm a passionate person."

"You're a jerk," Teneil said and stormed out of the dorm room.

The following morning, Bonnie promised her she would change. Deep down, she really wanted to change, but she was helpless around an attractive woman. By Hell Night, she was back to her old ways. Then it happened. The one woman she wanted didn't want her, and she began to realize that Teneil was right.

"Teneil, help me find out about her, I beg you," Bonnie asked.

"No, I won't. Do your own dirty work."

"I tell you, I've changed."

"No, you haven't. I've spent too many nights comforting crying women instead of studying. No more. I won't clean up after you."

"I've changed, I... um... er..." Bonnie stammered. "I've stopped, I swear."

"When? Last week?"

"I just want to know who she's seeing," Bonnie pleaded.

"I'm not going to help you break up someone's relationship," Teneil said. "Do me a favor, and don't talk to me until you grow up."

"You don't understand." Bonnie's words went unheard, because Teneil had walked away. "I think I have grown up," she whispered to the empty hallway.

March, 2006

"Shall I repeat the question?" Jennifer's tone was icy.

"No, I was just trying to think how to answer you without sounding like a complete lunatic," Raquel said.

Jennifer scowled. "Teneil Watts called me. She said you visited her to find out about the crisis center. After you left, she realized that most of your questions were about Bonnie Sanchez. Now I find you going over a list of dead Kappas. What kind of sick game are the three of you playing?"

"Hey!" Justine protested. Her shoulders slumped when Jennifer's cold gray eyes glared back at her. "I'm sorry, Ms. Lowell, but we really can explain."

"This had better be good."

"Bonnie didn't commit suicide," Raquel said. "She—"

"That's it!" Jennifer snarled, making the three students recoil in shock. "Bonnie did commit suicide. I don't know why, but she did. Do you want to know how I know? I found her. She was hanging from a beam in her room."

"There isn't a beam in that room," Raquel said.

"Not any longer. The ceiling was lowered and the beam covered up. The college was afraid someone else might do what she did."

"I hate this," Raquel confessed wearily, watching tears well up in the older woman's eyes. "Ms. Lowell, what if I can convince you to at least hear me out?"

"Too late." Jennifer began to walk away.

"The night before she died, she slept with you!" Raquel called after her, desperate to keep her from leaving. Jennifer stopped and turned to look at her. Raquel pressed on, hoping for the best. "She was wearing your clothes when she died because you tore her dress."

"How did you know that?" Jennifer asked, gaping. "I never told anyone about that night."

"Bonnie told me."

"I beg your pardon?" Jennifer looked angry again.

"This is where it gets really strange," Justine broke in.

"This is where it gets strange? At least in my day, we could blame it on drugs. What the hell is going on here?"

"I think you'd better sit down," Maggie said.

"I'm sorry to drag you into this," Raquel apologized. "You must have heard the stories about people seeing Bonnie."

"Yes," Jennifer said, taking a seat

"I'm in her old room," Raquel said. "I've seen her."

"I roomed there last year," Justine added. "I've seen her too."

"You know, it does sound like something she would do." Jennifer grinned wryly. "Lurking in the shadows so she could watch girls undress." She laughed. "Bonnie was a sweetheart, but she was also—"

"A pig," Justine and Raquel said together.

"We found that out." Justine said, blushing.

"She was starting to change," Jennifer said. "Bonnie was an enigma. Intellectually, she was Stephen Hawking. Emotionally, she was a teenaged boy. I had hoped that someday she would grow up, and that maybe after she graduated we could..." Her words trailed off. "I never got the chance to find out. That last night, when we were together, she told me she was falling in love with me, but I didn't believe her. She'd been through almost every girl in the house. How could I believe her? Does she really haunt your room? Can I see her?"

"No," Raquel said, sadly. "She disappears from the first of November until Rush Week."

"So she appears here from the anniversary of when she first arrived until the day she died," Jennifer said thoughtfully. "Why are you so convinced it wasn't suicide?"

"Let me start at the beginning,"

October, 1964

"Come join your sisters," Jennifer Lowell announced, amused as the five freshmen pulled the hoods from their heads. It was traditional to kidnap the new members and drag them across campus in the middle of the night. They looked idiots strolling around the campus in their pajamas, and they knew it. The startled looks and hair flying everywhere were icing on the cake. Only one of the new members had the nerve to look presentable. Jennifer snickered at Bonnie, the pledge who had been nothing but trouble since Rush Night. It amazed Jennifer that the girl had survived the torture the other Kappa girls had heaped on her.

"I can't believe my little sister made it," Carrie said, as they handed out hot chocolate and blankets. "I've never seen a pledge go through so much."

"She brought it on herself," Jennifer said. "But she made it."

"She's going to be a real asset," Carrie asserted. "Bonnie's brilliant, and capable of anything."

"Yes. Now if you can just convince her to curb her wayward attitude, she'll be an amazing adult," Jennifer said. "I'm serious, Carrie. If word got out, the entire house would be in jeopardy. I've never seen someone piss off so many women in such a short time. Still, she is—"

"Don't go there." Carrie laughed and gave her friend a playful nudge. "That's how all the trouble started. Speaking of my tawdry little sister—" Carrie chuckled as Bonnie approached them, while Jennifer sighed and excused herself. "Welcome, Bonnie, you certainly earned your place in this house. Now, promise me that you'll behave."

"I don't know what you mean," Bonnie said, grinning impishly.

"Oh, yes, you do. Your shenanigans have won you a room all to yourself."

"I thought only senior members have their own rooms? I was hoping that Teneil and I would room together," Bonnie said in a troubled voice. "We grew up together and—"

And college is a place where you can expand your horizons," Carrie cut her off. "Besides, Teneil isn't exactly on your side these days. Not a word. All the bullshit you went through was your own doing, and you know it. We've decided to put you in the small room in the attic. We rarely use it, since it's minuscule, but we felt it would be safer to keep you on your own until next year. Maybe by then you'll have learned to play well with others."

"Oh, but I do play well with others," Bonnie murmured, in a sultry voice.

"Yeah, I know, and that's the problem." Carrie groaned. "I'm proud of the way you rose to every challenge thrown at you. I've never seen a pledge targeted the way you were, and you never complained. I'm hoping that you've grown from the experience."

"But in the meantime, I'm banished to the attic." Bonnie laughed, then her expression turned serious. "Thank you, Carrie. I know you stuck your neck out to keep me from being blackballed, and I promise I won't let you down."

"I hope not." Carrie sighed, noticing the not-so-subtle glares being cast in Bonnie's direction as she walked away.

"Hi, Bonnie," Jennifer had sneaked into the kitchen to grab an after-hours snack and found her new sister already there.

"Hi," Bonnie said, shoving her sweaty palms into her pockets. She couldn't understand why she got so nervous around Jennifer. She had been with so many women, she knew just what to say and do to get them to fall into her arms. Around Jennifer, though, she felt clumsy and couldn't even form a decent sentence.

"I don't get it," Jennifer said, teasing the younger girl. "You're not the shy type, from what I've heard, but you blush like a schoolgirl every time I run into you. Maybe you aren't the tiger they say you are," she whispered in the stunned girl's ear.

Bonnie could only gulp in response.

"Just as I thought, all talk and no action." Jennifer ran her fingers down Bonnie's trembling forearm.

"You're playing with fire, *querida*," Bonnie said to the older girl.

"Maybe I like fire," Jennifer challenged, wrapping her arms around Bonnie's waist.

"You know what... um... what I've heard?" Bonnie stammered, "I've heard that you're spoken for."

Jennifer shook her head. "We broke up last spring, only she doesn't seem to understand that."

"I can understand why she would want to keep your heart," Bonnie whispered, snuggling closer, but Jennifer pulled away.

"You're as charming as they say," Jennifer chuckled. "But sorry, I'm not interested in being another notch on your belt." Bonnie was ready to protest, but Jennifer's fingers pressed against her lips and silenced her. "Goodnight, Sister." Jennifer flashed a cocky smirk and walked off, leaving a dazed Bonnie behind.

The following evening found Bonnie involved in a heated debate. "Goldwater? How can you even think about voting for him?" she said, disgusted. The presidential election was only a few weeks away, and it was all anyone on campus was talking about. Just over a year ago, everyone in the country had experienced a tragedy they still couldn't understand.

"Johnson will just keep us in the war," Regina argued. "And what about the space program? What's the point, other than trying to show the Russians up? We should be spending that money here, on Americans that need it."

"How unusually insightful of you," Bonnie said, complimenting the other girl. "I still say Goldwater will ruin this country."

"And I say the Democrats already have," Regina fumed.

"You would, but you still think Oswald acted alone," Bonnie said, laughing.

"He did!" Regina and Jerusha chorused.

"The gun was found where he worked," Jerusha argued. "He was acting strangely, and the shots were fired from the book depository. Who else could it have been?"

"Enough!" Mrs. Camden, the housemother, called out "It's late. Miss Sanchez, you have cleanup tonight."

"Yes, Mrs. Camden," Bonnie said, heading for the kitchen. "Oh, Regina, as a future doctor, you might want to listen to the Surgeon General." Bonnie nodded toward the cigarette Regina was about to light.

"Damn, I hate that." Regina grunted and tossed the unlit cigarette into the ashtray.

"Hate what?" Jerusha asked.

"The little twit really makes me think about stuff," Regina complained, her eyes on the cigarette she was craving.

"Is it true what they say about her?" Jerusha asked in a whisper.

"I don't know what you're talking about," Regina said, gathering her books.

"I've heard things. Carla and Sheila still aren't speaking to each other."

"I don't know anything about it," Regina lied. "I do know that she seems to have slowed down since she moved in here, if you get my drift."

"But if the rumors are true, we need to call a meeting," Jerusha suggested eagerly. "Have her expelled."

"And half the sorority along with her," Regina pointed out. "Trust me, don't say anything. I hate to admit it, but the little deviant really is a nice person. I have more important things to think about, like getting a new dress for Halloween. I was at Gorman's this week, and they had nothing."

"We should try Jordan Marsh," Jerusha suggested, and they made their way upstairs.

"You are really something else," Jennifer said, as Bonnie stepped out of the kitchen.

"That's what I've been trying to tell you." Bonnie played along, leaning against the wall.

"Everyone hates you and everyone loves you." Jennifer laughed lightly.

Bonnie shrugged, and tried to calm the rapid beating of her heart. "I'm complex."

"I can't believe you're eighteen."

"Why?" Bonnie asked. "Don't I act my age?"

"No," Jennifer answered. "Half the time you act like you're forty. The other half, you act like you're fourteen."

Bonnie struggled to find something to say. It amazed her how difficult it was to speak around Jennifer. "Come to my room," Jennifer invited in a sultry voice.

Once again, words failed Bonnie. She followed blindly. The moment Jennifer closed her bedroom door, Bonnie slid her arms around the older girl's body.

"Not so fast," said Jennifer.

"Huh?" Bonnie didn't understand why Jennifer was pulling away. Jennifer was a senior and had a single room; there would be no pesky roommate to interrupt them.

"Bonnie, do you ever take things slowly?" Jennifer asked, running her fingers through Bonnie's long, curly hair. "Just because I want to spend time with you doesn't mean anything is going to happen."

"It doesn't?" Bonnie was confused. Jennifer took her by the hand, led her to her bed, and they sat down.

"I like you," Jennifer said, stroking Bonnie's hand. "But that doesn't mean I'm going to jump into bed with you. I want to talk, so we can get to know one another."

"What?" Bonnie was still trying to wrap her mind around the unusual concept.

"You know, talk." Jennifer giggled. "Just because you're used to kissing a girl and having her fall at your feet doesn't mean that's what's going to happen with me. I'm not like other girls."

"No, you're not," Bonnie agreed. "What would you like to talk about?"

They talked for hours, until it was time for Bonnie to leave. "Good night," Bonnie said, feeling strange. The conversation had been enthralling, and she didn't want it to end. She was also trying to understand why the evening hadn't ended with both of them naked.

"Good night," Jennifer whispered, brushing her lips lightly against Bonnie's.

Bonnie reached out, only to have her advances nudged aside. "Good night," she repeated with an accepting smile, and stepped out of the room. *This growing up is going to take some getting used to.* For a moment, she thought she saw a movement in the hallway from the corner of her eye, but when no one came forward, she brushed it off as a figment of her imagination.

She pressed her fingers to lips that were still tingling from the gentle kiss Jennifer had given her. She wanted to rush up to Teneil's room and tell her everything, but it was too late. "And she isn't speaking to me," Bonnie grumbled, recalling their last argument.

She knew she would make up with Teneil, but that would have to wait. Right now, she needed to get some sleep. In the morning, she would have to review her notes for her first class. Somewhere between the nervous energy from spending the night talking to Jennifer and trying to get some sleep, Bonnie realized that Teneil wasn't the only woman in the Kappa house she needed to apologize to. *She's right, I'm a louse,* she thought, and drifted off to sleep.

As the days passed, tension remained between Bonnie and Teneil. Bonnie knew her friend would come around after she explained she really was changing. For the first time, it was the truth.

Spending time with Jennifer, she'd had an epiphany. She understood that Jennifer would be leaving in the spring, yet she couldn't resist either their late night talks or the good-night kisses Jennifer bestowed on her.

Bonnie smiled as she looked at herself in the full-length mirror in her room. "All dressed up," she murmured. "See, *Abuelo*, I'm doing it." Her beloved grandfather had lived just long enough to see her graduate from high school. "I'm going to make you so proud of me." She smoothed the pink satin dress she was wearing and donned a pair of gloves. With her hair neatly pulled back, and only a tiny ringlet caressing her neck, she exited her room.

She paused for a moment when she met Teneil and Mary. She and Teneil hugged quickly before joining the others downstairs, and Bonnie understood that the embrace was their way of apologizing to each another. Tomorrow, she would sit down and talk to her friend. Tonight she was caught up in the festivities of the occasion.

Another aspect of the elegant evening that captivated Bonnie was Jennifer. She looked positively enchanting, and they exchanged shy smiles throughout the evening. Bonnie made a silent wish that tonight she and Jennifer would finally become lovers.

At the end of the party, Jennifer gave her a simple nod, and Bonnie trailed after her, knowing by the look in Jennifer's eyes that tonight would be the night. Together, they quietly entered Jennifer's bedroom.

"*Bella*," Bonnie said and sighed happily as Jennifer cupped her face in her hands. Fueled by Jennifer's touch, she reached out for her, only to have her hands brushed away. "Please," Bonnie pleaded, her eyes fluttering shut as she spoke.

"You don't always have to lead the dance," Jennifer said, and kissed her.

Bonnie melted into Jennifer's kiss, clasping her waist as, for the first time, Jennifer parted her trembling lips. Bonnie moaned deeply, and her lover's velvet tongue slipped into her mouth. She felt safe in Jennifer's arms, and allowed her to lead their passion. Jennifer caressed Bonnie softly as she guided her toward the bed.

Bonnie chuckled when she felt her lover struggling with the zipper on her gown. "Tear it from my body," she said. "I need to feel you."

"You drive me insane," Jennifer said, kissing the nape of Bonnie's neck. She lowered her onto the bed and growled with frustration when the zipper still refused to yield. "This isn't happening." Jennifer gripped the zipper more tightly as they wrapped their legs around each other. Unable to temper her desires, she tore open the beautiful gown.

"Animal." Bonnie laughed, and Jennifer pushed the gown's straps off her shoulders.

"We'll get it fixed," Jennifer promised, sliding the dress to Bonnie's waist. The air left her lungs as she gazed down at her well-toned body. "Wow." Her fingers danced lightly across Bonnie's stomach.

"Can I see you?" Bonnie asked, running her fingers along the straps of Jennifer's gown.

"Yes," Jennifer said, giving her a brilliant smile, and turned around. Bonnie knelt behind her, and Jennifer trembled when she lowered the zipper of her gown and warm lips caressed the nape of her neck. She inhaled sharply when Bonnie's tongue drifted down her spine.

When Bonnie's nimble fingers released the clasp on her bra, she shivered. Bonnie kissed her shoulders tenderly, and she let Jennifer's gown fall to her waist. Warm hands slid along the curve of her body and cupped her breasts. Jennifer's body arched, and she turned to face her young lover.

She brushed her fingers along Bonnie's face and saw dark eyes linger on her half-naked body. Bonnie seemed to resist sharing control until Jennifer's touch coaxed her into it. Slowly, they undressed each other.

Jennifer hovered above her lover's naked body. She had seen fire in Bonnie's eyes before; an inferno blazed in them tonight. "I'm falling in love with you," Bonnie whispered.

Jennifer reluctantly dismissed the words as she lowered herself. She wanted to believe Bonnie, since she knew that she, too, was falling. But after hearing about Bonnie's numerous liaisons, she couldn't believe her. Then her mind emptied of reason as their naked skin touched for the first time. Their tongues and bodies became entangled, and they clung to each other.

Bonnie's senses went into overdrive as she allowed her lover to take things slowly. Everything about Jennifer mesmerized her, especially the gentleness of her touch and the way she curbed Bonnie's need to rush. The younger woman finally understood the difference between raw passion and making love.

Jennifer's body moved against her, painting the wetness of desire against her skin. Bonnie was gasping for air as soft breasts brushed against her. Jennifer kissed her face and neck in a slow, tantalizing way while Bonnie squirmed beneath her. "Jennifer," Bonnie gasped, her fingers kneading Jennifer's flesh. She tilted her head back as Jennifer's mouth fastened upon the hollow of her neck.

Bonnie's thigh moved up and pressed against her lover's wetness. Jennifer mirrored her actions. Their bodies moved together slowly as Jennifer captured Bonnie's nipple in her mouth. The rhythm of the dance grew more demanding, and they ground urgently against one another, seeking the release their bodies were screaming for. Bonnie felt her soul shattering as they climaxed in unison.

The hours passed quickly. They took turns leading each other's body into ecstasy, and Bonnie was nestled safely in Jennifer's arms when the window shade snapped up and revealed the faint glimmer of the sun struggling up to greet the sky. Bonnie started, certain she had seen a figure lurking in the tree just outside the window.

"What's wrong?" Jennifer asked.

"The light must have been playing tricks on me." Bonnie laughed at herself, and cradled Jennifer's naked body. "I thought there was someone watching us."

"Getting paranoid already?" Jennifer teased, and immediately drew Bonnie in for another lingering kiss. As they kissed, Jennifer reached across Bonnie's body and pulled the window shade back down.

The kiss deepened quickly, and their hands renewed their tender explorations. They entered each other, fingers stroking slowly until they were arching and crying out. Their hearts were racing, and they collapsed back onto the bed in a tender embrace.

The window shade snapped open again. "Time to go," Bonnie muttered regretfully, slipping from Jennifer's arms.

"I really need to have this fixed." Jennifer pulled the shade back down again while Bonnie examined her torn evening gown.

"Oops," Jennifer said, and grinned sheepishly when she saw the ruined gown.

"Could you lend me something to wear?" Bonnie laughed along with her. "I'm sure Mrs. Camden is already lurking around, and it might be hard to explain why I'm sneaking out of your room naked."

Jennifer dug through a pile of clean clothing while Bonnie carefully pushed the edge of the window shade aside and peeked out at the nearby tree. She shook her head, dismissing the notion that she had seen someone lurking in the branches. "Silly," she whispered, and turned back to her lover.

"Still looking for your Peeping Tom?" Jennifer teased, handing the younger girl a pair of jeans and a Sigma Kappa T-shirt.

"Maybe you have an admirer," Bonnie teased back as she dressed.

"One who likes to climb trees?" Jennifer scoffed.

"Curious George, perhaps." Bonnie chuckled and wrapped her arms around Jennifer's waist. "Have dinner with me on Sunday?" she asked, nuzzling her neck.

"Yes," Jennifer answered, and smiled before pushing Bonnie away. "Go on, before we get caught."

Bonnie sighed happily, took one last look at Jennifer and slipped out of the bedroom. She glanced around the empty hallway, then tiptoed up the stairs. As she made her way to the very top of the building and to her room, she listened for any noise. The room was dark. Bonnie reached for the light switch, only to feel a blinding pain. *Can't breathe,* she thought, hearing hateful words echo in her ears.

The next thing she was aware of was standing in her room and wondering why it was completely empty. "Not funny!" she yelled, certain her sisters were playing a prank on her. When she tried to leave, the door refused to open. She paced around the room as she watched the sun set. She was sure that many days had passed, but it didn't make any sense to her. She seemed to drift in and out of consciousness.

Then she noticed the door to her bedroom was open. Rushing out, she followed the sounds of a party coming from below. "I dreamed the whole thing," she said in wonderment as she entered the party. "Even making love to Jennifer." She looked around the room, noticing girls she had never seen before. "I need to get dressed," she told herself, and moved toward the staircase. For some reason, however, she stopped and headed back to the party.

She became aware that the mood of the party was surprisingly somber. She heard Sally whisper to Sheila, "I'll never understand. Why did she do it?" Bonnie detected the distinct aroma of marijuana when she passed Sally.

"Oh, girl, you really need to stop doing that," Bonnie murmured, making her way toward Teneil. Her friend looked so sad. "Teneil, something very strange is going on," she blurted. She was stunned when Teneil simply walked past her. "Fine, so you're still mad at me, but could you help me find my dress?" Teneil stopped in the center of the room, and everyone's attention focused on her.

Bonnie's shoulders slumped when her friend ignored her. "What happened to my dress?" she wondered, looking down at her clothing. She was surprised to see that she was wearing Jennifer's clothes. *If I'm wearing Jennifer's clothing, then it wasn't a dream. But where is*

Jennifer? Her rambling thoughts stopped as she heard Teneil address the group. She watched as her friend spoke eloquently, despite the tears rolling down her cheeks.

"At eight a.m. tomorrow, the Bonita Sanchez memorial hot line will open," Teneil concluded as Jennifer stepped up beside her. "I want to thank everyone for honoring the memory of our sister."

"Memorial?" Bonnie looked around the room at the solemn faces. Memories of a hooded figure and the feeling of the air leaving her body assaulted her, and she stormed over to Regina, who was also crying. "Okay, what's going on?" she demanded. "This isn't funny. Out with it, Regina!" she screamed, but Regina didn't acknowledge her presence.

"Big joke," Bonnie said, but they continued to ignore her. She couldn't shake the image of someone in a ceremonial robe gripping her throat, and the gold glimmer of a Sigma Kappa pin in the darkness. Bonnie had reached the limits of her patience, and she headed toward Teneil. She stopped suddenly when she saw the sheet cake set out on the table. It was just like the cake they had served the night before. *Was it last night?* Her jaw dropped as she read the date written with icing on the cake. "1965? It can't be."

Everything came flooding back to her: being struck from behind, falling to her knees, the robed figure grabbing her by the throat. She couldn't see the hands that were choking her, only the pin as the robe fell slightly open, and then darkness. "No!" she wailed, and several girls' heads jerked up.

"Did you hear that?" Regina said.

"Hear what?" Mary asked.

"Who did this to me?" Bonnie cried. Consumed with anger, she flipped over the table that held the cake and the punch bowl and sent its contents crashing to the floor. Some girls screamed and rushed out of the room, some shrank away from the table, and others tried to clean up the mess. Bonnie collapsed in a corner and watched the flurry of activity.

"I swear I heard her," Regina insisted.

"Maybe you did." Sally put her arm around the shaking woman.

"I heard her too," Teneil said, trembling.

"What a load of crap," Jerusha scoffed. "Regina, have you been smoking Sally's cigarettes?"

"Jerusha," Sally said, "Bonnie's spirit never left us. Can't you feel her?"

"Great, this is who defends me?" Bonnie suddenly realized that almost no one could hear her. "The stoner and the bigot. Man, this sucks."

"Her suicide was hard on all of us," Sheila said.

"Suicide?" Bonnie couldn't believe her ears. "Why would I kill myself, you idiots? I just had the best sex of my life, and lost my heart. As for you, Sheila, we slept together once, and just for the record, I showed up at your room that night looking for your roommate. Which is why I dumped you for her, later. Suicide, me?"

"Suicide," she repeated, and her heart sank. "Jesus, Mary, and Joseph, my poor parents." She sobbed. The Monsignor would never have allowed them to give her a Catholic burial. Not that she cared, but it must have broken her parents' hearts.

It was strange, listening to the nice things everyone was saying about her. Even people she would have sworn hated her had stories to tell, and they all made Bonnie sound nicer than she really was. At the end of the evening, she was tempted to throw a fit when Jennifer's new girlfriend arrived to take her home. "She's too skinny." Bonnie barely had time to sneer, before finding herself standing outside in the crisp morning air.

Day after day, she wandered around the campus, going wherever she pleased—except back into the Sigma Kappa house. No one was aware of her presence. Bonnie felt lost and alone. Then, at the start of a new Rush Week, she suddenly found herself back in her old room, which was still barren. She paced the floors day and night until Halloween, when she once again joined the party.

This pattern continued until the day she entered her room and found a couple of carpenters working on it. "A new ceiling," she remarked, inspecting their handiwork.

"Why did we have to cover the beam?" the younger carpenter asked, cleaning up the debris.

"Some Mexican chick hung herself a few years back," the older one said.

"I'm Puerto Rican, you jackass," Bonnie snarled, as Teneil entered the room.

"She was Puerto Rican, you asshole!" the dark-skinned woman yelled.

"You tell them, *querida*," Bonnie said. Then, "You're pregnant!" she exclaimed, as Teneil shooed the workmen away.

"This is really hard." Teneil sniffled, looking around the empty room.

"I'm here," Bonnie said, but Teneil didn't seem to hear her.

"Oh, Bonnie, I don't know why I came today," Teneil went on. "They're going to start using this room again."

"They should," Bonnie said. "Leaving it empty is just a waste of space, and I could use the company."

"I guess I came to say goodbye." Teneil sighed. "I owe you so much. I graduated with honors."

"I knew you would," Bonnie said, smiling proudly.

"And I'm married now."

"I would hope so." Bonnie laughed, and Teneil suddenly looked around.

"He doesn't look like Ringo," she said, smiling.

"Got tired of those skinny white boys, did you?"

"He looks more like Sidney Poitier." Teneil gave a soft laugh.

"I bet you're the only one who thinks that." Bonnie chuckled along with her friend.

"At least I think he does," Teneil added, almost as if she had heard Bonnie. "I'm still mad at you for leaving me, you know."

"I didn't!" Bonnie shouted, and Teneil shivered. "I know that on some level you can feel me," she said sadly. "I didn't leave you. I would never do that."

"Maybe if we hadn't argued..."

"Great, you blame yourself. I swear, if I ever find out who killed me, the bitch is toast."

"I miss you, and I pray that you're happy wherever you are," Teneil said, wiping tears from her cheeks.

"Bored, mostly." Bonnie watched her friend leave. She felt abandoned.

When a sorority sister moved into her room, Bonnie discovered something very interesting. She could be seen and heard. Of course, the first time she appeared, the girl went screaming from the room. Bonnie quickly learned how to keep her presence a secret, until one night when the girl was in bed touching herself. "Finally, some entertainment!" Bonnie said happily. She climbed onto the bed and cupped the girl's breast. Margo was so caught up in whatever fantasy she was enjoying that she didn't notice the extra pair of hands on her body. When she climaxed, calling out, "Stan!" Bonnie was so turned off that she decided to save her favors for her own kind.

The years passed slowly for Bonnie. There were some girls she shared her time with; some of them were very special to her, others weren't. She wandered around campus, occasionally catching glimpses of old friends attending alumnae events. It was hard for her to watch them going on with their lives and growing older. The only comforts she had were her memories, sitting in on classes, and hoping for a special girl to be placed in her room.

Then the attacks began. The first one shocked Bonnie as much as it did the poor girl who was sharing her room. Patty wasn't Bonnie's type, so the perky ghost left her alone. Patty's screams that Halloween night rocked the sorority. The sisters, of course, assumed Bonnie's ghost had caused the trouble, which irked her to no end. Not having experienced it before, Bonnie thought it was a fluke and forgot about it, until the same thing happened the following Halloween night. Every year from then on, Bonnie tried to warn whomever was living in the room to stay out of it on Halloween.

Most of the time, having a ghost advise a girl to get out worked, but whenever her warnings went unheeded, Bonnie felt sick. The attack on Justine had been particularly hard on her. She had enjoyed the girl's company, and it broke her heart when Justine was victimized.

October, 2004

The tall freshman had been one of Bonnie's favorites right from the start. Justine was lying on her bed drifting off to sleep when Bonnie curled up beside her. "Hello," she said, sleepily.

"Welcome, Sister." Bonnie smiled to herself. The girl probably thought she was asleep and dreaming, or that Bonnie was one of the Sigma Kappa sisters she hadn't met. Bonnie was still smiling when she brushed her lips lightly against Justine's. With a deep sigh, the redhead cupped the back of Bonnie's head and drew her in for another kiss.

Bonnie moaned into the warmth of Justine's mouth. "Are all of my sisters this friendly?" Justine asked in wonder after the kiss ended.

"Trust me, I'm not like any of the other Kappa sisters." Bonnie laughed, then looked chagrined as the window shade flapped up. "Time for me to go, *querida*."

Bonnie vanished, knowing she left behind a stunned Justine. They quickly became lovers, but Justine's interest waned when she realized that Bonnie was no longer among the living. She tried to shut Bonnie out; perhaps that was why she ignored Bonnie's warnings the night of the attack. Then came Raquel, and Bonnie knew, each time she saw Justine around the small blonde, that they were meant to be together.

March, 2006

"I can't believe this," Jennifer said, after listening to Raquel's story. Of course, Raquel had skipped over some of the more unique aspects of her experience. "If what you're saying is true, then someone I knew and was friends with murdered Bonnie. I just can't believe that anyone in the house that night was capable of such a heinous act."

Maggie frowned. "Can I ask you a couple of questions?"

"Yes." Jennifer looked like she was still reeling from what she had been told.

"How did Bonnie act right before she died? Was she depressed?"

"No," Jennifer said. "She was very happy. At least, I thought she was. We made plans to go out on the following Sunday, she kissed me, and then she sneaked out of my room. She was smiling the whole time."

"Okay." Maggie nodded. "Let me see if I can explain this properly. People who commit suicide often do so because they no longer feel any emotion. They usually aren't happy or overly sad. They've just stopped feeling, and they give up. In the weeks preceding Bonnie's death, did she seem to act that way?"

"Bonnie?" Jennifer laughed at the question. "No, she was full of life and energy. Her biggest concern was that Goldwater might win the election." Jennifer grimaced at the blank stares she was receiving. "This isn't ancient history," Jennifer said. "The '64 election was a big deal. A lot of people were worried that LBJ was going to keep us in Vietnam—which he did, by the way." The blank stares continued. "Fine, ask your parents about it."

"I don't think my parents were alive then," Justine whispered, earning a glare.

"Moving on," Raquel nudged her embarrassed lover, "would you agree that Bonnie didn't display any signs that she might have wanted to end her life?"

"You can't always tell," Jennifer argued. "But nothing in her demeanor even hinted she was about to end her life. That's been nagging at me for almost forty years."

"Did the police investigate?" Maggie asked.

"There wasn't much to investigate. They took a couple of pictures, and then an ambulance took her away. That's all I really remember..." Her voice trailed off, then she sat up straight and exclaimed, "Curious George!"

"Excuse me?" Raquel said.

"That morning, Bonnie thought she saw someone lurking outside my bedroom window. The window shade snapped open. It was always doing that, but this time, she thought she saw someone in the tree outside my window."

"Did you check it out?" Justine asked, excited.

"No," Jennifer muttered. "We got sidetracked." She blushed, and the others glanced away for a moment. "If what you're saying is true, then we need to find out the facts. Even if the killer's dead, she needs to be held accountable."

"How can she be held accountable?" Maggie asked.

"'Sincerity, Kinship, and above all, Honor is my pledge for myself and for my sisters,'" Jennifer quoted. "Or have you forgotten your pledge?"

"No," the girls replied.

"Dishonoring your house means expulsion from Sigma Kappa," Jennifer said.

"You want to have her retroactively blackballed?" Justine asked. "What good would that—" She stopped and smiled. "If she's blackballed, then she can't set foot on Kappa grounds. It just might work."

"And it might not," Jennifer said. "I don't know if your suspicions are true. All I know is that I've spent the last forty years wondering if I said or did something that led to Bonnie's death. I'm not alone. Most of us wondered if we'd somehow contributed. The alumnae tea is coming up, and I'll see what I can do about getting some of the other women to talk to you. For now, let me hear your list of suspects so I can tell you what I know about them."

"Thank you," Raquel said. "First is Regina Becker."

"Pompous ass," Jennifer snorted. "She and Bonnie never got along. Regina was from a conservative family, and she shared her parents' narrow views. You could have knocked me over with a feather when I heard she joined the Peace Corps."

"Sheila Collins?" Raquel continued.

"Sheila was very shy and insecure." Jennifer's smile looked sad. "Rumor was that Bonnie seduced her, then dumped her for her roommate, Carla. Sheila and Carla fought for weeks before making up."

"Carla Lipton?" Raquel asked.

"Yes," Jennifer said. "I heard Carla ended up with some guy, and Sheila ended up teaching kids in Harlem."

"Jerusha Davies."

"I can't do this," Jennifer said suddenly, her face ashen. "I can't examine my friends and try to figure out which one of them is a murderer. I need to think about this." She stood up, and her body swayed. "I'll be in touch."

"Ms. Lowell," Raquel said, "are you all right?" She chose her words carefully. "I don't think you should be driving."

"I'm fine. I'm going to take a walk around campus."

After Jennifer Lowell stumbled out of the house, the three exchanged glances. "Nothing like turning someone's life upside down," Justine said, and Maggie nodded.

"I hope we're doing the right thing," Raquel mumbled.

April, 2006

A few weeks later, Sarah Moorehouse called the three of them into the lounge. They stopped when they entered and saw all of the sorority officers awaiting their arrival. All the women in the room were seniors or juniors, since you couldn't run for office unless you were an upper classman. "Have a seat," Sarah instructed the trio.

Raquel fidgeted nervously as they sat down on the sofa. Knowing that she needed to steady her nerves, she fought the urge to grasp Justine's hand. There was something about her lover's touch that centered her, and she hated that they had to hide their feelings. She also feared that this was why they had been summoned.

"Chill," Denise, the house president, said. "We just need to talk to you about something that's been brought to our attention."

"Okay," Justine responded, and began tapping her foot.

"Jennifer Lowell and Teneil Watts contacted me about your little project," Denise said, "and we want to help."

"Huh?" Raquel was dumbfounded.

"We want to help," Sarah repeated. "Bonita Sanchez was a Sigma Kappa sister, and it would dishonor us if we didn't do whatever we could to put her spirit to rest."

"And it's a real mystery. How cool is that?" Tina, the treasurer, added. "Just like one of those *Law and Order* episodes."

"You watch way too much television," Sarah said. "Coolness aside, none of us have forgotten what happened to you, Justine."

"I had that room my freshman year," Denise said. "I thought I was going crazy when my stuff kept getting moved around. On Halloween night, I saw Bonnie for the first time, and she scared the bejesus out of me. Still, I'm glad she warned me to stay away that night."

"We've started contacting alumnae who were in that room," Sarah said. "Most of them swear nothing happened, but there are a few who are eager to talk to us. One of them is Gina Rogers, and as luck would have it, she's a local police detective. She said she would try to find the original police report."

Raquel was filled with a sense of excitement as the ten of them began comparing and assigning duties. The whole thing began to feel like a study project, although to Raquel it still felt very personal. Denise decided that the first order of business would be to track down the people who were in the house that morning. Raquel supplied her with the list of candidates and the twenty-five sisters. They divided up the list and began their investigations.

The following weekend, Raquel was walking around the sprawling campus grounds with Sally Connelly. The sixty-something-year-old woman seemed to be trapped in the nineteen sixties. As the over-aged hippie prattled on about her days living in a commune in Vermont, Raquel wondered if she was high on something.

"Of course she's stoned." Bonnie laughed, trailing alongside the unlikely duo. She was surprised to see Raquel in the company of her old classmate. She felt a familiar sense of disappointment when she tried to communicate with Raquel, only to have her presence go unnoticed. "Ask her about the time she mistook her driver's license for rolling papers and smoked it," Bonnie suggested.

"Ms. Connelly." Raquel tried once again to get the woman to focus on what she was saying.

"Sunbeam," Sally corrected her, and Bonnie laughed.

"My apologies, Sunbeam," Raquel said, forcing a smile. "Getting back to what I was asking about, how well did you know Bonita?"

"You want to know about me? How sweet." Bonnie smiled as she followed them around.

"My Don Juanita," Sally said with a blissful expression. "My Sapphic lover."

"So I fucked her." Bonnie shrugged. "Even though she's straight, she really got into it."

"You were intimate with Bonnie?" Raquel asked.

"She melded with my soul."

"I went down on you," Bonnie said, scoffing at Sally's flowery words.

"Were you in the house the morning she died?"

"Let me think..." Sally paused. "No, I wasn't. That night I went home with Truman, whom I thought was my soul mate. He turned out to be a jerk. He could score some kick-ass weed, though."

"The beatnik." Bonnie laughed at the memory. "Mrs. Camden threw a fit when he showed up in a smelly T-shirt and with hair down to his ass."

Raquel shook her head and wondered just how Sally had managed to survive all the substances she must have ingested over the decades.

"I was there when she came back," Sally rambled on.

"Came back?" Raquel asked.

"It was one year to the day," Sally said. "Bonnie wasn't happy."

"No kidding." Bonnie snorted.

"I heard her scream something, and she knocked over a table," Sally continued. "Regina was totally freaked."

"Regina Becker?" Raquel perked up.

"Yeah. Regina was really affected by Bonnie's death."

"The hell she was," Bonnie said with disgust.

"It was something Bonnie said to her..." Sally's focus seemed to fade in and out. "Words were weapons. Regina always wondered if it was something she said that drove Bonnie to do what she did."

"She gives herself way too much credit," Bonnie scoffed.

"Were they close?" Raquel asked.

"No," Sally said, and laughed. "Regina was blinded by her social class. Or at least she pretended she was." Sally laughed again. "I'll let you in on a little secret. One night, Regina was wasted on Sangria and let slip that Bonnie used to jerk her off."

"No kidding," Raquel said, not the least bit surprised that Bonnie had had a liaison with Regina.

"Martin Luther King," Sally said, yawning.

"Excuse me?" Raquel asked.

"Dr. King's assassination inspired Regina to change, and join the Peace Corps," Sally said. "She told me she never forgot what Bonnie had said, and when Dr. King was murdered, she decided to change her life."

Bonnie was stunned that she had actually gotten through to Regina Becker, the most uptight white girl she had ever had the misfortune to meet.

"What about the other girls in the house? What did they think about Bonnie?"

"Everyone really liked her," Sally said. "She didn't kill herself."

"Finally!" Bonnie shouted.

"No, she was a victim of an uncaring society," Sally concluded.

"Oh, brother."

Raquel sighed, knowing that Sally was drifting off into her own little world. "What about Rita Summers or Jerusha Davies?"

"What are you up to?" Bonnie asked Raquel. "Rita was fun, and I never touched Jerusha."

"What about them?" Sally asked.

"Never mind." Raquel could tell that Sally had given her all she could.

"Cool," Sally murmured as she inhaled the spring air. "Shame about Jerusha though."

"What, getting hit by the snow plow?" Raquel escorted her to a bench and helped her sit down.

"No," Sally responded with a dreamy expression. "That freaking cult she ended up in."

Raquel pressed for more, but Sally had drifted off and seemed to be asleep. Raquel busied herself with some notes while Bonnie looked over her shoulder.

"'Regina, Sheila, Carla, Jerusha, and Rita,'" Raquel read off. "I wish you could hear me, Bonnie, because I really want to know what's going on."

Justine came down the path toward her lover, who was still studying her notes. "Hi, Honey."

"Hi." Raquel looked up at the tall redhead happily.

"Who's this?" Justine nodded toward the sleeping woman.

"Sally Connelly, or Sunbeam, as she likes to be called. I think she's passed out or is in a coma, it's hard to tell."

"I'd vote for coma," Bonnie said.

"I aced my midterm," Raquel continued. "And I registered for that seminar this summer, so it looks like I'll be staying up here."

"Your parents are still freaking out, huh?" Justine's voice was full of guilt.

"I probably shouldn't have come out in the middle of Christmas dinner," Raquel said, grinning ruefully. "They'd prefer that I didn't come home for a while."

"I'm sorry, Raquel."

"No, don't be," Raquel said. "You're the best thing in my life."

Justine hugged her lover. "So both of us are going to be staying at the sorority house for the whole summer," she said, with a sly smile. "Did you know that after this semester you can move out of the attic?"

"Really?" Raquel was curious as to where the conversation was heading.

"Maggie's going home for the summer, and she'll be a senior in the fall," Justine continued, obviously trying to sound blasé about the whole thing. "She gets her own room, and I'll need a new roommate."

"Yeah?" Raquel's breathing increased.

"Do you want to room together?" Justine's voice trembled a little. "If it's too soon, I understand."

Justine's answer came when Raquel jumped into her lap and kissed her deeply.

"The two of you are so cute," Bonnie said, beaming. "I take full credit for getting you knuckleheads together."

"Do we have to wait until the fall?" Raquel asked, nuzzling Justine's neck.

"No." Justine laughed and helped Raquel off her lap. "You can request the new room assignment at the end of this semester. Now that's settled, tell me what Starship had to say."

"Sunbeam," Raquel corrected.

"Why would someone want to name herself after a loaf of bread?" Justine quipped.

"I always liked you," Bonnie snickered.

"She wasn't there that morning," Raquel said. "She did tell me that Bonnie messed around with Regina, and something Bonnie said helped pull the stick out of Regina's ass. Oh, and Jerusha ended up in a cult."

"How in the hell did that sweet girl end up in a cult?" Bonnie wondered. "Half the time, no one even knew she was around. She faded so far into the background, I even tripped over her a few times." But Bonnie's words were nothing more than a whisper on the wind. "Did you find out about Jennifer?" she asked in vain.

"Carrie Templeton was interesting," Justine said. "The only person she could think of who might have had a grudge against Bonnie was Sheila Collins. Apparently, Bonnie dumped Sheila for her roommate, Carla."

"Makes you wonder how she found time to go to class," Raquel noted with a grimace.

"You'd be surprised at what you can get away with in a crowded lecture hall," Bonnie said

"No kidding." Justine laughed. "Okay, we already knew about the Sheila and Carla love triangle, and yes, they did end up together, but very briefly. Carrie was certain that both Rita and Regina had a fling with Bonnie, but neither took it very seriously. I'm beginning to get the feeling that a lesbian affair was all a part of the times and Bonnie took advantage of it."

"Wouldn't you?" Bonnie challenged.

"She embraced the era with both hands," Sally said as she rejoined the conscious world.

"Evidently," Raquel said dryly.

"She is near." Sally smiled.

"How is it that this fruitcake is the only one who can sense me?" Bonnie grumbled.

Sally shrugged, as though answering Bonnie's question, and then said goodbye to Justine and Raquel. "I can't believe the two of you are doing this for me," Bonnie whispered, watching the couple stroll toward Higgins Hill.

Upon returning to the house, they went up to Justine's room. "Maggie must still be in class," Justine said, as they cuddled on her bed.

"I'm exhausted." Raquel yawned, and Justine curled up behind her and wrapped loving arms around her.

"No wonder," Justine said. "Between school, Bonnie, and us, you've been spreading yourself pretty thin."

"I'm okay." Raquel yawned again, then turned in Justine's embrace.

"I did find out something interesting about Bonnie," Justine said, nuzzling her neck.

"What's that?" Raquel asked, inhaling her lover's scent.

"One of the reasons Sigma Kappa was so eager to accept her, despite her free ways, was that she was really smart."

"We knew that."

"Not just smart," Justine continued. "She scored a perfect sixteen hundred on her SATs, and Mensa was courting her."

"Get out!"

"I'm not kidding. I told you she helped me with my homework. I thought she was so good because she told me she still sits in on classes. Carrie said that Bonnie was shy about her intelligence because of the pressure it put on her younger brother."

"Wait, Sally said she was close by."

"Sally was stoned."

"True," Raquel said, "but what if that's where she is for the rest of the year? Just wandering around?" Raquel fell silent as she traced her lover's face with her fingertips. She couldn't think about Bonnie anymore. At that moment, the only thing that mattered was that she was resting in Justine's arms.

The kisses began shyly as Raquel's hands wandered along her lover's body. Spurred on by the knowledge that in just a few short months they would be living in the same room, she moved her hands to Justine's breasts. Her lover's body arched in response.

Their kisses grew more passionate, and Justine's hand slipped between Raquel's thighs. Raquel moaned as her lover teased her clit through her jeans. She tugged Justine's shirt out of her pants and pulled it up. Her body rocked against her tall lover's touch, and she pulled Justine's bra up, revealing her breasts. Raquel's mouth watered as she began kissing her lover's skin. "You make me crazy," Justine gasped, as Raquel's mouth worshiped her flesh.

Raquel's blood was boiling, her hips thrusting urgently, her mouth suckling her lover's nipples. She trembled when she felt the buds puckering in her mouth. "Harder," Justine said, grinding the heel of her hand against Raquel's center.

Raquel's cries were smothered by her lover's breast as she convulsed against her. Justine held her tightly as Raquel's body erupted and she finally collapsed, all her energy spent.

"We have to go downstairs for dinner," Justine whispered. Raquel could only purr in response. "After things settle down, we need to go away for a weekend, just you and me."

"And a really big bed?" Justine chuckled.

May, 2006

"I am not reading this," Gina Rogers said, grumbling as she perused the dusty old file she had painstakingly tracked down.

"What's that?" Sam, her partner, asked.

"Unbelievable," Gina went on, handing Sam the file. He adjusted his bifocals and looked at it.

She had been surprised when Sue, an old friend from college, had called her. Gina had never forgotten about Bonnie. How could she? When she had first encountered Bonnie, she was completely freaked out. After a few days around the playful entity, she had learned to accept Bonnie's presence. The only troublesome aspect was the way the ghost kept flirting with her.

Gina was growing weary of constantly fending off Bonnie's advances. Bonnie was very entertaining, but Gina had a girlfriend. Or at least, she thought she had a girlfriend, until the day Judy called and informed Gina that she had met someone new.

She was alone in her room, crying. Then Bonnie's hands were holding her, Bonnie's breath was on her skin, Bonnie's soft caresses were teasing her, and Bonnie's curly tresses were tickling her thighs as the ghost's tongue plunged in and out of her wetness. She could hear Bonnie's words about how Judy didn't deserve her, and Bonnie's promises of how she would help Gina forget the pain.

Gina blushed as she recalled her face buried in the pillow, her hips in the air as Bonnie took her to new heights. Gina had screamed for more as Bonnie erased the memory of Judy's betrayal. Then, one morning Bonnie was gone. So was the pain, and Gina moved on with her life. Now Bonnie was back, and Gina was about to repay her for her kindness.

"What in the hell?" Sam said, dragging Gina back to the here and now. "Man, the captain is going to be pissed."

"Tell me about it," Gina said, taking the file back. "Like we aren't busy enough, I have to go turn a forty-year-old suicide into a homicide."

"Was the coroner sniffing glue?" Sam wondered. "A contusion on the back of her head, defensive wounds on her knuckles, and this crime scene. What kind of moron writes that off as a suicide? You can dump it on the Cold Case squad."

"No, I can't," Gina said. "She was a Sigma Kappa sister. Once a Kappa, always a Kappa. I owe her." Gina knew she owed Bonnie more than the loyalty of a sorority pledge.

Captain Briggs was ready to ignore Gina's visit until he looked at the old black-and-white photograph of the crime scene. "There's nothing under her," Briggs noted. "Didn't they even think about the fact that there was no chair or other piece of furniture even remotely close to the body?"

"Apparently not," Gina said. "The report is signed by Sheriff Bonner."

"Boomer Bonner," Briggs grunted. "That jackass. He wouldn't have bothered."

"Why not?" Gina asked. "You'd think that even in a town this small, the death of a student would have been a big deal."

"Back then, there were probably six guys on the force," Briggs explained. "Boomer was an ex-jock who wouldn't have broken a sweat over someone with the last name Sanchez. Not that we can ask him. The old prick died about twenty years ago."

"What about the medical examiner?" Gina glanced down at the file. "Hastings?"

"He wasn't a medical examiner," Briggs said. "He ran the local funeral parlor."

"What?" Gina looked exasperated.

"Remember, it wasn't uncommon back then for the local mortician to act as the coroner as well," Briggs said. "He might have suspected something, which is probably why he included such a detailed report. He passed on back in 1973, I think. Send the file downstairs to Cold Cases."

"I'd like to handle this myself, with your permission. I was a Kappa."

"Are you sure? Forty years, no clues, and most of the witnesses and suspects are probably dead."

"I'm sure."

"Good luck, then," Briggs said. "First, run the report over to the medical examiner. We need to have the death certificate changed, and if he doesn't agree, then we can't do anything. If he does, then you need to track down the victim's family. If the insurance company is still around, they need to change the claim. It would have been denied. Then you need to find out who was in that house when it happened. Still interested?"

"Yes," Gina said, her face grim. She had to do this, if for no other reason than because twenty-five years ago, she had never bothered asking Bonnie how she had died. Bonnie had given Gina her heart back, and she had never stopped to find out about Bonnie.

Early the next morning, Gina was already working on her third cup of coffee when the most attractive woman she had ever seen sat down across from her. Carlotta Kim Sanchez was Bonnie's niece and only living relative. With her caramel skin and almond eyes, she was nothing short of exotic.

"Thank you for driving up here," Gina said.

"I'm curious, to say the least," Carlotta responded, with a soft smile.

"Carlotta, did you know your Aunt Bonita?" Gina wasn't really sure where to start.

"Call me Carly," the woman said. "And no, I was born many years after her death. Why?"

"As of eight twenty this morning, the cause of your aunt's death was officially changed from suicide to homicide," Gina explained.

"Wh... what?" Carly stammered. "My God, if only my family were still alive to hear this," she blurted. "My grandparents raised me. Neither they nor my father ever believed that Aunt Bonnie took her own life. Her death changed my father in so many ways. He had always lived in her shadow, and that only got worse after her death."

Gina listened carefully as Carly explained how her father had enlisted in the army to escape his family, and ended up in Vietnam. There, he met and married her mother. He discovered horror during the war, and he also discovered drugs. Roberto Sanchez died at the age of twenty-six, from an overdose. Carly's mother had disappeared, so she was raised by her very over-protective grandparents.

"I'm sorry," Carly said. "I'm babbling."

"It's quite all right," Gina said. If Carly read the phone book, she would sit happily for hours and listen to each word.

"How did this happen?" the younger woman asked, still reeling from the news.

"Well, without going into things that would sound insane, someone at the Sigma Kappa house started to question Bonnie's death," Gina explained, sidestepping the ghost issue. "I'm a Kappa alumna, and I offered to look at the file."

"Are you sure it was murder?"

"Yes. Let me explain why." Gina was eager to spend more time with this intriguing woman.

One week later, Gina was standing next to a tree outside the Sigma Kappa house, looking up at a window on the second floor.

"My, didn't you grow up nice," Bonnie commented, watching the detective. "What are you doing here? Miss me?"

"Hello?" Raquel called out, breaking the detective's thoughts. "Can I ask what you're doing?"

"I'm Detective Rogers." Gina showed Raquel her badge. "And you are?"

"Raquel Albright."

"Ah, the troublemaker who started all of this," Gina said, and laughed. "Carly Sanchez is very much in your debt."

"Who the hell is Carly Sanchez?" Bonnie demanded.

"Carly?" Raquel asked.

"Bonnie's niece," Gina explained. "We need to call a house meeting. There will be some others joining us."

"Roberto, you're a Papá," Bonnie said, happily.

"Are the police looking into Bonnie's death?" Raquel asked.

"Not any longer," Gina said.

"Why not?"

"Yeah, why not?" Bonnie echoed furiously.

"The case is closed."

Raquel gasped in surprise. "Who did it?"

"Tell me," Bonnie pleaded.

"I'll explain at the meeting," Gina said.

"No," Bonnie wailed. "I can't go to the meeting. This sucks." Bonnie fumed in frustration as she watched them enter the house.

The entire house was gathered in the lounge, along with Gina, Jennifer, Carly, Sally, Carrie, Mary, and Teneil. Once everyone had settled down, Gina addressed them. "My Sisters, thank you for meeting with me," she said. "I've called you and our guests here tonight because one of our sisters has been denied justice."

"This is so lame," Claudette grumbled quietly, but her words were heard.

"Bonita Sanchez was murdered," Gina rebuked the rude young student. "It doesn't matter if it was forty years ago or this morning. I've managed to solve her murder, but I can't bring our sister justice. Her killer escaped, and she was one of our own. I've come here to ask the members of the house to ban this woman from Sigma Kappa."

"Who is it?" Teneil demanded. "I'll kill her."

"She's already dead," Gina said. "Her name was Jerusha Davies."

The moment Jerusha's name was spoken, Bonnie found herself in the lounge. No one noticed her appearance except a dark figure lurking in the corner.

"Jerusha?" Teneil gasped, and Jennifer's head bowed. "Are you sure? Bonnie never dated Jerusha."

"I wasn't interested in her," Bonnie said, her words unheard by everyone except the cloaked figure. Bonnie looked toward her. "You? But why?"

The figure merely hissed in Bonnie's direction. "Fine, don't tell me, bitch," Bonnie said, as Gina continued.

"I know," Gina explained. "But Jerusha was involved with someone Bonnie was quite taken with."

"Jennifer," Teneil said softly and looked toward her, understanding dawning in her eyes. "That's why everyone told Bonnie you were spoken for."

"Jerusha was very jealous of anyone who showed an interest in Jennifer," Sally recalled.

"Jennifer?" Bonnie shuddered at the very thought of Jennifer and Jerusha together. "My Jennifer?"

"My Jennifer," the figure growled.

"You really were a freak, weren't you, Jerusha?" Bonnie said, moving to stand behind Jennifer. "What were you thinking?"

"I broke up with Jerusha that spring," Jennifer tried to explain. "She didn't want to let go. She even followed me when I went to grad school in Illinois."

"I thought she was accepted to the same school," Carrie said.

"No, she didn't get in, but she moved a block away from my apartment. She followed me for years. She never threatened me, so I couldn't go to the police. I certainly never thought she was dangerous."

Bonnie watched the cloaked figure grow more and more agitated. "She still is," she whispered.

"She finally stopped, somewhere around 1981," Jennifer continued. "I was relieved until the letters started coming. They said she'd found God, that I should renounce my deviant ways, and that she blamed me for her sins."

"She had joined The Circle of Enlightenment," Gina explained. "That's a very interesting cult. They have a compound in the middle of Wyoming where, if the FBI is correct, they stockpile weapons. Apparently, they fund their cause by making jam and quilts while awaiting Armageddon."

"Charming," Justine sneered. "And what happens after Armageddon?"

"'God will cleanse the Earth of all sinners and undesirables,'" Gina quoted, rolling her eyes. "Fortunately, they're quite content to await God's wrath, so the Feds haven't had to raid the compound. The good news is, they're watching the group. They were able to get them to surrender Jerusha's personal effects, which have been in storage since her death. She liked to write things down. The stacks of notebooks we discovered dated back to when she was in high school. They weren't really journals, though. Her thoughts were often nothing more than ramblings." Gina grimaced.

"In her mind, she and Jennifer were still a couple, and she didn't like the way Jennifer noticed Bonnie. So, she decided to keep an eye on her. She described herself as being invisible to Bonnie, and how Bonnie never seemed to know she was there. When she saw Bonnie sneak into Jennifer's room that night, she climbed the tree outside Jennifer's window and waited. I'm not sure just what she was waiting for."

Bonnie nodded. "Then I really did see someone." Jerusha snickered, and Bonnie glared at her.

Gina continued. "When the window shade snapped open, Jerusha was sure Bonnie had seen her. She jumped out of the tree, crept back into the house and grabbed one of the robes from storage, and then waited in Bonnie's room. She struck her from behind and then strangled her. Then she staged the suicide scene, cleaned up the blood, went back to her room, and went to sleep. She called it justice. If anyone had taken the time to notice, they would have seen it was impossible for Bonnie to have hung herself. The chair was against the desk in the corner, and all the other furnishings were too far away for her to have hung herself in the middle of the room. For whatever reasons, the crime simply went unnoticed. The confession in these journals allowed me to close the case."

"Again, I have to say you are a fruitcake," Bonnie snarled at Jerusha.

"I never knew my Aunt Bonnie," Carly Sanchez said. "From the stories I've been hearing since all this began, I wish I'd had the chance. I was robbed of that, just as my grandparents were robbed of giving her a Catholic burial. I'm asking that you bring peace to her and my family by condemning her murderer."

"Ballsy kid you've got there, Roberto." Bonnie beamed proudly.

"I know," a solemn voice said from behind her.

"Roberto?" Bonnie gasped as she looked at the man her brother had grown into.

"Time for you to join us," he told her. "Our parents have been waiting for you."

"But?" Bonnie hesitated, looking around the room.

"Everything will be made right," he promised.

The room filled with light, and Bonnie's laughter echoed through the lounge.

"What was that?" Kate asked nervously.

"She's gone," Teneil said, and smiled broadly. "I think you got your wish, Carly."

"Almost," Gina said. "We need to deal with Jerusha Davies. She has dishonored the house."

"We've already prepared," Sarah said. "We researched what needs to be done. It has never been done before. Just as when a sister is initiated, the house must also decide banishment. We would like the alumnae to stay. Unfortunately, everyone else has to step out of the room."

Carly left the room as the sisters and alumnae formed a circle. Two wooden boxes were passed around, and each person removed one marble from each box until they each held one black and one white marble. "This has to be unanimous. If even a single white marble is cast, Jerusha Davies will remain a sister. Is everyone ready?" Sarah asked. The sisters nodded in response. "I hope this works," she muttered under her breath. "Jerusha Davies, stand before your sisters."

Everyone looked around, as if they expected Jerusha to actually appear. None of them noticed that Jerusha's dark figure had moved into the center of the room. None except Justine, who felt the hair on the back of her neck prickling and her lungs tightening.

"Are you okay?" Raquel whispered.

"She's here," Justine choked out.

"Jerusha Davies, you are accused of dishonoring your sisters, and must withstand the vote of banishment." As sorority president, Denise passed the ballot box around the circle. One by one, each sister dropped a marble into the box, her vote hidden from the others. "The vote has been cast," Denise continued, stepping into the center of the room and raising the box. A piercing scream invaded the room as Denise dumped the contents out onto the floor.

"Oh, p-peachy," Sarah stammered. The keening grew louder as black marbles, one by one, littered the carpeting.

"Justice," Teneil declared, once the last black orb had struck the floor.

"From this moment on, Jerusha Davies is no longer our sister," Denise proclaimed.

The scream increased to a fierce howl, the room began to shake, and the lights went out. A thunderous clap echoed, then silence returned and the lights flickered back on.

Carly stormed into the room, and Gina smiled when she wrapped her arms around her.

"What happened?" Carly asked.

"We kicked her out, retroactively." Gina enjoyed Carly's body pressing against her own, and returned the embrace with enthusiasm.

"Um... uh huh," Carly stammered.

"And quite possibly sent her to hell," Gina added, smirking.

"Speaking of cults," Carly said, releasing Gina, "don't any of you find this whole ceremonial, ritualistic thing a bit over the top?"

"No." Gina blinked with surprise.

"Not in the least," Marla agreed.

"Well, normally we just do bake sales and blood drives," Gina confessed. "Most of the ceremonial stuff is something someone came up with to creep out the pledges."

"But you still think it worked?" Carly asked.

"Yes, it did," Justine assured her.

"According to her journals, Jerusha took everything very seriously," Gina tried to explain. "Far too seriously. Being kicked out might be just the thing to get rid of her."

"Yes, Jerusha took everything seriously," Sally said. "Bonnie on the other hand…"

"I swear, if you call her Don Juanita again, I'm going to slap you," Jennifer threatened.

"She was more than that," Teneil stepped in to say. "But I think we can come up with a few exploits to share with you."

"I don't know if I'm old enough to hear this," Carly said, grinning.

"You might not be, at that," Gina muttered, putting her arm around Carly's waist again.

"Is it just me, or does Starship seem a lot more focused tonight?" Justine whispered.

"Gina told her if she showed up on anything stronger than a tic-tac, she was going to bust her," Jennifer replied, her eyes misty. "Justine, Raquel, Maggie, thank you," she said.

"For what?" Raquel asked.

"For finally doing what all of us failed to do for the past four decades," Jennifer explained. "You did the right thing."

"Yes, you did the right thing," Teneil added. "She was my best friend, and I still didn't see what had happened. For the first time since that day, I really feel that Bonnie has moved on to a better place. I'm just curious about one thing. So many of you claim to have interacted with her. What was she like as a ghost?"

"Um… um," Justine stammered.

"Friendly. Very friendly," Raquel said, blushing.

Later that evening, after the guests had departed and the excitement had faded, Justine pulled Maggie aside. "Any chance you'll be visiting my brother tonight?" she asked.

"No," Maggie said. "My God, the two of you are insatiable."

"What's up?" Raquel asked.

"She's trying to arrange another study session," Maggie complained. "Like walking in on the two of you once wasn't bad enough."

"Jealous?" Justine taunted. "Come on Raquel, I'll walk you to your room."

They lingered outside Raquel's door. Being so far away from the other rooms gave them privacy. "May I come in?" Justine asked.

Raquel blinked. "Yes," she said and opened the door.

She felt strange as they entered her room. Something was missing, but she couldn't quite figure out what it was. "Are you all right?" she asked Justine, who normally looked like a frightened rabbit every time she entered Raquel's room.

"Yes," Justine calmly answered. "That ominous feeling is gone."

"Bonnie's never coming back, either," Raquel said. "I'm going to miss her. I won't miss the way she moved my stuff around, though."

"I used to hate that," Justine agreed, wrapping her arms around her lover's waist. "I hope she's happy now."

"I think she is," Raquel answered. "Did you hear that laugh?"

"Yeah." Justine smiled as she nuzzled her lover's neck. "Promise me that forty years from now, you won't tell people that we ended up together because we slept with the same ghost."

"I promise," Raquel said. She moaned deeply as Justine's lips began to nibble her neck. She pressed against her lover's warm, inviting form, and sighed when Justine took a step back and cupped her face in her hands.

"Ever since the night of the attack, I've had nothing but bad memories of this room," Justine said. "Before that, it made me happy. I want that back."

"I'll make you happy," Raquel promised, running her hands down the front of Justine's body. "And the secret to true happiness begins with nudity." She yanked her lover's blouse out of her jeans.

"Really?" Justine smiled and began to unbutton Raquel's blouse.

"It's true." Raquel ran her hands up and under her partner's blouse. She sighed when Justine's muscles twitched beneath her touch. Her body arched as she felt Justine's hands cupping her breasts. "I love you," she murmured hotly in her lover's ear while she guided them over to the bed.

"I love you too," Justine whispered.

Raquel stepped out of her lover's embrace and lowered her to the bed. "Slow is good," she said, kneeling on the bed. Justine leaned back against the pillows and watched as Raquel slowly undressed her.

As Justine's body was revealed to her, Raquel kissed and caressed her skin, making Justine's breathing hitch as she traced every curve with her tongue. "Not fair," Justine murmured when Raquel cast off the last of her clothing and nestled between her thighs. "You aren't naked."

"I will be." Raquel nuzzled her face between Justine's breasts. The scent of her lover's body excited her. She could feel Justine's nails massaging her scalp as she kissed the valley between her breasts. Raquel's tasted Justine's skin while her hands ran along the curves of her body. Through hooded eyes, she watched her tongue snake out and flick Justine's nipple.

She felt her lover grind against her as she teased the bud and saw it pucker from her touch. She captured the nipple in her mouth, her own body burning. Justine rocked against her and moaned, her long legs wrapping around Raquel's body. Raquel nipped and suckled her lover's breast while Justine thrust against her.

She could feel Justine's body quivering. She allowed her long hair to tickle Justine's skin as she slowed her suckling. When Raquel's mouth abandoned her breast, Justine whimpered. Raquel pushed up on her elbows and looked down at her lover. "Are you wet, baby?" Justine was struggling to breathe.

Raquel rocked her hips in rhythm with her lover's demanding thrusts. "Tell me," she insisted.

"I need you," Justine managed.

Raquel panted heavily. They ground against one another in a frantic rhythm and Justine once again neared the edge. Raquel's body was screaming for release, but she slowed their dance as her lover squirmed beneath her. Her hips gyrated slowly against Justine's wetness, and her nimble fingers captured a nipple.

She pinched and teased the nipple while her lover begged her for more. She captured Justine in a fiery kiss, rolling the erect bud between her fingers. Raquel fought against her own needs as she slowly tormented her lover. There had been too many hastily stolen moments for both of them; tonight they would take their time.

Raquel unwrapped herself from Justine's hold and nestled beside her, running her hands over Justine's smooth flesh. They kissed slowly as Raquel's fingers explored the front of Justine's body. When her fingers brushed the damp curls of Justine's mound, she moaned into the warmth of Justine's mouth.

She broke away from their kisses and gazed at her lover's body, watching her fingers dance along the firm muscles. She dipped shyly into Justine's wetness, parting her slightly. Justine's desire coated her fingers as she teased the swollen nether lips, and she brushed Justine's throbbing nub before bringing her fingers to her lips.

She could feel Justine watching her as she licked her fingers, savoring the taste of Justine's desire as she swirled her tongue slowly around her fingers before plunging them into her mouth and sucking her lover's sweet nectar from them.

She glanced down at Justine's trembling body, then kissed her breasts. She suckled the nipples again, taking her time as she licked and tasted her way down her lover's long body. As she tasted the inside of Justine's thighs, she knew she was driving her lover insane. She blew a stream of warm air against Justine's mound and nestled her body between the long legs.

She could feel Justine's wetness on her neck as she kissed her lover's hips. She cupped Justine's ass and let her kisses drift lower. Drawing her closer, Raquel parted Justine with her tongue. She drank in her wetness; her tongue gliding along slick folds. Burying herself deeper in Justine's passion, she flicked her tongue against her partner's clit.

Justine's body thrust against Raquel as she curled her tongue and plunged deep inside her. As Justine gyrated against her, Raquel wriggled her tongue and thrust it slowly in and out of the delicious wetness until Justine cried out her name. She retreated when she felt her lover's body tightening against her.

Her tongue once again traced slick folds, and once again Justine begged for release. Unable to resist any longer, Raquel captured Justine's clit in her mouth and clenched her own thighs as her passion mounted. She released a strangled cry into her lover's passion as she made love to her with her teeth and tongue.

Fighting to hold Justine steady, she feasted on her. Trapped between Justine's body and her own needs, she drove her lover into ecstasy, grinding her hips into the mattress as she drove Justine higher and higher. Then she released her hold on the trembling body and lifted herself.

Moving over Justine, she plunged her fingers inside her lover, and Justine thrust urgently against her touch. She plunged in and out of Justine's center, teasing her clit with the pad of her thumb.

Raquel's body refused to hold still for Justine to lower her jeans. She continued to pleasure Justine as she felt long, slender fingers slip inside her panties. "Yes!" she cried out, as Justine stroked her. She felt Justine shudder beneath her, climaxing against her body.

Finally, Justine managed to remove her lover's blouse and bra. Raquel grasped Justine's wrist, moaning as she felt the long fingers slipping out of her body. Pulling Justine's trembling fingers to her breasts, she painted her nipples with the wetness of her own desire.

When Justine pulled her forward, Raquel pressed her breasts against eager lips. She braced herself as Justine slowly licked away every trace of her desire. Raquel was on fire as she felt her lover's lips and tongue teasing her nipples. When she couldn't stand it any longer, she pulled away from the warmth of her lover's mouth and tore off the rest of her clothing.

She climbed up Justine's body, kissing and teasing her along the way. Justine's hands caressed the back of her thighs, then squeezed the firm flesh of her ass. Raquel gripped the headboard and straddled her lover.

Justine drew Raquel down to her mouth and drank in her passion. Raquel groaned as her lover's tongue glided along her sex. With each flick of Justine's tongue, Raquel's body trembled. Justine drew her in deeper, and Raquel fought to hang on. She was gasping and rambling incoherently as Justine drove her into ecstasy.

Her ears were ringing and she struggled to remain upright as she climaxed. Before her body could still, Justine pulled her down onto the mattress. She covered Raquel's body with her own, and soon they were kissing wildly, stroking each other until they had nothing left to give.

Raquel kissed Justine deeply, then smoothed her hair back from her sweaty brow. "Happy memory?" she murmured.

Justine smiled lovingly. "Very happy."

"The first of many," Raquel promised. They snuggled under the covers and drifted off to sleep.

About the Author

Mavis Applewater was born in Massachusetts in 1962. As a child, she was an avid reader. Later, she honed her creative side majoring in Theatre at Salem State College. While supporting herself and waiting for her big break, she became a "resident" and well-known bartender at a nightclub in Cambridge, MA.

Mavis has done several commercials and lots of extra work, but her creative juices were still flowing, so she turned to another one of her hidden talents: writing. These efforts culminated in several manuscripts, the latest of which is this collection of Halloween stories.

Currently, Mavis lives in Massachusetts with her long-term partner.

Visit her website at: www.angelfire.com/ma4/findingmavis

Blue Feather Books is proud to offer this excerpt from Val Brown's provocative short story collection,

PEARL HAD TO DIE

Available now, only from

Bluefeatherbooks
LIMITED

www.bluefeatherbooks.com

Unlimited Sexual Favors

Part One: The conversation.

    The high-pitched siren of a fully functional smoke alarm whined throughout the large apartment. As the scent of charred lasagna filled the kitchen, Wilder McNeil sprinted across the room, switching off the oven and opening both windows. Smoking cheese clouded her vision and forced a cough past her lips. Frantically, Wilder flapped her hands around and looked down at the blackened remains of her supper. She grimaced and sighed deeply, running a hand through her shoulder-length blonde hair.
    "Just great! A night of being rushed off my feet at the bar, and then I kill my dinner. That really is the frosting on the cake." Readjusting her short black skirt, she gave the smoldering remains one last glare of disgust before walking back into the main room of her apartment.
    Rubbing eyes tired from a long shift, Wilder flopped down onto her overstuffed couch. The smooth fabric felt cool against the back of her bare legs. She hated wearing short skirts and skimpy white tops, but it was mandatory for all the girls who worked at Leather and Chains. The owner of the traditionally butch club liked all her girls to look feminine and "appear" available. Wilder really didn't mind being token "eye candy," especially with the tips that came her way every night. The amount of dollars slipped into the waistband of her skirt alone covered the monthly rent on her apartment.
    Wiggling her toes and glad to be out of restricting heels, Wilder looked across the room to her overflowing bookcase. She considered reading until she fell asleep but decided instead on the television. She picked up the remote control from the Quaker-style coffee table and switched on the set. With little enthusiasm, she commenced a lazy flick through the offerings, but at three o'clock in the morning, there wasn't much available.

Closing her eyes, Wilder let her head fall back against her cream-colored couch. The room's muted colors of pale cream and terracotta never failed to soothe her mind. After a night of constantly serving drinks and politely turning down offers for "company home," Wilder was more than relieved to retreat to the tranquility of her apartment.

The unexpected sound of the telephone ringing startled her. Frowning as she wondered who would be calling her at such an hour, she answered the phone.

"Hello?"

"You're the only person I know who would be up at this time of the night... or morning."

"Hi, Darcy. So does this mean you've just returned from your trip?" Wilder closed her eyes as she spoke with her friend.

"'Just' being the operative word."

Three miles away, in a plush San Francisco loft apartment, Darcy Gardner shook off the jacket of her black three-piece-suit and sat down on her luxurious black leather sofa. Ignoring the two navy suitcases she had literally dropped upon entering her apartment, she kicked off her Prada pumps and swung her legs up onto the sofa. Her brown eyes regarded the ceiling as she spoke with Wilder.

"I don't know why they wanted me to go to that 'Innovative Techniques for the Corporate Manager' seminar anyway. It's not like I haven't been running the entire West Coast Division for almost a year. It was a complete waste of my time. Three days in San Diego, and what do I have to show for it? A fog-delayed plane, a tension headache, and probably a huge pile of work stacked up on my desk when I get back to the office on Monday."

"Oh, you poor baby," Wilder said. "I know just what you're going through. The bar owner wants to send me to one of those courses to build my skills, too. I can't decide which one to go to though. Do you think I should attend 'The Cocktail Onion for Fun and Profit' or 'A Symposium on the Pros and Cons of Female Bar Patrons Grabbing Your Ass'?"

Darcy laughed at the gentle teasing. "You could always make me laugh, right from the start." She stood and headed into the kitchen as she spoke. "I remember the first day your family moved into the house next door. The movers weren't even finished unloading all your belongings when I looked out my bedroom window and saw a scrawny kid with a towel tied around her neck trying to get a mangy old dog to play Lois Lane to her Superman." Darcy plucked a bottle of water from her nearly empty shelves and frowned as she realized she'd have to go shopping the next day.

"Hey, I'll have you know Trooper had great theatrical range. Lois Lane was only a small part of his repertoire. He also played Cleopatra, Queen Elizabeth and Pocahontas." With a short groan, Wilder pushed herself up from the couch and went to her bedroom where she removed the clothes she had worn to work and dropped them into the wicker hamper in the corner.

"As I recall, Trooper would have played a virgin sacrifice in the temple of the Aztecs if a certain sharp-eyed babysitter hadn't intervened," Darcy said.

It was Wilder's turn to laugh. "You should have seen the look on your face when you found me chanting over Trooper with a plastic picnic knife for a sacrificial dagger. Until then, I'd never seen you as anything but the cool teenager my parents paid to watch me when they went out. Little did I know you were just a squeamish ball of mush. I think even Trooper was laughing at you."

Back on the couch now, Darcy said, "Yeah, and I'd never seen you as anything but an eight-year-old tagalong. It was then that I figured out you had homicidal tendencies and a flair for the dramatic." She rubbed her feet together, luxuriating in the feeling of the silky stockings moving against each other. "If you stop to think about it, it's amazing that we ever became friends."

"Not so amazing," Wilder said. "My natural charm won you over, same as everybody else. You didn't stand a chance against it." The last part of the statement was muffled as she pulled a well-worn nightshirt over her head.

"Getting ready for bed so soon?" Darcy guessed. "You don't still wear that ratty shirt I sent you when I was in college, do you?"

"Guilty as charged." Wilder glanced down at the Stanford Cardinal logo. "And it's comfortable, not ratty. I was pretty impressed when I got it, you know. You were my first crush." She slipped under the covers of her bed and slid up as she propped pillows behind her.

"I know, but I wasn't your last. Don't any of your women complain about your dilapidated nightwear?" Darcy moved to her bedroom, turning off the few lights that were on in the loft.

"No more than any of your men complain about yours. Besides, it isn't on that long anyway," Wilder said in a saucy tone.

"Wilder, you are such a dog, I swear!"

"What?" Wilder asked innocently. "I only speak the truth." She ended her sentence with a musical laugh. Burrowing farther down into the warmth of her bed sheets, she placed her free hand behind her head.

Darcy sat down on the silk sheets of her double bed. She allowed her body to fall backwards, and her slender frame undulated with the rippling waves of the waterbed. She groaned as the stress of the past few days slowly seeped from her body. "God, it feels so good to be home. As much as I appreciate five-star hotels, there's nothing like your own bed."

"Can't take the pace anymore?" Wilder smiled to herself as her comment crept dangerously close to their long-standing joke. "It must be your age."

"Ugh, how did I know you were going to say that? I know you far too well, Wilder McNeil, and FYI, an eight-year age difference is hardly enough to start looking through nursing home brochures." Darcy unfastened the tiny mother-of-pearl buttons on her red satin shirt. "Anyway, don't start with me. Jodie Tyler still works for me, and I don't want to accidentally let slip that you didn't join the Peace Corps and move to South Africa after all, now do I?"

"Oh, come on, what was I supposed to say? She started getting all serious and talking about us moving in together. She wasn't the one for me, and I knew that." Wilder also knew that she had only ever considered one person to be "the one," but as that person was unobtainable, she had resorted to a life of playing the field. Maybe it was a shallow existence, but it was all she had left to offer of herself.

Slipping out of her last item of clothing, Darcy slid her naked body between the luxuriously smooth sheets of her bed. The cool silk whispered softly over her body. "Don't you ever worry about bumping into her?"

Darcy couldn't see Wilder's smirk. "I did, but luckily for me she bumped into my twin sister."

"You don't have one."

"I do now."

Darcy shook her head. She had often wondered why Wilder never seemed to find anybody special. "Have you ever heard of Karma?"

"Of course." Wilder switched the phone to her other hand, allowing the feeling to return to her numb arm. "But this is what I figured… coming back as an earthworm in my next life might not be so bad. Look at it this way: I get both sexes, and although I do prefer the more femme-to-femme approach, at least I could have fun by myself. What would I care? I'd be a worm."

Darcy laughed. "Is that all you ever think about?"

"No," Wilder said. "So tell me, did you have fun in San Diego?"

"Fun? I wouldn't exactly call it fun. Oh, I had plans to have fun, but fate directed that it would be otherwise. You realize I'm blaming this on fate and not on my own poor judgment."

"Geez, here it comes, another 'Darcy picked a loser' story," Wilder said with a cackle. "I can't wait to hear what was wrong with this one. Let's see; you've already dated a man who didn't tell you he was married, one who wanted a last fling before entering the priesthood, a Republican, for God's sake, and of course let's not forget the guy with herpes... the gift that keeps on giving."

"Ha-ha, very funny, Wild. At least I found out about *them* before I slept with them." Darcy clapped her hand over her mouth and muttered an unintelligible curse.

"You slept with somebody and *then* found out his problem?" Wilder perched up on one elbow. "This I have to hear."

Removing her hand from her mouth and rolling onto her side, Darcy let loose an exasperated sigh. "You know I would have told you about it anyway. We have no secrets, damn it all."

Not many, Wilder thought, even as she verbally agreed with her friend.

Darcy continued. "I don't know why I trust you with all the dirty details of my life. Maybe because I know if I ever did find a great guy, I'm in no danger of you wanting to poach on my territory."

"You've got that right. Now, my poor straight baby, tell the nice lesbian all about your troubles." She leaned back onto her pillow and crossed one leg over the other, bobbing the free foot up and down. "Go ahead, entertain me."

"Yes, your Highness," Darcy intoned, "It's what I live for. Well, it was during one of those dry lecture sessions that I first noticed him. He was sitting with a small group from a Seattle company we've done business with. I hadn't seen him before, but I did know a few of the people he was with. He was cute in an 'I used to be a surfer dude' kind of way. You know, sandy blond hair, blue eyes, and a great smile that makes your knees go a little weak."

"Stop. Please. I'm getting all wet here," Wilder said in a dry, sarcastic tone.

"Well, maybe you aren't, but I sure was. He kept glancing over at me, giving me this appraising look. Now you know I don't usually just sleep around, but I was bored and I hadn't been with anybody in a long time, so I thought to myself 'why not?' and went over to the group. The manager of the Seattle company introduced us, and after a few minutes I asked the cutie out to dinner. I fully intended to have him for dessert, I can tell you." Darcy felt herself blushing a little at the admission.

"Ooh, you little tramp. Tell me more!"

"Dinner was okay. The conversation was about as deep as a thimble, but I didn't care. When I want conversation, I call you. I just wanted a little horizontal tango from him, and by the time dinner was over, it was clear he wanted it from me, too. We adjourned to my hotel room."

"And?"

"And fell straight into bed. The sex was passionate and hot. He had amazing stamina. There were mind-blowing orgasms, a couple of them as a matter of fact. It was fantastic except for one little thing."

"And that was?" Wilder was curious now.

"All the orgasms were his."

Wilder's eyebrows dipped in confusion. Turning onto her side she asked, "What... so you weren't really into it?"

"No, I was, believe me. I mean this guy was definitely easy on the eyes. I was after a quick lay, and he was an ideal candidate. It was just one of those things." Darcy shrugged. "I mean, it does happen."

Still confused, Wilder rolled once again onto her back. "Okay, let me get this straight. I take it Mr. Selfish wasn't much into sharing?"

"I'd say he wasn't... Still, you can't expect a mind-blowing orgasm every time, right? That's just the way it is." Darcy ran her manicured nails over the silken softness of her sheets. "It's easy for most guys, they can get there all the time. For us women, it's more like a fifty-fifty toss up... if you don't fake it, that is!"

"Whoa, whoa, whoa!" Wilder shot up to a sitting position, and stared incredulously at the receiver of her telephone. Her confusion was replaced by mild bewilderment. "What fifty-fifty toss up? Damn it, woman, who the hell have you been sleeping with? Please tell me you're kidding?"

Her friend's tone of voice surprised Darcy. "No, why?"

"Why?" Wilder echoed and fell with a light thud back onto her bed, her body rocking against the spring mattress. She wasn't sure how to respond to that question. In her experience, both partners had always been satisfied when it came to sex—often repeatedly so. What Wilder didn't understand was that as much as she and Darcy had discussed personal relationships, she had always assumed Darcy's were at least fulfilling. Now it sounded like Darcy's sometimes weren't, and she had believed that was simply the way physical relationships were.

Forcibly diverting her mind from her swarming thoughts, Wilder answered Darcy's question. "Because... well, it's just that in my experience, there's no fifty-fifty chance on whether or not both my partner and I hit the big one at least once."

Darcy laughed. "Sure, Wilder. It's hard enough for us to get there alone, sometimes, yet you expect me to believe two women together can hit the big one repeatedly? Keep in mind, I like to think my seniority in the age difference means I'm less naive than you think."

"You don't believe me?" Wilder was stunned.

"Of course not."

Shaking her head, Wilder rolled out of bed. "So you've never even wondered about it?" Wilder walked out of her bedroom and back into the kitchen. With the windows open, all of the smoke had dissipated. Taking the charred remains of her dinner out of the oven, Wilder kicked the door shut with her foot and dumped the ruined food, tray included, into the trashcan.

"Thought about what?" asked Darcy, although she had an inkling as to what Wilder was referring to.

Wilder closed her windows. "Oh, I know you've thought about it. I can remember a couple of times you questioned me on what it's like with a woman. Why don't you believe me now?" She opened her fridge and began rifling around in its contents.

"I thought you were just exaggerating a little. Anyway... what are all those clanking sounds?"

"I killed my dinner. I'm looking for something to fill a hole." Wilder pulled a small carton of milk from the bottom shelf and put it on the counter. She then opened a wall cabinet and pulled out a bottle of strawberry syrup.

"So, that means it's strawberry milk time."

"Oh, you know me too well." Wilder opened the milk and poured a generous amount of syrup into the half-full carton. She then shook the contents vigorously while holding the telephone in the crook of her neck.

"You've been drinking that stuff since you were a kid."

Wilder took a sip of the flavored milk. "And it just keeps getting better and better."Carton in hand, she headed back into her room and slid between the covers of her bed. "Okay, so where was I?"

"Keeping on the same train of thought, I think you were about to explain something else to me that keeps getting better and better," Darcy informed her.

Instead of laughing, Wilder took on a serious tone. "Darcy, when did you lower your expectations?"

"Of what? I still have high expectations of myself and my job. High expectations of life in general."

"So why not high expectations of sex, too?"

Darcy thought for a moment before responding. Finding her mouth a little dry, she reached for the water bottle that she had brought with her from the kitchen, unscrewed the cap and took a long sip.

"I suppose I haven't expected much from sex since the beginning. Once I figured out it wasn't the bells ringing, fireworks exploding, orgasm-every-time thing the movies led us to believe, I just haven't made a big deal of it."

Pausing as she lifted the carton of strawberry milk to her mouth again, Wilder clicked her tongue in sympathy. "I hate to break this to you, girlfriend, but sex *is* a bells ringing, fireworks exploding, orgasm-every-time thing for me. *With* me, too, I might add."

"Modest little thing, aren't you?" Darcy returned the water bottle to the bedside stand. "I guess next you're going to tell me the reason for the difference in our experiences is that you sleep with women and I sleep with men."

"That's exactly what I'm going to tell you," Wilder said, and drained the last of the milk.

"And what if the truth is that I'm just frigid?"

"Darce, if you've ever had an orgasm you're not frigid, and you pretty much said you have them half the time. What we need to do is figure out why you don't have them the other half."

Darcy laughed, in spite of this somewhat uncomfortable exploration of her sexuality. "Jesus, Wild, who died and made you Dr. Ruth? I can see you're not going to let this go, and I'd be lying if I said I didn't find this intriguing, so go ahead... figure it out for me. Just remember, I wouldn't be doing this with anyone else but you, so you should feel privileged."

"Compliment duly noted," Wilder said. "Now, let's get down to it. You say you have an orgasm fifty percent of the time. There has to be a common thread there. What are you doing during those times when you do have an orgasm?"

"Let me see," Darcy replied. "I had a fantastic orgasm about two weeks ago. It was very satisfying. I only wish someone had been there to share it with me."

Wilder grinned as she listened. "Okay, that's 'Darcy-speak' for saying you can come when you masturbate. What else?"

"The other time that's pretty consistent for me is during... um... you know... oral sex."

"Giving or receiving?"

"Giving or...?" Darcy trailed off when she realized her chain was being jerked. *Well, two chains can get jerked,* she thought. "Oh, receiving, definitely. Nothing like laying back with an eager partner who enjoys being between the thighs of a hot, wet woman."

Darcy's narrative had a jerking effect all right, but it was on Wilder's libido.

"Oh, really." The only response Wilder was capable of was breathily delivered about an octave below her normal range. She swallowed hard and after a second added, "Well, at least it proves the point I was trying to make."

"And that was?"

"You need to have sex with a woman."

An abrupt laugh rose from Darcy's chest. "So what are you saying? If a woman wants any chance of a good sex life, she has to sleep with another woman?"

"No, I'm saying that might be the case for you. Believe me, I have absolutely no experience with guys, so who am I to make that kind of judgment?"

Darcy's eyes twinkled, and a sly smile overtook her lips. Rolling onto her side, she said, "Oh, I don't know. What about when Handy Hubert took you to the Prom?"

Wilder covered her face with her free hand. "Ugh! I can't believe you brought him up. I swear that guy had multiple appendages." She shook her head in memory. Handy Hubert, otherwise known as Hubert Willis, was their neighbor across the road. Wilder hadn't wanted to attend the prom. She was pretty sure turning up on the arm of her then girlfriend would not have gone over well. Unfortunately, when her girlfriend had opted to attend with a boy, she had begrudgingly done the same. Although Wilder was confident in her sexuality, and had confided in Darcy even then, her girlfriend, Clare, had been less than open. Much to Wilder's later regret, she had attended the prom with Hubert and spent the entire evening trying to avoid his hands. It had taken a very convincing threat of actual bodily harm to get him to stop.

"You know, until you mentioned him, I was content to believe he was just the last vestige of an annoying dream I once had."

Darcy laughed again. "Nope, it really did happen. I remember seeing the fear on his face as you threatened him. He must have been about six inches taller than you too. Man, that was so funny."

"Yeah, but you didn't hear where I threatened him." Wilder paused. "Hold on, you saw that? I didn't realize you were visiting your parents that night. You told me you were at some conference."

Darcy cringed as she realized she had been caught out in a secret she had harbored for many years. Surprising herself at the time, she had cancelled the conference and visited her parents instead. She had presumed a hitherto unknown protective side of her had wanted to make sure her friend was going to be okay. "The meeting was cancelled so I visited my parents," she said. "I did think it a little strange that you went to the prom with him when you were seeing Clare." Darcy had never liked Clare. "I suppose I was just looking out to make sure you got home safely."

"How come you never came to see me that weekend?" Wilder asked, wondering whether she should feel hurt.

"I had to get back to work."

"Oh." Wilder picked up her empty milk carton and shook it as if looking for any last remnants of liquid. Suddenly realization dawned on her. "Aw, that is so sweet. You were worried about little old me."

Darcy rolled her eyes. "Like I had any reason to be. Anyway, what were we talking about?" She thought for a moment, trying to get off the subject. "Oh, yes. So you think if I want to enjoy sex more I need to 'do it' with a woman?"

"That's just my humble opinion."

Although Darcy had laughed at Wilder's suggestion, she was feeling extremely curious. It was something she had never fully admitted to herself, but the notion had played on her mind many times before this night. There was, however, the singular fact that Darcy still found it hard to believe sex could be as good as Wilder built it up to be. Was it really an unbelievable concept, or would she have to acknowledge that maybe she had been missing something all these years?

Darcy could feel temptation creeping into her veins but was too self-conscious to admit that fact. "I don't know, Wild. I find it hard to believe." She paused. "Okay then… I believe myself to be an open-minded person. How can you convince me that I should even consider this, let alone give it a shot?"

"What?" Wilder almost sputtered. "You want me to convince you? That sounds suspiciously like an invitation to me," she said in a teasing tone.

Darcy laughed and teased right back. "Maybe it was."

Wilder sat up in bed, covers dropping to her waist. "Don't play with me, Darcy. Number one, you may be eight years older than I am, but when it comes to sex with a woman, I'm the expert here. Number two, you couldn't handle me."

"Couldn't handle you? You're not very modest, are you? Look, I've been with enough men that one woman more or less wouldn't be any big deal."

"Maybe not," Wilder apparently conceded. "Unless that one woman was me."

Darcy was quiet a moment, considering what she heard. When she spoke it was in a low tone. "Tell me." With those two words, the entire tenor of the conversation changed.

"Tell you what? Tell you what it's like with any woman or what it's like with me?"

Darcy knew in her heart which she wanted to hear about, but she couldn't bring herself to say it. "Either," she said, taking the easy way out. Changing the phone over to her left ear, she adjusted to a more comfortable position.

Wilder smiled as she reclined again. *Darcy wants details? That's a breakthrough.* "I haven't slept with every woman in San Francisco, though not for lack of trying, so I'll just speak for myself."

Darcy felt her heartbeat pick up curiously at Wilder's statement, and she used her peripheral senses to study her own reactions even as she gave her friend her full attention. Almost without realizing it, she brought her free hand up and began lightly stroking the skin of her bare abdomen.

"When you're with me," Wilder said, "you are my total focus. There isn't anything on earth but you and me and what we're going to do together." She spoke slowly, deliberately using a seductive tone. "I notice everything about you. I see what causes your breathing to become erratic, watch as your nipples tighten beneath your clothing, and take every opportunity to touch you and communicate how much I want you."

Fascinated, Darcy listened and visualized the scenario in her mind. She had never been the object of such a single-minded seduction as she was hearing about. The men she had slept with had their own satisfaction as their primary goal, not hers. Her hand slipped down to her thigh, and her flesh quivered at the touch. "Go on," she whispered into the phone.

Wilder did. "You've come to my place, and you know why we're here. I lead you to the couch, and as we sit, I leave my hands on yours. I'm going to let you set the pace because your pleasure is what matters to me, but I want you to know how excited I am and how determined I am that you are going to be absolutely satisfied. I lean into you and bring my mouth to yours slowly. Tasting you, learning you." Wilder paused here and listened to the slightly ragged breathing on the other end of the line. "Darcy?"

Darcy swallowed a groan of exasperation and said, "Yeah?"

"Do you still think a woman can't beat out a guy any day when it comes to making love?"

Darcy knew her reaction to Wilder's short narrative gave her the answer to that question, but she was stubborn, and didn't want to let Wilder have the satisfaction of saying, "I told you so." Composing herself and moving her hand away from her now slightly spread thighs, she answered in a voice steadier than she felt.

"I'll admit your little tale struck a small chord in me, but I have to tell you I'm still sure a man would be a better lover for me."

"Want to bet?" The glove was hurled.

Darcy had closed her eyes as she concentrated solely on the soft tones of Wilder's voice. When the challenge so unexpectedly flew toward her, her eyes shot open. Licking suddenly dry lips, she opened her mouth to answer, but silence remained. She was becoming aware of an inner voice that was getting louder and more persistent. It was a voice that forced her to acknowledge something she had resisted for a long time—she really did want to experience that kind of intimacy with Wilder. In the past, she had always dismissed her feelings as those of a big sister. But what if they were something more? She had definitely been aroused by Wilder's words.

Taking a deep breath, Darcy composed her thoughts. "I have to say that also sounds like an invitation."

Wilder smiled, and a small part of her wondered when their innocent conversation had turned into obvious flirting. Still, her heart pounded rapidly in excitement. "Well, that would depend," she said.

"On?"

"On whether or not you would accept." Wilder held her breath in anticipation.

There was a long pause as Darcy's mind processed Wilder's words. There was no getting around the simple fact that she did want to delve further. "What if I were to say yes?"

Wilder pushed her seated body backwards until she was against her bed's headboard. She wanted to shout "yes" and "anything you want" and "I want you so much," but she needed to be sure Darcy knew what she was implying and that she really wanted that. "If you were to agree to let me prove what I'm saying? I don't know. Are you sure you have the ability to admit you were wrong?"

"Yeah, I see what you mean. You do have a point there," Darcy said. "I know you well enough to understand you can be a sore loser." She smiled as she waited for a response.

"Hey!" Wilder's voice burst forth as expected. "That's not what I was..." She paused as her mind suddenly changed directions. "Okay. You really do seem positive that I'm wrong."

Darcy wasn't positive at all, but she agreed on purpose just to see where Wilder's devious mind was heading. "Uh huh."

"Well, how about we make this a little more interesting?" Crossing her legs, Wilder plucked at the edge of her favorite T-shirt.

"What did you have in mind?"

"Just a little something to make this more... 'interesting'." Wilder couldn't believe what she was saying, let alone what was happening. She wondered where her bravado had sprung from. It certainly wasn't alcohol induced; she hadn't accepted any drinks from customers all evening. *Maybe I'm just overtired,* she thought fleetingly, unable to pull herself from the possibilities of their conversation.

Darcy herself was thoroughly engaged in what had definitely gone way past a mildly flirtatious conversation. "Interesting?" Brown eyes twinkled. "What do you have in mind?"

"A little wager."

"You want to make a bet?"

"Oh, believe me... the outcome can be anything you desire, and I do mean *anything.*"

That final word was spoken so enticingly that Darcy's body responded to its implications before she had even thought of a verbal reply. Both her curiosity and sexuality were being sparked.

"Spit it out, Wilder. Tell me, in plain English, what you propose."

Wilder turned over onto her stomach and propped herself up on her elbows as she composed her proposition. "Okay, this is the deal. You contend you have better sex with men than you would with a woman. I say you're wrong."

"And how do you propose to prove it?"

"You and I will have sex. Better sex with me means I win, but if you're not satisfied and pleasured to the point of admitting sex with a woman is better, you win."

"Satisfied and pleasured?"

"Yeah. Look, you said you only had orgasms fifty percent of the time with men. Most men can go maybe twice in an evening?"

"If I'm lucky," Darcy said and snorted. "Maybe three times if the moon is blue."

"So you have one or two orgasms on a good sexual occasion with a man. Fine. I say I should be able to double that in the same space of time. One evening, four orgasms."

Four? Darcy thought. *She's actually saying she can give me four orgasms in one night? I'm not sure my body's even capable of that.* Instead of giving voice to those doubts, she said, "And if I were to agree to that challenge, what are the stakes? Make it something good, because I'm positive I'm coming out on top in this one."

Wilder held back a comment about Darcy being on top, instead giving careful consideration to what would be the prize. "If you win, you not only get bragging rights, I'll throw in a weekend at that spa you like so much out in Napa."

Darcy realized this was serious now. Two days at The Ranch out in wine country would set Wilder back several hundred dollars, a huge sum on a barmaid's income. She had to give Wilder credit; she knew what strings to pull to get her interested.

Darcy asked the inevitable question. "What do you want if I lose?"

"Just one thing," Wilder said. "If I'm the winner, I want unlimited sexual favors."

"Unlimited sexual favors. Darcy tried out the phrase and found herself fascinated. "Tell me what that means."

"Just what it says. You and me, sex, anytime, anywhere. Think you could handle that?"

Darcy's competitive nature was out now in full force. "I won't have to worry about that now, will I? I plan on winning this little wager. Just tell me when and where."

Wilder chewed her lower lip as she thought. "This is Sunday, so let's say next Saturday. My place at seven. That gives you almost a week if you want to back out."

"I won't need it, but maybe you will," Darcy replied. "Saturday works for me just fine."

"It's a bet then," Wilder said. "Darce, this is going to change things between us no matter how it turns out, so I might as well tell you now. I've wanted you for a long time. If this is what it takes to make that happen, so be it." Wilder knew she wasn't telling the whole truth, but she had to be at least partially honest with her friend.

Darcy was stunned. She had no idea Wilder had been thinking about her in that way. *The way I've thought about her,* she leveled with herself.

"I'll see you Saturday, Wilder. Good night."

"Good night, Darcy. Sweet dreams."

After they hung up, Darcy reached up to turn off the bedside lamp. *Unlimited sexual favors. Oh, yeah, I'll have sweet dreams.*

Find this and other exciting Blue Feather Books
at

www. bluefeatherbooks.com

or ask for us at your local bookstore.

Blue Feather Books, Ltd.
P.O. Box 5867
Atlanta, GA 31107-5967

Tel: (678) 318-1426
Fax: (404) 378-8130